GILDED GLASS

TWISTED MYTHS AND SHATTERED FAIRY TALES

EXECUTIVE EDITORS

KEVIN J. ANDERSON AND ALLYSON LONGUEIRA

EDITORIAL TEAM

C.J. ANAYA, KAYE LYNNE BOOTH, AMY MICHELLE CARPENTER, JUSTIN CRIADO, MICHELE ISRAEL HARPER, MANDY HOLLEY, ANN MARIE HORMEKU, AISLEY OLIPHANT, ANNA STILESKI, SAVANNAH STUTTGEN, AND LIA WU

WFP
WORDFIRE PRESS

GILDED GLASS: Twisted Myths and Shattered Fairy Tales

Kevin J. Anderson and Allyson Longueira, Executive Editors

Editorial Team: C.J. Anaya, Kaye Lynne Booth, Amy Michelle Carpenter, Justin Criado, Michele Israel Harper, Mandy Holley, Ann Marie Hormeku, Aisley Oliphant, Anna Stileski, Savannah Stuttgen, and Lia Wu

EBook ISBN: 978-1-68057-344-2
Trade Paperback ISBN: 978-1-68057-343-5
Hardcover ISBN: 978-1-68057-345-9
Casebind Hardcover ISBN: 978-1-68057-346-6
Cover art image from Shutterstock
Published by WordFire Press, LLC
PO Box 1840 Monument CO 80132
Kevin J. Anderson & Rebecca Moesta, Publishers
WordFire Press Edition 2022
Library of Congress Control Number: 2022936375
Printed in the USA

Join our WordFire Press Readers Group for sneak previews, updates, new projects, and giveaways. Sign up at wordfirepress.com

CONTENTS

REFLECTIONS AND REFRACTIONS
INTRODUCTION

Once upon a time, nobody knew the phrase Once Upon a Time. Fairy tales, myths, and legends form the core of who we are, in our cultures and in our creative spirits.

Mirrors are at the very heart of many fairy tales, and gilded glass creates a more exotic and archaic type of mirror: with the application of thin gold leaves to the reverse of clear glass, the overlapping gold and the drying process creates beautiful variations in the image.

Reflections and refractions... One reveals truths, while the other bends light into varying shapes of deception.

This anthology was produced by our third cohort of graduate students earning their Master of Arts degree in Publishing at Western Colorado University.

As part of learning about the publishing industry, the eleven students developed the concept for an original anthology as their group thesis project. After energetic brainstorming sessions, they settled on *Gilded Glass*, exploring the variations of mirrors in fairy tales. They developed the call for submissions and spent the fall semester wrestling with the slushpile, sifting through 650 stories sent in for consideration (not to mention the five solicited manuscripts from big-name authors Sherrilyn Kenyon, Alan Dean Foster, Jonathan Maberry, Kristine Kathryn Rusch, and Michaelbrent Collings).

The anthology project receives funding from Draft2Digital, which gives us a very specific budget with which to buy stories. Out of those hundreds of submissions, they could buy only twenty-four, so they had to winnow down and winnow down, write rejections, and then move on to the next round.

The best of the best are the ones you'll read here.

After choosing the final stories, the students then had to decide on which order to place them in the table of contents. They copy edited the manuscripts, worked with the authors, chose the cover art, designed the cover and interior, and brought the book all the way through to publication. We celebrated with a gala release and book signing at the Gunnison (CO) Arts Center only days before their graduation ceremony.

But this is more than just a class project. As with the previous Western Colorado University anthologies, *Monsters, Movies & Mayhem* and *Unmasked*, this is a remarkable collection of outstanding stories.

The authors featured in *Gilded Glass* rely on their own creative mirrors to weave stories that reflect their roots, cultures, and backgrounds. The types of stories range from humorous to horrific, from subtle and lyrical, from fast-paced adventure to sardonic satire.

Enjoy!

—**Kevin J. Anderson and Allyson Longueira**
Graduate Program in Creative Writing
Western Colorado University

THE SILVER KING AND THE JADE EGG

NICOLE L. SOPER GORDEN

E veryone has heard of the Silver King. It's hard to ignore tales of a king with a magic axe so sharp it can cut a person in two without killing them. He is legend and boogeyman all rolled into one.

But it never occurred to you that he might choose you as one of his wives.

You stand now before the vanity mirror, viewing your reflection from the waist up. The wedding dress is beautiful and expensive, of course. But you look beyond the rich fabrics, colorless diamonds, and sterling silver to the face and body they cover. You study your reflection as you've been taught to study yourself all your life, finding the flaws in your complexion: the shiny skin, the slightly mismatched color of your eyes, the imperfect lay of hair—so many faults. You look at your reflection the way you know men look at you, examine yourself as if with the eyes of another, and you wonder why any man would settle for you, let alone a legendary king.

You stare your reflection in the eye, feeling wholly unworthy. You wish the Silver King had chosen someone else. You clutch the jade egg your mother gave you as a wedding gift and wish, too, she hadn't sacrificed so much on your behalf. The jade egg was made by a witch, and the price was your mother. As a child, your mother's garden of zinnias and potatoes was your sanctuary—the one place your father never looked for you. Those zinnias and potatoes would go untended now.

And yet, the jade egg gives you a chance. You only pray you'll know when to use it.

After the ceremony, when your hundred veils are removed and your marriage henna has been applied, when the red wine is drunk and the braided date breads are eaten, when the drums and bells have gone silent, and when the thirty sheep have been sacrificed in the name of a fruitful union, the Silver King takes you back to his room.

You know this is it: the moment you have been terrified of since the Silver King appeared to claim you.

He wears clothing of velvet and silk, the colors as rich as any gemstone, every seam decorated with tiny silver bells so that he moves like a song. His beard is braided with bells, too, and there is even one large bell hanging from the haft of his axe, which he always wears across his back. He stands you in the middle of the floor, strips you naked, and walks around you, eyes sharp and bells tinkling like laughter. Each turn around you is like being sliced by broken glass as he inspects every inch of your body. You hold the jade egg in your hand and consider unleashing it—but this was always inevitable. Better to save the stone's one use for a more propitious time.

Finally, the Silver King stops in front of you. As dispassionate and cold as the metal he is named for, he takes his magic axe and he cuts you in half.

It's easier for you to adjust to living in two pieces than you expected. Maybe it's the practice you've had all your life, the constant competing expectations of others pulling you in so many directions: be beautiful, be smart, be good at dancing, be a musician or a poet, be nurturing and motherly, be sexy but also be innocent. The world expects everything of women. At least now, you're only expected to be two things. Your upper half can be charming and sophisticated while your legs are busy with other pursuits. The other wives have been teaching you how to best maximize the assets of both halves, though they do so with whispered jibes and cruel smiles. It is more competition than help.

The wives' rooms are full of mirrors, on every wall and surface, on ceilings and floors, even on doors and windows. But all the mirrors are small—there is nowhere to see all of yourself at once. Each mirror shows only a disembodied section of a wife as she sits or lounges or strolls. You watch as a pair of dainty black ankles walk in a mirror nearby, thin silver chains circling each. Then you see the long, elegant, brown arm of another wife, netted with blood-red henna, stretch into a mirror across the way. On the ceiling, one mirror reflects the plump, bruised mouth of a wife as she talks, though you can't hear a thing she says.

The Silver King builds new women every day from his split wives. He mixes and matches tops and bottoms like changing his coat. He takes your legs to bed, attached to the top of his favorite wife, well before he beds your upper half. You're so disassociated from your lower half by then that you don't even realize it has happened until the next day, when the black-haired wife with perfect ebony skin smirks about it.

There is nowhere in these rooms where you can exist without the mirrors staring back. It's like being watched by a crowd of judgmental eyes every moment of every day. You spend way too long studying each of your blemishes and flaws, piecemeal, as they come into focus in the surrounding mirrors. It's like a meditation on imperfection. You think about how to be a better wife and wear the surface of the jade egg smooth as you run fingers over it, like a talisman against ugliness.

The first time your upper half is in the king's bed, he has attached it to the legs of a red-haired wife. You think he must not like red hair much, since she is his only wife with hair that color, and she is only there because she's the daughter of a neighboring king. Or maybe it's her too-sharp nose he doesn't like, or her unusually pale skin, or her tendency to talk too much. The Silver King wants a child with her for the prestige of her royal lineage but doesn't want to endure her face. You feel a strange sort of pride that it's your face he chooses instead, especially when the favorite wife scowls at you for it.

One day, the Silver King decides you will accompany him to a dance, and you feel a thrill of satisfaction in knowing he thinks you beautiful and poised enough to be seen on his elbow at such an event, even if he pairs your upper half with a more graceful set of legs. Still, though another wife's legs do the dancing, it's your hands he holds and your face he sees. It's your hair he adorns with white and pink mariposa lilies. It's your lips he brushes clean of red wine with a callused thumb. It's your smile he displays to the room, basking in the jealous leers of other men.

At the end of the night, it becomes clear he has brought you as nothing more than jewelry, an ornament to make himself look better. When another king openly admires your looks, the Silver King offers you to him for the night. You want to protest, but a good wife is silent and obedient. The Silver King gives you the bottom half of a wife he no longer cares for and sends you to the other king's bed. You feel as fragile and thin as a mirror when he leaves you there, ready to shatter the moment someone leans in too hard. You didn't bring your jade egg to the dance and wonder now if that was a mistake. The Silver King doesn't even look back as he walks away, his many silver bells flashing with a thousand tiny reflections of your eyes, wide with pleading.

Later, the other wives laugh at your naivete. Of course, the Silver King lends them out—anytime he is bored or trying to secure goodwill from another king. Party favors and bribes. You feel sick to your stomach, right at the place where the magic axe divided you in two. You stare at a mirror that only shows your mismatched left eye and wonder who is wearing your legs now.

The Silver King's tongue is as sharp and cold as the edge of his magic axe. He hands out insults dressed in compliments to every wife, and his aim is always true. No matter how lovely a wife is, he can find their flaws with unerring accuracy. The chestnut-haired beauty with the tiny scar under one ear. The tall olive-skinned wife with slightly uneven teeth. The busty wife with hourglass curves who only has a dimple in one cheek instead of two. He has a knack for illuminating any wife's deepest insecurities with pretended praise. He's never seen anyone with such a *striking* mole on their collarbone before. It's so *endearing* for ears to be at slightly different heights. The crook in a nose only serves to *accentuate* the rest of a wife's beauty. His words can wound so cleanly it's difficult to recognize the cut at first.

He finds your own personal, private faults too, of course, and speaks them into the open air to bounce between the mirrors: the slice of gold in one otherwise brown eye, the oily skin, the birthmark pale against the dark skin of your shoulder, and the left breast slightly bigger than the right. It's like being hit by the same arrow over and over again, thrown back at you by your own reflection and the gleaming eyes of the other wives. You hold the jade egg your mother gave you in one hand, rubbing a thumb over its smooth surface, and wish you could ignore the pain.

The other wives hide their cruel grins behind modest hands. You cover your own lips when he takes aim at others, as you are expected to do, even when you can't bring yourself to mimic the other wives' satisfied smirks and callous titters. It's like a game of war, one in which everyone is injured. Everyone except the Silver King, who delivers fatal blows as easily as brushing aside a new wife's hundred wedding veils.

The red-haired wife, the one whose bottom half is pregnant, is talking. She talks constantly to any of the wives she can accost. Some of the wives laugh at her words. Some turn them back on the redhead like weapons. The ebony-skinned favorite wife brushes her aside like she doesn't exist. The busty wife with only one dimple cowers away, too meek to even listen. The red-haired wife catches you one day, too, talking you into a corner. All the mirrors reflect her moving mouth back to you, a hundred sets of synchronous lips and teeth and tongue.

She is trying to tell you something about women and men, something about freedom and oppression, but you keep getting distracted by her too-sharp nose. She says that women should be treated better than prized silver cutlery, and you wonder if her blade of a nose has ever cut someone. She says that physical beauty and carnal appetites are both parts of the same woman, and that women shouldn't be disassociated from themselves. You can't help but remember what it was like to wear her legs in the Silver King's bed, long and shapely but slightly pigeon toed. Secretly you worry for her. Words are dangerous.

The Silver King hears about his red-haired wife's talking.

You suspect his favorite wife, she of the silky black hair, has told him. His anger is cold and sharp. His magic axe glints in the reflected light of so many mirrors. You think he will kill her, but that's foolish; her bottom half is pregnant with his child, and her father is a king of worth. Instead, he swipes the axe through her neck, separating her head from her torso. Without vocal cords, her head can no longer talk. For a moment, it lies on the floor, screaming silently, with only the sound of the Silver King's thousand bells ringing in the air, the bell on his axe haft ringing loudest of all.

Then he puts her head in a glass jar on a tall shelf, her neck resting on a bed of her own red hair. She screams and cries, mouth always open, but never makes a sound. You can't help but look at her every time you pass the shelf and wonder if you could have saved her with a warning to talk less. It's so easy to remove a woman's voice, you think. The Silver King can take any of you apart at any time. The disembodied head serves as a silent reminder of that. You palm your jade egg and bite your lip.

One of the wives tries to escape. She's the busty wife with the bright one-dimpled smile, but her smile has been absent more and more in recent days. You've seen the Silver King pinch every ounce of excess weight on her hourglass curves, heard his disinterested words grow sharper every day. It's been months since he last took her upper half to bed with him, and the other wives delight in pointing this out to her every evening. You watch the reflection of her chest heave in the mirrors as she cries each night.

And still, when the wife tries to escape, it shocks you all.

You know instinctively that there is no escape from the Silver King. There are no locks on the doors, no guards in the halls. And yet, everyone understands that you can't leave.

This is your life now; it's how life is. And even if you could get away, where would you go? Home, to a family who will know you've abandoned your duties as a wife? Who will know you're no longer a pristine prize to offer another man? Or go somewhere else? A woman on her own is as fragile as an eggshell, as breakable as a mirror.

Still, the busty wife tries to escape. She finds her original legs and uses them to walk out the front door. You and the remaining wives whisper about what will happen to her. Brigands. Rapists. Slavers. Maybe she will fall down a ravine and lose her legs forever. But secretly, in the quiet places of your mind, you hope she makes it somewhere safe, and builds herself a little cottage, and grows a garden of zinnias and potatoes. You let the other wives laugh about the awful fates that could befall her while running fingers over your jade egg and wishing her well.

The next day, the busty wife is back. She is blushing and her eyes are turned down. The Silver King keeps a hand at the small of her back as he guides her into the wives' rooms. His dark coat and tall form tower over the short wife like the grasping branches of a strangler fig. Your hand itches to pat her shoulder, but you don't dare, not with the Silver King there. He takes her legs and leaves her to the unkind stares of the other wives.

At dinner that night, you feel too queasy to eat, though you're not sure why. You try to hold down some bread and wine and watch the prodigal wife as she devours her plate of food. The busty wife is the only one at the table with a plate of meat, as red and tender as anyone could ask. The rest of you are given vegetable curry. She is sitting next to the Silver King this night, in the favored spot to his right, and keeps glancing up at him as if afraid he might take her plate of meat away. He remains silent, eating his own dinner of walnut and fig stuffed clams, looking at none of you as he drinks his blood-red wine.

For the last course of the meal, when you all usually eat candied fruits and flavored ices, only one dish is brought out: a silver plate covered by a mirrored cloche. You expect it to be set in front of the Silver King, that maybe it's some special treat that he wants to dish out to each of you individually. Instead, it is set before the busty wife. She looks at the king in confusion, and he motions her to open the dish.

The silver cloche rings like a bell when the wife drops it to the stone floor, almost loud enough to cover her scream. You feel sick but know better than to jump up from your chair like the busty wife does on her borrowed legs. You hold your stomach, glad now that you ate little, and hoping not to throw it back up.

On the platter, a feminine foot, roasted and glazed with honey and pistachios. The brown skin of the foot is decorated with henna lotuses in the same indigo ink as the busty wife's cinnamon-colored arms. The implication is clear: you can't run if you don't have legs. And these legs are gone now, consumed by the king's cruel punishment. The busty wife is busy retching up her own flesh she has just eaten.

The Silver King folds his napkin and stands, distaste written large on his face. He tells the rest of you to clean up the mess, then leaves the table, the sound of his silver bells harsh and bright.

You spend too much time lying down these days. You recognize the fact but can't quite bring yourself to get up and do anything. You lie on your back and stare at the mirror above you, wishing your left breast wasn't slightly larger than your right. You dread being asked to put on legs that aren't yours. You worry constantly about where the other half of your body is.

So many of the other wives seem to be in the same state.

Energy in the wives' rooms is low, everyone listless. The busty wife who no longer owns legs is in a state of near catatonia. Only the Silver King's favorite wife seems unfazed, brushing that glossy black hair of hers until it outshines the mirrors.

Everything is wrong, but how can it change? You stare at the jade egg, worn smooth by how often you rub its surface. You may be treating it like a good luck charm, but it is witch-made. Your mother explained this to you, explained how the egg works and what magic it contains. It can only be used once, but it might be enough to make the Silver King let you go.

But go where? There is still no safe place for a woman alone, just as there wasn't when the busty wife tried to escape. The Silver King will find you. So you rub the jade egg instead and hate the way your worry has made your eyes look puffy. You hate, too, the dark look on the Silver King's face every time he glances your way. His favorite wife's upper half rides your legs to his bedchamber, leaving the rest of you to stare at the mirrors. As he walks away, bells jangling, your eyes are drawn to the magic axe on his back: large and half-moon shaped, as polished as a mirror. You see your hand reflected in the blade, the jade egg between your fingers. And on the hundreds of bells of the Silver King's coat, you see the reflections of his wives arrayed around the room. And you realize, suddenly, the answer.

When the time comes, you find yourself restless. You walk by the busty wife, laying on her stomach and staring at the floor, as if trying to avoid the room's mirrors—but even the floors are mirrored here. You reach a hand toward her shoulder but stop yourself before you can touch her. Instead, you leave a plate of figs on the floor by her. You walk past the shelf and the jar with the silently screaming redhead wife, locking eyes with her for a moment. Her lips clamp shut, as if she knows what you will do. You resist the urge to look around at the other wives and loosen the lid on the jar, letting the redhead wife have fresh air for the first time in weeks. Her eyes are wide, her skin paler than usual.

The room is full of motion, like a shaken cage of butterflies. Wives exert petty cruelty on one another as a matter of habit. They wound each other, which injures the whole. You skirt around the favorite wife, feeling her gaze on you. Does she know what you have planned? Does it matter if she does? You're doing this for her, too. No woman alone.

When the Silver King comes in to make his choices for the evening, you come up behind him and crack open the jade egg over his head.

The jade egg's magic, your mother explained, will make a person's insecurities and self-doubts boil to the surface. As the yolk of the jade egg drips through the Silver King's hair, you imagine him starting to feel unworthy, or even worthless. You imagine him noticing for the first time all the shortcomings in his personality, physique, and intelligence. You imagine him thinking that he can never be anything important, that aspirations are futile.

You imagine him feeling the way you feel every day.

But the Silver King turns, eyes hard, and stares at you. And you suddenly realize your mistake. The Silver King has felt these things already. He has *always* felt these things. Everything he does—the fine brocade coats and silver bells, his cold anger and sharp tongue, the way he collects and trades wives like commodities, his need to control every tiny thing around him—it's all his attempt to overcome his own shortcomings. It's his way of compensating for his self-perceived inadequacies. Maybe it's the gray in his beard, or the lack of a true royal bloodline, or the half-hidden jeers of his kingly peers. Maybe it's anything else. His cruelty is a shield to make himself feel more worthy than everyone around him. You could spill every jade egg ever made in his hair, and all it will ever do is make him more himself.

You step back, suddenly panicked at the flash of anger in the Silver King's eyes. He pulls his axe free, holds it up to swing at you. The edge is so sharp it tapers to invisibility. Against a wall, you grab a mirror and throw it at his face. He dodges, the axe spinning across the floor. But he doesn't need an axe to hurt you. He has hands wide enough to encircle your throat.

He presses you back, presses you down. In the mirrors above, all you can see is the back of his head and your wide eyes. From the angle, he could be making love to you instead of strangling the life from your body. Your fingernails pry at his callused skin but find no purchase. Lights start dimming, and you think you'll die any moment now. He is stronger than you, will always be stronger. What were you thinking?

There's a shining flash, bright enough to blind you, and suddenly you can breathe again. You blink, trying to make sense of what has happened. A second later, the Silver King's head is pushed from his neck by a dainty silver-chained foot.

Behind him, the wives are arrayed like an army, row upon row of women made radiant by their fierce faces. They aim their wrath at the Silver King, holding shoes and silver chains, silk veils and ivory hairbrushes up to the light like weapons. But it's the Silver King's favorite wife who holds the magic axe, who has cut the king's head from his neck, and who is now holding out a hand to help you to your feet.

You don't know why they have helped—you didn't expect it. When you ask, the favorite wife explains: the way they all saw you use your most prized possession to disarm the Silver King, the way you spent special attention to the wives he has hurt in the past, the way you wanted to free them all instead of just yourself. The Silver King has spent years trying to make you all enemies to one another. But in this moment, as you all work towards one goal, you are stronger than the sum of your parts. No woman alone could defeat the Silver King, but together anything could be possible.

Later, after you each took turns swinging the axe at the Silver King, after he has been diced into uncountable living pieces, and after the castle is burned to shifting embers and the mirrors shattered to glittering dust, the women who were once the Silver King's wives come together. Some of the women travel home to their families, though you suspect most will come back when they realize they have no family waiting for them. Some of the women decide to travel farther afield, wanting to see the world and sail the oceans. The black-haired woman is one of these, unable to weather the lingering anger of the women she harmed in her position as the Silver King's favorite wife. Every woman who leaves takes a piece of the Silver King's living body with her to bury or drop in the sea, to feed to pigs or dump in a swamp, scattering his body to the four corners of the world.

The rest of you find a quiet place in the woods and build a cottage—large enough for dozens of women to live in, and with not a single mirror on its walls. Together, you build a chair with wheels for the busty wife and take turns lending her your legs when she wants a walk. The redhead gets her body back—both halves—and soon her newborn is underfoot to give you all the hope of innocence. You organize a garden, and together you plant zinnias and potatoes, and other things too—eggplants and peas, mallow and bleeding hearts, herbs both bitter and sweet. It makes up a beautiful, diverse, living patchwork—just like the women who tend it.

At the bottom of the garden, next to the big rock, you bury the Silver King's head, still silently screaming insults, deep enough that the hoes and plows will never disturb it. You plant a jade plant over the spot, to remember. It's not the same as the stone, but its waxy leaves are the same color and fleshy with life. You let the jade plant grow as wild as it wants, until it tangles with the weeds and shrubs. All the women touch the leaves as they pass, wearing the egg-shaped leaves smooth and shiny, like self-made talismans of good luck.

Nicole L. Soper Gorden is a speculative fiction author with a not-so-secret identity as a biology professor at a small liberal arts college. She has been reading and writing fantasy and science fiction stories her whole life and has a special soft spot for fantastical writing with nature or biology themes.

When not writing or teaching, Nicole enjoys growing heirloom vegetables, baking award-winning cookies, and plotting new ways to make people appreciate how wacky plants are. She lives in the mountains with her elderly puggle, affectionate black cat, playful goats, rescued box turtle, bearded husband, and dinosaur-obsessed toddler. Follow Nicole's writing at NicoleLSoperGorden.com

THE REFLECTION OF DARIA BLACK

MICHAELBRENT COLLINGS

I was surprised when she called me. Surprised, and a little in love again.

I'd given up on Daria—on *Dee*—a long time before, back when we were still in high school, right around the time she embraced the more sophisticated (and search-engine friendly) name of Daria Black.

YouTube was where she made her mark: makeup tips, five-minute beauty hacks, that kind of thing. Daria Black was the go-to girl to watch if you didn't know how to get your fake lashes to stick, or if you needed to know what color palette went with your skin tone or the best dress for clubbing.

We'd been friends to that point, me and Dee. The best kind. The kind that look at each other across the table during ten thousand lunch periods, who laugh and cry together over the little tragedies and triumphs that seem so epic, so critical and everlasting, when we're young.

I was ten the first time I thought of marrying her. Then we went to high school, and our freshman year I *knew* that was where we were headed. I'd marry her, we'd have a family. I saw it all so clearly.

Dumb, I know—but that kind of dumb is one of the definitional requirements of being a teen, so I'm not ashamed of it.

Sophomore year hit us like a tank with severed brakes. That was when she started doing the videos. When she stopped being my friend, just Dee, and became the rising star Daria Black.

I changed, too: I went from being her best friend, Joey Grayson, to being just one more follower. A blip. A flash on the screen between the numbers that she refreshed fifty times daily.

By the end of senior year, we were barely speaking. Not angry, just ... apart. I went to college, she went to the house she'd purchased the same month we graduated—fruits of her celebrity—and we stopped speaking at all.

I thought it was a joke when I saw the caller ID:

DEE

I hadn't spoken a word to her in almost ten years. Seeing that word, so far and yet in some ways so present surprised me so much that it didn't even cross my mind to ask how she got my number, let alone how it showed that way on my phone. I just answered the call and said it:

"Dee?"

She sighed. "No one calls me that anymore, turd-humper."

It was such a perfect expression, so very *Dee*, that all my questions disappeared as I stepped back a decade-plus into a moment where I was still in love with her.

I barely heard her talking after that. I barely remember agreeing to meet her at her place for lunch the next day. But I do remember thinking—and asking—"*Why?*"

She just said, "See you then," and hung up.

The second thing I noticed when I got to her house was the mirrors.

The *first* thing I noticed was the house itself: she'd upgraded to a place in the part of town we'd joked about living in, once upon a time before we grew apart and one of us came to realize how far out of reach a five-million-dollar home was and always would be for people like me.

I went through the security gate (the entry code she'd texted me was the ever irreverent 6969) and parked my crappy Dodge P.O.S. beside two Beemers and a Land Cruiser. Got out and slouched my way to a door taller than most houses.

I rang the button. Wondering what was happening, what I was doing here. Why Dee had reached out after all these years.

A buzz. The door swung wide.

I went inside, and saw the mirrors.

My first thought: *too much.* Too many mirrors, too many reflections of reflections, so many that as I walked through the empty entry hall in search of my old friend, I just saw infinite *me*s, trailing off until they dwindled to a singularity on eternity's horizon.

"Hey, Joey," came a small voice.

I looked up, saw her.

We remember things strangely. Details fade over time, and all we're left with is broad strokes; bold outlines that become caricatures in our minds: the lovers too perfect, the cheaters too wretched, the friends too loyal to be real.

It had happened to me, too—Dee had become a perfect shadow on those rare occasions when I thought of her. But as she came down the long stairway to join me in the hall of forever-mirrors, I saw the reality. I saw the little lines on her forehead, the bright spots in her eyes that spoke of years of triumph and tragedy in their measures.

She hugged me, and that *was* the same. The feel of her, so small it felt like I could have broken her in my arms. But so alive, so in motion. She trembled, even when she was at her most still—a breeze that would die should it ever fully rest.

She pulled back. "Look at you," she said.

"All growed up," I said. I looked around. "And look at this place."

She shrugged, but the light in her eyes brightened. She was obviously proud of what she'd done; how far she'd come.

"You hungry?" she said.

I nodded, though I hadn't come for food, I'd come for her, and to ask her why she wanted me here. Why, after all this time?

The "lunch" was a clear indicator that food wasn't the real point of this get-together for her, either. People using food as a subterfuge will always take pains not to let the menu outshine the agenda, and nothing was quite so dull as a chicken salad with a glass of lemonade.

I took three bites, then stared at Dee. She was looking everywhere *but* me. For some reason it made me angry. I pushed the plate away. "Well?"

"Well, what?"

"Why am I here, Dee?"

"I don't ... understand the question."

I waited. Waited. Finally, she looked at me. With a grimace, she said, "I needed something real." She sipped at her drink, then said, "It's all filters, you know? Just things that are almost real, but not quite, and we present them to the world and hope people love us enough to press a button or click a little bell and then we know we're loved because numbers tell us so and numbers don't lie. Right?" She laughed, a jittery, odd little laugh that I'd never heard from her before. "And then we wake up one morning and wonder if the numbers *did* lie, if the filters are hiding nothing but a hole, a darkness ... a monster." A tear tracked down her cheek as she said, quietly—almost to herself: "I'm still that real little thing so long ago. That thing I was before I grew up and Dee disappeared and there was only Daria left."

I started to feel cold inside. "You're scaring me, Dee."

Something in her eyes flickered. "Sorry," she said. "Just ..." She shrugged. "Things are about to change. I've made some big deals and some big changes are coming and ... I dunno. I wanted to talk to someone real. Someone I remember from before I was ... was ..."

"That one senior chick with all the subs?"

She laughed a stilted, wheezy laugh. That was when I noticed a group of pimples around her mouth. Nothing too terrible: just some raised bumps that were barely noticeable, but I remembered she'd always broken out when she was really stressed.

"Pimples," I said.

She colored. A little surprised, a little amused, a little angry. Any of those were fine with me—better them than the weird vibe I'd been getting. "Do you watch me?" she said suddenly.

For a moment I thought she was asking if I was some stalker who followed her every move, hoping to get a glimpse of things that would violate YouTube's content standards. I started to stutter out my own surprised, amused, angry answer, then realized she was just asking about her channel. I laughed a bit. Shrugged. "Not really."

"You should."

"So I can learn how to fix my combination skin?" I fluttered my eyelids. "It's not really my thing, Dee."

"You should do it anyway."

Silence. It grew and grew, until I said, "I will."

The rest of the "meal" passed awkwardly. I didn't understand what was happening, and don't remember now what we talked about. I do remember her walking me down that long row of mirrors, thinking this was the last time I'd probably see Dee—or rather, Daria. She was going to graduate from the big time to ... whatever came after that. Some level of celebrity mere mortals could never understand.

As we passed the last mirror, I took her in my arms and turned with her so we were staring at ourselves, at the infinite past selves in the mirrors behind, the uncounted future selves in the mirrors ahead. I whispered in her ear. "Dee, I don't know what's going on. But I know that the *woman* I see in the mirror—she was always smarter and tougher than anyone else could guess. You're my friend. You're —"

"The girl with all the subs," she said.

"Not what I was going to say, but yeah. That, too." I squeezed her. "You're Daria Black, and you've always been my favorite thing to watch."

She put her hand up. Covered her mouth. I thought for a second that she was holding back a sob. Then I realized she was just covering up those little pimples I'd noticed earlier.

I said goodbye. Walked out of the house.

As I opened my car door, she shouted from her porch, "Watch me tonight! I'll have new videos!"

I stopped, half in my car, half out. Half in her universe, half in mine.

"I will."

I kept my promise. I went to YouTube and, for the first time in forever, watched a few of her videos. Still the same stuff, those beauty tips and hacks that enrapture so many people. It always surprises me how many folks need that. I've never met a woman I thought looked better with makeup; I'd rather see the canvas than the painting, I suppose.

As for YouTube in general: I barely watched it at all. I preferred to read books and watch TV. Old-fashioned, I know. But I was happy that way, which few of my screen-leashed friends or coworkers could truthfully say, so I didn't see any reason to change.

If only I hadn't changed. If only I hadn't looked.

But I did.

I turned on her channel—*Daria Does It*. I watched a few videos. I watched Dee, and smiled a bit as my mind wandered and I remembered the things we'd done as kids, and how close we were and thought we always would be.

Until the last video.

I clicked it, and was shocked. It was Dee, but ... it wasn't. It was like I was staring at that memory of memory, that broad brushstroke of an attribute exaggerated to impossibility.

Dee was always a pretty girl. Relatable. Cute. But on the last video I saw, she was ...

"Daria," I whispered. For a second, I wondered if I was even looking at Daria, or if I'd somehow wandered onto someone else's channel, some model or movie star I'd never heard of but would watch everything she made from here on, just to see her smile.

But no, it was Daria. Under the strange beauty, it *was* her. But how did she look so different?

I remembered what she'd said earlier that day, about filters and fakery. Then I flashed to another bit of our lunch, a thing I hadn't remembered before: her constantly playing with her phone. It was a model I'd never seen, big and flat and strangely ugly on the table between us. Daria had twirled it around and around, a strange, platonic game of spin the bottle played out the entire time we sat there and stewed in unspoken moments.

Looking at the video, where she prattled on about the proper thickness of eyeliner, trying not to think about her body intertwined with mine, trying not to think of holding that beauty close and drinking it up into myself until it was gone, I thought of that phone. Of filters and fakery. I looked at the date stamp for the video. To my surprise, she'd uploaded it that day.

But there were no traces of the pimples I'd seen. She was live in super hi-def, but her skin was flawless, her face impossibly ...

Perfect.

Then I realized: "She uploaded it today. Doesn't mean she recorded it today."

Only ... only she was wearing the same clothes I'd seen her wearing at lunch. Her lipstick color was the same. Her hair was *exactly the same.*

I looked closer at the screen. At that one girl with all the subs.

I'd looked at her profile before I left for lunch. Just out of curiosity.

She had five million subs.

Now, barely a dozen hours later, it was up to ten.

Two days later. She posted two more times, and each time the effect was the same: I was in over my head, befuddled and besotted. It wasn't sexual, really. Sure, sex was part of it—I'm a straight male in his late twenties, and biology demands that I think certain things when I come across any beautiful woman—but it was more than just that. It was an intensity of thought and interest I'd never felt before. It was ...

Obsession.

I sat there, watching her videos all night. It never even dawned on me that I only watched the new ones, the ones where she wasn't Dee, or even Daria, but rather just that caricature of all her best qualities. Stripped of all her quirks and idiosyncrasies, painted large as a thing meant to represent beauty and desire in their purest forms.

The sun rose. I kept watching.

Two days, I watched. Two days, and at the end of it she had over twenty million subscribers.

I didn't know what I wanted. I just got in my car and drove, and when I stopped I was at Daria's gate and pressing the button and jabbering into the camera that swiveled to look at me. Then up the driveway, through the door, into the hall of mirrors.

I turned to look at myself in one of the huge glass planes, fidgeting with the tie I hadn't worn last time but had chosen to don for this second meeting. I looked like me, which was something of a disappointment because ... because ...

Because she's so beautiful, and I'm so plain.

I walked down the hallway, followed by the infinity of my selves that all wandered toward the thing that had suddenly become the center of our universe. A week ago Dee had been a memory, a phantom, a thought of what might have been.

Now, she was the brightest thing around. My star.

"Joey!"

Again, I saw movement on the stairs, a flurry of bright cloth and perfume flying toward me. She was in my arms before I even saw her, and the daisies I'd brought—her favorites—ended up crushed between us. But that was all right because she was here and I was here and that was all that I needed, and I finally looked down and saw her —

"Wait, what?" I shook my head. "Who ...?"

The woman in my arms looked up at me. "It's me, Joey." She laughed. "Don't you recognize me?"

"I ... of course ... of course I do."

It was a lie. Because when I looked down at her, so petite, so small, I didn't see the thing I'd come for, the thing I'd expected to find at the end of the mirrors: Daria.

I just saw ... Dee.

That wasn't what I'd come here for, was it? This girl with stress-pimples erupted around her lips, a few new ones on her cheeks, blazing hot and red and angry?

"It was so good to hear from you," she said. She pulled me to the couch. I sat down beside her—but not too close. *This wasn't who I wanted to see.*

This wasn't who I wanted to hold, to crush to myself like flowers and feel her petals spread across me as I inhaled.

She started talking. Bright and excited, and she talked and talked and talked and I didn't hear any of it because it wasn't what I wanted wasn't what I wanted *wasn't WHAT I WANTED*. It was just plain old Dee and I felt sicker and sicker until I couldn't handle it anymore so I spoke, saying the first thing I could think of so that she would *just. Be. QUIET.*

"Still stressing, huh?" I asked.

Her mouth closed with an audible clap. "What?" she said.

I pointed at the pimples on her mouth and cheek.

It might have been my imagination, but it almost seemed like several more had appeared, clustering under her right ear. "You always broke out when you stressed."

A tiny part of me thought how hurtful I was being. The rest of me told that part to shut up, or die.

Dee frowned. "I'm not stressed."

"You were the other day."

She laughed. No longer that jittery, jagged laugh from before: this one was bright and happy. "I don't know why I would've been. Everything's fine."

"Except the breakout. Doesn't that make it hard to film?" I

could hear the words, sounding like they were coming from someone else. And in a way they were. This wasn't me, really. It was the person who'd taken over, the man who'd come looking for Daria: the beautiful woman he'd watched for days on end.

I was just along for the ride.

"I don't have a breakout," she said.

I wanted to punch her. I settled for a grin and an emphatic, "Sure you do. Huge."

Dee grabbed a small purse that sat on the nearby coffee table. I knew what she was going for, and flashed to the million times she'd pulled out a makeup compact to check herself in the mirror before pressing play on some video she'd make during study hall or lunch. I'd given it to her when she was twelve, and she always had it. She'd look in the mirror, add a bit of powder or blush, then press record and would be gone from my life, even if I was in the same room with her.

Dee surprised me, though. She didn't pull out my long-ago gift, she pulled out that big ugly brick of a phone she'd spun between us.

As she withdrew the phone, I wondered how she'd managed to get the huge thing into her tiny purse. Only that was wrong, wasn't it? The phone wasn't that big. Not as big as I remembered it. It fit perfectly in the purse even though ... even though ...

It was bigger before.

No. Just a different phone. Different model.

It's the same. But smaller. It's —

(It's what it has to be for her to use it.)

I felt dizzy, my thoughts spinning as Dee held up the phone the way she had held her little compact mirror all those years ago. She tapped a button and the phone lit up, the homescreen looking like a billion others: apps and favorites and a background picture of Dee making a duck face.

Dee tapped one of the apps—must have been a camera

app, because now the phone showed the image of the painting on the wall opposite us. She tapped the screen and the image shifted to one of her: she was using the phone as her mirror, looking at herself to see the blemishes that I'd so rudely —

(Horribly, meanly. Why did I do that?)

— pointed out.

She ran her fingers along the blemishes. Tracing them, drawing small circles around the rage-red outbreak. One of the pimples—so big it was almost a blister—popped when she touched it. Watery pus dripped over her chin.

"See?" she said brightly. "No outbreak, no stress." She laughed. "You always did like to yank my chain, Joey."

Her refusal to admit what I saw fanned my anger to rage. I knew, that small part of me knew, that this made no sense. I didn't get mad like this. I was a calm, laid-back guy. But ...

But I'd come for *Daria*, not this girl with blemished skin and deepening lines on her forehead. My fists clenched, and I opened my mouth to shriek at her before I battered her lying, ugly face to nothing.

And that was when I finally saw what she was looking at. I saw her "mirror." Her phone.

Daria stared out from the screen. Perfect, pure. The broad strokes of perfection, of dreams within dreams.

I stared at the phone. I stared at *her* on the screen. "I love you," I said.

For some reason, the girl on the phone looked sad. "Everyone does," she said. "That was the whole point."

I looked away from the phone, and I ran.

I ran from the room, and was joined by millions in the mirrors as we fled from a place where my own eyes lied. I sensed motion, and turned to see that Dee was running after me. Her gait was strange, stilted. She ran like one of her legs was shorter than the other, or like she was getting over a bad sprain.

"Joey! What's —"

Whatever question she'd been about to ask died in her eyes as she caught sight of herself in the closest mirror. She ran her fingers over her chin—a new cluster of pimples had risen up, and I knew I wasn't imagining it this time, I *wasn't*—and sighed and said, "Oh," in a quiet, melancholy tone.

Some of the blemishes darkened as I watched. Deepened. Became black pits. Craters. One of her bright blue eyes blanched of color, then went as yellow as the eye of a corpse.

Dee started to cry, and the tears mixed with pus and spit and I almost vomited.

She was still holding the phone, and now she raised it and sighed and said, "Oh," again, this time in a voice of quiet triumph. "There I am."

I fled. Not because I was afraid but because there, on the phone, I saw Daria—not Dee, *Daria*—and I wanted her so badly I could feel it in my bones. One more moment in that house, staring at that image of beauty in the hands of a friend grown strange and wrong, and I would have gone mad.

It's been two weeks. I lost my job—unsurprising given that I haven't gone in once, or even answered their calls. I'm too busy.

I'm watching *her*.

I don't know or care what she's talking about, I just know she's beautiful. The most beautiful of dreams, the loveliest of delights.

Then today, another notification popped up on my phone and the only thing that registered was that the call had paused the Daria video—the newest one, uploaded today, and her more beautiful than ever. I cursed and swiped it away, and it wasn't until the third time it reappeared that I realized what the caller ID said:

DARIA

I answered, running from my bedroom to the small front room of my apartment. I flipped through trash and takeout boxes and dirty clothes—weeks' worth, a lifetime's worth—to find the TV remote. I turned on the YouTube app and brought up the Daria video I'd been watching. She was talking, but no words penetrated. It was just an ongoing, blissful cascade of sound.

The phone had picked up, but it wasn't until that moment that she spoke.

"You're watching me now?" Daria whispered in my ear. She sounded like she did online. I shivered.

"Yes," I said hoarsely.

"Come over," she said. "I want to celebrate."

"Celebrate?"

"One hundred million, Joey. I'm at the top, and still going higher." She laughed and my body clenched in ecstasy. "Come celebrate," Daria whispered.

I remember getting in my car. I remember her voice following me as one of her videos played from my phone during my drive. I remember almost crashing when the phone turned off, weeping until I got it plugged in and it was charged enough to start again.

Then I was through the gate. At the house.

The door hung wide. I ran inside.

That was the first time I realized that it was night. The lights of the house were off, too. The hall, so bright and becoming before, was now a murky corridor that led from dim to dark.

All the mirrors had been smashed.

I didn't care. I only knew that Daria waited for me.

Wanted me.

I walked down the hall, shadowed by jagged pieces of myself. They flitted in and out of existence between the cracks, the cobweb patterns that marred the once-bright mirrors.

I was almost there. She would be waiting on the stairs. Daria would reach out and I would run to her and we —

I froze. Something moved at the end of the hall.

The desire that had knotted my insides turned to molten lead as the shape, the *thing*, twisted upward, rising higher and higher. It was slimy, it was scaly. Parts were dry and cracked, others ruptured and running with rivers of dark ichor. It was pure terror made into broken, gashed, infected flesh.

It was shorter than me. The size of a petite woman.

The thing made a gibbering, whispering hiss that loosened my bladder and bowels. I didn't even notice. I was watching as the creature held out something in its ... hand? Tentacle? It reached out, and the thing in its grasp activated as that mad whisper-shriek sounded. The object it held grew bright, and a slick pseudopod on the creature's side quested blindly until it found and tapped something on the brightness.

Lights flickered, and I saw now that, though I had noted the smashed mirrors, I had failed to spot the phone taped crudely to each one. The same drab, ugly kind as the one Dee had held, the one the creature now clutched. And out of each screen Daria stared. She licked her lips, and whispered, "You came for me," as the monstrosity ten feet away opened a blood-coated maw and soughed like rotted leaves in wind. The thing's mouth opened wider, and as it did, Daria smiled through the myriad screens. "I'm so glad you're here," she said.

The thing came toward me, lurching on appendages that spurted out of its mass, pulled it forward an inch or a foot, then retracted with wet, sucking hisses as another slick tentacle would appear to pull it a bit closer, closer ...

I screamed. I screamed and screamed and screamed and didn't stop screaming as the thing's arms circled me. Not in fear, but because all I wanted was Daria, and she was here, all around me, on dozens of screens, dozens of our world's truest reflections, smiling and *living* for me.

Oddly enough, the desire was what freed me. It was too much. Desire shifts to fixation, fixation becomes obsession, and obsession—left untreated—transforms to madness.

I wanted her. I wanted all those Darias to dance around and with and for and through me forever, but it was too much and I was insane and in my madness I ran. I fled instead of staying with the thing I most wanted, lusted after, *needed*.

I ran, and I think Daria—or Dee, the thing at the center of the nightmare—would have followed. The thing lurched my way. Then she caught sight of herself on all the screens, the only reflections that mattered.

Dee the monster saw Daria the dream, and the monster howled and chittered and the phones took that sound and created of them the words I heard as I ran in my madness:

"I'm ... sooo ... beeeaaauuuuuutifullllll ..."

I don't know why she called me that first day, or why she called me back that last night. I'll never know, I suppose, and that's fine. It seems like you can find out anything these days —it's all just a touch of a button away—but sometimes we forget that there are things better left undiscovered.

I do know, however, that I've splashed twenty gallons of gasoline on the walls around her house, and have another three five-gallon containers to go.

I do know that I have to destroy whatever's happening in there.

It pours out quickly. All dry, all gone.

I light a match. I stare into it and listen to the chittering sounds that still emerge from the house. Thank God the phones' volume is lower, because if I heard Daria's voice I don't think I could burn her down. But all I hear is Dee, and that gives me strength.

Then I do hear it. Just a whisp, a phantom of Daria's voice. The match burns away to my fingers, and keeps on burning. I smell charred meat and barely notice.

I can't do it. Because horrific as it is to admit, I realize that Dee is the thing behind Daria's eyes. No Dee, no Daria. I have to spare the monster to save the angel.

But that's wrong, isn't it?

My body understands the truth before my mind does. My fingers move of their own accord. Another match flares. I touch it to the walls. Flames soar.

I'm content. The monster is burning, the madness gone. I'm sane now, I'm thinking clearly.

It's okay to burn her. To kill Dee.

Because all Daria's videos are still online. *She'll* never die. The beautiful, filtered reflection that mattered ... that's going to be around forever.

Michaelbrent Collings is an internationally bestselling author, and the only author to be a finalist for the Bram Stoker Award (multiple times), Dragon Award (multiple times), and RONE Award. He has also written bestsellers in science fiction, fantasy, thriller, mystery, humor, and more, but is best known for his horror writing: he has been one of Amazon's most-read horror authors for years, and was recently voted one of the Top 100 All-Time Greatest Horror Writers in a Ranker survey of over 15,000 readers. Find more about him (and get one of his books, free) at his website WrittenInsomnia.com.

BLOOD FOREST

GAMA RAY MARTINEZ

Ontar stared into the small pond. He saw nothing. Oh, there were fish and water plants, but other than that, he saw nothing, at least not until the dryad walked up beside him. Her emerald hair almost seemed to be leaves, and the smell of flowers followed her. The full moon's light gave her an ethereal beauty. He looked to her, and she smiled.

"How long has it been, beloved, since you looked into a pool and saw your own reflection?"

"Some five hundred years. Truth be told, Ishana, I don't even remember what I look like."

"If only you could see through my eyes..."

"Have you talked to the elders?"

She ran a hand along his cheek. He shuddered at her touch, his undead nature recoiling from the sheer power of life within her. She nodded. "It was a close vote. Four in favor and four against. Elder Varnia didn't want to vote unless she spoke to you. That's why I came. I'm to take you to her tree."

Ontar blinked. "Her tree? She trusts me enough to let me see that?"

"Not really, but her tree wants to speak to you, too. If they both agree, then the elders will grant you sanctuary."

Ontar pursed his lips. He had hoped to be given this chance, but he hadn't really believed he'd get it. The life-giving nature of dryad magic could be used to hold his vampiric nature at bay. He knew of no other way to have at least a semblance of humanity, and he was so tired of being a monster.

"Let's go."

Ishana glided through the forest, looking like she was walking but still moving through the foliage as fast as the wind. Ontar shed his humanoid form in favor of that of a bat. He screeched, and the sound bounced back at him, revealing everything around him. Fairies flitted from branch to branch, and a unicorn moved through the forest on silent hooves. Ontar took off. As fast as Ishana moved, it was all he could do to keep her in range of his peculiar sound-sight.

The pursuit was all a game, of course. No creature, alive or dead, could keep up with a dryad moving through the forest if she didn't want to be followed. As if in confirmation of that, her musical laugh drifted through the trees. He flew faster, and she squealed with joy. He screeched again, and the image he got back was not only one of trees and animals. There was also the sense of gentle power coming from up ahead, though he couldn't say how he knew that.

A tinge of joy brushed across his mind. If he'd had blood running through his veins, that would have made it go cold. That emotion had not come from him, but rather from an invader. Five hundred years of unlife had taught him a few things about defending his mind. He seized the intruder, but fear welled up inside of him when he felt how powerful it was. This could only be one person.

Ontar, your skill has improved. I did not expect you to detect me.

Markul, what are you doing here?

Markul? Is that what you're supposed to call me?

Ontar struggled against the mental compulsion, but it was no use. Obedience to this creature was a part of him, built into him from the first moment he had risen as a vampire.

Master.

That's better. I owe you my thanks, Ontar. Because of you, I know what the power of a dryad elder feels like. I can find the others now.

No!

You have my thanks, little pawn. Tell no one about me.

Then, the presence was gone from his mind. Ontar cast his own thoughts outward, trying to locate Markul, but this sort of thing had never been his strength, and if his master was anywhere close, he found no sign of it.

Ahead, Ishana slowed, no doubt in response to him slowing down as well. Ontar redoubled his efforts as she neared the elder's tree. She stopped about a hundred yards away. He landed by her and resumed his form. She extended her hand. He hesitated. He had to warn her, but as he tried to speak, Markul's command froze the words in his throat. Markul might be one of the vilest creatures to ever walk the earth, but the dryad elders were each powerful beings in their own right. If they had some advance warning, they could defend even against a creature like him. If he caught them off guard, however, he might well destroy them or worse.

Ontar couldn't even make his face twitch though. All he could do was smile and take her hand. He shivered at her touch. She did the same, but they had long since gotten used to their conflicting natures.

"It's best to approach an elder's tree slowly, even if she is expecting you."

Ontar nodded. "Does she know we're here?"

Ishana gave that musical laugh that made him feel like he was alive again. "Of course. She knew you were here as soon as you entered these woods. Nothing can surprise a dryad elder in her own forest."

Ontar desperately hoped that was true, but as they approached, the temperature dropped sharply, and dead grass crunched beneath their feet, something that shouldn't have been possible so near to an elder's tree. Ishana got a worried look on her face and walked faster. He smelled it before she did. Death was a smell no vampire could miss.

They saw their first ghoul a second later. It looked almost human, though its skin was mottled gray and brown. Patches of dark hair grew from a head that had a mouth a little too big to be human. It growled, revealing a mouth full of teeth that had been filed to a point. It charged, and for a moment, Ontar thought he wouldn't be allowed to stop the creature, but Markul's commands apparently didn't extend to not harming his minions. He moved almost as fast as he could as a bat, grabbing the ghoul by the neck while it was in midair. He threw it against a nearby tree so hard its bones cracked. It didn't move again.

"The elder," Ishana said and rushed forward.

Glad he was able to follow, Ontar kept pace with her. They came into a grove with a massive tree in the center. There were at least two dozen ghouls around it. Every eye turned to them, and their combined growl reverberated against his skin. He might have been able to handle as many as five or six, but with so many, he wouldn't stand a chance.

"Stay behind me, love."

"What are they doing to the tree?"

He hadn't noticed it before, but she was right. One of the ghouls dragged its claws across the bark of the great tree in designs that Ontar almost recognized.

"That's blood magic. I don't know exactly what it's meant for, but—"

"But we can't let it infect an elder's tree."

Without waiting for a response, she charged forward.

Ishana looked like a delicate creature, and she reminded him of a flower more than anything else. It was easy to forget that she had been alive almost as long as he had, and while she hadn't spent a great deal of time learning to defend herself, it was never a good idea to anger a dryad in her own forest.

The ghouls rushed at her, or at least they tried. Half of them were entangled as roots rose from the ground and wound themselves around the creatures' feet. The others hesitated, and that was all Ontar needed. He rushed among them, lashing out with his fists. In short order, ghouls littered the ground behind him, and in a handful of heartbeats, they had reached the trunk of the great tree. The ghoul hadn't quite finished whatever runes it had been carving. Black ichor oozed from the marks. Ontar ran his hand over them and gasped. The power was too much like his own.

"It's draining the elder's tree."

"Well, stop it!"

Ontar closed his eyes and concentrated. Markul was a master of blood magic, but Ontar had never spent much time practicing the art. Still, he thought he could feel something.

"I think the elder is still in her tree."

Ishana didn't wait for him to say another word. She stepped forward and placed a hand on the bark. It seemed to liquefy and flowed around her body. She was gone a second later. The bark writhed, and two figures fell out of it. One was Ishana. The other was the venerable form of Elder Varnia. She was coughing, and much of the color had drained from her skin. She glared at him.

"You did this."

"No, I—"

She wasn't listening. Instead, she got up and put her hand on the bark of her tree. The bark writhed, and the rune took on a brilliant green glow. Then, it simply vanished as the bark healed itself. The dryad elder turned back to him.

"This is because of you, isn't it?"

"No," Ishana said. "He helped me get to you. I never would have been able to get through the ghouls without him."

"What about the other elders?" Ontar asked. "If you were attacked, they might be, too."

"You just want to know where their trees are."

"Elder, what if he's right?" Ishana asked.

The elder closed her eyes and concentrated. Her tree seemed to shiver, and Varnia opened her eyes and gasped. "They're under attack. The other elders have been captured just like I was." She looked from Ontar to Ishana before shaking her head. "There's nothing else to lose. I'll go after Elders Misha, Colia, and Shatan. Ishana, save Phoban, Makili, and Staran. Vampire, Elder Labini's tree is three miles to the east of here. Elder Faria is two miles south of that. I'll go there as soon as I am done with the other three. If you truly are an ally, you'll help before I can do that. Now, let's go."

The dryad elder stepped into the underbrush and vanished. Ishana smiled before doing the same. Ontar took a step before a voice shouted so loud in his mind that he thought his head would explode.

STOP!

Ontar couldn't move so much as a muscle. An animal could have come by and knocked him down, and he couldn't even have gotten up. Mist coalesced in front of him, coming together as the form of a tall man with pale skin. His crimson robes billowed in the wind, and his raven-black hair seemed to suck in the light.

"You may move."

Ontar took a step back. "Markul." The vampire raised an eyebrow, and Ontar felt his mental command take hold. "Master. You're draining the dryad elders, aren't you?"

Markul smiled. "Yes, and you have no idea how much power they have." He laughed. "It's intoxicating. I will be invincible once I get it all."

"They'll stop you."

"Will they? Do you really think they'll be fast enough? I'm getting stronger every second."

Ontar tried to attack him. Maybe if there was a fight so close to an elder's tree, Varnia would notice. She might be able to stand against Markul, but it was no use. Markul's control over him was just too strong.

"I suppose it would be amusing to watch your lover try to stop me. She is at the elder's tree ten miles to the east of here. Let's go."

This time, it was Ontar who laughed. "Ten miles? Even you can't cover that distance fast enough. You're not faster than a dryad in the woods."

"But I'm taking their power, and you have no idea what I can do with it. Follow."

Markul faded away, leaving mist vaguely shaped like a human. Ontar tried to resist, but it was pointless, and he followed his master in the transformation. Mist wasn't nearly as fast as a bat, but a gust of wind blew through the forest, so fast it should have torn trees from their roots, but Markul apparently had precise control of it, and the wind simply carried them through the woods. In less time that Ontar would have believed, they had reached Elder Phoban's tree.

The ground was littered with ghoul parts. Ontar was a little surprised at the savagery of it. Before, Ishana had had to be careful to avoid hurting him, but with him nowhere close, she'd been able to unleash the full power of a dryad in anger, and the forest had torn the ghouls into so many pieces that the only reason he could identify them was that he'd known they were there.

Impressive, Markul said in his mind. *She's not an ordinary dryad, is she? The child of an elder? Answer me.*

The command took hold of him, and though he tried to hold back, the words spilled from his mind. *Yes. She is the child of Varnia.*

Ah, Varnia. I have heard of her. The seventh daughter of Elder Munilan, I believe. Tell me, does Ishana have sisters?

Six. She is the youngest.

The seventh daughter of the seventh daughter. Interesting.

Ishana moved toward the tree and placed a hand over the blood runes the ghouls had been carving. As before, the bark rippled, and a stately dryad stepped out. Her skin drooped more than Varnia's had, and she looked more tired. A chill ran through Ontar. Whatever else Markul might be, he was no liar. He was draining them, and they didn't have much time.

I'm sure they could handle any number of ghouls, but what about something a little more challenging?

Ice crept down the trunks of nearby trees, and a shadow passed over the dryads. They both looked to the sky, and for a moment, fear danced across Ishana's face. A humanoid figure stepped out of a nearby shadow. The elder pointed one finger, and the two closest trees bent and stabbed their branches into the apparition, but they passed harmlessly through it. Wraiths were creatures of shadows and could not be destroyed as easily as ghouls. The dryads could probably manage to face down one or two, but at least half a dozen were stepping out of the shadows. Vampires had many powers, but controlling creatures like this was generally not among them.

How did you get so many of them to follow you?

You can gather many debts over the course of an eternity. I admit I called most of them in for this attack. Shall we see what results?

The wraiths moved in, and the dryads stood back-to-back. A wraith drifted forward, as if carried on wind. Ishana extended her hand, but unlike with the ghouls, thin vines rose from the ground. They shouldn't have been able to entangle something as insubstantial as a wraith, but the vines wound around it. The leaves glowed brightly and the wraith wailed. In a second, the lights had glowed so brightly that the wraith faded away. The elder had dealt with two, but doing so had taken precious seconds, and the remaining wraiths were almost upon them.

Impressive. Markul thought.

No!

Ontar's weight returned to him as he retook his physical form. He jumped at the wraiths. The living couldn't easily affect spirits, but dead flesh was another matter entirely. He grabbed the spirit by the neck and tore it away, causing the wraith to dissipate. He leaped on another one, and dispatched it just as easily. The dryads had caught another two, but the remaining ones had focused on him. He groaned as fur sprouted all over him, and a wolf's growl rose from his throat. He took down another one before the others sank their ghostly claws into him. Strength drained out of him, but then the wraiths glowed green and two of them were torn away. It was all he could to do to get to his feet, but he did, and his teeth tore into the last of the spirits.

The elder glared down at him, but her face didn't have the cold distrust he had become so accustomed to. Instead, she gave him a half smile.

"I believe I owe you an apology."

"Ontar," Ishana said, "what about Elder Labini and Elder Faria?"

He shook his head. "I'm sorry. I couldn't help."

"What? Why not?"

Markul laughed as he too retook his physical form. "Because I commanded him not to."

"Ontar, who is this?"

A tree bent down, moving so fast it was almost a blur. It tried to stab Markul through the heart, but as fast as it moved, he moved even faster, stepping aside and grabbing the branch. He effortlessly tore it off.

"That," said Elder Phoban, "is a master vampire."

"Ontar? You betrayed us?"

"No."

"Silence!"

Markul's command froze his tongue. He struggled to speak, but the words refused to come. Elder Phoban scowled.

"Do not treat him too harshly, Ishana. He is your sire, is he not?"

Once again, Ontar tried to speak, but it was no use. He did manage a nod, though. Before anyone could say anything else, the trees tried to stab Markul, but he moved too fast. Ishana threw her hands forward, and roots gripped Markul's legs. He tore free of them as if they were made of paper. She glanced at him.

"Help us!"

Her words tugged at his heart. For the first time in half a millennia, tears ran down his cheeks. "I can't."

"I said silence!" Markul cried out.

"A vampire cannot disobey their sire," Elder Phoban said. "They rob free will of those they turn. It is one of the reasons they are so vile."

"Bold words from someone who has seized control of the trees." Markul slashed with his right hand, hitting a trunk so hard the tree exploded into a shower of splinters. The elder winced, and then Markul moved next to her tree and placed a hand on it. "Now, you will stop trying to kill me, or I will destroy you."

Ishana froze in her tracks, but the elder scowled. Her tree seized Markul, and for a second Ontar thought the elder would actually manage to destroy him, but Markul turned to mist for the space of a heartbeat. He returned to physical form before he hit the ground. He launched his fist directly into Phoban's tree. Splinters and sap went everywhere. Ishana screamed, and Markul seized her by the throat. He smiled and turned to mist, taking her with him. The elder coughed and fell to the ground as the wind carried the mist away.

"Go after her."

"What about you?"

She looked at her tree. Nearly half the trunk was gone. It would fall any second. She shook her head. "I am lost, but she is not. Go after her. Save her. Before I pass, I will tell the others that I have changed my vote. I am for you. Now go!"

"I can't. I can't disobey him."

"You already did."

Ontar blinked. She was right. Markul had commanded him to silence, but he had somehow managed to speak. It had only been two words, but he had spoken. He looked in the direction they had fled. It only took him a few seconds to realize where they were going. There was only one place they could be headed. Ishana's tree. It was miles away.

The elder seemed to read his thoughts. She picked up an acorn from the ground and held it out to him. "Take this. It will help you. There is more I can do. Take the form of a wolf again, and run."

The bat was faster, but he did as instructed, taking Phoban's acorn and putting it in his pocket. He transformed, and the elder closed her eyes. Power flowed up into Ontar from the ground. He recognized it, though it had been five centuries since he'd felt anything like it. It was the power of life. He wasn't alive. That would be beyond even a dryad elder's power, but for what might be the first time in history, life aided a vampire. He ran faster than he ever had, faster even than he had travelled as mist. The forest moved in a blur around him. In less time than he would have believed, Ishana's tree came into view.

The same blood mark Ontar had seen on the elder's trees had been carved into Ishana's. Though the rune had all the same lines, there was something different about it. It was somehow darker and more powerful. There were no ghouls around, which meant that this mark had been carved by Markul himself. Ontar rushed forward. He had tried to learn blood magic in the early years of his unlife, but he had never been particularly skilled at it. He might know enough, however, to wreck a construct. He ran up to it and dragged a fingernail across it, pressing his nail into the wood as it crossed certain lines. The rune flared and went out. Markul laughed as he stepped out of the shadows.

"Ontar, so predictable. You should have been more studious in learning blood magic. Back away from the tree."

Ontar obeyed, and Markul walked to where he had been standing. Then, the master vampire placed a hand on the tree and pressed. Ishana screamed as the vampire pulled her out of it. She was strong, but she was no elder, and Markul's magic had drained her nearly to death. It seemed to take all her strength to look up at him.

"Come here, Ontar," Markul said.

Ontar did as he was told. Markul laughed. "You know, it really is unfortunate for her that you ruined the rune. Their power can neutralize it and reverse its effects, but yours?" He shook his head. "You've left her permanently weak. She'll never even have the strength to stand." He laughed again. "Do you know what the worst part is? You stopped the draining magic, but you didn't sever the link between us. When she dies, what's left of her power will go to me." He smiled. "I think I would like that now. Kill her. Look into her eyes when you do."

Ishana was on the ground. Tears flowed from her eyes as she met his gaze. He had spent many nights staring into her eyes. His hands rose until he gripped her throat.

"I love you."

Her voice was as soft as a breeze, but it gave him the strength. He bent his will against Markul's and managed to stop his hand from squeezing. The other vampire snarled.

"Kill her."

He was too strong. Recent events had taught Ontar that given enough time, he could fight past Markul's commands, but he didn't have that time anymore. He looked into her eyes and squeezed. She grabbed at Ontar, but she was so weak she couldn't even hold on. Her hand brushed his pocket, and what little strength she had drained away.

For a moment, he saw *something* reflected in her eyes. It wasn't possible, but he didn't stop to consider it. He let Ishana go. As she fell to the ground, he reached down and seized a piece of root. He tore it free and before Markul could react, he drove the wood into the vampire's heart. Markul threw back his head and let out a scream that was part man, part bat, and part wolf. The world itself seemed to shudder as one of the oldest creatures in existence cried out for the last time. His body turned to fire, and in a handful of seconds, all that was left of him was ash.

Ishana's tree glowed brightly, and Ishana herself rose to her feet, all of her strength restored. While defacing the rune hadn't severed the link between Markul and Ishana, the death of the master vampire apparently had. She walked up to him and laid a hand on his shoulder. For the first time, he didn't shudder at her touch. Her hand went down to his pocket and she pulled out the elder's acorn. Then, her fingers brushed his cheek.

"Elder Phoban is dead, isn't she?"

"Yes."

"Even an elder can't long survive if her tree is that damaged, but it worked, did it? I had wondered about it, but I never thought we'd have the chance to try it. I can't believe it."

"What worked? Ishana, what's going on?"

"An elder's acorn, empowered by her dying act, is the most powerful healing magic under the sun. I had always wondered if it could heal a vampire."

"It couldn't. Not by itself. You gave it the boost it needed, but are you saying—"

She nodded. "You are alive."

Tears blurred his vision. He wiped them away and looked deep in her eyes. They were as brilliant as emeralds, but more than that. For the first time in five hundred years, he saw his own face reflected in her eyes.

Gama Ray Martinez lives near Salt Lake City, Utah, with his wife and kids. He moved there solely because he likes mountains. He collects weapons in case he ever needs to supply a medieval battalion, and he greatly resents when work or other real-life things get in he way of writing. He secretly hopes to one day slay a dragon in single combat and doesn't believe in letting pesky little things like reality stand in the way of dreams.

COMING OUT

KENZIE LAPPIN

S achi was not scared of ghosts. She didn't even believe in them.

It was just that in her mind there was no reason to *invite* someone to kill you for no good reason. Even if they weren't really going to kill you. Because they weren't real.

Things like dying a gruesome death could really ruin a good night in.

Which is why, the day after Sarah B. double-dared her to play Bloody Mary in the bathroom mirror, Sachi came prepared.

Sachi did not usually rise to Sarah B.'s taunts. They were eighteen now, and childish one-upping was, Sachi had thought, a thing of the past. But Sachi didn't have many friends these days. Her parents were out of town, leaving her alone in this big house. The idea of gaining some popularity for something that wasn't even going to work appealed to her. She'd post the video on Snapchat, get some acclaim, and maybe stop feeling so lonely all the time.

Everyone knew the legend of Bloody Mary. Stand in front of the mirror in a dim room, chant her name three times, and she appears. Sometimes she just shows herself to you, some-times, if she really doesn't like you, she kills you.

Usually violently.

Sachi might have been stupid for attempting it, but she wasn't dumb. When she went to summon Bloody Mary, she brought along a baseball bat.

It was, admittedly, a pink one. She'd gotten it for the Petals Junior Softball Team when she was in middle school, but it had served well since then. Made of metal, so no splin-tering. Brightly-colored, so you could find it in the dark. Sachi was always prepared.

Sachi shouldered the bat and turned off all the lights. They didn't have any candles in the house—she'd checked —but Sachi had found an old night light in the junk drawer. It was shaped like a fairy and it gave off a comforting purple glow, dissipating some of the shadows pooling on the floor.

She looked into the big mirror above the bathroom sink. It only reflected her own face.

"Don't be a weenie," she told herself and got out her phone, the record button blinking and blinking.

She looked herself in the eyes.

"Bloody Mary," she said, "Bloody Mary..." She took a breath. "Bloody Mary."

Nothing happened.

Sachi did not believe in ghosts. But she was relieved.

Something banged on the other side of the mirror.

Sachi screamed.

Bloody Mary, as it so happened, was a girl about Sachi's age or a little older. She had dark black eyes, lanky blond hair, and blood coming out of her nose, eyes, and ears. She looked at Sachi and bared her teeth.

She came out of the mirror.

Bloody Mary didn't move quite right, her limbs jerking, her head turning too far to the side, like an owl. She put one hand out of the mirror, then the next, then her whole torso, accompanied by a smell of death and mold.

Sachi screamed again, and also swore a little. She dropped the phone.

She tried the bathroom door, which held fast. That was more than a little alarming, especially because that door didn't even *have* a lock.

Bloody Mary hissed.

With all her might, Sachi swung her baseball bat right at Bloody Mary's face.

It hit her. But it seemed kind of like it was hurting Sachi more than Bloody Mary. The impact reverberated all up her arms and shoulders. It was like hitting a brick wall.

"Um," Mary asked. "What?" She turned, very slowly, to look fully at Sachi. She didn't really look mad, just confused. All the orifices on her face were still dripping slowly.

"Don't eat my soul!" Sachi said, as sternly as she could. "Um... begone!"

"Did you summon me... just to hit me with a bat?" Mary asked.

"Obviously that wasn't the intent. I mean, I didn't think it would *work*," Sachi said, a little embarrassed and trying to pretend that she wasn't. "So the bat was really just a precaution."

"Who brings a *bat* when they're trying to call a ghost?"

"A girl scout is always prepared," Sachi said sullenly. Then she remembered she was talking to Bloody Mary and hit her again.

Again, not a lot of impact on Mary, but Sachi's fingers tingled.

"Stop!" Mary said. "What's wrong with you? A hundred years I've been doing this and no one's ever tried to assault me, much less with a powder-puff baseball bat."

There was a brief silence, within which Sachi and Mary stared at each other.

"... what, really?" Sachi asked.

"Yes!" Mary said. "It's not normal! You don't even think I'm real, and you still bring a bat? You're not expecting me to come out but you still smack me with no hesitation?" Her voice had an odd little hiss to it, especially on the *S*'s. Not like a snake. More like a skipping CD.

"Not that," Sachi said. "Have you really been trapped in the mirror for a hundred years?"

"Oh," Mary said. "Well, yes."

"But," Sachi said. It seemed like she had gone through weird, passed through freaking out, and come completely out the other side. "But that means you've never had Cheetos." Without thinking about it, she tried the doorknob again. "There's some in the kitchen," she said, and the knob turned.

Mary had very sharp teeth, Sachi discovered. But she seemed to find the Cheetos an interesting challenge. The gummy worms seemed to perplex her a little, but that was probably par for the course when you were a hundred years old. They probably didn't even have food coloring back then.

They raided the kitchen then retreated to Sachi's room. Downstairs could be cavernous when she was home alone, dark and empty even with all the lights on. She always felt safer in her own space.

They sat across from each other on Sachi's bed, various snacks scattered between them.

Mary had wiped her face and the blood had mostly stopped dripping out. Sachi thought maybe it was just an intimidation thing, like how a cat's tail puffed up to frighten off its enemies. In the light of Sachi's room, she was still pale and tired looking, but somehow softer.

"This one's spicy, okay?" Sachi said, handing over a bag of Hot Cheetos. Her bat was leaned against the side of the bed, but she wasn't truly worried. Mary's fingers were stained artificial red and orange. "So don't spit them out like you did with the wasabi chips."

"It's your fault for not warning me," Mary said, but she licked out a pink tongue, slightly too long, to taste the chip before putting it in her mouth. "Okay, so then what happens?"

Sachi was explaining the plot to the TV show all the girls at school kept up with on Friday nights. It was, admittedly, kind of a bad show. But it was entertaining. "So then Vanessa —that's the secret princess undercover in the high school— finds out she has a *twin*," Sachi said.

"*No*," Mary said.

"*Yes*," Sachi said. "So, like, while she's dealing with that, it turns out there's a vampire loose at the school…"

"This show seems very complicated," Mary said.

"Oh, it is," Sachi said, leaning back. "That's kind of the fun part about it, you know? Escapism." Mary gave her a quizzical look. "Going somewhere else for a little while," Sachi said. "Where your problems don't seem so close, and all the drama can be solved in forty-five-minute chunks."

"That sounds nice," Mary said. "I like this show."

Sachi beamed. "Here, try this one," she said, assembling more food for her. "Fluffernutter sandwich. I practically live on this stuff."

"I don't live," Mary said solemnly, but she took the proffered sandwich anyway. Her fingers brushed Sachi's, cold but not uncomfortably. She took a bite, then made a noise like a dog eating a jar of peanut butter.

Sachi couldn't help it; she laughed.

"Ifff goo'f," Mary said, around a mouthful of food. "Kinda 'phticky."

Sachi put a hand over her mouth, hiding another giggle.

"Rude," Mary said, once she'd swallowed her bite.

"Sorry," Sachi said.

"No, it's nice," Mary said. "I don't usually have people talking to me like I'm a person. It's usually more like 'oh no, why, ouch, my eyes, why are you eating me?' That type of thing."

"I don't like to victim blame," Sachi said. "But it kind of seems like their own fault for not bringing their baseball bats along when they summoned you."

This time it was Mary's turn to laugh; Sachi found herself surprised by the delight it invoked—an ugly, snorting kind of laugh that was more real and genuine than anything Sachi had heard in a long time.

"You are a strange one," Mary said. "I don't think I've ever met anyone as brave as you."

"Brave?" Sachi asked, raising an eyebrow. "I almost peed myself when you came out of the mirror."

"Yeah, but you were willing to fight for yourself anyway," Mary said. "You didn't just give up. I like that."

"Oh," Sachi said. "Thanks."

"So?" Mary said. "What happens next? Do they find out that her mother is actually her from the future? That's my theory."

"No," Sachi said, "It turns out it was an alternate reality..."

When the pre-colors of dawn started to stream in through the window, Mary said she had to go.

"It's kind of the thing," Mary said, as they journeyed back to the bathroom. "Darkness, light. Creatures like me don't really go in the bright spaces. Not like you."

"I think you're plenty bright," Sachi said, and Mary ducked her head shyly. "You'd look good in pink," Sachi added, even though she'd left the baseball bat behind in the bedroom.

They reached the bathroom, and Sachi pushed the door

open. She kept the lights off again, with just the soft night-light shadowing their faces.

"Thank you," Mary said. "I haven't spoken to anyone in... a long time."

"Any time," Sachi said, and Mary gave her a faintly surprised look. Mary put one hand on the glass of the mirror. She didn't leave any kind of handprint behind.

Mary paused and tilted her head hopefully. "Is there anyone you want me to kill for you?"

"Well, the lunch lady at school keeps giving me regular milk instead of chocolate," Sachi said. "But I'm pretty sure that's not really a killing offense."

Mary smiled. There was still a little marshmallow smudged at the corner of her mouth. "Goodbye, then."

"Goodbye," Sachi said. "And, uh, thank you, too. It kind of feels like it's been a while since I've really spoken to anyone, you know?"

Mary smiled. Then she pressed both hands to the glass and drew it apart, like a curtain. She climbed into it and was gone.

Sachi pressed her fingers to the corner of her own mouth, thinking she should have wiped off the sweet taste from Mary's lips before she went.

Sachi checked the footage on her phone the next morning, still unposted. It was, as she had half expected, just a video of herself in the mirror, then her dropping her phone. Then it faded out into static. No one else.

She didn't tempt fate after that—she didn't go calling into a mirror again. But whenever she passed a reflection, she'd wave.

Sometimes the reflection would wave back.

It was Sachi's first date with a boy named RJ. It was not going very well.

RJ had been the one to ask her out, and Sachi, who had been in front of Emma Q. and Michaela and Isabella B., all cheering her on, had said yes. At the time, she hadn't had any real reasons to say no. She was regretting that now.

Sachi was still always prepared, if not a girl scout.

But having a taser in her purse and a couple of women's self-defense classes under her belt was nothing compared to the true reality. It didn't prepare her for being trapped in the car with a boy twice her size, or for being frozen with apprehension and the sudden realization that she had made a mistake. Her purse was in the backseat.

RJ slid a hand up her skirt.

"Stop it," Sachi said. "Let's just go to the movie."

"In a minute," RJ said. "This is fun, huh?"

"*No,*" Sachi said. "In fact, I changed my mind. I want to go home." She tried to pull RJ's hand off her leg but he was holding tight; tighter even the harder she pulled. It hurt. "Stop it."

"Don't be stuck-up," RJ said. "This is why everyone thinks you're frigid, you know."

His hand grazed her face.

Without much thinking about it, she bit him. He yelped and drew back, enraged, and slapped her. But she tasted blood. Not her own. His. It was almost enough to make her smile.

He pinned her down to the seat.

Sachi spied her reflection in the side mirror, her makeup streaked, her eyes wide. His hand went up her leg again.

"Bloody Mary," said Sachi, catching her own eyes in the mirror. "Bloody Mary."

RJ laughed; an ugly, mean laugh. "What are you doing?"

Sachi looked him directly in the eye. "Bloody Mary," she said.

Nothing happened.

Then the rearview mirror shattered, and Mary was there, clambering out of the windshield and into the front seat with them, limbs moving jerkily and eyes bleeding.

RJ screamed.

He jerked back off of Sachi as far as he could go, slamming into the door. He tried the handle several times, but it didn't open.

Mary crouched there, and turned slowly to look at Sachi.

"Do you remember," Sachi said, "When you offered to kill someone for me?"

"Oh, yes," said Mary. "I really, really do."

"Eating the body will mean there's no evidence to tie this back to you," Mary said cheerfully, with her feet up on the dashboard. "This is really just being practical."

"It's being *gross,*" Sachi said. She was going through RJ's wallet. He was dead anyway. He wouldn't miss the cash. Or the frozen yogurt coupon.

"The intestines kind of have the same texture as gummy worms," Mary said.

"Something I could have lived my life without knowing," Sachi said, but looking at Mary eating what was left of her date didn't bother her nearly so much as it should have. "Thank you. For saving me."

"I didn't do it for you," Mary said, blatantly lying. "I just like eating rapists."

"Okay," Sachi said.

RJ had a hundred bucks in his wallet in various bills. That pervy cheapskate had already told her she would be paying for her own stuff tonight, too.

But on the other hand that meant Sachi's funds had just increased greatly.

"Um," she said, "we were going to the movies."

"Oh," Mary said, looking at the last of RJ, which was halfway in and halfway out of her mouth. "Sorry I ate him then."

"What?" Sachi said. "Oh. I don't care about stupid RJ. But..."

"But?" Mary prompted.

Sachi, to her horror, felt herself blush. "Well, the evening doesn't have to be a *total* loss. You could come see the movie with me? And then we were going to have dinner after. I can pay! Or, well, RJ can."

"Oh," Mary said. "*Oh.*"

"Good 'oh' or bad 'oh'?"

Sachi watched with fascination as Mary blushed, too. Her skin was so pale and sallow that the red flush stood out prettily on her cheeks. "Good."

"Oh," Sachi said. "Good."

"Good."

Mary wiped a string of RJ's entrails onto the baby wipes Sachi had given her. Then, without looking, she slid her cleaned hand over to Sachi. Sachi took it. Her skin was cold but soft.

"I have to be home by morning," Mary said.

"I think," said Sachi, "that can be arranged."

Kenzie Lappin is a writer with a bachelor's degree in creative writing. She is published or set to be published with short stories in Wizards In Space Literary Magazine, Cemetery Gates Media, and with Brigid's Gate Press. Check her out on Twitter at @KenzieLappin.

MEMORIES UPON THE
EMERALD SEA
SAMUEL FLEMING

The wizard's tower of Ketteran Keep overlooked both the surrounding city and the misty falls that lined her edge. So high was the tower, that the city looked like a still painting beneath him, the people forgotten between the blocks. Even the mighty, billowing falls of Ketteran looked still from so high up, their turmoil reduced to a haze of white and gray.

Nighttime gave the only glimpses of movement. The street lanterns would illuminate, one by one, as workers lit the oil. Taverns were lit similarly. From the tower, each dusk looked like fireflies waking up.

Fane Rollus, the high magus of the realm, stood back from the window and peered out over the city—his home—and watched the evening fireflies alight. He stroked the long braids of his white beard idly, his hands always working, even when the wizard was not. Sun set on Ketteran, the falls, and the old wizard's keep, and Fane smiled inwardly.

The high wizard's study, by contrast, was awash in light and life. Everlit candles floated around the rafters of the pointed roof like fish, moving with minds of their own and congregating above their master in a school when he needed reading light. Blue electricity crackled around the room, contained by thin glass pipes. Sereel incense smoldered, the sweet, pungent aroma swirling in the updraft of the small warming stove. The latter doubled as a furnace for the old wizard in the wintertime and heated dinners when he forgot about them. The smell of wild rabbit filled the tower—as it had two hours ago when it was fresh.

And these were just the mundane curiosities of Fane Rollus's study. There were artifacts: curved swords from halfway across the world, leather tomes from lost cities, legendary staves whose names and makers were lost to history. Two winged skeletons of unknown creatures. And one mirror, most strange.

Sometimes Fane thought of what his tower must look like to a commoner below. That was, of course, if the commoners had the time to gawk at his tower. To hear his squire tell of it, the common Terran had not a moment to themself—and if they did, they silenced it with stiff drink. It was a wizard's privilege to gawk and wonder, his squire said.

That night, Fane Rollus's gaze turned from the solitary window to the mirror. It towered over the wizard, the height of it nearly brushing the rafters. Its sides were trimmed in fading yellow gold that Fane dared not buff. The surface was unlike any other mirror—the glass was green and had a rolling, curving surface, like a wave surging on a beach, cast and immortalized in solid form. The glass swirled from bright jade to deep emerald, and in the moving lights of the room, the mirror looked as if it were ebbing and swirling even though it was completely still.

Its name had been forgotten, much like the stave leaning against the doorway, the one made of elven wood the color of crushed blackberries.

The old wizard smiled at the mirror and, somewhere in the dappled waves, his incomprehensible reflection smiled back.

Fane's study of the mirror began innocently enough, as obsessions often did. Back then, Fane was a young, impressionable squire of the former magus, one still learning cantrips and simple hexes. It took only three times in gazing upon the mirror to unlock its potential—for the mirror to silently gift him with the words of power. This both worried Fane's master and endeared the young apprentice to him. Many times during his tutelage, Fane Rollus would work late into the evening, claiming to work on his studies, but really diving into the mirror.

The mirror was a place of perfect memory. One merely needed to say the magic words and think of a cherished memory to place it inside the mirror for safe keeping. Retrieving was much the same, except...

Fane Rollus gazed upon the mirror and said, "*By frozen warmth and captured dream, show me what thou has and what I've been.*"

And as the wizard spoke the ancient words, he was pulled into the mirror. The rolling green surface seemed to grow, stretching tall and wide in his view—but the old wizard knew it was merely a trick of the eyes. Even Fane's voice seemed to stretch as the illusion continued to nauseating dimensions—

Until the face of the mirror stretched out to the horizons as far as one could see, and the wizard stood on the face of it. The swirls and rises of the glass were hills and valleys to Fane. On this infinite plane, the ceiling of the tower was gone and replaced with a black and starless night. Beneath his feet, the rough green glass dropped down into a hollow abyss. It looked as if there was a space beyond the glass—though one that Fane shivered to contemplate.

Most nights, Fane came here—to this frozen, emerald sea. To this place of perfectly kept memories.

Finding the memory was merely a matter of *wanting* to find it. To think of a memory was to call it from the mirror.

Fane desired to see his mother and father, and they rose

from the depths beneath the ice. Flowing blue appeared from
below, those bright blue tunics they had always worn for the
week's worship. They fluttered to the surface like beautiful
fish. As they rose they brought the high singing of a wet finger
circling a glass. Then rose through the glass, to stand silently
before Fane.

His father was a towering fellow with a kind face and
deep-set wrinkles about the eyes. His mother was equally
imposing for a woman. They had both grown pale in their
later years and so that was how they appeared before Fane
now—regal and with hands folded beneath their loose
sleeves.

Fleeting scenes passed over the glass: Fane's bedroom in
his childhood home—scarcely more than a hovel. His father's
study to become a wizard and his insistence that Fane do the
same. His mother mending clothes and cooking spiced dishes
to cover up the poor texture of the meat. Each scene coming
and going with the rumble of distant thunder or muffled
waves. All the requisite emotions of warmth and fondness
passed through Fane as well and then vanished somewhere
across the green ice. His parents disappeared with it.

Others appeared too, dozens of faces rising from the
mirror's black depths to stand, facing him, each with the eerie
song of the mirror. This happened sometimes, unbidden. A
peasant family with dirty clothes, squat shoulders and kind
faces. Two looming warriors with unkempt hair, clad in steel
and cloaks, the woman wearing a necklace of trinket-gems.
Three nobles, gray faces half-hidden behind their deep, shim-
mering robes.

The old wizard supposed there was a connection between
the dozens of faces, but one he had forgotten, like all their
names. The older he grew, the more the absence of memory
troubled him. And so he walked past them as a king walked
past a crowd, with pale solidarity. Behind the people, scenes
swirled in the void: Market streets smelling of lamb and

spices, storerooms lined with grain barrels, marbled palace halls, and green fields and ominous dark sky. Places all as half-remembered as the people that filled them.

For that was the curse of the mirror—the mirror would remember perfectly, but the man would not.

One figure alone caught Fane's eye and kept it: His squire. A young man with a rough shaven face and a diligent mind. Had he chosen to be a craftsman instead of a magus, he likely would've been a journeyman and married by now.

Fane beckoned the squire to walk beside him, through the crowd and swirling scenes. A short walk away, a sheer-faced tower rose from the emerald ice—the wizard's tower of Kettering Keep. Behind the swirls of city streets, the billowing of the falls grew.

It was no night in particular, merely a night the two wizards had shared without study. Fane couldn't even remember what had prompted the evening or what the two said to each other as they walked up the winding stairs. But the mood was as light as mist and the bag of fresh rabbit felt heavy in his right hand.

The sun was bleeding orange when they reached the top. Fane lit the small stove for the rabbit, while his squire spoke alight the everlit candles and tidied the few items he knew the master wouldn't mind. When the stove began to crackle, the two sat and enjoyed the evening, sharing rabbit. Fane spoke of old spells and ill-received experiments, the squire of the city streets and news from afar. Only once did the squire ask about the emerald mirror, and only once did the master steer the young man away. As the evening drew on, they talked of childhood follies and hearty musings. The bustle of the city below faded until there was only the distant rumble of the falls.

And of all nights the wizard had spent in his study, late nights filled with work, this evening of levity had been far too short. For his squire had left when the streetlights were lit.

Alone in the tower, the old wizard had resolved to know his squire better, to learn about the man who had given so much time and dedication to his work and his master.

The old wizard lit sereel incense to clear his mind, the sweet, pungent aroma swirling in the air. It mixed pleasantly with the lingering spices of dinner. Then he looked out the window as he did so many other nights. The street lanterns and tavern lights emerged as the sun set, but soon the city and even the falls were reduced to a still painting of night. The wizard stroked the long braids of his beard idly as he stared out the tower window. Something he did because his hands were always expecting work.

That night, the old wizard's gaze turned from the solitary window to the mirror. It towered over him, nearly brushing the rafters and the breadth of it gave flat plane to the circular room, squandering a whole side of it. The green, rolling surface was as entrancing to him then as it was the first time he gazed upon it. Like a wave surging on a beach, cast and immortalized in solid form. Its name had been forgotten, like so many others. It was, perhaps, even larger and more captivating now than when he had first gazed upon it, all those years ago.

The old wizard smiled at the mirror, and, somewhere in the dappled waves, his incomprehensible reflection smiled back.

And he found himself wanting to relive again. So the old wizard spoke the magic words, as he did so many other nights.

"*By frozen warmth and captured dream, show me what thou has and what I've been.*"

So it was that the mirror grew and the man diminished, each time speaking a little more of himself into the swirled green face, his voice growing higher and more incomprehensible each time. For that was the curse of the mirror—the mirror would remember perfectly, but the man would not.

Until the frozen emerald sea was vaster than could be escaped and the old wizard was but another face beneath the surface.

Samuel Fleming is a Science Fiction and Fantasy author. He grew up in Maryland, spending most of his time swimming, lifeguarding, writing, and daydreaming about other worlds. He loves a good story no matter the medium and draws inspiration from books, TV, video games, comics, tabletop RPG's, and podcasts. He only comes up for air to share stories and dad jokes, much to the dismay of his wife and kids.

He's currently working on an unnamed dark fantasy universe comprised of the series *A Battleaxe and a Metal Arm*, *Tales from Another World*, and *The Sword of the Gray Queen*. This is his first professional sale. Find him and the rest of his stories at SamuelFlemingBooks.com

SKIN DEEP

ARLEN FELDMAN

My Grandpop took me to see my mother once. We had to sneak out of the house so that Grandmother wouldn't know. He didn't tell me why we were going at first—just that we were going to the circus.

Getting to ride in the front seat of the Studebaker was almost as exciting as anything I could imagine the circus had to offer. Just as amazing was leaving our house in Tennyson and driving two whole towns over—an unimaginable distance to me then.

Grandpop held tightly onto my hand, which was just as well because I wanted to go in every direction at once, enticed by the smells of food and animals, the gaudy colors, and the people. More people than I could have ever imagined in one place. But he took me past all of that, past the big tent—much to my disappointment—to a smaller tent tucked out of the way. Even then, I noticed the furtiveness of the audience, mostly men, as they paid their twenty-five cents.

Everyone knows about freak shows today, and this one had all of the standards—a bearded lady, a strong man, a midget couple, a wild-man, and a tattooed lady who, along with a mermaid wearing a skimpy top, drew whistles of appreciation from the crowd. To me, though, it was all new and all amazing. It didn't even matter that I could see the bad stitching on the mermaid's fake tail.

But the star of the show was the Mirrored Lady.

She came out wearing a cloak with a hood. The band went silent for a moment, stopping the constant oompah music that they played, regardless of what was happening on the stage. Then a guitar started to play a few simple chords and, with the slightest of motions, she dropped the cloak and stood motionless on the stage.

I remember everything about that moment. The silence of the crowd that was so amazed that they didn't even whistle. The slow turning up of lights that burnished her and reflected rainbows throughout the tent. And the sudden knowledge that there was someone who was, a little bit, like me. But oh so much more.

Then she started to dance. Slowly at first, the guitar keeping time. The lights reflected off of every single bit of her perfectly reflective skin. Even her eyes. She was wearing a swimsuit with a skirt that would be considered tame today but was pretty risqué back then.

A drum started and the crowd started clapping along to it as the Mirrored Lady began to spin, going faster and faster until it seemed impossible, the lights reflecting and blinding the audience, who didn't seem to care.

And then she disappeared. Probably through a trapdoor, but at the time it just seemed like magic.

There was silence for a moment, then the crowd erupted into applause. The tent started to empty almost immediately since the show was obviously over. Instead of following the crowd, though, Grandpop gently tugged me toward the front of the tent, where a muscular man was guarding the stage-side exit. Grandpop whispered something to the man that I couldn't hear and slipped something into his hand. The man glanced at me for a second, then moved aside to let us pass.

The exit led to a grassy area cut off from the regular trade. Several small tents and old trailers surrounded the space, along with stacked cages, piles of wood, and other random gear. Some of the people back there seemed busy moving things around, while others were resting after the show. Standing in front of one of the trailers was the wild man.

Fifteen minutes ago, I'd seen him running around on all fours, growling at the audience, his dreadlocks flying. Now he was dressed in a suit and tie and was smoking a cigarette. His hair was still wild around his dark face, though. He winked at me and I giggled.

It's not like I had forgotten the Mirrored Lady. Far from it. But I was still a seven-year-old girl.

"We're looking for Dot," Grandpop said. "Dorothy Maywell."

The wild man pursed his lips, then pointed at one of the trailers with his cigarette. Grandpop nodded at him, and we headed over, my hand gripping Grandpop's as hard as I could. My name was Maywell too. Ellie Maywell.

The door to the caravan opened after two knocks, and there she was—the Mirrored Lady. She was wearing a dressing gown that covered her up to her neck, but her face was uncovered and reflected the sunlight even more amazingly than it had the lights in the tent.

She frowned, and even that was beautiful—light bouncing around the little creases.

"Dot."

"Dad."

She didn't exactly invite us in, but she didn't slam the door in our face either. After a moment, Grandpop put his foot on to the laddered step and the Mirrored Lady moved back to let us in.

Normally I would have been wonderstruck at the inside of the trailer. It was a perfect little world, with a bed and tables covered with exotic trinkets. But at that moment I couldn't do anything but stare at the Mirrored Lady.

"I thought she ought to meet you. At least once."

She just grunted and sat down at a little dressing table, then started to apply some sort of powder to her neck and face. After a while she started to look like a normal person, not reflective at all. Except for her eyes.

I took off the dark glasses that I always had to wear when I was out and stared at the Mirrored Lady with my own silvered eyes.

"Mamma?"

Another grunt, but I saw that she was swallowing hard and blinking. The caravan was only lit by candles, but every time she blinked there was a flicker of light, then dark. Like she was sending me a code.

I think I may have been crying, but I never stopped staring. After a while she turned to me and actually smiled. She put out her hand and I took it. At first I thought she was going to shake it, like she was meeting another adult for the first time, but she just held it.

"Ellie. Nice to meet ya. I'm Dot."

I just nodded. I could see myself reflected in her hand—but distorted so that my face looked too short—like in the back of a spoon. I never wanted to let her hand go. And now the image was even more distorted by my tears.

The Mirrored Lady squeezed my hand, swallowed, and then started singing. It was a popular tune back then. *Too-Ra-Loo-Ra-Loo-Ral. Hush now don't you cry.* Just like everything else about her, her voice was beautiful.

I have no memory of leaving the caravan, or of getting home, although I think Grandpop got yelled at by Grandmother for sneaking us out.

The accident happened when I was nine.

I'd collected every mirror in the house that wasn't too heavy for me to carry. It was an old sprawling house that I'd spent years exploring, and I knew where all the mirrors were hidden—under cloths with old furniture, in cupboards and wardrobes, even one small one in Grandmother's room.

I used string to tie them to me. Two big ones made a sort-of sandwich board that covered my back and front. I'd spent hours making intricate string nets to hold others to my arms and legs, and I had a couple just sticking out of my drawers.

I tried dancing, but it was too awkward and heavy. I did manage to spin a bit. My room was too dark, though, so I went out into the hallway—dressed only in my underthings and all the mirrors—so that I could get to the big window.

Grandmother should have been in the kitchen. That is where she always was in the morning, but for some reason she'd come upstairs. She stared at me for a second, then started towards me, her hand raised.

"You slut. You little slut."

I didn't even know what the word meant, but I knew it was bad. I turned and tried to run, but the weight was too much. I tripped at the top of the stairs.

I don't exactly remember what happened next, either. They must have driven me to the hospital, I suppose. I know I was there for a long time. They managed to save my life, but the scars—the scars never left me. There was an ugly roadmap of scars over my entire body and my face, although miraculously, my eyes—which were already mirrors—were untouched.

I do sort of have one memory from the accident, although it may be a false one. I was lying at the bottom of the stairs, broken glass all around me making rainbow patterns on all of the walls, and I was sure that my mother had come for me.

When I was thirteen, my skin started to change.

I'd bled for the first time a month earlier and that had been a complete, miserable shock. Fortunately, I had been at school and not at home when it had happened. The one time I could say that I was better off among the teasing and abuse from my classmates.

The school nurse was sympathetic and kind, although it took a while for her to convince me that the bleeding was something that happened to all girls.

But my skin—I was pretty sure that was just me.

I first noticed it on my arms, but when I started searching, I found patches on my legs and on my back. The skin had gone from white to milky to gray. Only a few spots were truly reflective—true mirrors like my mother. But they were ruined before they formed. My scars twisted across the surfaces, showing horrible distortions of my already distorted face.

I hid it from Grandmother, of course. I was in the habit of covering my arms and body as much as possible anyway, so it wasn't so difficult. That worked until my face began to change. I brushed my hair forward as much as possible and just hoped that would be enough.

Grandpop had died two years earlier, which still hurts to think about. Things had gotten worse and worse between me and Grandmother. Whatever I did, it was never enough.

I'm not sure what she saw when she looked at me, but even then, I sort of knew that she wasn't seeing *me*—just some twisted reflection of her own misery and anger.

Eventually we just stopped talking to each other.

It was just the two of us at dinner one night. I had made soup, and Grandmother and I were sitting opposite each other, silently eating. I'd grown used to the silence by now. Preferred it.

But when I looked up for a moment, she was staring at me, and seemed to be quivering with rage. She stood and I actually backed up as though she was going to hit me.

Instead, she turned and walked out of the room. I touched my face and realized that the silvery-gray patches had spread farther down than I'd realized. They were clearly visible below my hair. Little areas of cool smoothness between the rough, ragged scars.

Not knowing what else to do, I finished my soup, then took both bowls to the kitchen and washed and dried them. Then I went out to the hallway. Grandmother was standing there by the front door. A small suitcase sat on the floor next to her.

We started at each other for a long time.

"I don't know how to stop it," I said. "Tell me what to do, and I'll do it."

"Go. Just go." She said it quietly, which I think made it worse. Crying, I moved toward the door, and she backed up as though I was going to attack her. I grabbed the suitcase and ran.

Grandmother had packed all of my clothes, and I found an embroidered wallet inside that held fifty dollars in shabby fives and ones—which seemed like a fortune to me. At first, I thought Grandmother was being kind. Then I thought she was giving me money so that I could get as far away from her as possible. It was only years later that I started to understand that a person's motives were often not so simple.

I took a bus to Chicago just because it was a city I'd heard of—and was less scary-sounding than New York City. It never occurred to me that they wouldn't sell a ticket to a kid. I guess it never occurred to them either.

The fifty dollars didn't last long. I tried to get a job—I was a pretty fair hand at sewing and could wash dishes as well as anyone—but I was rejected automatically for being too young. Or too scary looking. I went in to one shop that made dresses and had a help-wanted sign in the window. The woman at the counter took one look me and just started to scream and scream. I ran.

After that, I ended up begging. It was the one job where my scars were an advantage. Well, if I could have found a circus sideshow, maybe I could have worked there too, but I had no idea how to find one. As I grew older, at least I was spared much attention towards the *other* profession that young women on the street tended to drift towards.

I had a whole series of places to sleep. Some of the smaller parks worked okay in the summer, so long as you avoided the *bad* cops. A lot of cops would see me, see my face, then leave me be. I loved Grant Park where I could stare at Lake Michigan, watch the waves, and *not* see my reflection. But that was rich-person territory, so I generally couldn't sleep there.

In the winter, Chicago got cold, but, strangely, the cold didn't really bother me. I tried to stay out of the wind, but I usually didn't need to spend any of my small store of money on one of the cage hotels, with their chicken-wire rooms. I also generally avoided the religious shelters with all of their rules and lectures. It was in one of those where my little suit-case had been stolen.

One night I'd found a spot to sleep in a shed behind a tenement on the South Side. I woke to screaming—the main building had caught on fire. I quickly grabbed my things and circled the building, planning on getting as far away as possible. But something about the fire was mesmerizing. I couldn't look away.

A crowd was starting to gather, and I pulled my hair over my face. It was much longer now and completely covered my scarred gray features. But no one was looking at me right then anyway.

Most of the residents had managed to get out of the building, some of them coughing, many of them with ash on their clothes. A couple of people in the crowd were holding back a woman who was trying to run back inside. She just kept screaming: "My baby! My baby!"

I don't know why I did it. Perhaps it was the idea of a child who was actually loved. Perhaps it was just because of the beauty of the fire. Or perhaps it was because I had nothing to lose.

I darted past the woman and into the building.

The noise was what hit me first. The fire was a roaring tempest of wind, punctuated by crashes as pieces of the building gave way. And I felt the heat—knew it must be intense—but it was just a rough tickle on my skin.

The first flight of stairs was intact, but the second had half gone. I had to grab hold of a smoldering beam and pull myself up.

The little girl was hiding under her mother's bed. By some flip of a coin, the room hadn't yet been touched by the fire. The noise of the fire just sounded like a distant storm.

I tried to coax her out, but when she saw me, she ducked back under again. Thanks to my scars, I couldn't even save her life.

Then, for some reason, my mother popped into my head, and I remembered her singing to me. My voice wasn't good, but I gave it a try.

"*Too-Ra-Loo-Ra-Loo-Ral. Hush now don't you cry.*"

The little girl poked her head out from under the bed and looked at me. Then she reached up and touched my face. I managed, barely, not to flinch.

"Does it hurt?"

"No honey, it doesn't hurt anymore."

She nodded and came all the way out. I smiled at her the best as I could and picked her up. When we got to the hallway, I could feel her trembling against me, her arms wrapped tight around my neck.

The beam I'd used to get up was gone. I looked around desperately for some way out, but I couldn't see anything.

"Honey, I need you to be really brave, okay?" I felt her nod.

"I'm going to lower you down to the stairs below. When you are ready, you're going to drop a little bit. Just a little bit. Then you have to run as fast as you can down the stairs and then out the front door. Can you do that?"

Another nod.

I lay down on the smoldering wood and took her hand and held it tightly. She whimpered slightly, but didn't cry. I lowered her down as far as I could. She looked up at me and I tried to smile. "Let go, honey. You've got to let go." I had to yell for her to hear me.

She fell, and my heart lurched as she crashed into the stairs, but then she was up and running. I stood up and ran as well, into the front room. I was having trouble breathing now, but I could still stand the heat. The front window was half on fire, but through it I saw the little girl burst out of the front door and into her mother's arms.

The girl pointed up at the window and soon a half-dozen other people were pointing at me as well. I ducked back into the room out of reflex. I realized I was sobbing. A moment later, I realized that I was on fire.

My clothes had caught, and all of a sudden, as though it had crossed some threshold, I started to feel the heat. For a moment I thought it would be fine—that my strange flesh would protect me. But my skin was imperfect, and that let the fire in. I screamed and tried to get the ragged clothing off of me, but it didn't matter, because now the fire was in my flesh, crawling along my scars.

The floor collapsed, and I fell, still burning, onto the floor below. The pain was now beyond endurance, and I screamed again, rolling on the ground in a desperate attempt to put out the fire, fighting until I no longer had the energy to move.

Then, strangely, the pain started to diminish—some sort of merciful release before the flame took me completely.

I closed my eyes, waiting for the end. And kept waiting. I don't know how long I lay there like that. Seconds. Minutes. But eventually I opened my eyes. There was no pain, and the room was full of rainbows.

I looked down at myself in amazement. The scars were gone. Just gone. Instead of milky gray, my arms were perfect burnished mirrors. I pulled the charred remnants of my clothes off. Then I started to spin. The fire sparked and glittered off of my flawless reflective skin—and it was beautiful. I think I laughed—the first time I'd done that since Grandpop had died.

A massive beam crashed down beside me and I suddenly remembered where I was. I ran through a wall of flame to get to the landing. I could barely see through the inferno that the stairs had become, but somehow managed to make it down to the ground floor without falling. My mirrored flesh was glowing red hot as I ran out through the front door.

Into the freezing Chicago night.

I made it four or five steps, then the cold started to win against my heat, my arms windmilling out to try to stop me from falling. I was sure that I was going to crack into a million pieces, but instead I just froze in place, my mirrored skin transformed yet again into solid, unmovable glass. My arms held out as if they were wings.

I never moved again.

Time passed. I was aware and not aware. I felt it when the women of the neighborhood came by and polished my skin, could hear their laughter as my reflections caused rainbows to burst over the otherwise gray buildings. Just like my mother, I was the center of attention, but I hoped that it was more for what I had done than for what I was—or for what I had become.

As I stood and dreamed, I became less and less engaged with the world around me. But I still was conscious enough to recognize the girl that came to visit me every year. She would lay flowers by my feet, then hold my hand and sing *Too-Ra-Loo-Ra-Loo-Ral* to me.

It was enough.

As well as writing fiction, **Arlen Feldman** is a software engineer, entrepreneur, maker, and computer book author—useful if you are in the market for some industrial-strength door stops. Some recent stories of his appear in the anthologies *The Chorochronos Archives* and *Particular Passages,* and in *Penumbric, Vanishing Point,* and *Little Blue Marble* magazines, with several more coming out soon. He lives in Colorado Springs, Colorado. His website is cowthulu.com.

LOVE MY NEIGHBOR
LAURA VANARENDONK BAUGH

You know that scene in every horror movie? The one where the half-dressed woman is standing at the bathroom mirror alone, opens the medicine cabinet for something, and when she closes it, the mirror shows the monster is behind her?

There was no monster behind me. There was no monster. There was no me.

I stared into the mirror, and the face of an Indian woman stared back.

It was clearly my reflection, though not at all my face. No one else was in the apartment, much less in the room, and it moved in perfect synchronization with me. I stared at the foreign face with a sense of detachment, which probably kept me stable. I'd done enough psych in college to know that hallucinations are more common than is discussed, and from some remote distance I realized I was having one.

This woman was a stranger. She was beautiful, and I wondered if maybe I'd seen her in a trailer for some Bollywood production. Maybe my mind was replaying the obscure memory for some reason. I should probably make a note of this.

I went into the bedroom and tapped into my phone, "Saw self as Indic woman. Bollywood?" and then I methodically got dressed, concentrating on buttons and snaps as if they were puzzles.

When I went back into the bathroom, holding my breath, I was in the mirror again.

❀

The basket was full of embroidered pieces, old-fashioned samplers with old-fashioned sayings. "Home, Sweet Home," no kidding, like mid-century parodies of the early 1900s. "Live, Laugh, Love" too, just as laughably ubiquitous. And near the bottom, "Love Your Neighbor As Yourself."

The needlework was good, at least. "Neighbor" had a tight, smooth finish, with an oddly iridescent sheen to the thread or floss. The letters had neat serifs, and tiny roses made a border. It was old-fashioned and kitschy, but kind of ironically cute.

I had made the mistake of stopping at the crafts booth, and the nice old lady behind the table was smiling at me with far too much hope on her face, and the sign on the basket said "$2," which was certainly a mistake for handwork, but maybe they were just clearing out old projects. I dug two crumpled bills from my pocket, change from my earlier nachos, and bought my way out of guilt as I moved on.

I forgot the sampler until I found it in my jacket pocket that night. I unfolded it as I walked into my bathroom, smoothed it, and set it on the counter as I used the toilet. It wasn't a bad piece, if one liked that sort of thing. And there were worse lines on friends' apartment walls. "Dance like no one's watching." "In this house we pledge allegiance to the flag."

I propped the sampler atop the medicine cabinet, out of the way, and left it.

The next morning I staggered into the bathroom, used the toilet, made my bleary way to the sink. I brushed my teeth, spat, replaced my toothpaste in the medicine cabinet. I closed the mirror, and that's when I saw the Indian woman.

I went to the coffee shop to work on the novel that was going to make me famous someday, when I would be featured on all the major talk shows and make literary fiction cool. Someday, after I finished it. I did not think about hallucinating a different reflection for myself.

The next morning, my reflection belonged to a Black man. I traced his lips on my own face and felt my own skin, and when I looked at my hands, they were my own, still bearing the scar from Gramma's too-dull paring knife. But in the mirror, the stranger blinked back in time with my own eyelids.

I wrote down this hallucination too. Two points made a line, a pattern suggesting I should probably call someone. But was I supposed to just phone up a local urgent care clinic and mention that I was seeing different faces in my mirror instead of my own?

But it wasn't consistent. In the restroom at the coffee shop, or in the lecture hall toilet on campus, or in the reflective windows at the convenience store, I had my own face. Was it only my own medicine cabinet? How weird would that hallucination be?

Not as weird as actually seeing the man who had first appeared in my bathroom mirror.

He came into the coffee shop and got into line, like he was a normal coffee-drinking person and not an impossible physical incarnation of whatever was haunting my medicine cabinet, and I stared openly before I caught myself. I jerked my eyes away, but I didn't think he had noticed. He was fumbling through his pockets, first one hand and then the other.

I slid my phone to selfie mode and checked my face. My

own face. But I was sure he was the man I'd seen in the mirror that morning.

And then he was at the front of the line but stepping away from the counter. "Sorry," he said with an embarrassed laugh. "I thought I had my wallet, but I guess not."

I bounced up from my table too quickly. "I got you," I said, surprising both of us. "Go ahead and order."

He looked surprised, and he ran his eyes over me as if trying to recognize me—and for one terrifying instant I thought he might, because what if he had seen me in his mirror?—but he did not argue, only said, "Hey, thank you, I appreciate that." And I bought his Americano, and he thanked me again, and he went out the door, and I still didn't understand.

The next morning I avoided looking in the mirror at first, because if I didn't see anyone who wasn't supposed to be there, then I didn't have to find a doctor, right? But eventually I slipped, while spitting toothpaste, and there was a professional-looking white woman in a pantsuit, maybe forty or forty-five. I closed my eyes and looked back at the sink.

She was waiting on a bench at the metro stop, fussing with a sticky latch on her messenger bag. When she stood up to leave, her phone remained on the bench behind her. I grabbed it and ran after her. "Ma'am?"

"Oh, thank you so much!" she gasped when she saw it in my hand.

I passed back the phone and returned to the bench, where I dropped heavily on it to stare at the opposite wall, because multiple dots make a line.

I wasn't having hallucinations. I was seeing real people, real people I would meet and could do something for. That was terrifying and also a little...amazing.

It was a little less terrifying to think I was not just seeing things in the mirror. Now I was seeing things in the mirror, but they had a purpose. (As far as *why* I was seeing them—

that was another scary question, and I thought I should handle just one at a time.)

I would at least test the pattern. Like any good scientist.

Red-headed teen boy with acne (I lent him a charging cable for his dead phone). Young woman on the metro clearly trying to avoid the pushy dude-bro who couldn't take no for an answer (I gave her the seat by the wall and stood in front of her). A cute kid in pigtails, maybe five, who spoke only Korean (she was trying to make friends at the park with another kid who spoke only English, and I bought them two coloring books and a box of crayons from a vendor cart). A man with age spots over much of his face (his wheelchair caught on a door frame). A woman with an elaborate updo, like all of Southern Gospel had a contest for using the most hairspray (she had an outdated address and needed directions to the bank branch).

I was still writing down the faces I saw in my mirror, but I did not want to call a doctor. This was something amazing, something real, and I did not want to be medicated out of it. Besides, I knew now where it came from.

I framed the *Love Your Neighbor As Yourself* sampler properly and hung it beside the medicine cabinet. As the weather grew warmer, every morning I checked to see whose face I wore in the mirror, whose face I would recognize later that day.

Paid in advance for the hazelnut and caramel lattes the regular study group ordered at the coffee shop, because one of the guys kept trying to find ways to save money without the others seeing. Held a door for a man with his arms full. Passed a paperback mystery I'd finished to a woman at the next table who was reading another.

Where did this come from? Obviously the sampler—it had started after I brought it home—but what was behind the sampler? Was the ghost of the crafty stitcher sending me visions? Was it God? Was I a prophet now?

Woman with a package of toilet paper and bottle of bleach (l let her go ahead of me in the grocery checkout). Man with dreadlocks (needed a hand trying to hang an extension cord). Woman with a large mole on her cheek (I offered to mail her package so she could comfort the crying child on her hip without standing in line).

"Love your neighbor" was from the Bible, I knew. But I didn't know until I googled that it was Jesus putting some sassy hotshot in his place. "Who is my neighbor?" the guy had asked, like needing a specific instruction would get him out of obligation to be generally nice and decent. And that's where the Good Samaritan story came from.

Weird fact, "Samaritan" was an ethnic term; I'd never known that, just thought it was a word for good person. Apparently they were on bad terms with the Jews and that's why back then it was such a dramatic story of do-gooding.

I was doing good, too. My days ran differently now. I still went to work, went on my evening jog, went to the coffee shop to write, went to class, went to the grocery. But now I spent time watching the people around me, keeping an eye open for the face I had seen that morning. Once I had seen my target, the rest of the day held a feeling of happy accomplishment. I might not be able to shave thirty seconds off my mile, but I had made someone's day better, and which mattered more?

I kept recording the faces, but it was getting hard to describe them distinctly. *Girl in braid extensions. Man with star tattoo by ear. Missing front tooth boy. Bearded man. Model-beautiful woman. Heavy middle-aged woman. Androgynous person with pierced eyebrow. Adolescent boy with freckles.*

And then I looked into the mirror, ready for the day's assignment, and my heart twisted in my chest.

The face that stared back at me was white, shaved bald, with a swastika tattooed on one side of his bare head and, when I turned in slow shock, an iron cross on the other. There were silver rings in each of his ears—not my ears—and a chain about his neck. He had fuzz on his upper lip.

For the first time, I stepped back from the mirror and lifted my arms. The tattoos extended down shoulders and arms: a reichsadler, SS lightning bolts, a Totenkopf, a pair of boots with a menacing 8 on each one. It was a veritable catalog of hate.

I couldn't breathe. How could I look for this guy? How could I find a way to do something for a Neo-Nazi skinhead?

I left the bathroom and went to work.

I didn't see him at work. I didn't see him at the gym. It was on the metro that I finally realized he was sitting next to me.

He had hair, which covered his scalp tattoos, and long sleeves, which covered the ones on his arms. This made him nearly blend with the other riders. But the earrings were the same, and the fuzz on his lip, and he kept his eyes on the floor between his knees as he manspread, like he knew he couldn't look anyone in the eye.

I turned my head and stared at the opposite bench until he got off, one stop before mine.

The next morning I looked eagerly in the mirror, anxious for the next face. But the skinhead looked back at me again.

Again? How could this be? No one had ever been repeated before—not even the first woman I'd seen in the mirror but hadn't noticed in real life, the only other one I'd never helped. How could this skinhead be the first to repeat?

I opened the cabinet door so that I did not have to face him as I brushed my teeth.

He was on the metro again. He had on a red ball cap and a light jacket despite the warmth, but of course he'd want to keep his arms covered. I realized I was the only one who knew him for what he really was. He was hiding it from everyone else, but I knew.

No one would judge me for being nice to him, but I would still know.

This time we got off at the same stop. He went left, and I went right. It was only a little bit further to class that way.

In the bathroom, the sampler faced me blatantly, its neat needlework precise in its accusation. *Love Your Neighbor As Yourself.*

"He's not my neighbor," I muttered aloud. He was a horrible person who believed horrible things, and who knew what he'd actually done for those beliefs? Not my neighbor.

He came to my coffee shop. Sat at the table next to mine. Looked over at me a few times, as if he could feel my disapproval, and finally turned his chair to face away.

Good. Not my neighbor.

At home, I took the sampler off the wall. I held its frame in two hands, debating what to do with it. It felt wrong to throw it away; surely the previous exercises had been for good. But three days now it had given the me the same skinhead face, and I wasn't going to do it. I had standards. I held the moral high ground here.

And the sampler knew. The mirror could have shown me the man as he looked now, without the tattoos, and I would have picked up his fallen bag or whatever without a qualm. By showing me what he really was, it gave me knowledge I didn't need to just do something decent. Now I knew he wasn't decent, and I couldn't fall to his level.

But it felt wrong to throw the thing away. And maybe it would haunt me or something, more haunting than showing me faces in the mirror.

In the end, I propped the sampler's frame across the top of the trashcan. A threat, maybe, of what would come if it did not show me another face in the morning.

In the morning, the skinhead looked back at me from the mirror.

I struck the vision without thinking, and the mirror shattered over my hand and the sink and floor. I threw a towel down on the tiles to pick my way out for a broom, and the twenty minutes spent patching myself, sweeping up the shards of glass, and avoiding the Neo-Nazi watching me from the fractured mirror made me late to the metro, where I barely squeezed on as a final passenger.

It was crowded, and I cradled my bandaged hand to my chest. The starting jolt threw me back and I stumbled, stepping on someone's foot.

"Here," said a voice, and it was him, gesturing me toward the seat he was rising from.

I stared, speechless with surprise and revulsion and anger, but I could not shout at him because no one else knew. They just saw a guy being nice on the metro, and I would look like the anti-social freak. And while I hesitated, my stupid social conditioning hijacked my mouth so that I said, "Thanks," in a dull tone, and then once I'd acknowledged him, my legs put me in the seat, and he stood with his arm up on the grab rail—his right arm, I noted, how natural for him —while I fumed in the seat.

How dare he be nicer than me. How dare he!

...Was I *his* neighbor?

I fumed on that all the way to work.

At work, I could not concentrate, and I dropped a bottle of cleaning fluid (I blamed my injured hand) and accidentally locked my laptop in a filing cabinet (don't ask), and it was a relief to leave for lunch.

He couldn't be my neighbor. Besides, I hadn't seen any obvious way to do something for him, not like I'd seen the others drop a phone or need change or something. Of course, I'd been working hard not to see him at all, but still, no obvious need. Not my neighbor.

I ate soup, which I spilled on my shirt.

When I went into the coffee shop with my laptop, he was already there, and I almost left. But I didn't want to lose my coffee shop to him, not when I hadn't done anything wrong, so I defiantly went to the counter and ordered a cappuccino. Then I took a corner seat (the only one left, unfortunately near him, and I wondered if he remembered me from the metro) and sat sullenly facing across the room. He couldn't run me out of my regular coffee shop.

He was fine. He didn't need my help. He clearly had plenty of time and resources to make other people miserable.

There were a lot of the usuals today. I didn't know most of their names, but there was the college group reviewing together, a woman working on her laptop while her four-year-old drove toy trucks around her table, a man playing several games of virtual chess, against the computer or maybe online.

I didn't see exactly how it happened. One of the college kids was returning from the counter, pouring sugar into an open cup and apparently not looking where the child driver had just parked several toy cars. Foot met wheels, he stumbled to avoid the kid, and hot coffee went all over the skinhead's arm.

"Oh, man, I'm sorry!" The student snatched napkins from a nearby dispenser.

The skinhead had jumped up and was rubbing at his steaming arm. A barista dashed from the counter. "Here's a wet rag and ice. Get it on your skin, it'll help."

"No, it's—"

But she was already pulling at his sleeve, and she did not have to pull far to reveal the telltale SS lightning bolts.

She jerked back, and the college student stopped with his wad of napkins. Everyone went still for a moment.

He jerked his sleeve down. The mother pulled back the child she'd already jumped up to retrieve. Everyone stared—even those too far away to see the tattoo could see that something had happened.

Love your neighbor as yourself.

I stood up, took the ice water and rag from the surprised barista, and slapped them onto his table.

"What, you're not scared of me, like everybody else? Are you too cool for that?" Every word was a sneer.

"Not too cool," I mustered. "Just thought I'd treat you like you should treat other people." It was the meanest way I could think to be nice, and it wasn't a Hollywood-level quip, but it was the best I could do under pressure.

He scowled and slouched into his chair, looking away. I sat in mine, silence between us. I let a stream of epithets run across my mental screen.

Neither of us moved, and at last I risked a sidelong glance toward him. His chin rested on his hand, which partially covered his face, but I could still see how his lips were thin, the corners of his mouth turned down. Was he—was he fighting tears?

Had I made the skinhead *cry?*

I turned away, hoping he hadn't seen me looking, but his rigid posture told me he had. Then he grabbed his bag and launched out of his chair, heading for the shop door.

Fine. Good riddance.

I turned back and saw his phone lying on the floor under his seat.

Damn it.

I picked up the phone and followed him outside, hating myself and the mirror that wouldn't let up until I did this. At least I'd be done with it all soon. "Hey," I called to his back, already two dozen paces away.

He gave me the finger without looking back.

"Hey," I repeated, irritation in my voice. "I just want to give you your phone."

He slowed, brushed his pocket, and then stopped. When he turned back, his face was tight and pale. He stood in place and looked past me.

I approached and held out the phone. "You left this."

He jerked the phone from me, not even grateful. But I didn't need him to be grateful; I was done. I turned back.

"I wanted out."

The words were small, forced, angry. I hesitated.

"Just so you know, I wanted out. But that's not so easy. And not with—you know."

Damn it.

I knew now, knew what I had to do, and it was not returning the phone. I turned back. "I'm sorry."

He shook his head in a short movement. "You saw what you saw." He started walking away.

"Hey," I said. "See you on the metro tomorrow?"

His stride slowed. "Yeah." And then he was gone.

So maybe he wouldn't avoid me. Okay.

I went back to the coffee shop, one he probably wouldn't return to. I stopped inside the door, and a dozen customers looked at me with curiosity or resentment. I cleared my throat. "Tattoo removal is expensive."

There was a slow shift as the realization worked around the room. Some looked down at their tables in guilty surprise. Others grew defensive. "Shouldn't have gotten them in the first place," someone snapped.

"So no one can make a change for the better? You'd prefer people stay in their mistakes?" I didn't give space for an answer. "I've got fifty bucks I'm putting toward removal treatment. I know that won't get far, and I don't know what the cost is, but maybe it's something we regulars could do."

There was a moment of shock. I went to the counter, took a cup, and shoved a twenty in it. I wasn't carrying fifty, but I could get it.

"It cost me four hundred to lighten my ex's name," a woman said. "That's twenty people with twenty dollars."

"I'm not paying for Nazi bigots," someone snapped.

"No one's asking you to," I said. "Just an option, if you want to help out someone who needs a hand changing his life." I wrote *Tat Removal* on the cup and set it on the counter, looking to the barista. She nodded. "This'll be here if people want."

I went to my corner table and sat down, trying not to look at the counter. For a moment, no one moved. But then a man got up, ordered a brownie, and dropped his change into the cup. That was a start.

I couldn't concentrate on my laptop screen, but I pretended. I pretended through two refills and a sandwich. Four hundred wouldn't begin to cover the cost of removing what he wore on his arms, and maybe there were more on his torso, even if he kept what was hidden by his hair. But it would be a start, and most importantly it would be a message that there was a road back.

I stayed later than usual, and at last I got up and went to the counter. I asked the manager if she would keep the cup of cash, so people would know I wasn't running a scam. I peeked inside the cup, and it was full of bills, mostly small but with a dozen twenties and one fifty. And there were two business cards.

I pulled out the cards. The first was from a dermatology clinic, and on the back, in surprisingly neat handwriting, the doctor offered 80% off her removal services. The other was a black-edged card for a tattoo clinic, with an unspecified deep discount on cover-up work.

I dropped the cards back into the cup, snapped a lid on it, and passed it to the manager. I didn't say anything, because my throat was closing and I wasn't sure I had the words, anyway.

I would see him on the metro in the morning, and I would ask him to stop by the coffee shop. He would need some encouragement, but I could hint things were okay and there was something for him. And if he continued to refuse, I could take the money and cards to him myself.

I wondered what neighbor's face I would see in the morning.

Laura VanArendonk Baugh writes fantasy of many flavors as well as non-fiction. She has summited extinct, dormant, and active volcanoes, but none has yet accepted her sacrifice. She lives in Indiana where she enjoys Dobermans, travel, fair-trade chocolate, and making her imaginary friends fight one another for her own amusement. Find her award-winning work at LauraVAB.com.

WAR PAINTING

ELISE STEPHENS

"T hey make a man forge his own sword, then order
him to fall on it."

The warning haunted Nerr as the noonday sun
beat across his path. He paused at the open flap of the camp's
tallest tent and breathed through his mouth against the
stench of refuse and unwashed flesh. Why did this admoni-
tion plague him now? Just a year ago, he'd scrambled after
every scrap of wisdom his former teacher had offered, but
Nerr now viewed these words as fearful hyperbole, the
ramblings of a man who'd lost his stomach for war. And Nerr
wasn't Hallis's student anymore, so he didn't have to pretend
to listen.

"Enter," a voice called from within the tent.

The cool interior temperature prickled Nerr's skin. Twin
silver lanterns flanked Commander Jiskar Prusk, leader of the
Banner Lords regiment of the Royal Fornali Army. Behind him
rose an enameled desk and low shelves bearing thick tomes
with gold-lettered spines. Prusk's long, steel-gray hair was
twisted and braided, adorned with red, green, and blue glass
beads, and gathered into a tail at his neck. He wore a dark
robe, and his face was the hue of eggshell. Colorless. Like he'd

poured everything into his paintings. And this was Nerr's moment to prove his willingness to make the same sacrifice.

Nerr bowed and tried to discreetly wipe his sweaty neck.

Prusk said, "Nerramin Masson, I understand you want to join the Banner Lords. And that you've interrupted your training at Wessal Lumidden to do so."

Nerr nodded.

Prusk raised an eyebrow. "And what was your reason for leaving the lumidden?"

Nerr straightened his shoulders. "I wish to help reclaim Forna's ancient glory, not sit behind cold stone walls and paint lumastrations no one will ever see." Nerr had decided this sounded patriotic and purposeful, even if it wasn't quite the real reason he'd run away from Wessal.

Embarrassment kept him from adding, *I want to paint and be praised for it. And Hallis wouldn't teach me.*

Behind Prusk hung one of his Banner Lord recruitment lumastrations. The words proclaimed that Prusk considered all with employable talent, but the colors themselves had been imbued with another message. Nerr's throat tightened as the lumastration's influence overcame him. The scarlet border carried a sense of brutal purpose, and the upraised fists that brandished paintbrushes were shadowed with violet bruises, black blood, and cobalt splashes of burning zeal.

The Banner Lords' war paintings were said to wake lethal terror in the bellies of Forna's foes. Nerr wanted to be part of something powerful and world-changing like that. To be fearsomely visible. He'd had enough of being shoved outside of everything important.

Prusk crooked a finger and gestured Nerr forward. The twist of the commander's mouth might have been a sneer or a smile. "Are you ready to prove your ability?"

"Yes, sir." Nerr kept his eyes on the man's face.

At first, he'd just wanted to be a lumant. Lumanar Hallis

had let Nerr into his school as a kindness to the village outcast who could find no one else who'd apprentice him. Hallis had a benevolent reputation; he heard grievances, no matter how busy he was, and was known to give discounts to the poor who sought his lumastration services. There was no teacher more compassionate or honorable from whom Nerr would rather have learned the craft.

But Hallis had refused to begin Nerr's official instruction. Again. And again.

"Show me what you can do." Prusk gestured to a small easel beside his chair. It held a blank canvas. "Will you need supplies?"

That was a test in itself—to see whether Nerr had come prepared.

"No. I've brought my own." Nerr knelt and unslung his pack.

Hallis had never watched him use these lumidden paints. Nerr had painted with them in secret, against the lumidden rules. To know that Prusk, whom Hallis considered a warped monster, would first witness Nerr's work with them seemed somehow disloyal. But that was just the voice of weakness.

Hallis had once told Nerr, "You underestimate the greatness of your potential." The master's tone had somehow implied that this was a terrible potential. Hallis had added, "You'll hate me for delaying your training, but it's for your own protection."

Nerr opened his paint pots, one by one.

Hallis had never explained this lurking threat that he was protecting against. Was it external? From inside Nerr's own heart? He'd given up trying to understand it. The subject hurt too much to think about.

Nerr laid a few colors onto his palette and swiftly mixed his shades.

Lumastration was the only thing he'd ever been good at. It was his calling. When he filled his paint with sentiments and arranged them on a canvas so that viewers could look and experience the emotions in a balanced, blended form, Nerr knew he was offering his best gift to the world. If Hallis would block that gift, Nerr owed it to himself to take charge of his future.

Nerr felt Prusk's eyes on him as he selected two dominant sentiments for his lumastration—his yearning to serve a great purpose and his desire for knowledge—then fed them into his paints. Each color should embody just one sentiment, drawn from Nerr's consciousness into the paint held in his brush tip. The key was to hold the sentiment steady while he worked with a color or else he'd muddle the painting's clarity.

Nerr clamped his tongue between his teeth and moved his brush with fluid, deft strokes. The pangs of heat were already flickering in the bones of his brush arm, but he could easily ignore the lumastration symptoms for now.

If his parents received word that he'd been granted a place among the revered Banner Lords, helping to push back the Yukurish invaders, they'd have to forgive him for running away from Wessal. They'd have to be proud of him.

Nerr lifted his brush from the canvas and paused. His lumastration was a simple white pennant undulating in a blue sky with a glittering, topaz sunrise. He'd woven hopeful yearning into the light rays and filled the blank pennant with his anticipation for a deeper knowledge of war paintings. Nerr was still debating whether he'd put too much impatience into the ground shadows when he felt Prusk approach, almost brushing his shoulder. Nerr lowered his arm and waited for judgment.

"Unbridled ambition," Prusk said. He rubbed his wrinkled chin and returned to his chair. "Your desire to join is clear. You're likewise apt with form, color, and technique. What remains to be seen is whether you have the tenacity to make a real war painting." The eggshell face cracked as Prusk gave a thin, cold smile. "You shall undergo another test. Before sundown tomorrow you'll finish a war painting and present it to me, at which point I will determine your eligibility. I'll of course instruct the rest of the soldiers to leave you alone, to aid your concentration."

Nerr bowed. "Thank you, sir."

Prusk's eyes glinted like ice shards. "Gratitude may not yet be appropriate."

Nerr gathered his painting supplies, left his other belongings inside the sleeping tent, and set out to find a place to work.

It was a small camp, but loud enough to mimic a town. About fifty Banner Lords lived here at any time, cycling through in staggered intervals, with two dozen footsoldiers to run perimeter guard and manage food and maintenance.

Nerr passed a large tent with raised flaps and contents arranged like a classroom: rows of stools and low tables facing a blackboard. A hundred paces north of the instructional tent stood a large, velvet-sided one like Prusk's, set apart from the rest of the camp.

A man and woman emerged from it, headed toward the instruction tent, easels strapped to their backs. Both wore a black circlet with gold, indigo, and scarlet gems to mark their Banner Lord rank. Nerr had often wondered how such a circlet would feel on his own head.

He bowed low to them and murmured, "Clarity and color," the greeting between lumants.

The woman replied, "Shape and shadow," then frowned at him, as though she'd thought he was someone else and now scorned the imposter.

At the western edge of camp, Nerr climbed a small hill and found both fresh air and shade cast by a wild plum tree.

The hubbub had quieted here. He set up his easel and sat on the dry, crunchy grass.

This next part would not be pleasant. He'd have to dredge up his worst torments, the fears he'd fought his whole life to ignore: the aching loneliness, the broken dreams, the shame... everything that had, at one time or another, set ice to his heart.

He'd made many lumastrations, some sorrowful, some hopeful, but he'd never yet set out to create something explicitly destructive. After mentally sifting with gritted teeth, Nerr settled on a recurring nightmare from his childhood.

In this dream, he stood in a doorless room with just one window through which he could make out the lights of other homes. He would shout for help until he was half-weeping and pound on the smooth walls while, all along, something sinister stirred in the murky dark on the prison's far side. The weak lights through the window held it back from reaching Nerr, but with each cry that Nerr made for help, a light from outside would extinguish.

Nerr dropped his brush and wiped his eyes. The lumastration's fiery effect had already spread to the rest of his bones. Sweat stood out on his forehead.

A counter-ward! He'd completely forgotten to make a counter-ward. Nerr whistled in disgust at his own foolishness. He didn't dare finish this war painting without the proper precautions.

The sun was halfway down the sky as Nerr cut a wide strip from his shirt and bound it around his left forearm. Without the usual leather gauntlet on which to paint it, this tatter of shirt would have to act as his counter-ward's canvas.

He outlined a viridian oval on the counter-ward, then filled in the scene of a blue pond with a row of cream-and-brown ducks. He ringed the pond with a field of golden buttercups. Into the pond's blue waters he placed a memory of harvesting carrots with his mother. Into the buttercups he worked the enchantment of his first kiss with a girl named Glia. Onto the backs of the ducks, he pressed moments when he'd been certain his father was proud of him.

This finished, Nerr double-checked that the counter-ward was secure on his arm, then returned to his work. If, at any time, the war painting's unsettling sentiments were to savage him, Nerr could look at the counter-ward and unravel the damage.

By nightfall, Nerr felt light-headed with self-induced panic and his joints screamed at the slightest movement, as though the flames had seeped into his marrow. At least the burning sensation hadn't yet turned to ice, which would have signaled serious damage. He needed to find a hot bath.

Wessal Lumidden had been built near a natural hot springs so that its lumants could readily soak their aching bones after a day of lumastration to mitigate their craft's harsh effects. There had to be a similar set-up here. It was a Banner Lord encampment, after all.

Nerr made sure his canvas was dry, then shuffled back to camp with his shrouded painting pinned under one arm. He found soldiers sitting around rough-hewn wooden tables eating fish stew with rice and barley. The Banner Lords sat apart from the rest, but he wasn't invited to join them.

When he asked a footsoldier if there was a place for lumants to soak, she wrinkled her nose to imply he needed a bath for more obvious reasons, then said, "The Banner Lords have a bathing hut, but it's not for public use."

Nerr thanked her, gulped his stew, and stole a mugful of hot water from an untended pot. He hid himself in a dark corner of the sleeping tent, stripped down, and sponged himself. He'd escape the remaining ache with sleep.

Nerr was jerked awake in the full dark of night to the muffled sound of growling, weeping, and wild laughter. As the weird, heightened chaos grew clearer in his ears and the rest of the camp lay silent, a knot curled in his stomach. No one was rushing to investigate. Did that mean this was a normal occurrence? If so, what made such wretched sounds commonplace?

He tried to peer beyond his tent's flaps, but clouds blocked the moon and cloaked the campground in thick shadows. After a few minutes, the sounds quieted.

Nerr lay back down. The sleep that took him was troubled.

The next day, Nerr dragged himself to breakfast, trying to ignore the sensation of live embers sparking at each joint.

"Did you hear the sound of...mad laughter...last night?" he asked the man beside him. "I was wondering—"

The soldier's snort interrupted him. "You're the new Banner Lord try-out, aren't you? You'll get used to a lot worse if you want to stay on here!" He pointedly turned away.

Nerr wondered, for the first time, if Banner Lords were not as revered in their own camps as they were in the cities and towns that spread their rumored legend. He shuddered and asked himself whether he really wanted more people to hate him, but then pushed the quavering thought aside. He was used to hatred. What he wanted was to be worthy of notice.

Back at the plum tree, his second day of lumastration began as an excruciating uphill struggle. The fire in his bones scraped and stung as though raking him with hot claws and his color-mixing intuition felt halfhearted.

Once, he thought he fainted while painting, but no one came to help or investigate. His first war painting would be made alone. Camaraderie, if he earned it, would come later. Like the hot bath.

Nerr took to biting his left index knuckle to maintain focus. By midday, his teeth had cut into the flesh. The counter-ward helped, but only because he was careful to study no more than one quadrant of his canvas at any time, and even then he'd allow himself to fixate on just one color and sentiment in the quadrant.

He'd painted a place like his nightmare room, only this war painting prison was subterranean, dark, and the window hung directly overhead. He'd rendered a pair of hands reaching upward in piteous pleading, but they were the withered hands of someone who'd spent countless years in fear's thrall. He tried not to focus on specific details, but for some reason, the hands haunted him. Nerr kept looking down at his own hands, imagining them colored by dim dungeon light and crinkled with premature age lines.

Nerr knew if he surveyed this war painting all at once, he'd be bludgeoned by toxic fear and he wasn't sure his counter-ward could remedy that. Yes, Banner Lords had to be able to withstand the effects of their own creations, but surely they had been previously trained by intervals to build such endurance.

Nerr had suffused the gray shadows with the doom he'd felt ever since his parents had begun discussing his future in bleak tones. He'd dotted the stones in the prison walls with the uselessness that had trailed him after his unfair banishment by his village for making a tragic mistake. He'd edged the bars on the distant window with the blind anger that had tormented his sleep after each refusal from Hallis. First renounced by his village, then admitted into a school that had barred him from the knowledge he craved.

Nerr shuddered. This painting mirrored many of his darkest fears and held the power to destroy him. But that was the point: to cripple the foe with a blow so shattering, the enemy soldiers who saw it would freeze in devastation as it unfurled from its pole, and their minds would collapse into unspeakable horror and grief. They'd become husks, an easy harvest for the Fornali cavalry who followed behind the war paintings and cut down the paralyzed enemy like rice sheaves.

By the evening meal, Nerr had finished his painting and completely forgotten the sensation of hunger. He drank water and chewed some dried ginger as he tried to make himself presentable. On his way to Prusk's tent, he discovered the source of the previous night's commotion.

It was a woman, emerging just now from the Banner Lords' tent, hauled between two burly soldiers. The jeweled circlet had slid down across her face, pushing one eyelid closed. She laughed and cursed, bit and spat, and screamed in weeping bursts like a mother who'd seen the death of her children. Nerr stopped in his tracks and stared, mouth dry, as the fallen Banner Lord was led off to a waiting horse and cart. What would they do with her?

Two Banner Lords stood just outside the tent, smoking pipes and watching the exit of their disgraced colleague with blank expressions.

Nerr tightened his grip on his canvas and walked faster toward Prusk's tent.

He announced himself and stepped inside. The cold air grated on his bones. The commander had risen to meet him this time, a possible indication of favor, or perhaps a move to intimidate Nerr with his superior height.

Nerr set the canvas on the floor and leaned it against his shins. Even this slight contact made his leg bones ring as though struck by an iron bar. He bowed to Prusk and resisted the urge to bite his lip.

"Shall I show it to you, sir?" His own voice sounded like a crackling leaf.

Prusk took the war painting and turned his back to Nerr. He crouched before it and raised the veil halfway. The commander didn't shudder, but his neck muscles snapped taut for a moment. Then Prusk straightened and turned back to face Nerr. Nerr noticed a black-leather counter-ward on Prusk's arm that bore a complex lumastration of silvers, grays, and sea-blues. Prusk hadn't even glanced at it. The commander met Nerr's gaze. His face looked paler, but his eyes were sharp and hard.

"You're ready," Prusk said, "but I'm not your only audience."

Nerr felt the threat of another fainting spell as the commander added, "Your second test is complete. Your final one begins."

Nerr wanted to scream, to demand a hot bath. The human body couldn't withstand such exposure to lumastration, and Prusk should know that better than anyone. For all Nerr knew, his joints might have already sustained permanent injury.

Yet he couldn't embarrass himself with an outburst. Not now that he'd come so close.

He looked up and was astonished to see approval in Prusk's eyes. The commander was pleased. Nerr had managed to make him see his skill and his willingness to work, even to suffer for the process. Prusk had looked upon him and seen something valuable.

Nerr steadied himself. The test wasn't over, but his bones would eventually heal. The private bathing hut would soon be his. He only had to pass this last test and the pain would subside.

Prusk grinned at Nerr and the silver lanterns cast strange shadows on his teeth.

"For your final test, Lumant Nerramin, you must look upon your own creation with no safeguards to shield you. A Banner Lord stands by his own work without cringing. It's more than talent or technique or even the depravity that you put into the paints. It's the courage to face the worst in yourself."

Nerr's chest felt tight. No chance to rest or build up his strength.

Prusk held out his palm. "Give me your counter-ward. My Banner Lords must have the fortitude to withstand their own weapons."

Nerr unstrapped his counter-ward and passed it to Prusk,

not daring to watch what the commander did with it, for fear that seeing it vanish would make him lose his nerve.

"Take a moment to settle yourself," Prusk said. "Or find a comfortable place near the edge of camp, if you wish to be alone."

Nerr couldn't meet the man's eyes.

"Once you've looked at it," Prusk continued, "don't worry about coming back to tell me. I'll find you."

That probably meant he'd be easy to find. Nerr wondered if he would scream and thrash when he looked on his painting. How much had it taken to cause that raving Banner Lord to snap? Had her soul finally broken from exposure to the very things she'd made?

He'd heard that the Banner Lords who were dismissed from service were the weak and untalented, those unfit for the cause. Hallis of course, had claimed that everything about the war paintings was unhealthy, that no man or woman was strong enough sustain the creation of such depraved paintings.

Now that Nerr climbed the hill to the plum tree, feeling a bit like he was bound for his own execution, he knew what Hallis had meant with that story about making a sword and falling on it.

Nerr pushed the mental debate firmly from his mind. He'd chosen Prusk as his new master and he needed to act like it.

Nerr sat beneath the tree and took a moment to think of nothing at all. He listened to his heart and tried to breathe; he shut his eyes and raised his chin. He would be strong enough. He'd show the world his gift. True worth lay on the far side of this.

Nerr turned the canvas toward himself and tore back the shroud.

He stared into the heart of his own weapon with wide, unflinching eyes.

. . .

Elise Stephens credits much of her storytelling influence to a lifelong love of theater and childhood globetrotting. Much of her work focuses on themes of family, memory, and finding hope after a devastating loss. She is a first-place winner of *Writers of the Future* (2019). Her fiction has appeared in *Analog, Galaxy's Edge, Escape Pod, Writers of the Future Vol 35,* and *FIYAH,* among others. She lives with her family in Seattle in a house with huge windows to supply the vast quantities of light she requires to stay happy. Elise is currently seeking representation on her next science fiction novel. EliseStephens.com

THE MIMIC AND THE MANY MIRRORS

JD LANGERT

There once was a man who was famous for being able to see into and mimic the personalities of others. In doing so, he was able to give advice on who they were and what they should do in their lives.

When in front of a king, he'd become noble and resolute.

When in front of a thief, he'd become skillful and cunning.

When in front of a beggar, he'd become humble and resilient.

However, one day, the mimic was asked the strangest question yet:

"It's true that you can reflect the personality of all you see, but who are you truly?"

For the first time, the mimic was stumped. No matter how long he thought about it, he could not find a suitable answer. Thus, he began to ask those around him.

First, he went to his parents. In the reflection of their eyes was a lovable, dutiful son who would always honor them for raising him. While he was in agreement, it didn't feel like the answer he was seeking.

Second, he went to the woman he loved and who he knew

loved him. In the reflection of her eyes was a wonderful man that had always made her feel like no other. While he was happy, it didn't feel like the answer he was seeking.

Third, he went to strangers who admired him. In the reflection of their eyes was a wise man who always knew what to say and how to help them. While he was flattered, it didn't feel like the answer he was seeking.

Fourth, he went to strangers who despised him. In the reflection of their eyes was a foolish man with faults as limitless as the stars in the sky. While he was annoyed, it didn't feel like the answer he was seeking.

Frustrated from the many conflicting answers, the mimic went home and looked into his personal mirror to try and see what his true personality was. But just like the answers of those he'd asked, the person in the mirror seemed to change each time he looked.

However, looking in the mirror had given him an idea. It made sense that a typical, ordinary mirror wouldn't be able to show him what he was looking for. No, he would need to go on a journey and find a surface that would truly reflect what was inside of him. Only then could this conflict be resolved and he would know what to do with the rest of his life.

And so, the mimic left his home and ventured out into the world.

The first place he went to was a grand, towering waterfall. The waters were said to be so refreshing and clear that they granted clarity to all who peered into them.

However, when the mimic looked into the waters, he saw a calm, peaceful man who would achieve an existence with few worries or concerns. While envious of his reflection, it did not feel like the answer he was seeking.

Thus, the mimic continued his search.

The next place he went to was the home of a wealthy and extravagant dragon. The dragon was said to have a mirror made of priceless gemstones and metals that would show the glory of all who peered into it.

However, when the mimic looked into the priceless mirror, he saw a flamboyant and successful man who would achieve everything he'd ever desired. While envious of his reflection, it did not feel like the answer he was seeking.

Thus, the mimic continued his search.

The next place he went to was at the very top of the highest mountains in the land. These mountains were said to be so high that they gave a glimpse of the heavens who, in return for your hard work in venturing to the peak, would reward you with the answer you sought while peering into the clouds.

However, when the mimic looked into the clouds, he saw a spiritual man who would achieve enlightenment and always be devout in worship. While envious of his reflection, it did not feel like the answer he was seeking.

By now, the mimic was beginning to become desperate. He wondered if he would ever find the answer he sought, and began to wander aimlessly.

The next place he found himself was in the poorest, most desolate region of the land. While walking the streets, he found a homeless woman looking into a cheap, broken hand mirror. Believing he had nothing to lose, he asked to peer into it.

However, when the mimic looked into the cheap hand mirror, he saw a despondent and forlorn man who would always be plagued by doubts and uncertainty. While scared of his reflection, and hoping it was not the answer he was seeking, it gave him a new idea.

Determined, the mimic continued his search.

The next place he found himself was the home of an oracle in the deepest parts of the enchanted forest. The oracle had a crystal ball that was said to give you a glimpse of your future when you peered into it. The mimic believed that, if he knew what he would become, then he could become it now and save himself the time and effort.

However, when he looked into the crystal ball, he saw visions of multiple potential futures. Each version of him was more different than the last, with none of them feeling like the answer he was seeking.

More confused and desperate than ever, the mimic went to a place he knew he shouldn't search for answers, but he had no other choice at this point.

The next place he found himself in was the abandoned lair of a cruel villain who'd been defeated long ago, though his dark presence still lingered. To this day, in the center of the lair's crumbling remains, was a cursed mirror that would show you everything that you did not want to know about yourself.

And when the mimic looked into that cursed mirror, that was exactly what he saw.

But worst of all, it did not feel like the answer he was seeking.

In despair, the mimic hid himself away in the darkest caves where no light could hope to reach. He believed that, if he did not have to look at any reflection of himself, he would never have to wonder again about who he truly was.

It was then that he heard the voice of the woman he loved, calling out for him in the darkness. She'd become worried from how long he'd been on his journey and had tracked him down to this place.

While grateful to see her, he wasn't sure he could grant her request to return home. After all, who would he be when he got there? How could he live his life without knowing the person he should live as?

But after a moment, the mimic remembered the version of himself he'd seen reflected in her eyes — the wonderful man she saw.

He thought, *surely, as my lover, she knows me best. Thus,*

being the person she sees me as will make us both happy, so it doesn't matter if it's not the answer I'm seeking.

However, when he said this to her, she scolded him. She said that being what she wanted him to be wasn't the answer he'd gone through such effort to find, and, even if it was, she wouldn't be happy if she knew that she was deciding his life for him.

In misery, the mimic asked her what the right answer was then. After all, he'd been given so many, so which one was the truth?

She asked him, "Why can't you be all these things? You did or experienced all of them, so they're all a part of you."

She went on to tell him that no mirror can reflect all of what you are because living creatures are constantly changing and growing to add new parts of who they are. The person that he was before wasn't the same person he was today, but the person he was before didn't stop being part of the person he was now.

That, even when he chose to leave a part of himself in the past, it was still an important building block that made the person he'd be in the future.

"You are you," she told him, reaching out to hold his hand in the darkness. "So come home and be yourself—whatever all of that entails."

And so, the mimic took her hand and left the darkness, finally feeling like he'd found the answer he'd been seeking.

JD Langert is currently pursuing her MFA in Screenwriting at Western Colorado University where she also received an MFA in Genre Fiction. She has been published in John Hopkins' *Imagine* magazine, *The Drunken Odyssey*, *Flash Fiction Magazine*, and other publications.

Her favorite genre is YA Fantasy, but she can easily be drawn into any story where dynamic characters are thrown into an emotional blender! She dreams of one day working in animated television for children, but has an equal love for the world of novels. Some of her other favorites include cookie dough, musicals, and anime.

Feel free to friend her on any social media site, but if you'd like to find out more about JD, check out her website at jdauora2u.wixsite.com/jd-langert-website.

SEA GLASS

RACHEL MURTAGH

When I was a young woman, I married the man my parents wanted for me. If I had known who I was then, I would have chosen differently, but I had spent my life pleasing those around me. I wore their wishes like a second skin until I could not tell the difference between myself and others' visions of me. I reflected back desire like the depths of a wishing well. I became their perfect daughter, attending the university they wanted for me upstate, then following the career they wanted, until my body betrayed me.

Doctors could not tell me why my body simply refused to do as it was told. I would fall asleep, then walk freely, wandering the cold and foggy shoreline of the city until someone brought me home. The doctors gave me medicine to take every day, and the spells stopped. I had never been more than water, adapting to whatever was around me, never knowing who I really was, and now I did not even control my own body.

My parents came to believe that perhaps working life was not meant for me. They wanted someone to care for me so that I did not have to toil and could instead focus on raising a family.

They searched until they found their answer, the eldest son of my father's business partner who also worked with their law firm. We had seen each other and talked politely in church, but never had much to say. When they suggested we date, I obliged, and the son took me out to fancy restaurants once a week, his green eyes kind in the candlelight. I came to believe that I liked the idea, enjoyed the conversations that never steered toward work or health, or indeed anything personal on my end. I didn't have to want anything; he made all the decisions and wanted for me.

The week before our wedding, I was sick again. I begged it to behave, to do as I commanded, but it would not listen. I woke again and again from walking slumber, staring out to sea, sand on my palms and feet. I got through our wedding day in a haze.

Married life was not so bad. We moved into a nice apartment on the north side of the city not far from the beach. I went to the store in the morning, took walks by the shore, and collected bits of sea glass. I began to feel something, a stirring as I watched the waves crash onto the shore and carry themselves back out again, and again. I began to craft, my fingertips red and cut on edges of sea glass as I sanded and smoothed them. I made a mirror from the pieces to hang on our living room wall, a gorgeous dark green mosaic large enough to see my face within it. When I gazed into it, I saw a woman I almost recognized.

My husband began to change, then. Everything I did he did not like. How I folded the laundry, cleaned the dishes, the roast I made for dinner. Everything seemed to upset him. We fought all the time. I began to speak up, whispering how I felt in bursts, but it only ever made him angrier. We had dinner with our families every week, mine on Fridays, his on Sundays. No one seemed to notice a thing. I would think the dinner went fine, and once we were back in the car my husband would begin to scream.

You would think I'd remember the first time he hit me, but I don't. His anger and violence seemed to increase minutely, like drops upon drops, and before I knew it, I was drowning. I looked into my mirror and could not meet my own eyes.

One night he was angry about dinner again, or maybe the car, or work, and he smashed my mirror. I watched as his fist sent the pieces shattering to the ground that I had so lovingly put together. I screamed, trying to collect the shards with frantic fingers. He held one to my throat, the whites of his eyes too wide.

I didn't beg or struggle. I grabbed the piece sticking out of his hand and squeezed until warm blood trailed down my wrist.

Something calmed in him then. I'd never stared into his eyes without backing down before. He let the shard go, excused himself, and told me to clean up my mess. I did, picking up each piece individually, and cleaned them as well as I did my new wound. Not bad enough for stitches, but enough to hurt.

They wouldn't go back together the same way. Instead, I strung them up into suncatchers and hung them on every window, save for one piece. It was the largest I had, nearly the size of my palm. I smoothed its rough edges, rubbed the surface with oil until it shone, and when I looked into the mirror, I saw a face that was definitely not my own. I thought I must finally have gone crazy.

"Is this really the life you want?" the strange new woman asked. Her eyes gleamed green like the light off my suncatchers, her hair as dark as mine but longer, falling well past where I could see.

I swept my eyes around the room. No sign of him. I shook my head, not caring if I was crazy, if this woman could give me a way out.

"Let's make a deal," she said, and her voice was like the waves, pulling me down and out into the sea.

I didn't ask for much, only for means of protection. At first, I accomplished small things, unable to dream of or ask for more. She taught me what words to say, how to call upon the wind and let it take my prayers into the aether. I whispered my husband to sleep so that he would not have his fill of my body. But once I saw what I was capable of, I began to want more.

"What else can I do?" I asked my new friend.

"What do you dare to do?"

I tested my limits. I called the birds to me. The seagulls that I fed by hand would caw and peck the windows when my husband came home to warn me. The right words said over my stew would make my husband amenable, almost sweet. And when he pulled me close, all it took was a touch to his brow and he forgot his intentions. I began to revel in my new power, this new sense of freedom and autonomy. The world seemed larger, in full color. I began to daydream of another life. When my husband kissed me before going to work, I began to imagine the taste of my witch friend instead.

"Can I meet you?" I asked her one morning after my husband had left, the stale taste of him still on my lips.

"Already?" Her plump lips curved into a smile. "It's cold where I live."

"It's cold here, too," I shrugged. "What is your name?" *What do you like? Are you married, too?* I wanted to know.

"You will find out one day, I'm sure."

"Tell me," I begged. For all I'd learned how to do, and how much more there was to learn, what I wanted most was this.

"Do you really want to know?"

"*Yes.*"

My suncatchers shook and glinted despite the closed windows. A shadow moved just out of sight, and she stepped into the light.

The morning sun caught her face, yet still she appeared no more than a shadow upon the sea.

"Are you real?"

She held out her hand. I took hers in mine and felt her chill, like coastal rocks at night.

"You're so cold," I whispered.

"Then warm me," she smiled, and I pulled her into my arms.

I wanted nothing more than to keep her with me, to walk hand in hand by the shore collecting shells and speaking to gulls. But she lived far away, she said. One day, I would visit her home, she promised.

I would call her when my husband left for work. She would teach me the songs of the sea, and I would sing her what I heard on the radio. Perhaps I got a little carried away. I was smiling more, so sure of my protection, and giddy with puppy love I'd never felt. I should have known it would have to end.

My husband became harder to trick. She had warned me. *A clear mind is hard to trick,* she had said. *When a man wants the truth, he will find it.*

He watched me closely. *Why are you smiling? Why do you keep going to the shore?* He took my phone, searched it through until he threw it down in frustration. *I'll find out what you're doing,* he promised.

I decided I wouldn't wait that long. I would go to her now. Forget my husband, forget family dinners. I wanted to look in my mirror and not be able to look away.

I took only my most precious possessions, my little mirror and a photograph of my parents hand in hand. I left my phone behind.

There was a storm brewing far out on the waves, dark gray clouds rushing forward. Seagulls cawed and circled above. The icy water lapped at my feet, and I wrapped my coat around me tightly and held my mirror close to my lips.

"I promised I would come. I'm coming now. How do I find you?" I whispered.

But it was my husband who answered.

"Find who, darling?"

I spun around to find him just behind me. How had I not seen him coming? The gulls had tried to warn me, I realized. It wasn't the storm they were warning about, it was him.

He grabbed my arms, holding me tight in a painful grip. Terror was ice in my chest.

"I'm sorry," I gasped, and I was. Sorry I had agreed to a marriage I didn't want. Sorry I didn't realize who I was and what I wanted sooner. Sorry that I had forgotten what real fear was.

Ice-cold sea water filled my mouth. I sputtered and pulled at his arms, trying to climb up his body and out from under him. His voice was rage itself, clear even above the now monstrous claps of thunder.

"You'll be sorry," he promised. I gulped in air as I broke topside, my fingertips digging at his throat until it was red with blood. His eyes were bloodshot, the veins in his temple pulsing with madness. He shoved me under again, and I stopped trying to climb to shore, and began to pull him down.

Salt water filled my lungs, and I could breathe. I stopped fighting the water, and let it pull me downward. My husband's grip loosened, his strength waning under the pressure of the waves. I watched him sink, and I felt weightless.

Smaller, warmer hands touched mine. I turned to see my sea witch, dark hair billowing up above her.

"You came," she sang, for all words were like music under the waves. She would teach me many songs in the years to come. We would lay together upon the rocks and sing them to the stars.

"We made a deal." I pulled her close, and let the tide pull me down.

Rachel Murtagh loves to explore the dark depths of the human heart and the beauty hidden within. Immersed in myths and fairy tales since childhood, she now endeavors to write her own. They usually have a happy ending—so long as you're rooting for the witch. Rachel has been writing for over fifteen years but has just begun to share her stories with the world. When she's not writing, she enjoys developing her oil painting techniques, stargazing in the desert, and hiking the many beautiful local trails. A member of the League of Utah Writers, she lives in Salt Lake City with her twin sister and black cat, Magpie. You can find her on twitter at @rimurtagh or outside feeding the crows.

AMONG THE CANNIBALS
ALAN DEAN FOSTER

As his guest settled himself in the chair on the other side of the desk, Ealing Rutherford-Jones glanced at the small mirror that stood to the left of the reading lamp. The mirror was there so that he could ensure the few hairs on his head were properly emplaced, his eyes were clear of orb muck, and that nothing untoward was dangling from any of several orifices. Content that all was correct, he smiled amiably at the visitor.

"So they're going to remake the story—again."

"That's right, professor." The honey-voiced visitor leaned back in the chair and crossed his legs, thereby exposing the sole of half his pair of three-hundred dollar tennis shoes. Rutherford-Jones took note of them. He'd purchased the sneakers in which he played squash at the faculty club at Walmart and, like the old rhyme said, they served him very well. Not that he would have objected to owning a pair of three-hundred dollar sneakers. "Only this time it's going to be done *right*, with all the talent and production value that the greatest novel ever written in America deserves."

"Well, I'm certainly very glad to hear that." Outside on the quad, the post-adolescent hormonal burble of eager

students blended harmoniously with the high-pitched stac-
cato of newly arrived birds. It was Spring, when an elderly
tenured professor's fancy turned to convivial faculty dinners
and required contemplation of new academic papers. Rutherford-Jones was bemused but in his element. "But why come
to me?"

"We want your help, professor. Your help and advice." If
earnestness were a fresco, Rutherford-Jones thought, his
visitor would be badly in need of restoration. With his faux
casual attire, earring, and expensive haircut he wasn't
deluding Rutherford-Jones for a minute. *Does he think we're all
idiots here, just because we don't work in his over-prominent
"industry?"* Rutherford-Jones thought with amusement. "We
want you to be a part of this tribute to American literature."

"You want me to be your 'technical advisor.'" Utilizing
another quick glance at the desk mirror, the professor
adjusted his glasses. They were thicker than he would have
liked, but for someone in his position, utilitarianism super-
seded appearance.

His visitor, the jocose Frank Letts, looked relieved, like a
man who had just learned he would not have to begin
educating the natives on the basics of the alphabet and could
instead proceed directly to words of more than one syllable.

"That's right."

"On a new film version of *Moby Dick*."

"That's right."

Rutherford-Jones nodded thoughtfully. "Tell me about it.
Which production are you remaking and improving? The
silent version with Barrymore, the Huston-Bradbury from the
1950s, or the TV miniseries with Patrick Stewart?" He waited
impassively for the response.

"None of them." Clearly, Letts was fired with the energy
and enthusiasm common to any producer who had already
been guaranteed a preproduction budget as well as cancel-
lation insurance. "We're going to start from scratch,

working from the original book. For the first time, a production will do justice to this pillar of American creativity."

"You're going to pillory it?" Despite himself, Rutherford-Jones was having fun. Especially since he already knew the answer to his visitor's question and therefore did not have to waste time or brainpower on it as a viable option.

Letts grinned. "You're a funny guy, professor. That's good. *Moby Dick* is a funny book. Not everybody sees that. That's because they haven't read it."

For the first time since his visitor had entered and announced himself, Rutherford-Jones experienced a modicum of surprise. Also interest. But not so much interest that he failed to notice something decidedly odd in the little desk mirror. Not for the first time he was glad he had picked it up on a whim at that Paris antiques market. The mirror was not of French manufacture, though. He never had been able to properly place its origin. Nor had any of his colleagues. "Congolese," one had surmised. "No, no—it's plainly Persian. Note the scrollwork on the frame," declared another. "Moche," insisted his friend Amy from the Archeology Department.

"Professor?" Letts sounded uncertain. "Are you okay?"

Rutherford-Jones pulled himself away from his reflection. "I'm fine. Just slightly in shock. You've actually read *Moby Dick?*"

Looking to one side, Letts gave a slight shrug. "Well, not yet—although I plan to when I can spare the time. So far I've just made it through the film treatment." He brightened. "But it's all there, I'm assured. In the treatment. And I have read portions of the book."

"What portions?" Despite the promise implied in this meeting Rutherford-Jones had to fight a sudden diminution of interest.

"I'm sure you'll be okay with them, professor. If not, you

can advise us how to modify them. That's what your fee is for."

"Ah, yes. My fee."

Something drew his gaze again to the mirror. His brows drew together, and not just in the mirror. Were those new hairs on his head? Why had he not noticed them before? Furthermore, why had he not noticed they were dark brown instead of gray?

"There are a couple of lines—just a minute." From a handsome leather and prominently logoed carrycase, the producer extracted and proceeded to consult an ePad. "That one about 'It's better to sleep with a sober cannibal than a drunken Christian.' That's a great line!"

"Yes, it is." Rutherford-Jones decided not to bring up the chapter in *Omoo* where Melville relates the tale of the itinerant doctor who fakes illness in order to fraudulently obtain opium from a local doctor. His gaze flicked to the mirror, he noted that the bags under his eyes appeared to have shrunk down to next to nothing. *Must be the humidity*, he told himself uneasily.

"Of course, I'm not sure yet we can use it. Those Christian Coalition people don't have a real sense of humor, you know. And then there's the part where the two sailors debate if it's fair to ask sharks to eat people, and if so, what kind of people."

"So you're going to joke it up?"

This morning he had put on a navy blue tie emblazoned with the image of a small reptile. The mirror showed his shirt secured with a flush of gold silk. Furthermore, the shirt appeared to have acquired a pale pink hue. Rutherford-Jones grimaced slightly. He did not much care for the color pink, especially in male attire. But there was something attractive about it on his shirt. Seductive, one might almost say.

"Hey," Letts responded, "do you think if Melville had been offered some great gag lines appropriate to the story he would've turned them down? No way! Rest assured we'll add humor only where it's appropriate. To leaven the drama. Just like Hitchcock."

"Like Hitchcock," an increasingly conflicted Rutherford-Jones mumbled. "Who do you have in mind for the main roles? The principal characters?"

The producer fought to contain his enthusiasm. "Only big names! I mean, Melville was a great writer and all, but let's be honest: he's got no marquee value. So to justify the budget we're going to have to go with some major talent. Not that we wouldn't try for name value anyway. We're looking at Malanese Okando to play Ahab."

Rutherford-Jones frowned. "I know that name. Wasn't he recently in a comedy about an African king who abdicates his throne to become a breakout hip-hop artist in Philadelphia?"

"That's the one." Letts met the other man's gaze. "You're okay with that, aren't you?"

Fee, Rutherford-Jones reminded himself. Fee. Fee-fi-fo-humdrum. You bum. He struggled to drown the alliteration. As he did so, he found his eyes glazing over slightly. Confused, he took off his glasses and looked to the mirror.

He could see just fine without them. There seemed to be more hair on his head, too. The bags beneath his eyes were now completely gone. If Letts noticed, he did not let on.

"It's just—I'm not sure I see him in a stovepipe hat."

"No problem." Rutherford-Jones grinned. "We'll lose the hat. It's just costuming. And get this." He winked. " Darlette is really interested in playing his wife."

Rutherford-Jones frowned. "Darlette who?"

"Just the one name." Letts was plainly amused. "Don't you ever watch music vids on the net?"

"Not really, no. No time, no interest."

"No interest?" Reaching into the case once more, Letts pulled out an 8x10 and passed it across the desk. "As the picture's consultant, you'd get to meet her."

The woman in the publicity photo appeared to be twenty-five, maybe twenty-six. Less than thirty, certainly. Her smile covered about as much of her as her clothing.

"I could meet her?"

"Sure, sure! Everyone wants to meet Darlette."

"She—she looks a little young to be Ahab's wife."

"Won't matter to the target audience. Especially after we build up her role."

"Build up her role?" Rutherford-Jones swallowed. Outside, and through no fault of their own, the newly nesting robins were starting to sound slightly brittle. "Ahab's *wife*?" A flash in the mirror caught his eye. Something was glinting on the desk. Looking down, he saw car keys. New car keys. Attached to the ring that held his apartment, office, and other keys. He didn't own a car.

"Who else? Melville said in the book that he had a wife, didn't he?"

"Um, yes, but she didn't exactly figure prominently in the story."

"I told you: we'll build up her role. That's what script doctors are for. To fix holes in the continuity, bring things together, tighten the story up."

"You're going to 'fix' Melville?"

Letts had endless reserves of patience. "Now don't go snaky on me, professor. Every great story can do with a little reworking. That's not what people remember about a film, anyway. When people think of *Bambi*, do they think of Felix Salten, or do they think of Walt Disney? When they think of the *Wizard of Oz*, do they see that Baum guy, or Judy Garland? When they think of the Ten Commandments, do they think of God, or Charlton Heston? See what I mean?"

"Yes, I do. I really do," murmured Rutherford-Jones. He wanted to terminate the visit right then and there, but found he could not. It continued to possess for him the same fascination that scrutinizing the aftermath of a car crash did for the morbidly inclined. Also, there was the new hair, and new vision, and unlined, far more youthful face. And car keys— don't forget the car keys.

The mirror on his desk gleamed brightly.

"All right, then. Now, what do you think about changing the title? There are some PC concerns there, you know. Physical inferences, and like that."

Rutherford-Jones almost choked, but managed to reply with aplomb. "What did you have in mind to 'fix' it? *Moby Dave?*"

"No, no." Letts chuckled. "Man, you English guys have more of a sense of humor than I was led to believe. Melville's subtitle was *The Whale.* We're going to call it *The White Whale.*"

"Oh." Rutherford-Jones was a little abashed. Had he perhaps judged his visitor just a smidgen too harshly? Especially in light of what he was seeing in the desk mirror. "That's probably all right, then."

"*The White Whale's Revenge!*" Letts had risen from his seat and, striving to work off the surfeit of energy that was characteristic of his particular sub-species, had begun pacing back and forth from one side of the office to the other. "It gives us a terrific direct tie-in to the old *Free Willy* movies, to which my group owns the rights. You have to understand: we're not making a movie here, professor. We're trying to make a franchise."

"A what? You mean, like McDonald's?"

"Like that, yeah. Only with an aesthetic. I'm glad you're staying with me, professor."

"Why not just call it *Free Moby?*" In the mirror, some of his new hair turned gray.

Letts shook his head slowly. "C'mon, professor. Think. Don't get ahead of yourself. That title's already been tapped for one of the sequels." He turned toward Rutherford-Jones's desk so sharply that the professor flinched. "Wait 'til you see the preproduction sketches, and some of the designs for the special effects. When you see this movie, you'll believe a whale can sink a ship!"

"They have." Rutherford-Jones grasped the edge of his desk as firmly as any Briton defending his land against the invading Hun. "One such actual incident is what gave Melville the idea for the conclusion of the book."

"Yeah, *you* know that, and I know that, but the audience doesn't. We're budgeting twenty mil for the SFX alone!" His voice fell sharply and Rutherford-Jones wondered if perhaps he shouldn't put in a pre-emptive call to Security. "But everything I've been telling you so far is nothing, nothing at all."

"Nothing at all? I thought the movie was everything." The newly grayed follicles on his head turned dark brown again.

Letts chuckled politely, as one would to a six-year-old who had just asked his father for a quick explanation of superstring theory. "It hasn't been, not for a long time, professor. The main thing today is tie-ins. Ancillary rights. *Synergy.*" He pronounced the word as if he was sure Rutherford-Jones had never encountered it before. "We've got forty-five million in advance commitments already, not counting video, streaming, and cable sales, which we're still negotiating. Taco Bell will be bringing out their first fish taco, the Moby Grande. Pepsi will introduce the whale-sized aluminum soda can—forty ounces of cola with all the refreshing power of the open sea. Nintendo will do the home videogame. I've seen the prototype, and the graphics will blow you out of the water. In one set of screens, Ahab kills the whale. In the other, the whale kills Ahab and then gets to sink the *Pequod.* For really good players, there's a hidden bonus round where the player gets to use a boss whale to destroy Nantucket." He smiled widely. "Lot's of blood in both. This time, the sharks get their due."

"Astonishing," was all Rutherford-Jones could mumble in the face of Letts's onslaught.

"I'm just teasing you, professor. Ten percent of every game and theater ticket sold goes to support environmental causes."

"Like Greenpeace?" Rutherford-Jones wondered.

"C'mon, Eal! I can call you Eal, can't I? Everybody knows those people are nuts! There are safe, responsible environmental organizations that do fine work and will be glad to receive the money—and credit us for the donation. Respectable groups based in Washington, with important ties to Congressional leaders, who get things done. It doesn't hurt that some of those elected officials also vote on issues essential to the entertainment industry. Call it *our* bonus." Leaning further forward, he rested both hands on the table and looked Rutherford-Jones square in the eye. Much as Ahab, Rutherford-Jones mused, must have eyed the whale.

"I'm telling you straight out and with complete confidence, professor: this film will *make* Melville." He stood back. "It's been done with Shakespeare. Now it's the turn of an American author." Raising a hand before Rutherford-Jones could reply, the producer turned and dug a sheaf of papers from his carrycase.

"Here, just have a look at these designs for action figures! Think what it will mean for Melville's reputation—and sales—to have half the kids in America playing with these. See, this is the Ahab figure—press down on the left arm and the right arm throws the harpoon. Child-safe, of course. And look here—a dozen customized removable peglegs!"

Overwhelmed, Rutherford-Jones swallowed. "Ahab only had prosthetics made of whalebone."

"Get with it, professor! Don't you want the kids to have any fun? Sure, there's a 'whalebone' leg. But what's the harm in letting the kids screw in a gold one? Or one made of steel? Here's one of my favorites—it converts to a sawed-off harpoon. And check out this figure of Queequeg. See—he has removable, overlapping tattoos!" He eyed the professor slyly.

"Even the soccer moms can't object to them because they're a part of Queequeg's culture."

"He has too many muscles," Rutherford-Jones protested feebly. The new car keys on his desk quivered slightly.

Letts sighed heavily. "Don't you watch the WWF, or any professional wrestling, professor? Kids these days just won't accept heroes without the right volume of muscle mass. So maybe he's a little more buff than Melville might have imagined him. He's a harpooner, right? He needs those muscles!" Dropping his voice to a whisper for the second time, he added, "Don't tell this to anyone, and I mean anyone, but you can guess which company has signed on to a formal tie-up with the character of Starbuck!"

Not knowing quite what else to say, Rutherford-Jones muttered, "Ishmael. Where's Ishmael?"

For the first time since he had launched into his spiel, Letts looked slightly disconcerted. "Well, you know, professor, that kind of presented a problem for us. I mean, Ishmael's not exactly a flash name, you know? And frankly, just between you and me, the character's kind of a wuss. Doesn't really do much of anything in the book."

"He's Melville's voice!" Rutherford-Jones reached up to adjust his glasses threateningly only to realize he no longer needed them. Although a faint fogginess was beginning to creep back into the left one. The one closest to the mirror.

"In the book, in the book, sure," admitted Letts placatingly. "But in the film, it's the director's voice that counts. That's just the way film is."

"And the writer? What of the writer?"

"Oh, they'll get their credits, don't worry. We're very conscientious about such things."

"Excuse me?" Rutherford-Jones peered over the top of his glasses. "They?"

"We've got four of the best taking the story apart and putting it back together right now. I've seen the initial twenty pages of the first draft, and I can assure you they're killer, just killer! Of course, it's only a first draft. But by the time they're finished, we'll have one of the great screenplays of all time! Sweep, action, adventure, love, everything a great picture should have!"

"Uh, love?"

"Sure. I told you about Ahab's wife." At the stricken look on the professor's face, Letts felt compelled to explain. "Look, be reasonable professor. I mean, Darlette is getting *points*, for god's sake! You don't think we can just stick her in bed with Ahab at the beginning and forget about her for the rest of the picture, do you? Put her on the *Pequod* with all those whalers, and the opportunities for dramatic action are just all over the place! I'm sure Melville would have done exactly the same thing. If he'd thought of it."

"Oh, indubitably." Rutherford-Jones was gradually regaining his composure. "What—no action figure of the whale?"

Relieved, Letts hastened to expound. "All kinds, all sizes. One that submerges in a pool, one that spouts water. Got a slick toothbrush design that lets Moby Dick fight tooth decay above and below the surface. Breakfast cereal too, of course."

"Of course," echoed Rutherford-Jones.

"White whale, whole milk—Nature's natural healthy combination. With mini-marshmallows in the shape of the *Pequod* and all her mates. I've already promised our principals that if it doesn't outsell Captain Crunch by twenty percent three months into general distribution, I'll eat one of the boxes!"

"I'm not sure that's quite what Melville had in mind. Tell me, Mr. Letts—what about the enlightenment and revelation about the human condition that the book speaks to?"

"Well, I mean," the producer shrugged, "don't forget, this is a *movie*. That's what the book is for, right? And whatever else you may think of everything I've been telling you, consider how many people will be driven by the release of the film to go out and buy the book."

It was true, Rutherford-Jones had to admit. Mightn't it all be worth it, after all? All the hype, all the gloss, all the alterations and sham, to introduce tens of thousands to Melville's masterpiece? Might in this one instance, the end after all justify the means?

"Maybe—just maybe—you're right," he confessed hesitantly. The sun seemed to be shining directly into the desk mirror. A key to a safe deposit box appeared on his key ring alongside those for the car he supposedly didn't own.

"Of course I'm right! And wait until you see who we've got to do the novelization!"

"Novelization?" Something rose in Rutherford-Jones's throat. Possibly gorge. In the mirror, the reflection of the safe deposit box key vanished.

"Well, duh. You don't think people are actually going to plow through all that heavy 19th-century prose, do you? I mean, if you want to enlighten people about the human condition, you have to make it palatable. Streamline it a little, throw in some more action, cut out some of that unnecessary exposition. It's not unlike writing the script. Alan Dean Foster's agreed to do it. You know, the guy who novelized *Star Wars* and *Alien* and those other sci-fi epics?"

"Sci-fi? Is that really Melville?"

"It's all action-adventure, isn't it? Besides, this guy Foster can do it in three weeks, so we can hold off on the book until the last minute and make sure all the final script changes can be incorporated."

"But there already is a book!" Rutherford-Jones roared, somewhat to his surprise. Roaring was generally not his style.

"I know, I know." Letts made placating gestures with both hands. "And don't you worry, we'll make sure that Melville gets credited on the cover of the novelization, and in the film, right after the script writers and before the director. Even if he doesn't have much name-recognition value." Once more he leaned forward anxiously, reminding Rutherford-Jones of the squirrels that every morning and evening emerged to beg for nuts among the oaks of the campus quadrangle.

"How about it, professor? Can I tell them in L.A. that you're fully on board?"

"You can tell them ..." Rutherford-Jones began portentously.

"Oh, and one more thing. I've been authorized by the executive producers to endow a chair in English literature here at the university. Fifty thousand the first year, more when the production goes into profit."

Rutherford-Jones hesitated, a man without a car. "Fifty thousand?"

"That's just for the first year. When the film hits, the endowment will go up." Letts was beaming, much like Walter Huston in the film version of *The Devil and Daniel Webster*. "Fifty thousand to start. In your name." Gazing skyward, he drew his hands slowly apart, as if distributing letters on a theater marquee—or among the clouds in heaven. "The Ealing Curry Rutherford-Jones Chair in American Literature."

"I don't ..." Rutherford-Jones blinked. He felt light-headed, as if Mandrake was working on him. The magician, not the root. In the mirror, he looked twenty years younger. Perhaps even young enough not to repulse someone like Darlette. "In my name?"

"In your name. Fundable immediately upon your agreeing to lend your expertise to the production. And your name and title, of course."

"My name." He had tenure. What could they do to him? And who knew? The film might actually induce a few people to go out and buy the book. The real book, not the "novelization." Anything was possible. He felt himself wavering. But in the mirror, his reflection held steady.

Letts was repacking his ePad. "Of course, if you choose

not to participate, we'll understand. Professor Atkinson up at Yale has agreed to."

Atkinson! That goateed fraud, that perpetrator of unwholesome myths about Melville's adolescence, that publisher of papers fraught with innuendo and badly-written footnotes! How could they even consider him a legitimate expert on Melville and his work? How could they possibly ... ?

"I'll do it," he heard himself say.

Letts's smile expanded until it filled the office, leaving little room for anything else. "Outstanding! I'm really glad to hear this, professor. I've got some papers for you to sign, and in a week you'll hear from my secretary about travel arrangements to bring you out to L.A."

"Los Angeles?" Suddenly everything was moving very, very fast. Rutherford-Jones felt like a man who had just agreed to donate some blood to a worthy cause, but who had neglected to verify the quantity promised. "But my schedule, I have classes ... "

"Oh, don't worry about a thing, Eal. It's only for a weekend."

"A weekend? But I thought, as technical advisor ..."

"We'll call you whenever we need you. Don't worry about that—sign there, and there, that's right—these things take time to get underway. We're still bringing all the talent and financing together, you know." He tapped a form filled with what looked like cuneiform. "One more time, there —that's it."

"But Ishmael," Rutherford-Jones protested, as if suddenly remembering something vaguely important. *"What about Ishmael?"*

"Didn't I tell you? He's out. We've written him out of the storyline—he detracts from the focus on Ahab. And Ahab's the big role, isn't it? Even Melville wouldn't have been fool enough to deny that. We've added a giant squid—sperm whales eat giant squid, and Moby Baby was a sperm whale, so it all works out great. Don't worry—we'll do it better than Disney did. We've got better squid tech now." He was at the door. "Welcome aboard Pequod Productions, professor. And don't worry—with the whale we're digitizing, and the cast we're assembling, and the costumes and the music and the SFX, nobody'll miss a wimp like Ishmael. The story'll be all the stronger without him." He closed the door behind him before Rutherford-Jones could comment further.

Leaving the professor sitting silently behind his desk, contemplating the demise of something significant that had just been replaced, as skillfully and slickly as if by Houdini. After sitting motionless for just a little while, he happened to glance yet again at his reflection in the mirror. It showed a much younger man, with a smooth-skinned face and a full head of dark hair, clad in a sharp dark suit complimented by an Italian silk tie. It was a handsome visage, and only one thing that had been there before seemed to be missing.

Until that moment, Ealing Rutherford-Jones had not realized that one could see one's soul in a mirror.

Alan Dean Foster's sometimes humorous, occasionally poignant, but always entertaining short fiction has appeared in all the major SF magazines, as well as in original anthologies and several "Best of the Year" compendiums. His published oeuvre includes more than 140 books, including excursions into hard science fiction, fantasy, horror, detective, western, historical, and contemporary fiction.

He has also written numerous non-fiction articles on film, science, and scuba diving, as well as having produced the novel versions of many films, including *Star Wars*, the first three *Alien* films, *Alien Nation*, *The Chronicles of Riddick*, *Star Trek*, *Terminator: Salvation*, and both *Transformers* films. Other works include scripts for talking records, radio, computer games, op-eds for the *New York Times*, and the story for the first *Star Trek* movie. His novel *Shadowkeep* was the first ever book adaptation of an original computer game. In addition to publication in English, his work has been translated into more than fifty languages and has won awards in Spain and Russia. His novel *Cyber Way* won the Southwest Book Award for Fiction in 1990, the first work of science-fiction ever to do so. He is the recipient of the Faust, the International Association of Media Tie-In Writers Lifetime achievement award.

REFLECTED IMAGE

A MONK ADDISON STORY

JONATHAN MABERRY

-1-

I hate mirrors.

Really fucking hate them.

Any kind of mirror. Any reflective surface.

Hate them.

Hate.

Hate.

Hate.

I hate the one in my bathroom. I can see it watching me. Them, really. Not the glass itself. I'm weird but I'm not actually crazy. And, yeah, side note ... crazy would be useful. Being out of my goddamn mind might soften the edges. That's a big thing to say, I know that, but there are times when the real world is Olympic-level bizarre, and no personal level of insanity is going to compete in that league.

So, no, it wasn't the physical mirror that tore at me.

It was the reflection.

My reflection.

And theirs.

All those faces.

Watching me constantly.

Every day. Night and day.

All those faces on my skin.

-2-

It was a Tuesday.

Tuesdays generally suck. They're like Monday hangovers but without the memories of joyful excess. A greasy, grimy, headachy Monday. That's what Tuesdays are.

I spent a lot of time in the shower that morning because the night before hadn't been a good one. Tears, blood, spilled whiskey, and pain. Sometimes there isn't enough soap, you know?

Of course you know.

I took a half bottle of breakfast beer into the shower and drank it while the water pounded me. I set the temperature to boiled shellfish, had my Echo playing Delta Blues, and leaned my forearms against the tile. Even in that position I could see the faces. There were more than eighty of them now. Faces, I mean. They started just above the wrist, spiraled around my arms and then cascaded down my chest and back. Black and white faces. The only color in any of my ink are the older tats, the ones I got back when I was a sergeant pulling triggers for one of Uncle Sam's no-name agencies. Several wars back. That was when people still called me Gerry. Or Sergeant Addison.

I started getting the faces around the time someone hung the nickname "Monk" on me. They're not random art. God damn, but that would have been fine. I had a buddy back in Iraq who had the face of every girl he'd ever dated tattooed on him. Fourteen faces, ranging in age from fifteen to thirty. It was only because of those faces that we were able to ID him after his Stryker rolled over an IED.

Mine are different.

With my buddy, the faces on his skin were of women who were alive but now he was dead. For me it was exactly the opposite. The women who looked out from my flesh were all dead and I was alive.

I'd never met a single one of them when they were alive. That's not how this works.

Well, that's not exactly true. The first one, the little Vietnamese girl. I met her and even played Frisbee with her in the yard behind her family's tattoo shop in the village of Tuyên Quang. I was a friend of her mother's. I was in town when the little girl—Tuyet—went missing. I was there when the police found her body. What was left of her after the gang of bastards had used her up and disposed of her like garbage. Her mother, Patty, tattooed Tuyet's face on me and on the back of her own hand. For her it was the memory, to have that face since she'd lost everything else.

For me ... well, that's how this all started.

Patty had mixed some of Tuyet's blood with tattoo ink and sunk it onto my skin. The process changed me. Changed my world. Stretched it into a new shape. Darker, bigger, uglier, scarier. More heartbreaking.

It also kicked open a door in my head and through that door stepped Tuyet. Or, maybe it's more accurate to say that I stepped into Tuyet's life. I was in her mind and connected to all five of her senses during the last hours of her life. I felt what she felt, endured what she endured, screamed when she screamed, begged when she begged.

And I died when she died.

Then I was me again.

The tattoo was some kind of magic. Even now I can't really explain it. All I know is how it works. When a tattoo of that kind—blood and ink—is drawn onto my skin I always have that experience. I relive—right alongside the victim—their death. What she saw, I saw.

It painted the faces of the men who'd raped and murdered her into my head. It shoved me in their direction.

I was a soldier before that. Sometimes for the good guys. Sometimes for whomever signed my checks as a private military contractor. I had blood on my hands and more marks against my soul than I can count.

And then that fucking tattoo.

Her death was the start of a new war. The tattoo was the gun, and I was the bullet.

I found those men.

I ruined them.

They died very, very badly. But, let's face it, not badly enough. Nothing could redress what they'd done. To take a young life, a happy and innocent child, and destroy her faith in the world, tear away her hope, violate her on every level, and then to snuff her out, to erase her from the calendar of her own life.

Vengeance is not restitution.

Here's the real kicker, though. Here's the punch in the balls.

That magic is devious as hell. It's not kind. When I killed those men, it's not like Tuyet just went into the light and cue inspirational music. No. She lives with me now. I see her in my house, when I walk down the street, when I turn around.

I see her in the mirror.

Her, and all of the other lost ones. Those whose spirits came to me after their own murders. The ones who were not looking necessarily for revenge. They wanted their killers stopped so no one else had to die like they did.

I was fired again and again and again at the same kind of targets.

There was so much more blood on my hands. I didn't mind that. Those men deserved everything I did to them. Every. Damn. Thing.

But the ghosts were stuck here. With me. My entourage,

my family. Whatever it is.

Stuck.

And I see them. No one else can. I can see them. Hear them. Feel their pain, even after their monsters have been cleared off the board.

Some of them are screamers. That's fun. Ask the guy at the liquor store how much I enjoy that shit.

Most nights they're quiet though, and that's been the case lately. So, I've even gotten some sleep. Mind you, I wear noise-cancelling headphones and those blinder things. I play music, too. Distraction therapy to keep what sanity I have left.

The mirrors, though.

No hiding there.

Sure, I could take the mirrors down. Learn to shave without one. I mean it's not like I need one to put on my face or do my hair. My face looks like an eroded wall. It looks like I've been punched at least once from every possible direction, and with enthusiasm. Which isn't entirely inaccurate. And lately I've been keeping my hair buzzed down to almost nothing. Losing it, anyway, so there's no loss there.

The mirrors are still up because taking them down feels cowardly. It feels disrespectful in a way I can't quite phrase in my own thoughts.

So, they watch me. And in the mirrors, they see themselves. Wish I knew if they liked that, if it made them feel like they still existed. They can scream but they can't actually talk. Not to me. Maybe to each other, though that adds another layer of creepy over my life.

Why am I telling you all this?

Well, one of the faces on my skin was looking at me through the mirror's reflection.

I mean really looking. Eyebrows raised, mouth working as if she was trying to tell me something. Maybe something important. There was an urgency in her expression I hadn't seen before. It was as if more of her personality had suddenly come awake.

Alive.

The other faces seemed to go still, as if maybe *they* could hear her. Their eyes were filled with strange lights. Fear and something else I couldn't define.

You wouldn't think that sort of thing could scare me anymore.

You'd be wrong.

-3-

I leaned on the edge of the sink and stared at her.

She looked the age she'd been when she died. Twenty-seven, though if she hadn't been killed, she'd be closing in on thirty-five. Medium brown skin and pale eyes. A mixed-race art dealer from New Hope, Pennsylvania. Fifth victim of a ritualistic killer who targeted women in that world. First was an artist, then a gallery owner, an art critic, a model, and then her. Gabrielle Toussaint was number five. Born in the suburbs of New Orleans, got a BA in art history from LSU, and then an MBA from Wharton in Philly, moved to New Hope to open her gallery, and died.

Left behind a three-year-old son and a husband whose grief at her funeral was so profound that it silenced all conversation. Last I heard he was still single and looked like he was twice as old as he was. Their kid, now in junior high, was a skinny little ghost who drifted along the fringes of life. Two more casualties of the monster who'd killed her.

Yeah, I keep tabs on some of the families. Those I can. And, yes, that's probably going to put me in rehab or a twelve-step one of these days.

I stared in Gabby Toussaint's green eyes and tried to read her lips.

I'm no good at that sort of thing, but there was one word

that she seemed to say over and over again. I finally said it aloud.

"More ...?" I asked the face in the mirror.

Her answer was a scream.

She'd never been a screamer before.

She was now.

And the scream hit me like a punch. Like a bullet. Like a fucking freight train. I reeled back, clapping my hands to my ears, slipping on tiled floor. Falling. Slamming the middle of my upper back against the rim of the tub. Rocked my head back. Saw stars. The room spun like a drunken dervish. I screamed, too. In pain and in shock.

Then the mirror exploded.

It didn't just crack. The whole thing burst outward as if there was a hand grenade in the medicine chest. A thousand glittering splinters razored their way through the bathroom, slashing the shower curtain, scratching the tile, sticking like throwing knives into the door. Cutting me.

I barely got a hand up in time to save my eyes. Splinters lacerated my palm and inner wrist.

Then everything was absolutely silent.

I sprawled on the floor. Feeling like an accident victim. Like some kind of victim,

More.

More?

Jesus Christ.

-4-

The ER staff here in Pine Deep are probably second to none. God knows they've had enough practice. Some of it with me.

I spent five full hours there, trying to be patient while doctors used tweezers to pick glass out of me. Not sure if they believed the story about me slipping on a wet floor and bashing the mirror in an attempt to keep from falling. Best I could do at the time.

My friend, Malcolm Crow, the chief of police in that town, once told me that the ER staff approaches unusual injuries in almost the same way as doctors who patch up underworld criminals. They smiled and nodded, and either worked in silence or filled the time with meaningless chitchat. They did not ask probing questions.

After they were done, I looked like I'd been auditioning for a new sequel to *The Mummy*. It didn't spoil my looks any more than it improved them. I have that kind of face.

Afterward I went to see Crow and found him in his office, feet up on his desk, reading reports and listening to John Lee Hooker. There's something about living in Pine Deep that cultivated a love of the blues.

He waved me to the Mr. Coffee and then to a chair.

"You look like shit," he said.

"Feel like it."

He studied me. He's a little guy a bit north of fifty, and he had his own collection of scars. I knew where some of them came from, but not all. He knew some stuff about the faces on my skin, but not all. I brought a cup for him and we sipped for a few minutes while he finished a report. Then he tossed the papers onto his desk.

"You want to tell me about it?"

I debated that, but then did. I told him all of it, including the backstory on Gabby Toussaint. He listened without comment or judgment because that's who Crow is. He's both been there and done that and after some events we went through together a few years back, we'd become family. Sort of. Not brothers. Cousins, I suppose; and with the clannish attachment and tendency toward mutual support that comes with all that.

"More," he said, making it a statement rather than a question.

"More," I said.

"Well, hell. That's unnerving."

"Yeah."

"You know what she meant?"

"Not yet."

He nodded to my shirt and raised an eyebrow. The office was empty except for the dispatcher, who was on the far side. I took a break, raised my T-shirt, and touched Gabby's face. It was as still as a tattoo should be. Always was with other people.

"Beautiful woman," said Crow, his eyes sad.

I pulled my shirt down.

We drank coffee.

"What was the name of the perp?" he asked.

"Henry Sullivan. Thirty-eight at the time of his death," I said. "Architect living in Frenchtown, New Jersey. No family."

Crow did some tappity-tappity stuff on his keyboard and pulled up a photo of Henry Sullivan. It was the only photo of him I ever saw; the one that was used by the papers when what was left of his body was found in a dumpster behind a 7-11 in New Hope. Ordinary guy, with reddish-brown hair and blue eyes. Utterly forgettable features except for a large port-wine stain birthmark covering most of the left side of his face. What my grandmother used to call a 'stork bite.' The eyes that looked out of that photo were flat and dead despite the smiling mouth below.

"How can I help?" he asked.

"'*More*'," I said. "That's ringing a bell with me."

"What kind of bell?"

I said, "There was some thought by investigating officers that Sullivan wasn't working alone."

Crow pursed his lips. "I ... um ... thought you were *there* when she died. In the way you do that sort of thing, I mean. Like ... you saw it."

"I did. I saw the guy who killed her, yes."

"Then ...?"

"I saw what she saw," I said. "That's how it works. Only the vic's point of view. Nothing else."

"Okay," he said. "I mean, it's creepy as shit, but ... okay. I get it."

"So, there could have been someone else."

"Serial killers are usually solo acts," said Crow.

"And you know that it's not always the case."

"Sure, Monk, but you think that's it? Maybe she was trying to tell you that there were other victims. Women whose bodies were never found, or women whose deaths were not obviously connected to the ones they know of. A lot of killers have those kinds of kills."

I nodded. Many ritualistic killers work up to that pattern, and when they're caught it's more often just the ones that fit the pattern who are directly connected. Exceptions are when there's DNA.

"Yeah, maybe that's it. Can you check for me?" I asked. "More DNA gets collected all the time and added to your databases. Maybe there's something else we don't know about or didn't back then."

"Sure," he said. "And if I come up dry?"

I shook my head. "I don't know," I said. "Not yet."

We sat and talked about it for a while. I went over every detail of the case that I could remember. That's always a bit of a challenge because I tend to come into it after the fact. I'm not the investigative officer. I'm not a cop and I'm not even that kind of P.I. Mostly I chase bail skips and do some personal protection work. I'm a hired thug.

Sure, I've picked up some tricks along the way, and the bondsmen I mostly work for gave me access to a bunch of databases and websites that help me find the skips, but I never did the investigator course work or logged the apprentice hours with a licensed dick.

Back when I lived in New York I had no real friends in

NYPD. Rather the reverse. But here in Pine Deep, Crow was on my side for sure.

He looked at the wall clock. "Give me the rest of the afternoon. I need to make some calls and it's Sunday, so it might take time for me to catch up with folks off the clock."

I thanked him and went out.

The autumn sun was a cold yellow ball in a bright blue sky. I went to the Scarecrow Diner, stuffed myself into a booth in the back corner, ate some eggs, drank too much coffee, and made a lot of calls of my own.

First was to one of the bondsmen I work for, J. Heron Scarebaby, and yes that is his real name. His partner is just as unfortunate—Iver Twitch. Proving that some people are really unlucky in terms of heritage, and that occasionally parents make it worse when it comes to naming their kids. Personally, I'd have changed my name to literally anything else.

"Can you do a background check for me?" I asked.

"Because why?" said Scarebaby. "Because I have nothing better to do? Because the only thing on my day-planner is running errands for skip tracers who don't know how to use the Internet?"

"Because I'm in a jam and I'm asking nice," I said.

He heard the tone of my voice. Scarebaby is not nearly as much of a dick as he pretends to be. He likes the drama of complaining and feels that, as a bail bondsman, he is professionally required to *act* like a dick.

His sigh was elaborate, but then he said, "Okay. Give me the details."

I gave him just a bit. Nowhere near what I shared with Crow. Different kind of relationship. Scarebaby and Twitch know some of what goes on with me, but they don't know the scope of it. Nor do they want to know, which is cool with me.

He told me to wait and rang off.

I waited. The coffee at the Scarecrow is first rate even by

diner standards. There was an Eagles-Broncos game on the big screen. I watched Jalen Hurts do some real damage.

Then Scarebaby called back.

"Got something on Henry Sullivan," he said.

"Tell me."

-5-

I paid my tab and walked back to the police station. Crow saw me and waved me once more to the coffee pot. My nerves were already doing the Macarena, but I poured myself some and brought the cup to his desk.

He finished a call he was on and peered at me.

"You have a look," he said.

"A look? No, I don't. What kind of look?"

"Like you know more than you did when you were here before."

He was a sharp little S.O.B.

"I called a bondsman I work for."

"Twitch?"

"Scarebaby."

Crow chuckled. "I can't take that name seriously."

"Yeah, well," I said. "He came through. And maybe it's the same thing you got. Turns out Henry Sullivan was a foster kid. Went into the system out of an orphanage. Bounced around from one home to the next and was never adopted. Kicked loose when he hit eighteen. Dropped off the radar for a couple of years and then resurfaced in Philly. Got a degree in architecture from Drexel, then moved to Jersey and joined a firm. Background checks came up zip on his family, though. But I have the name of the orphanage and that's a start. Going to poke around there and see if I can get info on the foster homes. Maybe he made a friend there. Someone who might have shared his ... *proclivities*."

"That's a nice euphemism for murderous psychopathic

asshole," said Crow.

"The rest is implied," I said. "Is that what you got, too?"

"In part," said Crow. "First things first. I talked to a friend in the FBI who ran some numbers for me. It would break your heart to know how many young women go missing every year. In 2021 alone the number of missing girls and women under 21 who went missing was 209,375. Over 21 the number is 59,369. There are all sorts of statistical models postulating how many are runaways and drug addicts living homeless and how many are dead but unidentified because there's no DNA or fingerprints on file. Of the rest, it's anyone's guess what happened to them. My guy at the Bureau says the pervading theory is that only one in ten serial killers follow a pattern. It's virtually impossible to track and quantify patternless murders. Now, your boy Henry Sullivan was close to being patternless, and had it not been for your ... um ... *special gift* ... he'd likely have never been caught."

"Yes," I said. "And, no, it's not a gift."

"Whatever it is," said Crow, "my point is that we can't look at the numbers of missing women and easily tie any of them to Sullivan's M.O."

"Which means that if he had a partner," I said, "we're not likely to find him by looking for similar murders."

"Right."

"Balls."

"I know," he said. "So, I went the other direction and, yes, I hit the edges of the foster home thing, but I have something your buddy didn't get. Sullivan isn't his real name. He was a classic—dropped off in a basket outside of a fire station. Right out of every hard luck TV movie you ever saw. A note was pinned to his blanket that said, *'I'm sorry. I can't.'* And a little card that read Henry Mathew."

"Mathew?" I asked. "Sullivan's middle name was Joseph. I saw his driver's license. And it was Henry J. Sullivan in the news."

"Ah," said Crow, "I noticed that, too. The firefighter who found him and contacted child protection services was Joseph Sullivan. The orphanage named the kid after him."

"Keeping only the first name and replacing the middle? That's odd."

"It is. Never heard of an orphanage changing what amounts to a known, or presumed, legal name. I can see the addition of a surname, and it was a nice nod—at least at the time—to name him after the firefighter. No idea why they tossed the kid's original middle name."

"Any chance you have the firefighter's contact info? He'd be old but maybe he remembers something."

"You'd need to hold a séance," said Crow. "Joe Sullivan is deceased. Died of smoke inhalation four years after he found the kid."

"Shit. I guess I'll have to wait until Monday and then talk to the people at the orphanage."

"Yeah, well ... that's the other thing," said Crow. "The orphanage burned down two years ago."

We looked at each other while the wall clock ticked very loudly. The skin on my chest felt crawly, as if the faces beneath my shirt were reacting. My version of Spider sense, I suppose.

"Yeah," said Crow after a while, "that's one of those things that make me go *hmmmmm*. I mean, if the fire had been set *before* Henry Sullivan died, then the first thing I'd have done was look at troubled kids who came out of there."

"Because serial killers often do shit like that when they're growing up," I said, nodding. "Setting fires, killing local pets."

"Uh huh. Often enough that it's factored into the psychological profiles," agreed Crow.

"And if it burned during the years we know Sullivan to have been active as a killer," I said, "it'd be likely him scrubbing his back trail."

"Yes."

I smiled. "Now *you* have the look."

"I expect I do," he said.

"You're going to tell me the place was torched, aren't you?"

He grinned. "Yes I am."

"Shit."

"Yeah."

"Did the arson team look at anyone in particular?"

"They did," he said, looking smug. "The guy who reported it had some moderately bad burns. He said he got them when he tried to go inside to try and rescue people. None of the staff or kids said they saw him go in while it was burning, though. There was enough reasonable doubt—dark night and lots of smoke, general confusion—that no one could either confirm or deny. No charges were filed."

"Who was this guy?"

Crow took a sheet of paper from the printer tray and handed it to me. "Kevin Lane. Currently living in Lambertville, New Jersey. Address provided by your local public servant."

"Thank you, Officer Friendly," I said, plucking it from between his fingers.

"Keep me posted," said Crow.

-6-

The drive from Pine Deep to Lambertville is about twenty minutes. A-32 to State Route 32 and over the bridge in New Hope.

Yeah. A stone's throw from New Hope, where Gabby Toussaint lived. And where she died.

There are coincidences in life, but I tend not to believe in them.

Kevin Lane lived in an old Victorian house on a side street in Lambertville, within easy walking distance of shopping but far enough away for privacy. I parked and spent a couple of minutes walking the neighborhood. It was not the fashionable part of town, though. The houses were all old and there wasn't as much attention to yard work as elsewhere. Nothing had gone wild, but there was an unkempt feel to everything. The weeds were tall but withering now as autumn kicked in. The last of the summer grass had been allowed to go stiff and brown, and unpicked apples were left to rot among the fallen leaves.

Most of Lambertville was dressed for Halloween, with strings of orange lights, inflatable spiders and ghouls on the lawns, and decorative skeletons leaning out from around oak trees.

Not Lane's house, though. No decorations except for an uncarved pumpkin on the porch. Only one light and that was on the second floor. It was still technically afternoon, but the skies had darkened and there was a thin gray cloud cover, so it felt later.

The info Crow gave me was thin. Lane had six parking tickets in ten years. Nothing for speeding and no other violations of note. No criminal record. The fact that he was interviewed about the arson at the orphanage indicated that no follow up was anticipated. There was a photo of him showing a face mostly covered by bandages, which was about as helpful as no photo at all. And it was in black and white.

I decided to give a face-to-face a try.

The chance of this guy being *the* guy was slim bordering on none. I am never that lucky.

I knocked.

It took him nearly a minute to answer the door.

The man who answered was bald as an egg and he leaned around the edge of the door to peer at me. The photo of him with a bandaged face did not do justice to the burn he'd received. His face was a distorted moonscape of lumps and bumps. He looked melted. The brow hung down over his eye and heat damage had warped the tendons around his nose and mouth, flaring the former and giving the latter an unpleasant uptilt. A bit like a mix of The Joker and Two-Face from the Batman comics.

"Yes?" he asked nervously. The fingers curled around the edge of the door were scarred, too. That news article hadn't come close to reporting how badly he'd been hurt. And from the lights in his eye and the tremolo in his voice, I wasn't getting the "bad guy serial killer" vibe. Not at all. Not even a twinge.

"Excuse me," I said, "are you Kevin Lane?"

"Yes?" he said again. The door was open only a few inches, enough for me to see a bit of an old-fashioned entrance foyer. Wainscoting with molded plaster images of flowers, faded floral wallpaper, a bit of a mirror in a heavy cherrywood frame, and one corner of an unlit lamp in a wall sconce. It looked like my grandmother's house. Old, worn out, and sad.

"My name's Gerald Addison," I said. "I'm an investigator and wondered if I could ask a few questions."

"About what? Is this more about the fire? I answered everyone's questions a hundred times."

"No," I said. "It's about Henry Sullivan. Does that name ring a bell at all?"

He stared at me. "Who?"

"Henry Joseph Sullivan," I said, watching the one eye I could see. "He had been at that orphanage as a child."

"They never said anything about any kid dying in that fire," said Lane.

"No, sir. He died a few years before that. Nothing to do with the fire. Would you mind if I came in? It won't take much of your time."

"No," he said. "No more questions. I'm not feeling very well, and I don't know you."

The door closed.

I heard the lock click.

I stood on the porch for a full five seconds, feeling very acutely that I had mishandled things. Which is a fair assessment because I really had no actual plan. As I said, I'm not a private investigator in the classic sense. I chase people who skip out on court appearances, and I look for murderers I see in the shared visions of the dead. This was outside of my skill set and on first pitch it showed.

So, I turned and walked down the steps and down the street to my car.

And then stopped halfway there.

I turned slowly and looked at the house again. I saw a curtain fall into place as I turned and knew that Lane had been watching me go. Nothing unusual about that.

Something was bugging me, though.

As the autumn wind blew past my face, I went through everything that had happened in those few moments on his porch. The timbre of his voice told me nothing. As for the burned face, well ... it's impossible to read the expression in melted meat. He had been brusque, but not actually rude. I had, after all, knocked on his door at nightfall on a Sunday. And I hadn't had the sense or forethought to flash an ID at him.

So, what was it?

I closed my eyes and replayed the moment.

The door opened. Just a little. He looked out, but all I saw was the burned side of his face.

That was a bit odd right there. Was it common for someone with extreme facial disfigurement to only show that side of his face? Wasn't it more common for said person to show the other side? Maybe. I don't know enough about the psychology of physical trauma to make an assessment.

But there was something.

The bit of hallway I saw. Wainscoting, wallpaper, mirror, light fixture ...

And then something in my mind went *clunk*.

At the same moment the face on my skin seemed to writhe. I could almost hear her yell at me. And I knew that if the tattoo had a voice, then I was certain which word she would be yelling. Earlier she'd told me that there were more. More victims, of that I was certain. And maybe a double meaning, more killers.

But the feeling of her trying to speak on my skin—as awful and nightmarish as that is—seemed to shape a different word. And I spoke it aloud.

"Mirror."

In that edge of the old dusty mirror, I had seen the other half of his face. A shadowy ghost of an image in the unlighted foyer

I went to my car and drove away. As I did, I called Malcolm Crow and asked some fresh questions.

-8-

He woke when I spoke his name.

"Mathew," I said.

Not Kevin.

Mathew.

His eyes snapped open and he nearly screamed.

I stood beside the bed. The room was dark, with only a little light from the outside streetlamp to separate me from the shadows.

"What the fuck," he snarled.

His voice was no longer timid. Now there was steel in it.

I stood there, naked to the waist. All those faces looking at him.

Her face looking at him.

I saw his eyes go wide. I saw the horror and confusion turn to recognition and understanding.

"I killed Henry," I said. "I killed your brother."

He stared at me.

"That was what the note meant. Henry Mathew. Henry and Mathew. The firefighters found two kids on their doorstep. Joseph Sullivan turned them both over to child protection services. You burned down the orphanage because that's where the records would be of what happened to both. What happened to you. Maybe there were fingerprints or footprints on cards, like they do with kids. Maybe there were records of a Mathew Sullivan. How did it work? Did the Lane family adopt you and not Henry? Or did you both cycle out and start doing what you did? Yeah, I know I'm missing a lot of pieces of the puzzle, but I also know I'm right. And I have a police buddy who'll be calling Philadelphia child protection services first thing Monday morning to verify what I already know. You and Henry. Twins. Cut from the same cloth. Twin brothers, twin killers. Rare, but not unique. Sad, too. I mean, I can grieve for the babies you were, but ... damn ... I hate everything about the men you became. Tell me ... why the women?"

He said nothing.

"How many are there we don't know about?"

"No idea. I'd like to say 'none,' but—."

I looked at him. "You know how this ends, right? You know this is all over."

He whipped back the covers and came up off the bed. The poor light flashed dully on something metallic he'd snatched from under the pillow.

A knife.

Six-inch serrated blade.

He moved with cat quickness—fast and precise and deadly, going from dead sleep to instant action. The blade moved so fast it blurred.

Had I been someone else, maybe a cop come to arrest him, I'd have likely died right there. He was that fast, and he moved with absolutely no hesitation. A rare and deadly quality. The very best SpecOps soldiers move like that.

So do I.

He moved fast but I moved just as fast. And I moved first.

He went for my throat; I went for his arm. My blade sliced through the muscle and tendon of his knife-arm, cutting the biceps to the bone. My other hand clamped over his mouth. Screams were inconvenient. I bet he already knew that. Was he the one who kept the women silent while his brother ruined them? Or did they take turns?

Doesn't matter.

He never got his screams out.

Not then.

Later, in the quiet of his soundproofed basement, I let him scream all he wanted to. All he needed to. And in that ugly darkness he told me about the other women. Where they were buried. Where I could find his trophies. God damn, but he really didn't want to tell me. He wanted to keep those secrets with him, even knowing he was going to die. He tried, too. He so wanted to have the last win here because it would mean all those families would never know where their daughters and mothers, sisters and wives were buried. That would have put a grin on his face all the way down to hell because he would have carved off a piece of every survivor, every grieving loved one, and taken those as trophies with him to the pit.

He would have gotten that, too, if I'd been a cop, or a real P.I. or any kind of decent human being.

I'm cursed with what I do because of what I've done. Fate or the Universe whoever could have picked millions of nice guys.

They picked me.

For a reason.

And, yeah, Mathew fought me there in his bedroom. Before I took him downstairs.

He fought real damn hard while the face of Gabby Toussaint watched. While all of the faces watched. Watched me. Watched what I did.

And at one point I caught sight of my reflection in the bedroom mirror. All of the faces on my back were watching. Their eyes were alight. There was a kind of crimson joy in their smiles. I saw them reflected. Saw the awful delight.

I hate mirrors.

Hate them.

Most of the time.

Jonathan Maberry is a *New York Time* bestselling author, five-time Bram Stoker Award-winner, three-time Scribe Award winner, Inkpot Award winner, and comic book writer. His vampire apocalypse books, *V-Wars*, became a Netflix original series. He writes in multiple genres, including suspense, thriller, horror, science fiction, fantasy, and mystery; for adults, teens and middle grade. His novels include the Joe Ledger thriller series, *Bewilderness, Ink, Glimpse*, the Pine Deep Trilogy, the Rot & Ruin series, the Dead of Night series, *Mars One, Ghostwalkers: A Deadlands Novel*, and many others, including his first epic fantasy, *Kagen the Damned*. He is the editor of many anthologies including three X-Files anthologies, *Aliens: Bug Hunt, Don't Turn Out the Lights, Aliens vs Predator: Ultimate Prey, Hardboiled Horror, Nights of the Living Dead* (co-edited with George A. Romero), and others. His comics include *Black Panther: DoomWar, Captain America, Pandemica, Highway to Hell, The Punisher, Bad Blood*, among others. He is the president of the International Association of Media Tie-in Writers, and the editor of *Weird Tales* Magazine. Visit him online at jonathanmaberry.com.

THE REFLECTOR
E.W. BARNES

C handee saw the blow coming, but neither tensed nor dodged as the man's fist struck below her eye. She relaxed into the hit, feeling the cold metal of brass knuckles before the sensation dissolved into icy-hot pain that spread across her face. She allowed her body to reel as she absorbed the blow, the bright lights above the ring flashing into streaks as she spun. Her opponent faced the crowd and waved his arms with a triumphant howl when she dropped to one knee. Exactly as she expected.

Chandee got to her feet. He smirked as he scrutinized the damage from his blow, and then frowned slightly. She knew why. When preparing for this match, she learned that his brass knuckles had an "x" carved onto the outside edge. He used them to leave an x-shaped scar to remember him by, thus earning him the nickname, "The Exer."

This time, his signature move failed. She had known how to take the hit; there would be no "x" left on her skin and he would not get another chance to mark her. He growled as he swung his fist again, striking under her chin and confirming her suspicions. He had not researched her and had not learned of her dense bone structure, or her jaw of granite.

He failed to prepare, and so the Exer would lose.

Chandee needed no tools or weapons, relying only on her experience and skill. She responded with a sequence of punches designed to confuse him. Many fighters watched their opponents' feet, torsos, or eyes to determine from where the next strike would come. She had trained herself to hide those tells. Now the widening of his eyes as she landed solid hits told her everything.

She could smell the desperation in his sweat as he delivered a rapid series of blows like a jackhammer on her midsection. Chandee almost felt sorry for him. A lost Barter Fight could mean disaster for an under-funded merchant ship. When he failed—when, not if—his ship would lose trade opportunities in the sector for one full rotation. Many, including the ship's fighter, could find themselves in a welfare compound.

There was nothing she could do about that. What she could do was not prolong the Exer's suffering. Chandee took advantage of sloppy footwork that knocked him slightly off balance and used her height and reach to land a powerful blow. He dropped to the floor. She could tell by the way his eyes rolled he would stay there for a while. Her work was done.

She ignored the cheers and yells from outside the ring, sitting heavily next to her employer. Captain Aurum stroked his beard, wearing an expression like a satisfied cat as he pocketed currency shoved at him by numerous hands. Having secured exclusive rights to trade in this sector, he was now guaranteed a small fortune. Winning the betting pool was a bonus.

Chandee's mind was on the match, as always, analyzing her performance and looking for ways to improve her skills. *The jackhammer maneuver was new*, she thought. It was an interesting technique, one she considered adding to her repertoire—until she remembered that after today, she would enter the ring no more.

"Hold still." Dr. Khanya reached up and clasped Chandee's chin in her hand. "This laceration is deep. Unless you want a scar, stop moving."

Chandee stilled herself and held her breath. She did not really care if the cut left a scar, but she respected Dr. Khanya and understood her desire to do the best work she could. It was a quality they shared, though their goals were the reverse of each other: Dr. Khanya repaired while Chandee destroyed.

Destroyed was not the right word, Chandee decided. She didn't enter the ring with the purpose of destroying her opponents—her objective was to win; but the means often resulted in damage and destruction. She regretted that side of her work and was more satisfied by the matches she won with minor damage than those when her opponent was seriously injured. She felt pride that there were more of the former than the latter.

"There," Dr. Khanya smiled, a twinkle in her black eyes. "You can breathe now."

Chandee inhaled deeply, feeling the bruises on her ribs and abdominal muscles.

"Do you want to see?"

Dr. Khanya held up a mirror, and Chandee examined her reflection. Brown eyes stared solemnly back at her. This latest scar was almost invisible amidst the fine lines, crow's feet, and outright wrinkles that graced her face. These were echoed in the streaks of silver in her crewcut hair, which flashed brightly amidst the mix of iron gray and what her mother had called "old ivory" blond.

"This was your last match, wasn't it?"

Chandee nodded as she handed the mirror back.

"Where will you go?"

"Sannus."

"I've heard of it. That's one of the pastoral planets, right?"

"Right," Chandee chuckled. "No Barter Fights there."

"It sounds peaceful," Dr. Khanya said. "The perfect place to retire." She set the mirror on her instrument tray. "Is someone waiting for you?"

"My brother and his family have a farm there."

"Sannus is a long way away. How will you get there?"

"I've booked passage on a transport leaving from Ziyo."

Dr. Khanya sighed. "So soon." Her smile was sad. "Then I will say my goodbyes now. Good luck, Chandee. I will miss you."

Chandee stood, towering over the petite doctor. She took a long look around the sickbay. This was the last time she would see these bright, clean walls. Stopping at the door, Chandee crossed her arms in front of her, palms against her broad chest, and bowed in the traditional gesture of respect on her world.

"Thank you, Doctor."

The command deck of the *Merchant Ship Mercuria* was impressive—gleaming with glass and chrome and replete with up-to-date technology. Chandee could remember when the *Mercuria* was only one step up from a garbage scow; over the years as his wealth had grown, Captain Aurum upgraded and improved her until his ship was now the envy of the Mercantile fleet.

As she entered the bridge, Chandee nodded respectfully to Brower, the new crew member retained to replace her as the *Mercuria's* Barter Fighter. Purchasing the services of not only Dr. Khanya, but a strong contender in Brower had been a master stroke by Captain Aurum. Brower was also the ship's pilot. Chandee envied him a skill besides throwing punches. All she knew how to do was fight.

"Reporting as ordered, Captain," Chandee said.

"We're approaching Ziyo," Aurum said. "But something's come up." He paused, his face inscrutable. "Another Barter Fight has been set."

Chandee frowned. "The last match secured our trade rights in the sector for a full rotation."

"A protest was filed."

"By the Exer's captain?"

"No, by another captain. He's convinced his fighter can win and demanded a new match. The Mercantile Ministry agreed."

She exhaled. "Is Brower ready? I can advise him if you approve."

"Of course, I'm ready," Brower called out with a grin, but the captain shook his head.

"It's not that simple. The protest was filed by Captain Cissus of the *Syllicia*. His fighter is the Reflector."

"The Reflector?" breathed Mura, the communications officer. "I've heard of him. A non-human who always mysteriously wins, right?" Mura made eye contact with Brower, confirming Chandee's guess that they had become a couple since Brower's arrival on board. "He's undefeated."

"I can take him," Brower said, but Chandee saw his doubt in the shift of his shoulders and heard his fear in the slight rise of his voice.

"We can file an appeal," Captain Aurum said to Chandee, ignoring Brower's protests. "Your match was clean. Your win was fair."

"How long will an appeal take?" Chandee asked.

"Days, maybe weeks."

Chandee ran her fingers through her hair. Without sector rights, she could not leave the *Mercuria* to catch her transport. If the captain appealed, there was no guarantee the

Ministry would decide in his favor, which meant the match would still happen. Either way, her ride to Sannus would be long gone.

"I can do this, Captain," Brower insisted.

"Can you?" Aurum pinned him with his hawk-like stare. Chandee knew what the captain was thinking: Brower was good, one of the best to come out of fight training; but he was untried and inexperienced. "Are you really ready to risk this ship and the livelihood of everyone on board against an undefeated opponent?"

Brower scowled and did not answer.

Chandee took a deep breath. She saw only one option.

"I'll do it, Captain. I'll fight the Reflector."

Aurum nodded his acceptance, his eyes glinting as he stroked his beard. The betting on this match would be legendary.

Chandee was sitting at her computer when someone knocked on the door to her quarters.

"Come in."

"I heard about the match," Dr. Khanya said as she entered. To make room for her visitor, Chandee moved off the end of her cot the bag she had been packing when Captain Aurum called her to the bridge. Dr. Khanya nodded her thanks as she sat down. "You didn't have to volunteer."

"Yes, I did."

Dr. Khanya looked around curiously. Chandee's quarters were cramped but private, a quality she valued. Most of the *Mercuria's* crew slept in shared living spaces, except for the captain (who entertained guests at every port), and Dr. Khanya (who insisted on private accommodations as part of her contract). Early in her career as Barter Fighter, Captain Aurum had given her a converted storage closet for quarters.

There was enough room to train without accidentally injuring her crewmates. When Chandee left, this would become Brower's quarters and then Mura would value the privacy.

Dr. Khanya peered at the photos on Chandee's computer screen.

"Is that your brother? He looks just like you."

"We're twins."

"That explains it!" She leaned forward to take a closer look, pushing a coiling lock of black hair out of her eyes. "Are you originally from Sannus?"

"We were born on Nakara."

Dr. Khanya's mouth dropped open. "Nakara! Goodness. How did you survive there? How did you escape?"

"Captain Aurum."

She raised her brows. "Really? I never guessed he was philanthropic."

"He's not." Chandee grunted in amusement. "Before he became a licensed merchant, he smuggled refugees off Nakara for a price."

"How did you become his fighter?"

Chandee cleared her throat. "We had to pay bribes to get to the spaceport and by the time we were delivered to Captain Aurum, we didn't have enough currency left to pay his fee. He saw me disable an Obsidian Guard and was impressed. He wanted to go legit, and for that he needed a Barter Fighter. In exchange for delivering my brother and his family to Sannus, I agreed to fight for him until our debt was paid."

"How long ago was that?"

"Many years."

Dr. Khanya narrowed her eyes and pressed her lips together.

"What's he like?" She gestured at the image of Chandee's brother.

"Latif is everything I am not. He is gentle, and a talker, and a family man."

"While you're a fighter and a loner."

Chandee nodded.

There was a pause and then: "What have you learned about the Reflector?"

"There's very little that's useful," Chandee sighed. "He's a good fighter, but average. Video recordings show no unusual moves or strategies. His opponents seem to just ... give up. And when asked about the match, they can't explain how they lost."

"Do we know anything about his species?"

"Only that they call themselves the Lyuud and that their planet is on the outer edge of Mercantile space."

"Why is he called the Reflector?"

"Because his fight unitard is made of a dark, shiny material. He's covered head to toe with it."

"You can't see his face?"

"No."

"Hmm. Could the material be the reason he always wins?" Dr. Khanya asked, but Chandee was already shaking her head.

"It's been tested. It's an ordinary fiber found in many markets, commonly used for ornamental clothing."

"Maybe the way the lights hit it, or maybe he uses telepathy ... "

Chandee grinned at her enthusiasm. "You know the ring blocks all emissions from inside and outside, including telepathy."

"There's got to be a reason, something out of the ordinary. Like something he brings with him into the ring."

"He uses no tools or weapons in his matches." She exhaled. "Every angle has been examined. Whatever his advantage is, it's a mystery."

Dr. Khanya focused again on the picture of Chandee's brother.

"What happens if you lose?"

"I don't know. I spent all my currency on the transport ticket. If I miss this one, I can't pay for another." She laughed sadly. "The captain won't keep me on. He's already paid for Brower, and no one wants to say it, but I know I'm getting too old to fight. I don't have any other skills to barter with. I'll probably end up in a welfare compound, I guess."

Dr. Khanya shook her head in dismay.

"It wouldn't be that bad," Chandee reassured her. "I learned how to survive with very little on Nakara."

"I can buy ... "

"I won't accept it."

Dr. Khanya swallowed and looked at the ceiling. "Ok," she said, blinking rapidly. "Ok. Then you just need to win."

The intense lights overhead made it impossible to see outside the ring, but the low rumble of voices and a heaviness in the air told Chandee it was standing room only in the spectator sections. She sat alone on a low stool, watching her opponent. The Reflector was so still, he might have been a work of art. Art was a good word, she decided. His shining unitard appeared to absorb light, and yet he seemed to glow. Her unitard, once a deep black now faded to a dark gray, was dull in comparison; except for the *M.S. Mercuria* insignia on her left shoulder—Brower had given her his brand-new badge "for good luck"—which blazed gold and silver against the gray.

The Ring Master welcomed the spectators, who quieted to listen to the opening recitation. Knowing the story by heart, Chandee only half-listened as the Ring Master described how the Barter Fights were established to stop deadly battles between merchant ships, offering a fair and non-fatal means of deciding trade rights throughout Mercantile space. She customarily used this time to concentrate on her opponent's weaknesses—except this time, there was nothing to think about.

She was caught off guard when the Ring Master announced her name. As the Reflector stood to cheers, there was no body language to read. She could not tell what he was thinking or feeling. A frisson rippled through her, a sensation so unusual that she at first assumed the floor of the ring was vibrating. The bell rang to begin the match, and the Reflector came out, dancing.

Chandee met him and threw the first punch. She allowed his responding strike to make contact so she could measure his strength and energy. It knocked her back more than she expected.

I'm getting old, she thought.

Chandee aimed several blows to his head. Unhurt, the Reflector responded in kind. She tasted blood and danced away to regain her equilibrium. Then she waded in with a series of hits to his abdomen and chest. The darkly shiny unitard flickered and shimmered with each blow, but he neither gasped nor grunted. Chandee felt lost with no facial expressions to read, no telltale flicks of the eyes. He was a cold surface that gave her nothing.

I'm going to lose. The thought flashed across her mind without warning as he pummeled her midsection. She deflected, punched, deflected, punched, over and over. The harder she hit, the harder she was hit. Her strength was waning, and the Reflector matched her, blow for blow.

I'll never see my brother again.

The bell rang for the first break. Chandee swayed in shock. Her matches usually ended quickly, and she had not fought through to the first break in years. Yet she felt as though she had been fighting for days. She dropped onto her stool, weak and uncoordinated.

"Here," a voice said, handing her a towel.

Bleary-eyed, Chandee discovered to her surprise that instead of Captain Aurum, Dr. Khanya was kneeling next to her.

"How's it going?" she asked, her tone suggesting she already knew the answer.

"I'm too old," Chandee muttered, breathing heavily as Dr. Khanya handed her a water pack. Every part of her hurt.

"You weren't too old during your last match," the doctor replied, taking the towel and dabbing at crusted blood on Chandee's lips. "What's changed?"

"I don't know," Chandee shook her head. "I'm going to lose. I'll never see Latif again." She stared at the floor, a weight in her chest more painful than any bruise.

Dr. Khanya frowned. "This isn't right."

"I agree. I never should have volunteered for this match."

"That's not what I mean." Dr. Khanya's eyes darted from the Reflector in his corner, then back to Chandee. "You don't talk like this."

"Like what?"

"Like you've given up." She inhaled suddenly, her eyes wide. "Remember what you said?" she whispered. "About how the Reflector's opponents seemed to just give up? And here you are, talking like the match is already lost. That's not like you." She stared with narrowed eyes across the ring. "Maybe it's not about the shiny suit..."

Chandee looked up at her. "I don't know what you're saying."

Dr. Khanya held Chandee's eyes in her own. "You are brave and strong and smart. You saved your brother, you saved your family, and you have brought honor and wealth to your ship. You are a hero, and you will win."

Time seemed to stop. There was no sound, no movement,

only the depths of Dr. Khanya's eyes. Chandee took a shuddering breath. A warmth filled her, and her eyes prickled. It was as if her brain had been wrapped in a thick blanket that was now removed. Her mind was clear again. Her arms felt strong again. There was pain, but it no longer dominated her. She followed Dr. Khanya's gaze and looked at her opponent with fresh eyes, and she understood.

The Reflector brought nothing into the ring to use against her—she had brought it herself.

"He mirrored my own fears back to me," she said in a hushed voice. Dr. Khanya eyes sparkled as she nodded in agreement. "A trait of his species, perhaps."

The bell rang to resume the match.

"Do you know what to do?"

"Yes, I think so."

Chandee stood. She repeated Dr. Khanya's words to herself as a mantra and they worked like a crisp breeze, keeping her cool and sharp. She waited for the Reflector to make the first move, but he only bounced and watched her. Exactly as she expected. She now saw his limits in the emptiness of his stance. Always letting his opponent make the first move was one of his weaknesses. He was a mimic, incapable of original ideas or creative thinking. He would let her do the work and then take advantage of it until she collapsed.

No more.

She waded in with steady hits, changing her angle and position each time, not giving him an opportunity to find a pattern. With each blow she sent out strong, clear thoughts:

I am brave. You are empty.

I am strong. You are nothing.

I will win. You will shatter.

There was a gritty, crunching noise as she struck his jaw with all the power she had. The Reflector flung his hands out toward her and then fell stiffly backwards. His unitard glittered and distorted as he hit the floor. He did not move.

Chandee stepped back and staggered. She was falling. Hands grabbed her, pulling on her. They were helping her to stand. There was a roaring in her ears. It was the spectators. They flooded the ring, cheering her, cheering each other, cheering the ageless tale of the underdog succeeding against the undefeated. Captain Aurum was crying, as was Dr. Khanya who, through hiccupping sobs, ordered the spectators to unhand Chandee and whisked her out of the ring.

Chandee opened her eyes to see the polished walls of the *Mercuria's* sickbay. She groaned.

"How do you feel?" Dr. Khanya was beside her in an instant.

"Sore." Chandee flexed her hands and stretched her arms and legs. "My head hurts. But it's not too bad. Why am I here?"

"Your injuries were considerable, and you were near exhaustion. You've been asleep for a long time."

Chandee sat up quickly, ignoring the surge of pain in her head. "For how long?"

Dr. Khanya lowered her eyes. "The transport left without you."

Chandee rubbed her forehead. "Are we still in Ziyo orbit?"

"Not anymore. Why?"

"I need to disembark as soon as possible," Chandee said, gingerly pulling herself off the bed.

"No, wait ... " Dr. Khanya began, but she stopped speaking when Captain Aurum and Brower entered.

"Captain, I request to leave the ship at your earliest convenience," Chandee said, grimacing as she stood.

"May I ask why?"

"I am no longer your Barter Fighter, which makes me a passenger. I cannot pay for transportation."

Captain Aurum stroked his beard. "I see. I was under the impression you were a patient of Dr. Khanya." He looked at the doctor. "Is that no longer the case? Is she no longer under your care?"

"She can use more rest, but she's free to leave if she chooses."

"Will you grant my request?" Chandee insisted.

"Certainly," the captain said. "But we won't reach our next stop for a while. You'll have to remain on board until then."

There was an odd inflection in the captain's voice and a definite twinkle in Dr. Khanya's eyes—something was going on.

"What is our next stop, Captain?"

"Our next stop is the planet Sannus."

Chandee's mouth dropped open.

"I cannot pay," she said when she found her voice.

"You'll earn your keep, as always," Aurum said with a grin and pointed a thumb over his shoulder at Brower. "You'll spend the time training him. Teach him everything you know, and we'll call it fair."

Blood thundered in Chandee's ears. She blinked as she tried to speak around a lump in her throat.

"I don't know what to say. Thank you."

"He should be thanking you," Dr. Khanya laughed as she ushered them out of her sickbay. "He won the betting pool. He can afford to give you a free ride."

The suns were low in the sky as the *M.S. Mercuria* touched down on the planet Sannus. Captain Aurum and the rest of the crew hung back as Chandee walked down the ramp with Dr. Khanya. There was a large crowd milling on the edge of the grassy field that served as the local spaceport. Chandee assumed they were there for a market or a fair until she saw her brother Latif standing at the head of the group and realized they were all facing the ship. Every one of them was smiling at her.

Latif met them at the foot of the ramp and hugged her tightly, laughing with joy. When they broke apart, each studied the other's face. She saw his eyes linger on her scars, but she did not care. To her, he looked the same as the day they parted, despite the lines in his weathered skin and the silver streaks in his hair.

"Who are all these people?" she asked.

"These people are your family," he said with a proud smile. "My children and grandchildren."

Chandee blinked. There were more people there than the entire crew of the *Mercuria*.

"Eve told us what you did," Latif said as he hugged her again.

"Eve?"

"Dr. Khanya," Latif jutted his chin at the doctor, who was squatting with one of his grandchildren, smiling and laughing. "She sent a message before you arrived, telling us how long and hard you fought for us." He pulled out of their hug and faced the group, his arm still around her shoulders. "Beloved family," he called out. The animated chatter faded into a respectful silence. "This is my sister, Chandee. She sacrificed to save us, to protect us. Without her, I would not be here. None of us would be here."

Latif turned and faced her. He raised his arms, palms against his chest, as did all her family and the *Mercuria's* crew. As one, they bowed to her.

"Welcome home, sister."

Captain Aurum and the crew said their farewells to Chandee, one at a time, until only Dr. Khanya remained.

"Goodbye, Chandee," she said, reaching up to give her a hug.

"Thank you for everything you did for me. I ..." Chandee paused, at a loss for words.

"I understand," Dr. Khanya said. She hesitated and then: "I'd like to come visit sometime, if that's ok."

A warmth flooded through Chandee. "Yes, Doctor," she said with a delighted smile. "That would be ok."

"Eve. My name is Eve."

Eve kissed Chandee on the cheek and returned up the *Mercuria's* ramp, stopping at the top to watch Chandee and her family leave the field. She waved until they disappeared from view in the golden light of the setting suns.

E.W. Barnes writes science fiction and fantasy, loving equally adventures in time and space, along with magical journeys accompanying elves and dragons. Originally from Los Angeles, California, she grew up outside of Washington, D.C., and when she was not reading all the mythical stories she could get her hands on, she was exploring museums and soaking up history at monuments and battlefields along the east coast of the United States. Now retired from a legal career, she lives in the Range of Light, which is what John Muir called the Sierra Nevada—where the deer and the antelope play, and wild horses roam freely. She is married with one offspring and an opinionated 75-pound lab/border collie mix whose nicknames include Princess, Missy, and Zuul, the Minion of Gozer. Learn more at linktr.ee/E.W.Barnes

MIRROR SEEKER

ROSE STRICKMAN

Hi, Inkspot." Otis scratches me behind the ears. I stretch out in my warm patch of sun and purr, my eyes slits of pleasure. He's such a good scratcher, Otis. Around us, the shop smells of dust and furniture polish and warmth.

"Ah, you're happy, aren't you?" His fingers travel down my neck. Oh, wonderful man. I purr still more ecstatically.

Then, sadly, his phone sings its little tune and he takes it out. "Hello? ... Oh, the shipment's coming tomorrow? Great! ... 8 a.m., fine ..."

He wanders off, into the labyrinthine aisles of the shop. I guess scratching is over. I sit up, stretch some more, and thump down after him.

I've really enjoyed my sojourn here in Otis's antiques shop —maybe a little too much. But it's been so good to stay in a warm, dry place, quiet and with a million little nooks and crannies I can explore and curl up in. Otis's shop is always full of old furniture and old books, ugly lamps and hide rugs, ancient sewing projects from forgotten craftspeople. Mice too, in the farther reaches. It's a cat's paradise, even without the lovely Otis.

Now he's finishing up his call. "Excellent!" He pushes the end call button with a jaunty thumb. "We've got some real treasures coming our way, Inkspot!"

I rub my head against his ankles and purr. He's so cute when he's excited.

He rushes about the shop, humming, fussing with the antiques, entering something on the laptop, packaging stuff for shipping. We even get a couple of customers in the afternoon. Otis shows them around, and one of them leaves with an order. It's been a good day.

Which makes the evening's disturbance all the more unwelcome.

Otis lives in a small loft above the shop. I've lived up there with him for six months now. He closes up and then goes upstairs to cook himself dinner. I eat my cat food while he munches on lasagna, flipping through an old paperback.

Then the phone rings. Otis looks at the incoming number and freezes. "Oh, God."

Reluctantly, he hits the button and puts the phone to his ear. "Hello?"

In shrieks the tinny voice of Charis, Otis's ex-wife. Otis leans his head on his propped hand, closing his eyes, and I glower in sympathy. If my powers were any broader, I would use them against the woman now shrilling furiously at Otis while he makes abbreviated efforts to get a word in edgewise.

"I know, but...Charis, I...It's not like the shop is making a lot of money, you know..."

Wrong response. Charis's voice grows louder and shriller. I growl, my fur standing on end.

"Fine, then...Bye, Charis." Otis hangs up and places his phone limply on the tabletop. He props his forehead in both hands, eyes tight shut. He lets out a groan.

I come over, jumping fluidly into his lap. I curl up in the warm space, leaning against him and purring. Miserably, he scratches me.

"Oh, Inkspot," he says softly. "I...She's so unhappy, Inkspot. And everything I do makes it worse."

Oh, Otis. If only I could talk, I would tell you that it's Charis who makes everything worse, who is preying on his guilt and his good nature to try and squeeze money and misery out of him, while he aches with unhappiness and unrequited love. He'll go to bed early tonight, I know from experience, and he'll shed a few tears that he'll wipe away, embarrassed, in the dark.

He gathers me close. "I'm so glad you're here, Inkspot."

I'm glad I am, too.

The next morning, the new shipment of antiques arrives. Otis and his brawny young assistants run around at the docking bay, gathering the carts, helping the large, muscular truckers roll the packaged furniture, portraits and rolled-up rugs into the storage area. I stand back, watching, while Otis and the men unwind the wrapping and cut into the boxes. Otis hops around like a flea, so excited that his hands are shaking. I purr a little. It's so good to see him happy, especially after last night.

"There we go!" One of the truckers stands back, admiring the unwrapped antique, beaming light across the room. "Eighteenth-century mirror, as promised."

I freeze, staring at my own image in the glass: a small black-and-white cat, perched on a box, fur standing on end, green eyes wide with horror. I recognize that thing. That *mirror*. It's not eighteenth-century.

It's not even really a mirror.

"It's beautiful," Otis says, running a hand over the silver frame. "Look at that scrollwork! I've never seen anything like it."

Of course he hasn't. That style is not native to this universe.

I still haven't moved. The glass, only slightly fogged, seems to ripple, waves of brilliance under the surface. *Come, Seeker, come, Finder,* it whispers. *She is not in this world. It's time to move on.*

Sometimes, that mirror has been a welcome sight. Sometimes I've thrown myself into the glass headlong, desperate to escape whatever world I'm in, ignoring any chaos my sudden exit prompts. But not this time. Oh, not this time.

"Not a chip anywhere." Otis continues cataloging the mirror's virtues. He notices my upright fur, my fixed stare. "What's the matter, Inkspot?"

It's too much. I hurl myself down and go streaking off, back into the main shop, where I hide under a low embroidered chair, safely out of sight and beyond any human's reach.

But not beyond the mirror's.

I spend a restless night prowling around the loft, growling to myself and trying not to think of the mirror downstairs.

The next day dawns sunny and bright. For once, I wish it wasn't: the brilliant light bounces off every reflective surface in the shop, including the mirror's. I just can't get away from it: everywhere I go, whether I'm crouching under a sofa or jumping among the lamps, it twinkles and shines at me, somehow catching every beam of light and reflecting it to my every hiding place. Even when I leave the showroom, hiding in the loft or the backroom, I can feel it tugging at me.

She's not here. It's time to move on.

"Hey, Inkspot." I'm so disordered that I can hardly take pleasure in Otis's scratching fingers. "What's the matter? You're so restless today!"

I mew and rub against him. I wish so much that I had human words to tell him what the matter is. But I suppose he wouldn't believe me.

In the corner of my eye, the mirror flashes again. This time I catch a glimpse of another world—the world I must travel to next. I spring away, hissing.

"Oh, Inkspot!" Otis straightens the crystal ashtray I've knocked askew. "Be careful."

The mirror winks at me. I hiss again.

"Okay, be like that." Shaking his head and chuckling, he goes off to get the mail.

He comes back with a heavy white envelope in his hand and a strange flat look in his eye. He sinks down at his desk. He takes out the letter, scans it quickly, and puts it down. He picks it up again. Puts it down.

I hop into his lap, purring. He pets me, but with a heavy, stiff hand.

"I'll have to find you a new home, Inkspot." His voice is flat and blank. He's still as stone, as though he'll never move again.

"Hey, boss." John, one of Otis's shop assistants, a beefy young man who does a lot of the heavy lifting, comes in. "What's the matter?"

Otis pulls himself together. "Nothing, John." It's *not* nothing; John and I can both see that. "I wonder if you could help me move some of the stock..."

I jump off his lap and watch while he moves off, giving the good impression of a man about his normal workday, with just the occasional hint of a stricken child.

That evening, we eat dinner together as usual. Otis doesn't read. He just stares into space, mechanically chewing.

When he's done, he takes his dishes to the sink, where he abruptly drops them.

"Oh, God! God..." He leans over the sink, tears rolling down his cheeks. I trot over and lean against his ankles, mewing in concern and confusion. Charis didn't call, so why is he like this?

"I'm sorry, Inkspot, I'm sorry ..." He leans down to scratch my ears. "I should've known. I went to the doctor, after all ... But I guess I didn't want to believe it."

He kneels down, still scratching. "Don't worry," he says in a soft, hoarse whisper. "I'll find a good home for you before it's all over. You'll be okay."

It's then that I know, and my heart falls down an endless abyss.

The mirror's getting impatient. I know, because it's started to invade my dreams.

Seeker, it says, floating toward me like the mouth of a grave, *it's time to go.*

Not yet, I plead.

Now. She's not in this world.

No, but he *is. He needs me.*

He is not the one you were sent to find.

I growl in my sleep. I can feel the mirror tugging me through my slumber.

I care nothing for her. *She ran away of her own free will, crossing the worlds and breaking her mother's heart. Otis has hurt no one. And he needs me.*

This is your mission, Seeker. For this you were made.

The mirror's right. I was made for this. And I cannot long resist.

Go to hell, I tell the mirror, and spend the rest of the night awake, sprawled on Otis's sleeping chest.

The next morning, the mirror's call is worse than ever. I move restlessly around the shop, stressed and sleep-deprived, feeling the damned mirror pulling at me every minute. Otis is in little better shape. He's distracted and preoccupied, paying little heed to the shop assistants or the customers. I wish he'd tell someone about his condition—John at least. It might make him feel better. But that's not Otis's way.

"What a pretty cat!" A woman customer stops to admire me. "What's its name?"

Otis shakes himself. "Her name's Inkspot." He pets me. "I found her about six months ago, out in the alley, and adopted her."

I remember that. I was cold, hungry, and had given up all hope of my quarry in this world. I was hoping desperately for the mirror to appear and release me. Instead, the side door to the shop opened, and I found Otis.

"She's beautiful." The woman reaches out to pet me. Normally I'm fine with humans, even strangers, petting me, but today I hiss, showing my teeth. She freezes.

"Sorry," says Otis with an apologetic grimace. "She's not normally like this."

"It's okay." The woman forces a smile and turns away. "I'm looking for a nice big ornament for my office's lobby. Something we can hang on the wall, like a painting or a mirror. I wonder if..."

They go off together, deep in discussion. I don't waste time hoping she'll choose the mirror and take it away. Nothing is going to take the mirror away. Not before it's ready. *Seeker...*

I mew miserably. But there's no point in fighting. For this I was made.

I will go with you, I tell the mirror. *Tonight. But first there's something I must do.*

Otis takes a nerve-wrackingly long time to go to sleep. He works late, and then he's restless, barely eating anything but moving around his loft, reading and re-reading the papers the doctor sent him. Naturally, Charis has to pick tonight to make a particularly long, shrill call. He sits crumpled on the sofa, listening to her screech, but doesn't say a word in response. He hangs up on her mid-rant, puts the phone down, and doesn't respond to its repeated angry call-tunes.

Finally he gets up to shower, listlessly pull on pajamas, and crawl into bed. Even then, it takes a long time for his eyes to close and his breathing to fall into that somnolent rhythm.

It's time to make my move.

Silently, I slink in around the partially-opened door. I leap onto his chest. It rises and falls gently, and I feel his steady heartbeat against me. Putting down my chin, I let its rhythm enter me.

Beat...beat...beat. On and on, loosening my mind. *Beat... beat...beat.* On I go, traveling deeper, losing all sensation, as I finally wash slowly into Otis's sleeping mind and there spin my tale for him.

There are other worlds, other universes. A vast array of them, strung out on existence like gems or beads. And in those multitudes of worlds, a multitude of beings, cultures, cities, continents, forests, oceans. A brilliant net of jewels, scattered over the black velvet of eternity.

And in one of those worlds, a world of golden plains and high temples, where women's hair flashed with diamonds and the priestesses danced for the gods, where magic was as common as dust or wind, there lived a sorceress and her daughter.

The sorceress was perhaps not the best mother. She was distantly related to the royal family and very gifted at her craft, but she did not have a good relationship with her child, especially as the daughter grew older. They clashed more and more frequently, and the stubborn sulky pout on the daughter's face grew ever more pronounced.

Why won't you teach me anything? she yelled at her mother.

Because you don't have the concentration or the intelligence, the mother said brutally. *You don't have the strength of mind needed for my craft.*

I'll show you! the daughter screamed as she fled the room in a clash of bracelets and a ripple of silk.

The mother thought nothing would come of it. But the next day, the daughter was gone. There was only a mirror, displaced from the mother's workroom, still rippling with the strength of the spell the daughter had cast. Still showing, dimly, the world she'd disappeared to.

The mother was overcome with grief and horror. There was no telling what dangers her daughter would face in that other world. And there was no coming back that way: the mirror only worked in a single direction. The sorceress could feel her daughter too, far away, leaping from world to world, heedless with ease now she'd opened that first door. The younger woman had more talent than her mother had ever credited.

So the mother sat down in her workroom, and she thought, and she planned, and she finally stood to cast a mighty magic.

She fasted, she sang, she chanted, she danced. And from her exertions came a white light, glowing in the center of her workroom. Hours passed, and the light solidified and resolved, until a small, female, black-and-white cat fell to the floor and bowed before her creator.

You will be my Seeker, the sorceress said to her. *You will travel the worlds until you find my daughter, letting nothing stop you, no danger stay you, until you bring my daughter safely home. This mirror will be your gate. It will transport you from world to world, appearing only when you have searched a world and found she is not there. For this will be your task evermore: you will search, and never stop searching, until you find her. Then the charm I place upon you will bring her home to me again. Do not fail me, Seeker.*

And the Seeker swore she would not.

With a wave of her bell-sleeved arm, the sorceress ushered the cat to the mirror. Without hesitation, the Seeker jumped through. The glass rippled and wavered, and showed, briefly, another universe. Then it fell still, reflecting only the sorceress's workroom, and the cat was gone.

That was you? Otis doesn't manifest himself in the dream, but his question emerges with the dim but inexorable focus of a dreamer.

That was me, I confirm. My physical form, now barely felt, cuddles closer to Otis. Oh, it's so good to actually talk to him. *My mistress made me for one reason only: to find her daughter and bring her home.*

Why you? His sleeping voice is slightly indignant. *Why couldn't she go herself?*

I have often wondered that same thing. *A cat has more mobility than a human,* I say, giving him the politic answer. *A cat can go places a human is barred from. A cat can go unnoticed, and travel through city or forest with equal ease. And she invested in me the charm to bring her daughter home. She may not have been able to, herself.*

Around me, his mind contracts with a sudden, painful emotion. *So now you're leaving,* he says.

Yes, I say. *The mirror has appeared. I must leave, go to the next world, keep up my search.*

Let me come with you. His mental voice is sharp with pleading.

Otis. I withdraw slightly. *That's not possible.*

Why not? We have the mirror—

I can't bear this. *Goodbye, Otis. I'll miss you.*

No! Inkspot, wait—

I'm already gone.

Slowly, my consciousness floods back into my own brain. For a long time, I stay on Otis's chest, basking in his warmth, his presence. His sleep is restless, his head tossing on the pillow. He may not believe the dream's message. But he will remember it all his days, however long they last. And I will at least have told him the truth of why I had to leave.

Oh, Otis. A hundred worlds I've wandered, and I've never loved anyone as much as you. If I had the choice, I would stay. You are worth a thousand times more than the pouty, spoiled sorceress's daughter I've been chasing from world to world. You are worth a thousand times more than the sorceress who was too cowardly to search out her daughter herself.

But I have no choice. I can feel the mirror calling, tugging, more insistent with every heartbeat.

I lean over to give him one last nuzzle, one last purr. He murmurs something in his sleep, a groan.

Slowly, I leap off him back onto the floor. His warmth leaves me as I trot across the room back to the door.

Down the stairs I go, to the silent shop. In the darkness, the mirror glows silver. Lines of gold run across the glass, and again I glimpse that other world, the next world I must travel to, on the quest I am bound to, the endless, endless search that precludes all rest, all happiness, all love.

I breathe in, taking one last gulp of Otis's scent. Then I leap.

Midway through the leap, I hear the pounding footsteps behind me. Otis's voice calling out. Oh, Otis, why did you have to do that? You should have stayed sleeping, so you wouldn't have to watch me leave—

The mirror shimmers around me, and I fall out onto the ground of another world. But this time, not alone.

A thin gray cat lands beside me. He's not used to his new body, so he barely lands on his feet, but at the last minute he twists in midair and lands four-paw, his fur standing straight. His yellow-brown eyes are wild.

It's a moment before I can speak. *Otis?*

He blinks at me. His ears swivel, and a shiver runs down his frame. *Inkspot?* His mental speech is faint, tentative. *What —what just happened?*

You followed me through the mirror. I hiss in incredulity. *I didn't think that was possible. You actually followed me through!*

Yes, he says slowly. *Yes, I did.* He looks around the autumn wood we stand in, a grove of red and gold trees, shining in the afternoon sunlight. *Are we in another world?*

Yes. I slump as new knowledge sinks in. *Otis, why did you do that? Now you're bound to the quest, the same as me!*

I had to. He prances a little, experimenting with his new body. Already his psychic speech is stronger. He's a hundred times healthier in this magical new cat-form, all his age and illness washed away. *I didn't have anything to live for, back home. And...* He stops to look at me. *I couldn't let you go on alone. Not all alone, like you've been for so long. You're my friend, Inkspot.*

At this, a tide of warmth washes over me, melting away my dismay and apprehension. Yes. Friends. Friends forever now, it would seem. For the quest may go on forever, hopeless and pointless, but we will be together. And that makes all the difference in the worlds.

Come on, then, I say, springing away. *Let's see what this world has to offer.*

And together we go.

Rose Strickman is a fantasy, sci-fi and horror writer living in Seattle, Washington. Her work has appeared in anthologies such as Sword and Sorceress 32, Nightmare Fuel and Air: Sylphs, Spirits, & Swan Maidens, as well as e-zines such as Luna Station Quarterly and Aurora Wolf. She has also self-published several novellas on Amazon. Please see her Amazon author's page at amazon.com/author/rosestrickman or connect with her on Facebook at facebook.com/rose.strickman.3

JARJACHA ENGAÑO
SAM KNIGHT

J acinta's eyes gleamed as she waited in the dark. She raised her hand-rolled *siyaru* and, with pinched lips, pulled in the strong smoke of the *mapacho*. The ember lit her ruddy cheeks against the night, showing deep lines etched into her aged face. The cold rock she sat upon was jagged and hard, but she ignored it. Her whole life had been jagged and hard, and she no longer paid attention to being uncomfortable. There was a worse discomfort to be found in soft things: the terrible knowledge they wouldn't last.

Movement caught her eye. A shadow left the house Jacinta watched over and nestled itself behind bushes. And then quiet crying began, just as Jacinta had feared.

Slowly burning into Jacinta's soul, the sound summoned unbidden tears to the old woman's eyes. She'd thought the old wounds long healed, but despite the velvety softness of the sobs, the sounds burned deeper and harsher than the smoke filling Jacinta's lungs. The too-familiar sound dredged up despised memories and a wrenching gut she hadn't felt in years.

Worst suspicion confirmed, her face hardened, and she pushed the feelings away.

She took another drag from her *siyaru* and ritualistically waved it around herself, letting the heady smoke cleanse her emotions and fill her thoughts. The shadow, a young *cusqueña* of only ten years, named Dayana, had just discovered how hard life really was; as Jacinta had feared, the death of Dayana's mother had only been the beginning, a door that had opened to let in even worse.

Would Dayana leave the village after this, run away to the city? Jacinta could not blame Dayana if she did. Jacinta herself would have left when the same horror happened to her those many years ago, had she been able.

Dayana would be leaving for a much different reason than merely to escape a mundane life and enter into the modern world as so many others had, but the effect upon the village would be the same. So many children left now, there would soon be no village at all.

Though her heart hurt for Dayana, Jacinta could do nothing to undo what had been done to her. She knew from experience nothing would make it better. But that did not mean nothing could be done at all, that Jacinta could not lay a path for Dayana.

Yes, life was hard, but some hard things were not to be endured; they were to be dealt with.

The dawn found Jacinta wrapped in her best *lliclla*, sitting upon a blanket in front of her stall in the village marketplace. Her fogged breath floated through the cool air to join with the blue sky as she spun fleece into yarn with her boney fingers. She occasionally squinted into the sunrise to keep watch over Dayana's home. On the blanket beside her lay an obsidian mirror in an ornate setting. The relic had been passed to her by Adoncia, the village mother, the healer who had trained Jacinta in the old ways. The mirror had been handed down for generations, and in it, those who knew how could see the truth of the deeds of men

As morning sounds grew within the waking village, Jacinta struck a match and lit her *siyaru*. She drew deeply of the smoke and then lit the ends of several palo santo incense strings she'd laced around the ornamental edges of the mirror. She waved the *siyaru* around herself, stuck it in the corner of her mouth, and then lifted the mirror and repeated the process of spreading the cleansing smoke. When she was satisfied, she turned her back to Dayana's home and began watching it in the reflection of the mirror.

Soon four men, their distorted reflections wavering, appeared in the doorway. Jacinta could hear them talking as they stepped out into the road, but their voices were low and somber. Their reflections blended into each other, merging and coming apart as they moved through the ripples in the mirror. Jacinta tried to discern who was who, but at this distance, the mirror did not reveal enough details. Suddenly one of the figures seemed to reach out and strike two of the others, who fell to the ground and vanished.

Jacinta gasped and quickly turned to look directly at the men. Who had struck whom? Dayana's father, Ignacio, and her three brothers, Ronzo, Dario, and Brayan, strolled on as though nothing had happened. Jacinta could not tell whose misdeed had been revealed.

Dismayed but unsurprised, Jacinta turned back to the mirror and waited. She puffed on the *siyaru* absently as she contemplated the meaning of what she had seen. It was not the vision she had expected, and it revealed nothing of the crime she already knew. Perhaps, though Jacinta had not truly thought it possible, Dayana's situation was even worse than Jacinta feared.

She focused her attention on the reflection in the mirror as Dayana appeared hefting a sack of dirty clothes onto her back as she left home

Even in the distorted image, Jacinta could see the girl had pulled her *lliclla* up high around her neck and pinned it tightly under her chin, as though she wished to hide in the brightly colored shawl. Eyes to the ground, Dayana was slow to follow the other women to the river. It was apparent the young *cusqueña* had no song left in her heart.

It hurt Jacinta to recognize nothing of the girl who had once run along the path giggling as she played tag with her brothers and hid within the pleats of her mother's colorful *pollera*. Since the death of Dayana's mother, four months ago, Jacinta had feared this day; the day this beautiful little girl would skip the best years of her life and suddenly become old in a young body. The day Dayana would be cursed to the life Jacinta had.

The girl would not leave the village after all. Youthful exuberance stolen, Jacinta could see Dayana did not have the spirit or determination to try for a new life in the city.

Jacinta puffed on the *siyaru*, this time inhaling deeply and letting the smoke clear her thoughts. What more would the poor girl have endured were Jacinta not here to have recognized what happened and know what to do?

Jacinta had long worried that when she died, the village would die with her. Perhaps that was no longer so. Jacinta would take Dayana under her wing, protect her from the harsh looks and sharp tongues. She would teach the girl the old ways, train her to become matron to the village, as had been done with Jacinta after she'd endured the horrors Dayana now went through.

Within moments of Dayana leaving home, the babbling voices of the other women and their playing children were lost over the hill ahead of her. Jacinta watched in the mirror as the girl slowed even more, apparently reluctant to catch up. Though Dayana continued on, she bent as if the sack she bore contained the weight of time without end.

When Jacinta could no longer make out Dayana in the

mirror, she found herself looking into her own reflection—a twisted, hideous face, half her father's, and half llama. She dropped the mirror.

But what it had shown her should not have been a surprise. The mirror never lied.

I am old, she thought, and then shook her head. She opened her bag, stowed the mirror, and took out special *ojotas* she'd made. It had taken her arthritic fingers all night, but she'd carved the bottoms of the tire-rubber sandals into the split-moon shape of llama feet. Then she'd used sticks to add long fingers and a thumb to the front of each sandal. It had taken several tries until the sandals left the tracks she wanted.

Jacinta looked to make sure no one was around. The sun was up, and the village was quiet. The men in the fields, the women and children at the river, Jacinta had an hour until anyone would come around.

She donned the bizarre shoes. They were uncomfortable, but Jacinta paid no attention. Slinging the bag onto her back, she teetered drunkenly as she walked, carefully staying on her heels and leaving the imprints of llama tracks in the dirt. When she made it to Dayana's, it took only moments to stomp out full tracks in the dirt around the house. Though it made her old back ache to beat at the ground so, the awkward *ojotas* left satisfying half-llama, half-human hand tracks.

After circling the house, she caught her breath and began leaving a trail heading toward the mountain.

The men came with the sunset, laughing and carrying on with vulgar jokes as men always did. The sound of children and the smell of woodsmoke and cooking food filled the village. The evening was lovely, peaceful.

Jacinta hesitated.

Did she really want to do this? While it would put the fear of wrongdoing into those who deserved it, and give affirmation to others who needed it, it would also cause nightmares. And not just for the children. She remembered how the village had reacted when it had been her: chaos, confusion, fear, and, in the end, bloodshed.

It seemed a terrible thing to contemplate against the backdrop of laughter and the golden clouds of sunset. But a terrible thing had happened. And it had to be stopped. A warning had to be put out to others who would do the same. A reassurance to those who feared it happening to them.

There were few in the village who would remember what had happened before, but she was sure their knowledge, their memories, would spread like mice through untended maize.

And then the evil would be revealed, and that revelation would end it.

Jacinta turned weary eyes to Dayana's home. Smoke rose from the stovepipe. Dayana was making dinner for her father and brothers. The *cusqueña* had done well taking over her deceased mother's duties. Too well...

Jacinta pushed the thought down, sickened for letting the insults of others travel through her mind. She, of all people. To blame poor Dayana... Jacinta knew what it was like, even if others did not.

Her jaw set. There were four men in that house—which meant three of them could have stopped it.

She had to do this. The village needed reminding there were consequences for actions. Otherwise, those actions could tear it apart. And though this would, for a while, make things even worse for Dayana, Jacinta would make sure the girl would eventually command the respect of the village, just as Jacinta had.

❀

The sun had been down for an hour. The glow through the windows lit the street enough to walk, but not to clearly see faces. The village would sleep soon.

Dressed in black to conceal herself in the shadows, Jacinta took a deep breath and readied herself. At her age, this was not going to be easy, but it had to be done.

She double-checked the raggedy bindings she had wrapped loosely around the llama to create the illusion of clothing. She wanted them to fall off quickly, but not too soon. Some plastered on and wet, some painted with chicken blood, they gave the gentle animal a horrid appearance of parts missing and internal organs revealed. Jacinta placed a three-sided mask onto the llama's head, covering the back and both sides, and acting like blinders. The animal, at least for a little while, would run in the direction Jacinta wanted, and the grotesque faces, one on each side, would make anyone think the llama was looking at them—and that it had a human face.

Jacinta had only a glimpse of the beast when she'd been a child, but it had terrified her. In the dim of the night, she was sure she had re-created the creature.

She secured her black *lliclla* and made sure she had a good grip on the rope around the llama's neck. "Forgive me, my friend," she whispered. She hefted a large wooden spoon and slapped the llama's testicles as hard as she could.

The scream carried throughout the village, followed by the haunting cries *Jarjacha* was named for: *Har! Har! Har!*

Startled faces appeared in windows. Old faces only long enough to slam shutters, young faces only until elders pulled them away and covered their eyes. *Jarjacha* could steal a person's soul with just a gaze.

Many saw the ghastly creature racing through the village,

coming from Dayana's family home, crying out demonically. *Har! Har! Har!* Its horrid, twisted visage looked upon all who saw it. Tattered, bloody clothing streamed around it, falling away like the last shreds of its humanity. The beast galloped lurchingly through the village before heading for the mountain.

None saw the old woman running behind, fast as she could, barely holding onto the rope lead. Her hoarse voice cried out, *Har! Har! Har!* until she tasted blood in her throat and fainted from exhaustion.

The village was terribly quiet. No one came out of their houses until the sun was full in the sky. It didn't take long for Jacinta's planted tracks to be found, and people gathered around quickly. Wild-eyed and talking in low voices, they shared stories of what they had seen and heard the night before. The few children who ventured out stayed close, many refusing to let go of their elders' legs.

Jacinta approached, limping terribly and hiding her rope-burned hand. She wouldn't have to explain anything. The word *Jarjacha* could be heard as each newcomer confirmed their suspicions with the others and were shown the horrible, half-human, half-llama tracks. That would be immediately followed by sideways glances at the home Dayana lived in.

It wasn't hard to read the thoughts of the people at that point. Who had it been? Ignacio? Ronzo? Surely not Dario or Brayan!

But no one doubted the meaning of what had happened. Jacinta's plan worked. The village knew someone in that house was guilty of incest.

No one came out of Dayana's house. As the sun climbed and the day grew hot, the villagers debated what to do. Only a handful were old enough to remember the last time the evil of *Jarjacha* had cursed the village, and those who did quickly deferred to Jacinta.

No one mentioned or asked about her involvement, then or now, but she saw the looks in their eyes and felt bared and naked anyway. What had happened so long ago was a fresh wound once again.

But it had to be done, and she had done it.

She kept composed and answered their questions.

Yes, *Jarjacha* had come when she was a girl. No, she did not know if it stole souls with a gaze or ate the brains of the innocent to keep itself alive. Yes, it was the embodiment of the sin of incestual lust. Yes, it had been dealt with very quickly back then.

"What do we have to do to get rid of it?" a desperate voice carried over the others.

The memory of Jacinta's father, stoned to death as people chased him from the village, came back to her, vividly as if it had just happened. The horrible mixed feelings returned as well.

Was that what she should tell them? Was that truly necessary? Did there have to be bloodshed?

Of course there did.

Jarjacha had to be killed, or it would get worse. If not in reality, then in the minds of the people who now looked to her for guidance. But she didn't know who the culprit was. The mirror hadn't revealed it. Did it matter? Should it be different for Dayana's violator than it had been for Jacinta's own father? Should the punishment be different for a father than for brothers, or even for those in the home who knew, and could have stopped it, but didn't?

And why hadn't anyone come out of the house yet?

Jacinta did her best to keep everyone calm. Surely those

inside knew what was going on and would push the guilty party out soon.

Tension rose. People became restless and began to ask more questions.

What if they waited too long and *Jarjacha* returned? Was it in the mountains, or had it returned and resumed its human form in the night? What if it really did eat the brains of innocent people? What if it really does steal souls? Could it do that in human form? The children were in danger!

Jacinta found herself weary beyond what age and the previous night took from her. Last night had been difficult, and her aching, barely mobile body proved it, but this was worse. Adoncia never had so many questions from the villagers. They had always been quick to do what she told them to do.

But then, Adoncia had always been quick to tell them what to do. Jacinta was hesitating. She needed to be quick and decisive.

And Dayana needed her

Though the village wouldn't realize it, they would never look at Dayana the same, never treat her the same. When the time was right, Jacinta would tell Dayana how the same thing had happened to her, show Dayana she could overcome this, could be strong and respected, as Jacinta was. But Jacinta needed to protect her quickly, nurture her, train her in the old ways so the village learned to respect her, as they had Jacinta

And that had to start now, by setting an example Dayana could follow, just as Adoncia had once set an example for Jacinta.

Jacinta pushed through the crowd and rapped upon the door. When no answer came, she unlatched the door and pushed it open.

The smell of blood, of death, washed thickly over her and out into the warm day, pushing the people behind her back with a collective gasp.

Jacinta covered her mouth and nose with her hand and stepped in, letting her eyes adjust.

Dayana's father, Ignacio, belly split open, eyes wide and filmy, lay in a pool of drying blood on the earthen floor.

Her brothers, Ronzo and Dario, were on the bed, holding each other in tight embrace, comforting one another from the terror of their dead father—until Jacinta saw their slack faces, the blood, and the knives each still held.

In the corner, Dayana sat holding her youngest brother's head in her lap, cradled like a child, though he was bigger than her. His throat had been cut, his lifeblood captured in the pleats of her skirt.

"It's my fault." Dayana didn't look up. "I tried to stop them. They wouldn't listen." She brushed Brayan's hair. "Papa said *Jarjacha* proved I was lying. Proved they were lying."

"Lying about what, little one?" Jacinta asked, though she knew.

"When I couldn't sleep, when I couldn't bear not having Mama ..." She choked on a sob. "I would go outside and pray. And cry. I thought they wouldn't hear. But they did.

"I worried that Papa was alone, that my brothers would never marry, never be happy ..." Tears broke through, overwhelming Dayana's words and retracing dried tracks over her cheeks. "But we *were* happy. I just didn't realize ... It's all my fault.

"Papa said *Jarjacha* meant one of my brothers—" Dayana shook her head, unable to say it. "They fought. And they wouldn't stop! They wouldn't stop ..."

"No ..." Jacinta whispered, stepping forward numbly. Could what Dayana said be true?

What would happen when Dayana told the village? Would they call Dayana a liar? Or think *Jarjacha* was someone else, someone still out there?

Jacinta could no longer tell Dayana this had happened to her too—because it hadn't. She couldn't tell Dayana ...

She couldn't tell anyone ... that ... this was what the mirror had shown her. That, like her father, she would destroy a family with *Jarjacha*.

Jacinta's legs gave out and she found herself upon the cold, hard floor. Despite the velvety softness of Dayana's sobs, the sound was unbearably jagged against Jacinta's soul. "What have I done?"

Shadows filled the doorway again as others pressed closer to see what had happened. *"Jarjacha* is gone," a voice called out, before Jacinta had time to think, before she could say anything

Jacinta's own voice betrayed her. Words meant to silence the man before he said more never passed her quivering lips.

"They are all dead. It is over," he cried loudly, pushing back into the crowd, telling everyone what he had seen.

But it wasn't over.

For Jacinta it would never be over.

Sam Knight is publisher of Knight Writing Press and author of six children's books, five short story collections, three novels, and over 75 stories, including three co-authored with Kevin J. Anderson.

A Colorado native, Sam spent ten years in California's wine country before returning to the Rockies. When asked if he misses California, he gets a wistful look in his eyes and replies he misses the green mountains in the winter, but he is glad to be back home.

Once upon a time, he was known to quote books the way some people quote movies, but now he claims having a family has made him forgetful, as a survival adaptation. He can be found at SamKnight.com and contacted at sam@samknight.com.

TIPS FOR A BABY WITCH
KRISTEN S. WALKER

There are so many guides for new witches and tips for beginners that it's hard to know where to start. That's okay. You try something and see if it works for you. If it doesn't, try something else. It's how we learned before there was the internet full of lists and social media aesthetics.

You can't hurt yourself with witchcraft. Some guides will warn you against doing advanced things until you understand them better, but you can ignore them. It's not like a spell is going to blow up in your face if you use the wrong crystal or didn't gather your pondweed exactly at midnight.

First tip: don't buy a lot of expensive tools at first. Look around your house for things you can use, or buy cheap items. Good things to start are candles, salt, a cup or dish, a mirror, and something to write down what you've learned. I like to gather natural items like seashells or sticks. Do you ever see a cool rock on the ground and feel the urge to pick it up? You can use that!

Oh, and don't look into the mirror during the dark of the moon.

Herbs are another useful tool, but don't go buying a

whole bunch just to make your house look like a medieval apothecary. Start with what you already have in your spice cabinet. Basil can be used for money spells, and rosemary brings good luck. Don't forget the salt. Cayenne pepper can—

Wait. I told you not to look in the mirror. Yes, that movement was trying to get your attention. Don't fall for it.

So after you've covered your mirror with a dark cloth, start by casting a basic circle. Sprinkle salt and charge it with your wand. Your wand can be a stick, a crystal point, a pen— anything that helps you direct your energy. Make sure you give yourself enough space to move around inside.

Did you just lift the cloth to look at the mirror again? Whatever you do, don't look at your reflection—

Shit. Now you've seen it.

Don't freak out. Your reflection just looks a little distorted. Do you start to notice all those little things you hate about yourself, like the nose that looks like your dad's? Don't focus on the way your eyes narrow, like when your mom criticized you. It doesn't help to remember how she told you that you were wasting your time instead of going to college. She was right that your boyfriend was a loser, but she doesn't know everything. If you graduated and got stuck in a crummy corporate job, you wouldn't be where you are today, owning two cats and studying witchcraft. We all have our own journey.

Put the cloth back over the mirror, and let's move on.

Okay, so the vibes are getting kind of weird in here now. Let's cleanse the space. Some people smudge with sage or Palo Santo, but I would try something more neutral, like incense or even a room spray. I knew this one girl who used expensive perfume, but that triggers my asthma. I like moon water with a little lemon juice to freshen the place up.

Try playing some music to block out that scratching sound from the mirror. Something soothing, like Celtic harp or EDM. Turn up the volume. Louder.

Don't look at it. Don't look at it. Don't—

You had to lift that cloth, didn't you?

Crap! That thing looks like you, but the eyes are glowing red and those claws look really sharp. I don't think you can stop it now. Tell it that it can only enter in perfect love and perfect trust.

No? Crap, what's that line again... You have no power over me!

It's still coming? This is really bad. Don't make any sudden movements, and whatever you do, don't break the circle. Back away slowly...

Run!

Go downstairs. Kitchen. Get the biggest knife you can find. Stop screaming, you're just making it mad. Get ready, here it comes.

Aim for the heart! Left side, a little lower. Try again. Stab it again. Just keep stabbing! Kill it! Now!

Whew, that was close.

Okay, so the body should be dissolving now into ashes. Those bloodstains stick around, though. We need to clean those up before they can set in.

You may be a fan of natural, organic cleaning products, but now is not the time to mess around. The best thing to clean up blood is bleach. A lot of it. Start buying in bulk.

Take a deep breath. Ground and center. If you feel drained, eat something to restore your energy.

Congrats! You've defeated your first inner demon. Doesn't it feel like there's a weight off your chest? Things should get better around here now. I see new love in your future.

Last tip: keep practicing, especially your circle casting. Bad vibes shouldn't be able to get inside a circle of salt. See how else you can brighten up your space. Affirmations are basically spells, so try a sign that says "Good vibes only" or "peace" to help you manifest those positive energies in your home.

And just in case, don't look in the mirror during the dark of the moon.

Blessed be!

Fantasy author **Kristen S. Walker** dreams of being a pirate mermaid who can talk to sharks, but she settles for writing stories for teens and adults. Her self-published series include the Fae of Calaveras trilogy, the Santa Cruz Witch Academy, the Divine Warriors, and Wyld Magic. Her works have appeared in several anthologies including Tales of Ever After, Flights of Fantasy, 2019 Christmas Spirit Short Stories, and 2019 Halloween Short Stories. She's proudly bisexual, Wiccan, and a liberal feminist, incorporating these identities into her stories. She grew up in and lives in northern California with her family and two rescued pets. To find out more about her stories, please visit kristenwalker.net.

THE BROTHERS THREE
AARON OZMENT

Three fair brothers crept at night
Hiding from the pale dim light
They were not to make a sound
They had sworn to not be found

Up the walls and down again
Past the city's watching men
Down the road across the way
In a race against the day

Underneath the crescent moon
They would reach the forest soon
Though they all were at their best
This would be the night's first test

When the trees had closed around
And a path could not be found
Said the eldest to the two,
"I can handle this for you."

After this he drew his ax

All the trees like candle wax
Melted fast beneath his blade
And so thus a path was made

So they pushed on in their rush
Ripped and torn by underbrush
They had hoped to make this quick
But the forest was too thick

Soon the clearing was no more
They were trapped just as before
Said the middle of the two,
"Let me show you what to do."

Carefully he climbed a tree,
"Let me tell you what I see:
Just a dozen yards from here
I have found a path that's clear."

So they pressed on twice as fast
Thinking this path was to last
But it simply wasn't so
Soon there was no way to go

As his elders stood distraught
Thinking all had been for naught
Said the youngest brother, "Please
Let me listen to the trees."

Silence, silence, nothing, then
Steadily it rose again
Feelings from the world around
And their path as good as found

"Here's the way, so said the trees.

Come with me, my brothers, please.
I can feel the way to go
But don't ask me how I know."

So they trusted what he said
And they followed where he led
Soon the forest was no more
And they reached the river's shore

Mighty fast and broad it swept
As the three along it crept
Searching for a way to cross
Coming to a total loss

When they'd sat and sulked their fill
Jumped the eldest up, "I will
swim and reach the other side
Then some help I will provide."

Jumping off the sandy bank
All at once his body sank
Pulled beneath the river's flow
Sinking deeper down below

Then the middle brother said,
"I won't see my brother dead!"
He pulled off his lovely cloak
In a single simple stroke

"Take this corner in your hand,
Find a steady place to stand
Count to ten and reel us in.
Ready brother? Let's begin!"

Just at the appointed time

He began to pull and climb
Up the bank with all his might
Praying it may end all right

Sure enough his brothers rose
Gasping air, in near death throes
Off the youngest brother went
Since the other two were spent

Down he kneeled beside the stream
Eyes half closed as in a dream
Searching for that silence still
Calling in the deadly rill

Silence, silence, nothing, then
Steadily it rose again
Feelings from the world around
And their path as good as found

"Here's the way," the river said,
"I can show you where to tread.
I can feel the way to go.
But don't ask me how I know."

Unperturbed, they did their best
Pushing on with little rest
Soon they reached the other side
Of the river deadly wide

Now before them was at last
Doors whom ancient kings had cast
Full in bronze and burnished clean
Shining with a light unseen

First the eldest felt the draw

Summoned by the light he saw
His own face in bronze and gold
Something splendid to behold

Tightening his princely wrist
Iron strong he balled his fist
First he gave a mighty yell
Then he rang them like a bell

Here is what the eldest saw
Shining from the glowing maw
Three great armies in alarms
Springing forth from out his arms

Three gold dragons bound and chained
To his carriage tightly reined
Shrieking to release his grip
Cowering beneath his whip

But he could not leave a mark
And so, crumpled. In the dark
Pushed beyond what he could bear
Once again he gasped for air

While the second brother said
Nothing, but just scratched his head
Staring till his eyes were shot
And his brow was red and hot

Seeking what it would reflect
Hardly daring to expect
What his piercing eyes would find
In the mirror of his mind

Planets three and stars the same

Each to chart and each to name
Astrolabes, glossaries
Lore of herbs and lore of trees

But the rivets came apart
And the tools and the art
Soon were rendered leaf from leaf
Silver buried underneath

So he fell onto his knees
Breath constricted to a wheeze
If the visions did not cease
He could barely hope for peace

So they sat and not a word
Passed between them, how absurd
They had not thought yet to ask
Why the youngest kept his mask

True the doors were glowing bright
But the youngest, cloaked in night
Stood as if he did expect
What the brazen doors reflect

In the east as if by cue
Suddenly a navy hue
Called the brothers to their cause
Giving one a moment's pause

First the oldest looked behind
But the youngest didn't mind
Then the second brother too
Looked at him as if he knew

"It's your turn!" they said as one

"You must go before the sun!
Just what are these skills of yours?
Try your all upon these doors."
Then the youngest brother said
Nothing, but with downturned head
Reached out to one brazen door
It fell back unto the floor

Speechless stood the elder two
They did not know now what to do
They did not know how to know
What the brazen doors would show
What was left but now to try
entering and then descry
what was there inside the cave
Now the brothers must be brave

In the dark the elders peered
Searching for just what he feared
Past the gap now in the wall
They could see nothing at all

"Brothers, I must ask of you
one more time: Do what I do
Harken to the silent fear.
Let us go away from here."

"No, we'll stay until we see
What's behind this mystery
Why build doors with naught behind
Ripping deep into one's mind?"

So the brothers, now transfixed,
Put their youngest now betwixt
Their strong arms and crushing grips

Tried to silence his two lips

Silence, silence, nothing, then
All at once it rose again
Bronze light growing ever stronger
Mirrored shadows ever longer

With his face bare to the light,
Youngest brother, now afright,
Calls with fear, "Avert your eyes!"
But they stare with blank surprise
One face, two eyes, three men gape

Three have turned to one
Looking for a moment at
The light from eastern sun

Staring down at six wet feet
Counting each his hand
Three and one in bronze light meet
Where the brothers stand

"How I warned you," says the one
In the other's voices
Now he knows the sense of it
And their futile choices

Vanishing within the cave
Goes the hole beneath
And the bronze cleaves to the air
Cenotaphic sheath

Navy sky and black night
Covered by the doors
Shining with the heaving mass

Of three and one on fours

"Look away," a lone mouth calls
No foot steps to leave
Silent faces in the bronze
Three are left to grieve

So it was and so I'm told
So then it shall be
One and three make one again
As three and one make three
And nights that live behind the doors
That guard themselves alone
Will claim as theirs what you said yours
In the bright unknown

Sometimes doors are what we seek
And glitter over gold
Forests dark without a path
And stories seldom told

Sometimes we are who we are
Sometimes we are others
Sometimes we're the youngest
Sometimes we're the brothers

Sometimes dreams will die in us
Sometimes they live on
Some dreams live beyond their hosts
Most are dead by dawn

But still we dream and still we seek
And still we pass away
And still we bar the doors of night
Against the coming day

And if we keep within us
Nothing more than simple dark
We'll stare at walls built thick of dreams
And quaver from the spark
Of what we built and what's within
And whether they are one
And what collapse of all we've built
Is hastened with the sun

So the sun rises
So the sun sets
So with it vanishing light
In the same city
At the same time
The brothers are off in the night

Aaron Ozment was born in Royal Oak, Michigan and currently resides in Kagoshima, Japan, where he studies classical Japanese music and poetry. His previous works have been published in the *Asahi Shinbun* Newspaper, and in *The Journal of The International University of Kagoshima.*

He developed a love of Japanese poetry at an early age and majored in Japanese Literature as an undergrad. Having researched a great deal of western poetry during his time in graduate school, he was inspired to experiment in classically inspired poems within the western tradition.

SLIVERS

KRISTINE KATHRYN RUSCH

I saw her for the first time on the last day of church camp. We were in the great room. Through the arch and down the stairs, the sparkling windows of the extra large dining room had a spectacular noontime view of Green Lake. The lake had been our center, the bane of our existence, our refuge, for the past three weeks.

We'd cooled off in her, frozen in her, rowed across her, and hidden in her. We dipped our feet in her from the dock and got sunburned on her shores.

The lake was the reason we were there—not the pretty gold church buried halfway in the woods.

And now it was over. I'd said goodbye to the lake twice already; once at Polar Bear swim at dawn, and again, with Ben. We sat under the weeping willow just up the hill, hidden in the branches, the lake just barely visible. The scents of loam and green rose, and competed with the slightly stagnant smell of this side of the lake.

We didn't cry—Ben and I prided ourselves on being the only ones in camp who never cried—but we leaned on each other and stared at the water, knowing something important had come to an end.

He wasn't in the great room. His parents had arrived an hour early. They didn't want to stay for the final hour of festivities. They had some appointment, and they wouldn't listen to him when he told them the entire experience was supposed to culminated in that final hour.

They whisked him away in a gray Oldsmobile. He leaned out the open window in the back, his blond curls blowing in the wind, and his lips moved in the shape of my name. He might have yelled *I'm sorry* or maybe it was *I will miss you* or maybe it was *I love you.*

I'll never know, because we never saw each other again. A year of letters (oh, such an innocent time before the internet) and then nothing. I can't even remember who stopped writing—him or me. The letters are long lost, the sentiments forgotten, but I'll never forget his face framed in that back window, his sunburned cheeks making his blue eyes sharp, his hands clutching the door as if he was being held against his will.

Weren't we all then? Aren't all children?

Not that we thought of ourselves as children. We were in between—fourteen, both of us. Old enough to be dangerous. Young enough not to understand what we were playing with.

His face, so clear. And then that moment, not an hour later, as I was hugging all the friends I'd made at camp, people I thought would be essential to my future, lifelong companions, kids I loved (although not in *that* way)—and yet, there it was, a feeling so profound I can still capture it: the sense that I would never see any of them again, that they weren't really important, that this moment in time, which had felt so momentous, really wasn't.

But that glimpse I had in the mirror—that had been momentous. And life-changing, and not important at all.

Mirrors have since become a source of fascination and fear for me. They're all different, even if they seem identical. Pick up mirrors in a furniture store, a row of mirrors with the same frame, and you'll realize each one has a slightly different reflection of the world around it.

People will tell you that's because the mirrors are sitting in slightly different places on the floor or the shelf or the wall. And while that might be true, it might also be true that they are as individual as snowflakes, and that what each mirror's reflective surface sees or draws upon is something unique, something no other mirror can replicate.

That first mirror, the one in the great hall, had seemed unimportant to me three weeks before. The great hall, just off the entry in Spruce Lodge, smelled not so faintly of mildew. Its green carpet was stained white along the edges from water that kids had tracked in all summer long. The mismatched furniture was mostly green and gold plaid, no longer on-trend colors, probably replaced with light gray with faint pink or blue pinstripes in living rooms all over the Green River basin.

All forty kids in our age group would spend two long summer nights in that room, listening to lectures on venereal disease and types of birth control from realistic counsellors who knew that the woods were filled with opportunities. In those days, Christians—at least of that particularly liberal ilk —understood that unwanted pregnancies reflected badly on the camp, the church, and the teachings. Later, those things would not be tolerated, and useful life knowledge—the kind that protected a kid's future—became not only taboo, but an instrument of the devil.

We also watched movies in that room, projected on a screen that unrolled and had to stand on its own little tripod. More than once, the screen would come unhooked on the bottom and roll upwards, usually at the most terrifying moment of some old Bela Lugosi film.

All those nights in that room, and never once had I noticed the mirror. It ran the length of the room, from arch to arch, and it was at an angle with the ceiling. The kind of mirror that had a different purpose than most. It wasn't there to reveal anything about us or let us primp in front of it. It wasn't there to make the room bigger or to act as one-way glass so that someone could watch us from the next room.

Instead, its angle allowed someone who knew it was there to see the entire room at a glance from inside the dining room. The counsellors could serve dinner or conduct their evening shows while making sure no one was sneaking out of the building.

For some reason, on that late morning, just before noon, when all the rest of our parents would arrive, and we would have to come to terms with "real" life once again, I looked up from a hug to see the room at the oddest angle. I saw dozens of people I knew, many kids I had come to know well, all of us slightly rumpled and bleary-eyed, many in tears, and everyone professing that they didn't want to leave, not now, not ever, and smack in the middle of it all, a girl-woman I didn't recognize.

She had an angular face with a sharp chin and even sharper eyes. She looked older than almost everyone in the room, but she wasn't one of the counsellors. Nor was she one of the attendees. I would have known. I knew everyone at that camp.

Finally, I recognized her by her hair. It had been chopped haphazardly, longer in the front than in the back because no one at camp knew how to cut hair. The hair was brown with blond highlights, not added by a stylist, but designed by the sun. The girl underneath that mess had nut-brown skin that had also come from sunlight. Push up her sleeves and it would become clear that her normal skin tone was a pale white.

I knew that, because it was my skin tone. That fox-faced

girl, looking older and just a little lost, was me. The distinctive hair chop had come from a rather scary evening in the woods when my ponytail got caught on a bramble of some kind. The more I struggled, the worse the tangle got.

Six of us tried to free me and only succeeded in tying me in deeper. Flashlights were trained on my hair, solutions were offered and rejected, because they all involved waking a counselor and confessing to spending half the night around an illegal campfire.

We hadn't been drinking beer and fornicating—it was a church camp, after all. But there had been long meaningful conversations of a type only teenagers just discovering the world could manage. Marshmallows stolen from the kitchen, sodas taken from a refrigerator in one of the closed lodges (which Davis knew how to break into), were evidence of what we thought of as our rebellion.

Seems small now, but then, we were afraid of our own shadows—and even more afraid of the larger shadows cast by the counselors.

So when someone suggested using a knife to cut me free, I didn't argue. I leaned my head as far forward as I could, the pull on my scalp almost unbearable, the stickers from the bramble jabbing me in the back of the neck and the spine.

Someone—Ben?—covered my scalp with his hand, what remained of my ponytail threaded through his fingers. The pull got worse as someone began to slice—*Upwards and away,* Margot had said, *so that if you yank, you don't cut her head off*— and then, suddenly, blessedly, I was free.

Most of my hair remained in that bramble, evidence of our perfidy—as if the terrible haircut wasn't more of the same—but with me no longer attached, Sadie was able to pull most of my hair free.

She offered to give it to me, but I didn't want it. I didn't need it. Instead, I had to fix the chop into an approximation of a wedge cut which wouldn't become an actual fashion statement for another twenty or so years.

The next morning, no counselor commented on it. Maybe girls cut their hair in frustration every summer or maybe no counselor noticed. But the other kids did. A few offered to help me make it even, and they tried. But nothing could hide the big hole near the back of my neck, the way that my hair looked like someone had taken a huge bite out of it.

I was afraid of what my appearance-conscious mother would say about it. I couldn't see the damage—it was in the back after all—and given the wavy condition of the mirrors in the girls lavatory, I didn't even try.

Later, I pieced it all together. I hadn't looked in a mirror, really looked, in three weeks, so of course I didn't recognize myself. I hadn't seen the transformation from pale washed-out girl with long mouse-brown hair to a brown-skinned girl-woman with blond highlights and muscles on her upper arms. I had changed, and I hadn't realized it.

Such an adult observation. Rationalization, really. Because it hadn't been like that.

It *wasn't* like that.

That moment wasn't rational at all.

I was looking at another world from a different angle, and instead of me standing there, *she* was there, the fox-faced girl with the knowing eyes.

And I would see her a few times throughout my long and somewhat strange life.

As frightened as I'd been of it, I have no memory of my mother's reaction to my mutilated hair. Or of the car ride home or of the year afterwards.

Sometimes I had nightmares about Green Lake. My hair wasn't caught on a bramble. There weren't other kids and flashlights, just a boy's face and a hand holding my ponytail, forcing my head back, and a mouth, wet on mine, braces cutting the skin near my lip.

I would get free by kicking him and ripping out my ponytail by the roots, blood on my face from the slice along my lip, and a mad scramble through the woods that left me bleeding and cut from a dozen branches.

And Ben would show up at the end, holding a flashlight because he heard me scream. He would talk to me, only I couldn't hear him or the girl he was with. At the end, on the last day, he would smile at me, and thank heavens his teeth did not have braces.

The dream didn't feel like my memories, but it felt real enough to shake me up and make me wonder.

Later, in my real life, I spoke to a colleague, a psychologist, about distant odd memories and not recognizing your own face in a mirror.

Did you have a head injury about that time? he asked.

No, I said.

A traumatic experience that might cause dissociation? he asked.

No, I said, even though I wasn't sure what he meant.

Some kind of out-of-body experience? he asked.

I laughed. *Of course not,* I said.

Hmmm, he said. *Might be worth seeing someone about,* which of course I did not do.

It had only been a moment, that day at camp, and none of the other times I saw her was like that—where she was nearly me only with knowing eyes and a fox-face.

The other times, she was someone else entirely, with more control and something of a better life.

The second time I saw her in a bathroom mirror in the old vaudeville theater downtown. The upstairs ladies' bathroom had a lounge that dated from the 1920s, where women could sit on upholstered stools and fix their hair.

The stools remained, along with some gold carpet that had clearly been added forty years later, as had some make-up bulbs that framed the mirrors, ruining the lighting.

I had gone to the theater with a new boyfriend, and he had insisted on the balcony, where I had never sat before. I was naïve enough to think he wanted to see the movie, and stunned when he wanted to sit in back, where it was impossible to see the screen.

The back of that balcony smelled of spilled Coke, Old Spice, and cum, even though I didn't really recognize that smell until much later. Maybe if I had, I wouldn't have sat down, but I did, and he lunged for me, and I slapped him, and that was how I ended up in the bathroom, trying to figure out how to get home without telling my mother what had gone wrong.

She didn't like any of my boyfriends, which, in hindsight, probably showed good judgement on her part, but the other problem was that she really didn't like me either, so it was hard for me to separate her advice from her unnecessary criticism.

I wasn't crying when I went into that bathroom. I was mad. My right hand still stung from the slap, and my wrist hurt from the force of it all.

A woman sat on the divan in the middle of the room, puffing on a cigarette, its smoke curling around her head. She wore green stretch pants and a gold top that clashed with the gold carpet. Her hair was in tight ringlets that she clearly hadn't changed since she was in high school.

She didn't ask me if I was all right. She watched me walk in, got a vicious half-smile on her face, and stood. She stubbed the cigarette out in the cut-glass ashtray she had carried from the counter encircling the lounge. Then she set the ashtray on the divan, and left, leaving the horrid stench of her menthol cigarettes behind.

I watched her go, wishing I'd thought to ask her where the pay phone was. I had expected it to be near the bathroom and it hadn't been. She looked like she worked there, but I might've been wrong about that, too.

I saw a movement to my left, and turned that way.

The girl who looked back at me from one of the mirrors had the sharp angled chin and startling green eyes of the girl I'd seen at camp a few years before. She raised her eyebrows at me and then lifted a champagne glass. It was full of gold liquid that bubbled.

She wore a red gown that was cut low over her breasts—something I would never wear—and her waist, already small, was cinched tight. A gold necklace glittered around her neck. She wore only a smattering of make-up, but it matched the dress and glittered in the light—a style that wouldn't be acceptable for another ten years or so.

I squinted at her, but couldn't tell if she was older than me or if the dress and the make-up made her look older.

She appeared to be alone in her bathroom, and she was alone in the mirror. The other mirrors around the room only showed my wrinkled shirt, the front half-open where that horrid boy's quick fingers had yanked. The buttons were probably still on the balcony floor, but I wasn't going to search for them.

And, I realized, their loss would mean some kind of conversation with my mother, no matter what. The shirt was new enough that she would notice.

The fox-faced woman's bathroom lounge didn't look seedy. It had a gold-and-black art deco rug, with gold art deco frames around the mirrors. There were chairs instead of stools, and the chairs had the same art deco pattern on their backs as the rug and—I finally noticed—the wallpaper.

She silently toasted me again, sipped the champagne, and then beckoned. I walked toward that mirror, only it really wasn't a mirror, because I didn't see myself in it. Only her, and that strange ladies' lounge.

The glass in front of me was old, the silvering peeling, leaving a bit of black around the edges. I extended my hand to touch that edge when the door banged open and that hideous boy entered.

"There you are," he snarled.

He was tall and thin and his back curved forward ever so slightly. He had a wiry strength that had surprised me, and muscles on his thin arms that were real. I had initially thought the grease under his fingers made him an adult, but nothing did, not really.

His mouth was turned downward, his square face red with anger.

"You're not supposed to be in here," I said.

"Who's gonna stop me?" he asked. "This is a lot more private anyway."

I thought about the woman with the cigarette, and wondered if she would return. There was no one else in the lounge or in the stalls, and there hadn't been many people in the theater in the first place.

He came for me, just like I knew he would, and I had braced myself, not to fight him, but to run.

But he was too quick. He grabbed my shoulders before I could even move, and started to turn me toward him.

I shoved him away as hard as I could. His own move had placed him off-balance, and he hit the counter, gasping in pain. His eyes narrowed, and his anger grew worse.

He was about to push off that counter when a hand came out of the mirror and grabbed him by his slick-backed hair.

The hand had long red fingernails, and a gold chain on the wrist. It yanked his head back. The fox-faced woman looked at me, her eyes familiar and strange at the same time.

She mouthed *Here or there?*

I didn't understand the question, and it must have showed on my face.

She raised her eyebrows and smiled. The smiled was slightly crooked and I realized she had a white scar running along the edge of her mouth.

Here, then, she said, and pulled him through the mirror. As she yanked, he screamed, and the scream cut off as his face went through.

He kicked and grabbed for the edge of the glass, but there seemed to be no edge.

And suddenly, he was in there, with her. She forced him onto the ground by shoving his head downward.

I got this, she said, and then the mirror went dark.

My heart was pounding. The cigarette smoke still lingered. The black area where the mirror had been reflected in all the other mirrors now, but I didn't want to touch it.

He was gone, not in the lounge at all.

I wiped my hands on my jeans, then looked around. My own face—my reflective mirror face, looked at me from every single wall. Behind me or on the side of me or on the other side of me, depending, was a black square where that mirror had been.

I looked at the counter, and saw no broken glass. But there was an oily stain that looked like it came from hair tonic and the faint smell of Old Spice.

I breathed shallowly through my mouth, and moved away from the counter. If this happened—and I wasn't sure it had —I needed to have a story, an excuse as to why he wasn't with me.

The truth was the only thing that worked—up to a point. I had run from him into this bathroom, and then, I hadn't seen him again. As far as I knew, he was still in that sticky balcony, fuming because I wouldn't let him rip off my shirt.

I pushed open the lounge door, and didn't see anyone.

Not other patrons, not the woman. Just a wide open hallway that had, once upon a time, been filled with the eager vaude-ville crowd waiting to go inside and watch—what? Ventrilo-quists? Magicians? Bad comedians who said *Take my mother. Please.*

Please.

I let out a small snort, which was more nervous energy than real energy, and walked down the wobbly grand stair-case. There wasn't anyone in the real lobby, not even someone at concessions, although they'd recently made fresh popcorn. I walked uphill toward the double doors, then stepped into the twilight.

The street looked like it always did—rundown and dirty, with only a handful of very old or very cheap cars parked badly against the curb. If I walked, I could get home by the time the movie ended, and no one would be the wiser.

So that was what I did.

And then I convinced myself that the lie was the truth—that I had run out of the theater clutching my shirt in place, and left him there. Which was more or less true. I had left him there.

All of him.

So much of him that I couldn't ever really remember his name.

I saw him sometimes, in really old bars all across the country. The first time, I'd been in college. My dad showed up unex-pectedly and took me to dinner at a supper club just outside the city. The club had a famous old bar that I was too young to go in, but as we waited for our table, I could see the mirror behind the bar, and in it, a tall, thin boy-man who hunched over his drink.

I knew on some gut level that was him, but I figured that was guilt talking.

So I didn't say a word, but I never went back there, not even when my father showed up unexpectedly the following year to take me to dinner and then tell me that he was moving to Chicago, alone, which was not a surprise.

It meant I never went home, because there was no longer a home to go to, and I didn't miss it. I graduated, started working, and got sent to conferences all over the country.

Inevitably, in the older cities, there would be a fancy dinner at a fancy restaurant and often that restaurant would be in a restored building decorated with antique furniture, and usually that meant an antique mirror.

Most of the mirrors simply showed my aging face. Time had not been kind to me, adding a crepe neck by thirty-five and more than a few grays by forty.

But sometimes, particularly in old hotels, refurbished into boutiques so that someone could charge a small fortune for a historically accurate room, I would see him.

Once he was adjusting a tie in front of the mirror and I moved to the side, so that he didn't see me. His face had become concave, and his eyes haunted. He had a small badly done tattoo of a cross on his hand that I later learned was prison ink.

A few other times, he huddled at the bar, nursing a drink, and the last time, he had his face smooshed into the bar by a bouncer, who had one hand on his face and another yanking his wrist toward his shoulder, a woman sobbing at his side, her blouse ripped halfway and her hair ruined.

But I didn't see the fox-faced woman again for years, not until my second divorce, the one that gave me more money than I deserved. I did the round of charity galas and in one of the old hotels near the Algonquin in New York, there she was, in a mirror that ran the length of a wall on the mezzanine level, her hair piled above her head, her jewelry much more expensive than mine.

She still favored red dresses, but they covered her clevage this time instead of revealing it. Her make-up accented her face, and if she had early wrinkles, they didn't show.

She seemed to be the focus of a group of people who were all so thin that their designer gowns looked proper and their jewelry hung just right. She quick-glanced into the mirror, the way people did when they were making sure their clothing was just so, and did a double take when she saw me.

She excused herself, and threaded her way through the conversation groupings until she stood on the opposite side of the mirror from me.

I looked around, saw no one close, and saw none of the people at my gathering reflected in hers. Up close, it became clear that her sharp chin had softened, the fox look of her features had become something lost to time.

She grabbed a glass of champagne from a passing waiter, and raised it at me. Her fingernails were still long and red. Mine were short and stubby, because I didn't have the patience to grow mine out and I didn't like wearing fake nails.

You all right? she asked.

I nodded.

No more troubles? she asked.

A million of them. The wrong men, always. It made me wonder if Ben had been wrong too, all those years ago. The way I held him up as an ideal, one I couldn't achieve.

I'd tried to find him, years later, and couldn't. There was no record of him anywhere and what had been in my splotchy memory hadn't been enough to find him.

He didn't appear in the camp photos someone had posted of our year online either—those curls, that handsome face, those startling Paul Newman eyes.

I thought I'd conjured him, like I'd conjured her, like I conjured these mirrors.

She was watching me as if she could read my mind.

"What are you doing?"

I jumped and turned at the same time. The hostess, who wore the same red dress as the woman in the mirror, stood behind me. Only the hostess was much older—eighty, maybe —and exceptionally famous.

"Just checking the mirror," I said.

"Sad, isn't it?" she said. "Something that old and that lovely. You'd think mirrors would reflect but the silvering is gone and no one wants to risk a repair for fear of ruining the value."

I turned toward the mirror again, saw the splotches of silver against a black background. Nothing more, nothing less.

"Yes," I said. "Sad."

She put her hand on my shoulder, her bony fingers digging into my skin.

"For women our age," she said portentiously, "mirrors are no longer our friend."

I was not her age, and was about to correct her, when another woman on the periphery of the conversation laughed and said, "Don't be silly, darling. Mirrors are never our friend."

I looked at that one, saw in my mind's eye the mirror in the ladies lounge of a now-destroyed theater, saw the long mirror in a closed-up lodge, and thought that wasn't true.

Sometimes, mirrors revealed a friend, one who maybe wasn't there.

Do I have an explanation? Of course not. I have theories.

The real-world theory: The nightmares *are* memories. Mine. And Ben did not exist, just someone I made up to wipe out the memories of another boy, one who wore braces and lured me into the woods at night, and was the first in a life-time of bad choices.

The other boy, the half-forgotten boy in the theater, got slapped and left behind and I never spoke of him again.

The fantastic theory: Old mirrors, certain mirrors, reveal other worlds and other lives. The fox-faced girl and I were the same person, different worlds/universes/existences. She pulled her ponytail free, because she was (then and later) very strong.

I got caught in brambles while walking in the woods with friends. My test would come later in that theater, and she—very strong—would save me.

So the boy/man I saw in the bar mirrors all over the country was drinking his life away after a stint in prison, maybe because she had accused him of something.

She became someone, while I didn't. Her strength maybe. Her willingness to take action. Or maybe I've guessed wrong, based on expensive jewelry and a few images across time.

The truth: I don't know. I know what I want to believe (the fantastic theory) and I know what my life hints at (the real-world theory) and I know the mystery shall remain unsolved.

Because I don't look in mirrors anymore.

Not because they aren't my friend, but because I don't believe they show any truths. I don't believe in mirrors the way I don't believe in the God they taught us about at that church camp.

The problem is that I don't believe that I am special enough to warrant a fantasy version of my life, and I don't believe that my experience in Green Lake was anything but benign.

I have thought of returning to the lake, and seeing the remains of Spruce Lodge and the places where I had once been happy. Or thought I had been happy.

But I don't want to trigger anything.

And besides, what are memories if not a reflection of the past? They're not truth, any more than an image in the mirror is truth.

They are but one sliver of a life, a life that no one else can understand, a life that we ourselves can't understand, in a world that will continue on without us—that does continue on without us—whether we want it to or not.

Internationally bestselling author **Kristine Kathryn Rusch** writes in almost every genre. Her work has appeared under a variety of names, including Kris Nelscott for mystery and Kristine Grayson for romance. She has won awards in all of her genres, including a large number of reader's choice awards. Her work also appears in 20 best-of-the-year volumes. Find out more about her work at kriswrites.com.

THE SEMICENTENNIAL WOMAN

ANAÏD HAEN

There's a magpie against the trunk of the tree across the street, sharply dressed in its black-and-white plumage, pecking into the moss. It's autumn, I can make out the bird very well, but am annoyed I can't see what it's digging up out of the moss. Insects? Larvae?

"I need a telephoto lens." I point my fork at the tree in the distance. "That magpie is eating something, and I don't know what."

"A telephoto lens?" Portio, my Love, takes another helping of potatoes. "There are some binoculars in the top drawer of the dresser."

"An internal one." I point at my eye. "They exist, you know." Attentively, I pour some gravy onto his taters. If there's anything I know about love, the way to the heart is through the stomach.

"Of course they exist, Martina." Love stabs his fork haphazardly into his food. "But do you mean implants? Honey ... then they have to cut into you."

Ignoring the tone and content of his objection, I put the brochure onto the big screen. "For a few digicoins more they can even install a camera. Film and photos." When *the* frown appears, I quickly keep talking: "Henrietta has one too, in her left eye. Five thousand by seven and a half thousand pixels, dear. Twelve hundred dpi, do you know how sharp that is? And a thirty-four times zoom!" I show some pictures made by our neighbor.

"Cutting, honeybun. They have to cut into you. In a healthy eye, for crying out loud!" The fork disappears heavy-handedly into the potato with gravy. "And how does that work with those images? Where are they stored? In your brain perhaps?"

"Of course not. How could that work?"

The potato is mashed. While it absorbs the gravy, the fork is hanging above it, just as still and straight as the look he gives me from those sea-green eyes. "So?"

"I'll get a wifi-connector. Behind my ear."

It's my body, on that we agree. And I've worked for it myself, we agree on that as well. But that's about where the consensus stops. The more I want to talk about it, the more I'm interrupted and stopped until an ignoring silence ensues, colder than a night on Io. On the one hand I hate that stiff back sliding away from me in bed when I want to snuggle up against it, on the other hand it does give me the chance to put my thoughts straight and reach a decision.

"Are you going to come along with me?" I softly ask the seventh night. "I want it very much."

"What is it you want much?" the back asks. "That damn implant or me accompanying you?"

I risk our little joke: "Yes."

His sigh is deeper than the Mariana Trench. "Okay, then."

The thing about *one* eye implant, as I gradually discover: depth perception is a problem. "When I zoom in very much, I have to close my right eye, you see?" I show it. "Otherwise I can't judge the distance."

Portio grumbles something from behind his newspaper. It's from 2017, part of the inheritance of my in-laws. I hate the stale smell and the cold shiver-inducing dry crackling of the old paper. *Trump Wants to Go to the Moon* the headline on the front page reads. I believe a lot of people would have liked to have seen him go there.

I zoom in on the little letters under the headline, but the fingers of my big dear cover part of the article and I can't read it. I quickly take a few pictures and project them onto the screen. "Look."

Perturbed, Love looks at the screen.

"You see? Out of focus."

"Then you should be more patient, sweetheart. Carefully zoom in first, and don't snap until you're in focus."

I shake my head. "That's not it. I just need my other eye..."

"No way!"

It's my body, on that we agree. And I've worked for it myself, we agree on that as well. And this time it doesn't take that long until I get my way. Not that I'm waiting for permission of course. But it's rather pleasant if we agree.

It's beautiful, beautiful, beautiful. Yes, I do trip over things when I'm walking around in zoom-in mode, but boy, am I making lovely pictures and movies. So, that magpie eats beetles. I can see the little paws wriggling in its beak. The only thing is: when you have very sharp sight and can zoom in thirty-four times, it's really annoying you can't hear what's going on in the distance. At least, that's how I feel. Not to mention that I don't have any sound with my movies. As I get more used to my implants, "annoying" turns into "irritating."

"There are sound amplifiers, did you know that?" We're sitting next to each other on the couch looking at a series I picked out to soften him up for what I want to ask.

"Sound amplifiers?" He gives me a "You're crazy" look. "So I can whisper all day because your hearing is too sensitive?"

"Teething problems. They've been fixed." I pull up my legs and, sliding them underneath me, I pull my auricles out from between my hair. I want to tell him how small those modern implants are. And how reliable. And ask which ear would be best: my left or my right.

"They're cute." Quasi-startled he puts his hand over his mouth. "Do you mean you're going to have some elephant's ears put on?"

It's no fun getting mocked. Especially not now, especially not about my ears and most certainly not about improving my senses. From which we would both profit, by the way.

I flop down on my bum again, cross my arms and give him the silent treatment for the rest of the night.

That helps.

Of course I have both ears done at the same time. The stories Henrietta told me, that you can't judge the direction if you only have one ear improved, make that a necessity.

"Beautiful auditory canals, Mrs. Andrew." With a big smile doctor Malaki gives me a playful tap on the tip of my nose. "You'll soon see how good you're gonna hear."

"Hear, you mean?" Portio looks at me with his lips pursed, like Donald Duck.

Just like the doctor, I ignore his remark. I'm glad I didn't have to go to the clinic on my own. And of course I know he'll be himself again in a little while: sweet and caring. "Can I make sound recordings as well?"

"Not with the standard unit. You can if we implant the enhanced one. Then it's best to install new cochleas as well." The doctor is staring at the 3D-holo of my skull. "Because of your balance."

I'm glad the doc starts about my balance, because now Love doesn't have any time to think about the standard or the enhanced unit.

"Balance?" Portio shows his frown again. "But surely there's nothing wrong with her sense of balance?"

"No, not really." A projection of me appears on the wall. "But as you can imagine, with all that extra weight in her head ..." The projection bends forward. When it reaches some ninety degrees "I" lose control and bang the forehead against the floor. Love and I are both startled by the sound.

"You'd better throw in those cochleae then." Never before have I seen Love's face that white.

It's a shame the wifi-connector has to be moved to the bridge of my nose, but according to Malaki I won't regret that. "The reception is much better there."

The love of my life is less than impressed. "Did they have to place that antenna right under your skin on your forehead? Behind your ear it was almost invisible."

I try not to be annoyed by his nagging; my own pain is enough to deal with. I never knew the bridge of the nose had so many nerve ends. In hindsight I should have had to inquire how painful an operation like that is, then maybe I wouldn't have gone through with it. It's giving me a headache. The sounds are as well, coming in sharp and raw. There's something wrong with the attenuation, but I don't dare to say it out of fear we would then go straight back to the clinic to have all of it removed. It is my body after all.

"And you did work for it..." Spread out on the table are cogs and sprockets and all kinds of brass thingamajigs. Used to be a clock, will be one again it seems. He puts down the magnifying glass with a very deep sigh. "Your spine has to be replaced? Why?"

I try not to emulate his sighing, but fail.

"Cut that out. You're way too good at that. You imitate people, you mirror and manipulate them. And all that with a faint smile, so they don't catch on what you're doing."

"But you do know, don't you?" I sit down on his lap and try not to move anything on the table. "You know I do it and that I'm good at it, so you're immune to it."

"Honey, you're heavy. You've become heavy."

I kiss those exquisite lips, jump off his lap and bat my seductively long eyelashes, especially fabricated when it turned out the light entering my lenses was too bright. "Are you coming?"

"Where to?" He isn't giving in easily today.

"To bed. Together." I turn around and start by taking my sweater off. When Love remains seated, I play my trump card: "I'll switch on vibrate mode."

There's nothing nicer than dozing in each other's arms after making love. I zoom in on the little smile lines next to Portio's eyes and study the layout of the pores next to his nose. It's like a bee home ... what's it called? A honeycomb.

"Sweetie?"

"Yes?"

"Do you love me?"

The arms pull me in tighter against the delightful body. "Of course, honey. Very much." A kiss lands somewhere behind my ear, on the scar. It hurts, but I don't even flinch.

"About my spine, you know?"

It's as if I'd poured liquid nitrogen on us. The arms freeze up, breathing stops, eyes snap open. "Stop it."

"What?" I'm getting hot under the collar. Disagreeing with me is one thing; ordering me around is something else.

"Stop disfiguring yourself. You've reached the limit already."

"Your limit, maybe. Not mine." Furiously, I jump out of bed. "You were already against the very first procedure."

Love sits up straight. "That's not true, honey."

"Don't call me honey! And it *is* true." I extend my left arm to grab my clothes from the chair. "You didn't want me to take lenses. Didn't want me to improve my hearing. Didn't want me ..." I push my right foot through my trouser leg, but forget to pull in my nails, which are very handy for climbing trees. Aghast, I stare at the enormous rips in the fabric.

"Didn't want you to what?"

"Never mind!" I yank my trousers off my leg. "But that you never have to cut the hedge anymore... I never hear you talk about that." I make cutting movements with the index and middle finger of my right hand. The metal blades of the scissors slide over each other. Razor-sharp tools, very useful.

His jaw drops. "Do you mean that your modifications are for *my* benefit?"

"Of course!" I cut off the shreds of the trousers and decide to keep the other trouser leg long. Colored stocking under it, and it'll be fine. "I have three jobs! You're benefitting off my robotization without even having to invest a cent."

"Not a cent? And what about my time? And my caring?" He jumps out of bed as well. "You've been at it for twenty years! Every time I have to go along to the clinic, watch how painful it is for you, help you rehabilitate and take over your jobs and chores as long as you're recuperating. Those things don't count?" He stands with his clenched fists against his sides, his elbows wide.

Speechless, I look up from my cut-off trouser leg. His time? His cares? About me? For a moment, I feel something behind my sternum softening. He's such a dear. But the anger about his selfishness flares up again when I see the frown bringing his eyes so close together, darkening his glare. With a jolt I straighten up to say that he doesn't have to invest anything in me anymore. No time, no cares, nothing.

CRACK.

My legs feel as if they are cut out from under me.

"Martina?" Portio jumps forward and grabs me. Like a wet rag I'm hanging from my armpits. I mumble about pain-in-my-back or something.

When I come to, he's sitting next to me. Red eyes, chaffed nostrils.

"Hey," I say. "What's up with you?"

"With me? With you, you mean." My hands are grabbed and kissed. "I thought I'd lost you."

"Lost me? No, that's not possible. I mean, you've got that tracker I gave you." I have a dreadful headache. Not at the front of my head, but in the back, in my neck. When I try to move my hand toward it, I notice I'm strapped in. "Where am I? What's happened?"

"You're in the clinic. I brought you here when you ... snapped."

"Snapped? Me? What?"

"You'd better stay comfortably in bed, Mrs. Andrew." Doctor Malaki comes into the room. "You're very lucky." In a few sentences he explains what's happened to me. My vertebrae couldn't cope with the weight of my arms and head ("Especially your head, those electronic connections are heavy.") anymore and gave way to the pressure.

Although I know that the adaptations that are coming, especially the jumping mechanisms in my legs and the grabbing tail, will necessitate a new spine, I'm very surprised that this could have happened. "But all the implants I have are lightweight, aren't they?"

The doctor smiles. "That's true. But you did choose to have your arm extensions done in Turkey, right?"

Portio sits up straight with a contorted face. Our fights about foreign operations are fresh in our minds.

Guilt-ridden, I nod. "It was cheaper there and ..."

The doctor raises his hand. "I understand. And what they've done is excellent work."

"Really?" My Love slumps back, relieved, like a deflating balloon.

"Sure! First-rate materials, can't be faulted." Malaki raises his finger admonishingly. "Only, they should have taken all previous procedures into account. All in all, the weight of your implants was just too great for a natural spine."

I try to process it and then ask in a faint voice: "And now?"

Doctor Malaki cheerfully pats my bedspread. "Fortunately, your partner stabilized and transported you in the right way. No connections, nerves you would say, neither organic nor artificial, are damaged. We can just proceed as planned."

"Proceed?" Portio jumps up. "Are you mad? Martina..."

"Dear, listen," I softly say. I could use my megaphone to shout him down, but I don't.

"No, I'm not listening! I want you to have all that crap taken out of your body. All of it! I want you to be my sweet, soft, beautiful girl again. I want ..." Tears flow down his face. Shaky, Portio, my partner, the love of my life, flops down into his chair. "I want to have Martina Andrew, my wife, back." The beautiful face disappears behind the delightful hands, shoulders juddering.

Doctor Malaki rolls his eyes. "I'm sorry, stopping is impossible and reversal is out of the question." He spreads his hands. "Your original body parts and organs were replaced during the operations. They haven't been saved, that's impossible. You don't have real eyes, auditory canals, vestibular systems, vocal cords, arms, hands..."

"Enough!" Love's voice breaks.

The doctor doesn't stop talking. "And if we don't do anything, you will remain immobile." He turns to my husband. "So we have to replace the spine anyway. There's no other option."

We're sitting across from each other and I give it a try to explain why I don't want to stop, that the last bit of replacement, my brain with an artificial brain, is *important*, but I'm not successful. For some reason I just can't get it into his head that changing my body feels good. That I'm glad with every bit of skin that disappears and is replaced with shiny metal, so beautiful I don't want to wear clothes anymore. That I love having access to the internet and other data right away. That I put up with my heart not beating anymore, and with updating and charging taking several hours a day, because I've become stronger, faster and smarter. Yes, I understand that our meals have become somewhat less sociable, and I honestly feel for him, but isn't it crystal clear that I'm much happier now? That I've finally become myself?

"Yourself?" Portio laughs in a scornful way. "There's not an ounce of you left anymore. Everything's gone."

"You're exaggerating, honey." My wrist creaks a bit when I pat his hand. "I'm just as much myself as you are yourself." I get up to grab the can of lubricant and lube up my hinges. "Since you were created, you've been replaced countless times as well."

"Sorry?" Love gets up and takes the can out of my hands, and pushes the straw into my neck. "Here?"

I let him inject the grease and turn my head a few times. "Wonderful, thanks." I turn toward him. Since my last operation I'm taller than he is, but I obscure that by keeping my knees a little bit bent when I talk to him. "I mean that every cell of your body you were born with has already been renewed." I shrug. "All things considered, you're not yourself anymore either."

Flabbergasted, he stares at me, squinting a little. "You've been saving this one, haven't you?"

"This what?"

"This argument. About those body cells." He seems very tired. His shoulders slumped. His graying temples and beard tell me he's getting older.

Getting older … that's not happening to me anymore. Another argument I don't pull out, but which has been bothering me for some time now. I'm overcome by a wave of tender feelings, mixed with sorrow because in the end I will lose Portio. Apparently there's still some oxytocin in my body, because I haven't felt this for a long while. "No, I haven't been saving it. It just popped into my head." I reach out and caress his cheek. "Shall we make love?"

His face slowly contorts from tired to disgusted. He steps back and pulls his head to the side, freeing his cheek from my fingers. "Make love?" He pulls up his upper lip.

His reaction amazes me. I can't remember ever being rejected by him.

"When?" His voice is hoarse.

"When what, dear?"

"When is that operation?"

Yes! He's changed his mind, he gets it. To make sure, I ask: "Why do you want to know? Are you coming with me?"

He nods.

I feel joy. From head to toe. "Next Wednesday."

Portio emits a scornful laugh. "Next Wednesday?"

Overjoyed, I look at him. "On my fiftieth birthday."

It's the first operation where I don't feel any pain when I wake up. Nothing hurts anymore, nothing can hurt me anymore. I sit up and look at my hands, at the fingers, the phalanges that can each move individually. The tips of my thumbs easily reach the tips of my fingers. For a while, I play tag with my fingertips, ever faster and faster, both hands at the same time and then my toes as well. I feel joy that everything is working, that this body is doing what it's supposed to do, that it has become exactly what it has to be.

Portio is sitting in the corner of the room, looking at me head to toe. This time I've also had my skull replaced with a cover made of titanium graphene, so my whole body has the same look. Not that appearance matters, but I know that the human eye appreciates esthetics.

"How do I look?" I ask. Force of habit: I always asked.

"Are you in pain?" Portio gets up and comes toward me. He reaches out to my head, a tear glimmering in his eyes. "Your beautiful hair ..." As he blinks, the tear rolls down his cheek.

I smile in understanding mode and softly take his hand. "I don't feel any pain. Shall we go home?"

As Portio ages and I keep functioning better, our relationship changes somewhat. We don't make love anymore, and Portio doesn't want me to come sit with him at the table, or next to him on the couch, watching a series. He doesn't want me with him in bed to sleep, not even if I change my armor for surrogate skin. "I prefer lying alone."

I don't care, I don't have to sleep anyway. I vaguely remember enjoying our nights in that bed. Spooning, our legs entangled. I remember I would have felt rejected, but now I don't feel anything but ... nice, then I can go to work. I work a lot: waste sorter, sewer cleaner, powerline technician, gardener, and other jobs that are dirty, dull, or dangerous. Now that the operations are complete, our expenses have drastically dropped. Shovel-loads of money are coming in, he sometimes jokes.

I laugh about it, but don't understand the joke.

Portio dies at almost a hundred. I do feel something. I can't call it grief; it's more like the memory of grief. I carry his casket to the grave and listen to the reverend speaking about Portio's pain when he lost me, about the cares my Love has had in his life, and how difficult it must have been for him to get used to the new situation. I listen to the man, my head cocked, as I make recordings of the squirrels in the large chestnut trees in the cemetery.

Home is empty. I clear out everything that belonged to Portio. It's no use to him after all and I don't need the furniture either. While emptying the cabinets, I find albums full of printed photos. Photos of me, back when I was still of flesh and blood. Pictures of us together. On vacation, here at home

... The last photo is one of me in bed at the clinic. I still have my hair, but the rest of my body is completely transformed. The picture must have been taken just before the operation where I had my brain replaced. *In a little while, she will really be gone, my dear Martina,* the caption says. The photo has ripples and smudges as if it's been dripped wet very often.

I close the album. Something slides out. An obituary. It's dated on my fiftieth birthday.

Dearest,
I've watched you
Piece by piece
Leaving me
I supported you, because I thought
It was the right thing to do
It was your body after all
And you worked for it very hard

In loving memory of
Martina Andrews
The woman who lived half a century

I stick the obituary back into the album and put it with the stuff that needs to be chucked out. Portio was wrong. I mean I'm already a hundred, and I can last for many more centuries.

Anaïd Haen is a Dutch author, specializing in science fiction and fantasy. Her stories have appeared in virtually all Dutch SF/F/H magazines and various anthologies. She's won three major story awards (the Unleash Award 2010, Trek Sagae

2018, and Waterloper 2021) and has been a Finalist and a six-time Honorable Mention winner at Writers of the Future. Over twenty Dutch novels, story collections and children's books written or co-written by her have been published by various publishers (like "De Vier Windstreken," "Averbode," "EigenZinnig," "Zilverspoor," and "Quasis"). "The Semicentennial Woman" is her first publication in English.

TANGLED UP IN CONTUSIVE BLUE

BRIAN RAPPATTA

I f you'll check under your seats, you'll find a little plastic bag with some tissue and a couple of band-aids in it. You'll need those. Because, well ... this could get a little messy. But not to worry; we're all here for you.

In order to fully understand what you're about to see, we have to go back to the beginning. To the first of its kind.

There are plenty of explanations as to how it works. Pick your poison; I've heard them all, and could tell you any theory you might want to hear. There's a half-dozen pseudo-scientific hypotheses ... and plenty of supernatural ones, too: demon possession, haunting, gypsy curse ... it even appears in way more *Harry Potter* fanfiction than you'd probably care to read. But as far as I'm concerned, how it works isn't nearly as important as *why* it works.

Its particular effects weren't widely known until about fifteen years or so ago, but best estimates think that it was painted maybe five years or so before that. By that time, it had been bouncing around a bunch of regional museums and galleries in their rotating collections, and any record of the artist has been completely lost.

We're pretty sure that its current title didn't come from the artist herself. That dates back to its stint in a Minneapolis gallery. According to their records, when they'd dug it out of their storage and put it up for display, the placard just said *Untitled*, by "Artist Unknown."

Ada McIntyre was the volunteer docent who first began to notice its effect. She didn't think much of it at first; she was retired, and when you get older, sometimes strange bruises just pop up out of nowhere on your body. Something for us all to look forward to.

But eventually Ada started to put two and two together. She'd get home after every one of her volunteer shifts with a new ache for her efforts. At first she attributed it to standing for so long at a time, but then, the severity and random locations of the bruises she found didn't add up. She mentioned it to some of the other docents, and the rest is ... well, art history. Whether or not Ada actually came up with it or not, she's commonly credited with the title by which it's been known ever since: *Contusive Blue.*

Ada and the other docents talked it up to the gallery's visitors—hell, we probably have the gallery staff to thank for half the apocryphal stories about it. But when the patrons started reporting mysterious bruises after visiting the gallery, it didn't take long for it to gain some notoriety around the Minneapolis area. One of the local news stations did a piece on it and ran it on Halloween—which is probably where some of the rumors of it being haunted came from.

After that, it spent a couple of years bouncing around various regional museums as its notoriety grew, until finally it came to rest here in Chicago. Not quite the Art Institute yet—it wouldn't get wall space there for another couple years—but there were plenty of other smaller museums who were eager to cash in on its quirky fame. And that's where I first experienced it.

At that point, I was a college sophomore, and *The Metropolitan* was a tiny little museum on the west side with delusions of grandeur. I wasn't an art history major—Business Marketing, of all things—so I didn't quite fit the portfolio of the usual college kids who came to *The Met* for part-time jobs. But I fudged the truth a little bit on my application and said I was studying Art History. I had a grand total of six credits on my transcript in Art, if anybody bothered to check it out—I took the classes because I thought the professor was kind of hot. But that's another story.

When the bowtie-wearing curator hired me, he gave me a tour of the place, and he pulled a pair of sunglasses out of his pocket when we got to the room where *Contusive Blue* had its own wall. He put them on, and then pulled out another pair and handed them to me. "You're going to want to wear these, my dear," he told me. "Mutes the impact—not entirely, but close enough for government work."

Bless his heart, Bob could pull off the dad phrases and the *my dear* without sounding creepy or condescending at all.

When you see it for the first time, it's easy to be unimpressed. I mean, the various shades of blueberry-blue *could* kind of resemble a particularly ugly bruise, if you use your imagination, even though they're all kind of jumbled up in a rather inharmonious mishmash that's kind of like a blow to the face in itself. I distinctly remember making some kind of comment to that effect to Bob. I was trying to sound witty, you see. Give me a break. I was only a sophomore, remember? But I remember Bob just chuckled and said, "Wait till tonight."

In retrospect, I'm pretty sure he knew I wasn't an art history major. He's passed on, so I can't really ask him to make sure, but I think that's probably why he gave me the job.

As the employee with the least seniority, I got assigned a

lot to the gallery with *Contusive Blue*. I learned about its back story, and all the legends and rumors so I could chat it up to patrons, but I wasn't a believer at first. I thought it was just some kind of really clever marketing gimmick to jump up a mediocre piece of artwork past its sale value. I was a sophomore marketing major; cynicism came with the territory.

That lasted for about a week. By the end of my first few shifts on the job, in which I stubbornly kept taking off my protective shades, even though they did make me look like a badass, it was obvious after waking up to new bruises every morning that *something* was beating the hell out of me. And even though I wasn't quite ready to have my faith in the rational ordering of the world shattered, there was really only one explanation as to what that was.

Most of my fellow employees just shrugged and wore their shades when they were stationed in that particular gallery, but, well ... I was stubborn. I was in an abusive relationship with *Contusive Blue*, and I was determined to find out how it worked. So I spent a good chunk of time chatting with the patrons about their perceptions of it. Like with any other work of art, they ran the gamut, from revulsion to horror to grudging admiration even to morbid fascination—which is basically where I landed. I spent a good deal of my shifts staring at it, trying to suss it out, and earning a good deal of aches and pains for my efforts.

But after a while, I realized that I wasn't alone. A certain subset of our patrons shared my fascination—enough to drive up our gold memberships a good ten percent after we put it on display. Their faces slowly grew familiar to me as they returned for regular visits. They were the ones who lingered there in front of *Contusive Blue*, mostly oblivious to the other patrons who would come up, give it a few seconds of consideration, maybe lean in to read the information on the placard, and then wander away to see the museum's Mondrian, the second-biggest draw.

I instinctively kept my distance from the connoisseurs, though, for lack of a better term. It was mostly out of respect for their experience—they hadn't come to chat about it, or listen to lurid ghost stories. I think they appreciated my distance, too. Most of them would give me a thin little smile when they'd finally had their fill of it for the day and wandered on to the next gallery.

Until one day. She was a regular. I distinctly remember her face. Always perfectly made up to match her expensive clothes, like one of the *haute couture* trophy wives who maintained their gold membership to impress their friends. Except she always visited alone, and spent up to twenty minutes at a time in front of *Contusive Blue*. Sometimes she even circled back to it more than once on a visit. I kept meaning to strike up a conversation with her, but the moment just never seemed right.

It was in December, I distinctly remember, when she visited for the last time. I didn't know it would be her last time, but, well ... you never really know these things, do you?

It was on that visit that I realized, toward the end of her communion with *Contusive Blue*, that a single tear trickled down her cheek, which was discolored with a fresh bruise. Had that been there when she'd walked in?

That bruise couldn't have been caused by *Contusive Blue*, though. It never left its mark in such visible spots.

I came up beside her so as not to seem like I was creeping up or anything, and I put a hand on her shoulder. "Are you all right, ma'am?" I asked.

I'd tried to be gentle, but I still spooked her out of her reverie. She flinched. Blinked twice, to break the spell of the painting. She turned to look at me. Another tear followed the first one down her cheek. She searched my face, and in that moment, I was worried her composure was an instant away from shattering, and that I was about one eyeblink away from having my first full-scale meltdown to deal with on the job.

And maybe I was. But instead, she smiled at me. It was an expression of profound relief, like when the doctor tells you your tumor is benign. She put her hand to her cheek to brush the bruise with the backs of her index and middle finger.

And then she reached out and hugged me. Tight. "Thank you," she said. That was it. Just: "Thank you."

"I—" I couldn't find words. Fortunately, she didn't seem to expect any. She just held me tight, and I instinctively put my arm around her and patted her on the back. And we stood like that until she finally pulled back. She flashed me another smile, then, and wandered off, as if just to take in the rest of the collection.

That night, I got the best sleep I'd had after a shift in a long while. All the tender spots were still there on my body, I could feel them, but it was as if they were muted somehow.

From that day forward I ditched the shades. I'd never quite felt right wearing them indoors, anyway, and they just made me look distant and unapproachable.

And I soon grew adept at spotting those like her. Oh, anybody can spot a regular's face once they visit enough times, but I could tell who was going to come back usually even on their first visit. You see, for most people, a bruise is just a boo-boo, something you get maybe from tripping over a chair going to the bathroom in the middle of the night. But then there are people for whom a bruise is a memory. And you can see it on their faces if you know how to look.

I started carrying business cards with the phone numbers of women's shelters on them to my shifts. I was terrified when I slid the first one quietly into a patron's hand. I was certain she was going to take one look at it and take umbrage at how I'd misread her and get me fired, and there went my cushy little job. But no, she just looked at the card, then at my face, and I could tell she wasn't used to looking anyone in the eye, and I was oddly touched that she made an exception for me. She just gave me a nervous little smile, and said "Thank you" in a tiny voice, and continued on.

I'd never see them again after that. But as my sophomore year turned into my junior, I never once had any complaints to Bob.

It wasn't always women; men have bruises in their pasts, too. There were plenty enough of those regulars, too; I got so I could spot them instantly, as well. They usually came at *Contusive Blue* the long way round, taking their time with all the other works on the other walls of the gallery, especially the Mondrian. They'd spend an exaggerated amount of time bent over reading all the information placards, and then come before *Contusive Blue* like *hello, what have we here?*—even though they had to know ahead of time. They'd come looking for it. Their guards took longer to come down, but they always would eventually. I started carrying business cards to a licensed specialist counselor. I discreetly handed a few out —even got a few hugs in return over the year and a half that I worked there.

What we didn't get a lot of was kids. The gold member-ship granting unlimited visits was over a hundred bucks, after all. Of course, we'd get plenty of kids who came through with their parents, but not really repeat visitors, unaccompanied. So even though, by the time my second semester of my junior year rolled around, I flattered myself into thinking I was ready for anything, I was completely at a loss when the kid started showing up.

He was maybe thirteen or fourteen, but small for his age. It was a Saturday, I remember, when I saw him for the first time, so the gallery was at its busiest—which means there were something like half a dozen to a dozen or so people moving through at any one time. I just remember turning around and seeing him there, captivated by *Contusive Blue*. That in itself was hardly out of the ordinary, but I remember looking around at all the other patrons for his parents, 'cause what kind of teenager spends their Saturday by themselves in an art gallery, right?

Most of the other patrons made their circuit of all four walls and moved on to the next gallery, but he still stood there for what must have been like twenty minutes. The other patrons would come up next to him to get their looks in at *Contusive Blue*, but he hardly seemed to notice them. He just stood politely off center a bit to let other people in while he seemed ... lost.

Well, soon enough one of the other patrons distracted my attention with a question, and when I looked back the kid was gone.

Of all the people I'd approached over my time at *The Met* —you know, those special few for whom *Contusive Blue* is just a bit *too* intuitive—there were plenty of others who'd gotten away, or ones who maybe I might have approached if they'd ever come back. I certainly never expected to see this kid again.

But a few days later, on a school night, there he was again, his feet planted on the same stretch of floor. There were fewer patrons this time, so I started my customary circling, non-threatening approach, working on my reassuring smile and the opening line I'd use when I got up beside him. But just before I got there, the spell broke. He took his eyes off of the painting, turned straight toward me, even smiled at me, without a trace of self-consciousness. Which *really* confused me, because I expected to see layers and layers of baggage there. I think I smiled back at him, and I hope I didn't look like a total dumbass, but while I was mentally discarding everything I might have said to him, he just ambled away, cool as you please.

He showed up again on Monday night the next week, same as the other times: alone. What kind of kid used his allowance to go to an art museum? Maybe his parents had a gold membership, and Patty at the front door was letting him through on it? I resolved to ask her about it, but I never got a chance. That last time, he loitered as always in front of *Contusive Blue*. I respected his communion, but this time I timed my swoop a little better. I was standing next to him when he came out of what was almost a fugue state. I remember him blinking up at me. There were no bruises that I could see— not out in the open, anyway, but his left cheek did have a prominent half-healed scratch that went from just under his eye halfway down to his chin.

I tried out my reassuring, non-threatening smile, and hoped to hell it worked on kids. "You must be just about black and blue all over, as much as you've been staring at that thing," I said. I forced a chuckle at my own remark.

His eyes got round. "It's not just a myth, is it?" he said. "It really works?"

"You mean you don't know by now?" I rolled up my sleeve to show him my latest bruise. He gawked at it, then looked back at *Contusive Blue* as if comparing them. I frowned. "It doesn't do anything to you?"

He shook his head. "It's brilliant, though," he said.

"But ... if it doesn't ... you've never... why do you keep coming back?"

He shrugged. "I just want to be an artist someday." He took one long last longing look at *Contusive Blue*. "Like my mom."

I never saw the kid again, even though I looked for him, every shift from then on. I asked our entrance monitors about him; one of them vaguely remembered a kid by that description, but wasn't paying any attention to the membership card they swiped to admit him—not to mention that looking into patrons' personal data without a clear, compelling reason was a big no-no.

I changed my major, by the way. Late junior year, which meant it took me another whole year to finally graduate. I was never really cut out to be a business marketing exec, like

I'd thought, so it turned out for the best. I still picked up shifts at the museum into grad school, at least until The Art Institute poached *Contusive Blue* out of our collection. By then I was ass-deep in working through my clinicals.

There isn't a day that goes by that I don't wish I had a *Contusive Blue* to hang up in my office, so I could just instruct my patients to look at it for however long they need, but then, that would be selfish of me. I think it needs to be on public display, open to anyone.

When I began, I told you that how it works isn't as important as *why* it works. I apologize if I led you to expect some easy answer; I'm afraid I don't really have one. As far as I can tell, it works because ... well, why does any art work? It works because we all look to it to get what we need out of it. Some of us just need a little not-so-gentle reminder of our own fragility. Some of us need a whole lot more ... we need to look into it to know we're not alone; and that everybody's bruises sometimes threaten to leap out of the frame. And some of us even need to look into the bruises and show them who's boss.

Which brings us here today. I'm very pleased to have been asked to return to the museum where it all started for me, all those years ago, for today's unveiling.

The work in question was left outside *The Met* over a month ago, with no note, nothing to identify the artist. The management wasn't even sure they wanted to display it, but, well, I like to think I played a little part in convincing them. Just like *Contusive Blue* before it, this one sometimes hurts, but people need to see that at times, too.

So without further ado, it's my privilege to introduce to you *Lacerative Scarlet*. Please be mindful and respectful of others as they are experiencing it for the first time, and ... maybe just be there beside them to offer them a tissue or a band-aid if they need one, eh?

· · ·

Brian Rappatta is an expat writer currently living in South Korea. His short fiction has appeared in *Analog, Baffling Magazine,* and *Amazing Stories;* in anthologies such as *Writers of the Future, Chilling Ghost Stories* (from Flame Tree Publications), and *Life Beyond Us* (forthcoming); and in multiple genre podcasts such as *Curiosities, Tales to Terrify,* and *StarShip Sofa.*

POST REFLECTION

SHERRILYN KENYON &
MADAUG HISHINUMA

Attorney Larry Robb prided himself on being the commander of his boring universe. A scrawny, balding little man who was neurotic about every minuscule detail of his pathetically ordinary life.

From the fact that he demanded his breakfast be served every single morning the same exact way—

Two eggs, sunny side up. Two slices of bacon cooked extra crispy, not burned. One piece of lightly browned toast, with a thin layer of grape jelly, to coffee ... no sugar, but enough milk that it turned the same color as his plain, boring khaki pants.

The only variation in his life was the color of his button-down shirts. Though they, too, were as plain and boring as his toast and taste in bland music.

Just like his personality.

Indeed, Larry knew exactly just how boring he was. How average his intellect. Average his taste, and how below average his humor and tolerance for others.

That made him constantly angry. Bitter.

And scheming.

Something he took out on the world around him. Such as the poor waitress who'd made the mistake of serving him toast this morning that was a little too brown and eggs that were a bit too hard in the middle.

Like the bitter little man who eyed her with disdain.

"How stupid are you? No wonder you're stuck here, making below-minimum wage. And you people think you're worth fifteen dollars an hour! Ridiculous!" Snarling at the poor girl, he tossed his payment down on the table and snatched up his phone as he left her there with tears in her eyes and no tip.

And all because the cook had been overburdened with orders and Mr. Robb had been too lazy to make his own toast at home.

It hadn't been the waitress's fault and if he'd taken a moment to use his feeble little brain, Larry Robb would have known that. But sadly, his lizard brain was occupied with such novel contemplations as where he'd left his car and what he might want to eat for lunch that he couldn't be bothered with anything as trivial as sparing a moment's compassion for another human being.

So, he headed for his office down the street. An uninspired place, really.

Just like its owner.

Drab gray walls. Austere furnishings that had been purchased in whole from a catalogue because Larry had no taste or ability to put together anything from an imagination that had failed him as a child and abandoned him as an adult.

"Mr. Robb? There's a call—"

"I don't have time for it. Tell them I'm in a meeting." He brushed past his secretary, heading for his office.

Sighing, he pulled his car keys out his pocket, still unsure of where he'd put his car on the street, and dropped them in his desk drawer. He had a designated spot there because if he didn't, he'd never remember where they were later.

Just like his missing car.

Oh well, that was why he had an app.

Wiggling his mouse, he sat down in his chair and waited for his computer to awaken.

But instead of his bland background, something odd appeared.

GREED. GREED.

Stupefied, he stared at the screen and the single word that was repeated over and over.

What in the world?

"Charlotte!" He shouted for his secretary.

The tiny blond rushed in. "Yes, Mr. Robb?"

"Is this a joke?" He pointed at the screen.

Eyes wide, she shook her head. "What is that?"

"How should I know? Who was in my office?"

"No one."

He arched a brow at her. "Someone was. Obviously. Someone did this!"

"No, sir. Check the video feed."

"Trust me. I will and whoever did this will be fired!" After all, he had no measurable sense of humor.

Everyone in the office knew that about him.

"Do you want to know who called?"

He glared at her. "I don't care." Then he rudely waved her off as he pulled up the surveillance feed for his office.

But as he reviewed the hours from when he'd left the night before until he sat down, it was just as she'd said.

No one had ventured into the room.

No one.

"It must have been done by remote."

That was it. That made sense.

Picking up the phone, he called downstairs to the IT department.

Peters picked up. He was the head of the department. A cranky little twerp of a man Larry had hired five years back. Not for any particular skill other than he was as boring and crabby as Larry was. Plus, he didn't intimidate him physically or challenge him mentally.

Larry liked those characteristics in a person, especially in an underling.

"Yeah, Robb, what'cha need?"

"I want to know if someone hacked into my computer as a prank."

"Is something missing?"

"No. They left me a rude message. I want to know who did it."

Peters smacked his lips, then yawned. "All right. I'll look into it and get back to you."

Fury darkened his gaze. *Look into it ...*

Putz! He should fire the imbecile, but it was too much work to replace him. So he suffered the fool.

Sighing, Larry got up and went to the small fridge near his window where he kept his waters and Cokes. As he reached down for a drink, he glanced into the mirror that was hung on the wall next to it.

Shock riveted him.

Instead of his own face, he saw an ugly, warted gremlin there.

Gasping, he turned around and saw nothing.

He looked back in the mirror. Again, he saw the hideous face of a beast he didn't recognize.

"Charlotte!"

His secretary came running back into his office.

He gestured at the mirror. "Do you see that?"

She scowled at him. "It's the antique mirror you

purchased last week and wanted hung. Is there a problem? Did they not put it in the right place?"

"No! Look at it. What do you see?"

She glanced at the mirror and shrugged. "Me?"

He held his hand up, which also appeared warted in the glass. "No. Look at me."

She did.

"In the mirror, you idiot. How do you see me in the mirror?"

"The way I always see you."

Rolling his eyes, he scoffed at her. "Get out! Go! You're useless."

Without a word, she left him alone.

And still the gremlin stared at him. Was this some sort of filter?

"Someone's playing a prank." This was a deep fake or some other kind of screwed-up gimmick. He had no doubt.

Turning his distorted, wrinkled face side to side, he snorted at the ugly image of himself. "Fine. Whatever."

But as he stared at the mirror, words began to write themselves over the glass.

REPENT. REPENT. REPENT. REPENT. REPENT. REPENT.
REPENT. REPENT. REPENT. REPENT. REPENT. REPENT.
REPENT. REPENT. REPENT. REPENT. REPENT. REPENT.
REPENT. REPENT. REPENT. REPENT. REPENT. REPENT.
REPENT. REPENT. REPENT. REPENT. REPENT. REPENT.
REPENT. REPENT. REPENT. REPENT. REPENT. REPENT.
REPENT. REPENT. REPENT. REPENT.

What the hell?

"Repent what?"

It didn't answer.

This was insane. What kind of madness had consumed him?

His land line buzzed. Disgusted with the trick, he grabbed a water and headed back to his desk. "Yes?"

"There's a call on line one for you."

"I'm busy. Take a message."

"She says it's urgent."

"I don't care." That was the shit about clients. They all thought they were important. They all assumed they were the only one he had.

To them, it was a matter of life and death.

To him, they were just another file in his drawer. He didn't give a shit about their concerns or their cases. Sure, he'd grease their egos whenever they came through his doors. Tell them whatever bullshit they needed to hear to get them to put down a retainer for his law firm.

But once he had their names on his contract and their checks cleared the bank ...

They could take a number.

This was just a job. Another day. Another dollar. All cases were basically the same. The client did something wrong. Or someone did something wrong to them. Both sides lied, and he had to tell some made-up bullshit to the judge and file paperwork while arguing with another asshole like himself over inconsequential matters so that they could amass as many billable hours as possible out of whatever case they had.

Win, lose, or draw, he got paid and so did his opponent. What the idiot client didn't realize was that every time they called or sent an email, he charged them hundreds or thousands of dollars just to listen to their bullshit and say, "uh-huh."

It was good to be a lawyer.

But at the end of the day, they didn't pay him enough to care.

His line buzzed again.

Growling, he hit the button. "Do you want me to fire you?"

"It's Chad Shaddix, Mr. Robb."

"Oh. Put him through." Sadly, he needed to talk to that asshole. Their case had been going on for almost three years and they'd bankrupted their clients. Now they had to settle the matter.

Pity. It'd been a good run that had netted them both some nice vacations and retirement plans.

"Hey, Chad. You have your terms?"

"No. Did you hear?"

"Hear what?"

"Your client gutted himself last night."

Larry froze at those words as disbelief went through him. "What?"

"Yeah. He realized that we'd taken him to the cleaners and that he was fucked. So apparently, he locked himself in his office, wrote a note to his family and committed ritual suicide right there."

Damn. "So where does that leave the case?"

"Well, unless you want me to sue his widow for his actions, which would make me an even bigger asshole than I already am, we're screwed."

Not that it really mattered. Both of their clients were turnips at this point. There was no need to keep trying a case when no one had any more money to pay them.

Larry growled deep in his throat in frustration. "No shit."

Chad sighed. "Let me talk to my client and see if I can get them to withdraw their suit."

"Fine. I'll try and calm mine down. I'm sure she's beside herself with hysteria. I know Kazama was always saying he and his wife were soul mates, yada, yada, yada. No doubt, she's all kinds of torn up over this. You know how women are."

Chad snorted unsympathetically. "Yeah, well, they should

have had insurance. Damn it. What kind of asshole doesn't have insurance for their store? Could the bastard have waited to kill himself until my clients paid their latest bill? They still owe me about twenty grand. I'm sure I'll never get it now."

"No, kidding. Mine owes me about sixty. Hope he had some life insurance I can snag. Provided they don't cancel it over his suicide."

"Maybe we could—"

"Don't even go there, Chad." Wow, he was an even bigger asshole than Larry was. "The judge would hang you if you tried to sue a grieving widow for her husband's life insurance."

"Depends on the judge. Bubba would give it to us. All we'd have to do is get the case moved to him."

Larry considered it for a moment. He wasn't wrong. "Let me think about that. I'll get back to you."

"You do that. But don't wait too long."

Narrowing his eyes as he credited Chad for his resourcefulness, Larry hung up the phone. There might be a way to get more money out of their turnips, after all.

Yeah, leave it to Shaddix ...

His monitor flashed.

GREED. GREED. GREED. GREED. GREED. GREED. GREED.
GREED. GREED. GREED. GREED. GREED. GREED. GREED.
GREED. GREED. GREED. GREED. GREED. GREED. GREED.
GREED. GREED. GREED. GREED. GREED. GREED. GREED.
GREED. GREED. GREED. GREED. GREED. GREED. GREED.
GREED. GREED. GREED. GREED. GREED. GREED. GREED.

Curling his lip, he turned his monitor off and buzzed for Peters again. "Get up here and fix this damn thing!"

"Be there in a bit. Have something I have to do first."

Sure, he did.

I need to fire that asshole.

"Mr. Robb?"

"What now, Charlotte?"

Before she could answer, his door opened. A small, beautiful Asian lady walked in. Dressed in an elegant black suit, she was the epitome of high fashion, right down to her vibrant red Jimmy Choo shoes and matching handbag. She bled high brow.

There was something about her innately peaceful. Graceful.

Timeless.

He was instantly captivated.

"Sorry, Mr. Robb. She rushed past me."

"It's all right, Charlotte." He rose to his feet as the woman stopped in front of his desk to eye him with a gimlet stare.

The intelligence there unnerved him.

"How can I help you ..."

"Kazama. Wanaka Kazama."

Oh shit. This was the widow.

Who knew the old man had married so well. But then, it figured. At the beginning of their suit and before they'd drained the man's estate with legal fees, Kazama had been worth millions.

As old as he'd been, that would have made him attractive to any woman.

No wonder he'd made sure to keep this little honey hidden.

Offering her a sympathetic smile, Larry came around his desk and shooed away his secretary. "Can I get you anything, Ms. Kazama? I was just about to call you."

"Really? I've been trying to call you all morning. Your secretary said you were too busy to take time for me."

"Yeah ... sorry about that. I just found out about your husband. Such a shame. He was a good man."

Tears swam in her dark eyes as she licked her red lips. "Yes, he was. And he was innocent."

"I know."

"You allowed them to lie about him and you never once stopped them."

"I tried."

She shook her head. "No. You didn't."

Larry sighed. "The law is complicated, Ms. Kazama."

"But the truth isn't."

"Sadly, the law isn't about the truth."

She laughed bitterly at that. "Tell me, Mr. Robb. Have you ever heard of if an *ungaikyo*?"

"A what?"

"*Ungaikyo*."

"Is it a watch?"

She tsked at him. "No." Setting her purse on his desk, she walked over to his newly purchased mirror to adjust her hair. "They're very special in my culture."

"How so?"

"In Japan, if an object is held onto long enough or if it's something someone loves enough, it can acquire its own soul."

"Really?"

She nodded. "In some cases, some items can even be loved enough that they can grow to love their owners in return."

"That's a nice fairytale."

"Hmm." She smiled at him. "But the *ungaikyo* is a little different. They can only be created in *Hazuki* on the fifteenth night during the light of a full moon. Only with glass or crystal so consecrated can one be made."

"What are they, exactly?"

She hesitated before she answered. "Demon mirrors."

"Demon mirrors?"

An odd light darkened her gaze. "Long ago, my people used them to trap yokai and demons that caused trouble in this world. To banish them back to their own realms."

"Interesting."

"Yes, but that's not the most interesting part, Mr. Robb. Do you know what is?"

"No idea."

She crooked her finger.

He stepped closer to her as if pulled by an unseen force.

Leaning against him, she whispered in his ear. "*Ungaikyo* ... the mirror always shows demons and people for who and what they really are. No one can hide the truth from them. Whatever you're hiding, it reveals."

Before he realized what she was doing, she shoved him toward the mirror on his wall.

There, he saw himself as the gremlin and instead of a beautiful woman, he saw Wanaka as a walking mirror herself.

"My husband found me in his store and his love gave me life and purpose." She wrapped her mirrored arms around him.

Larry tried to scream, but his voice was frozen. Against all efforts, he was dragged from his office and into a cold, deep darkness.

All sound stopped and everything ceased ...

Charlotte opened the door to Larry's office and froze as she found it empty. "Mr. Robb?"

No one had come out of it. Yet there was no one inside it now.

Weird.

Stepping toward his desk, she saw nothing out of the ordinary.

At least not until she neared his new mirror. Was that ...

Blood?

She wasn't sure, but there did appear to be a deep crimson smear across the center of it.

Even stranger, there was a small silver hand mirror lying on the shelf in front of it. One encrusted with black and red crystals that shimmered in the light.

What the ...

The door opened behind her, startling her so badly that she actually shrieked.

"Jesus, Charlotte! What the hell?"

She covered her heart with her hand as she saw Peters coming into the office behind her. "Sorry. I just ..." She gestured at the empty desk. "Larry was here and then he ... vanished."

"He does that."

"Not like this."

"Whatever. Asshole's been at me all morning to come look at his computer. So here I am." He went to his desk and wiggled the mouse.

A second later, he gasped. "What is this?"

"What?" She stepped over and gaped at the screen.

JUSTICE IS SERVED. JUSTICE IS SERVED. JUSTICE IS SERVED. JUSTICE IS SERVED. JUSTICE IS SERVED. JUSTICE IS SERVED. JUSTICE IS SERVED. JUSTICE IS SERVED. JUSTICE IS SERVED. JUSTICE IS SERVED. JUSTICE IS SERVED. JUSTICE IS SERVED. JUSTICE IS SERVED. JUSTICE IS SERVED. JUSTICE IS SERVED. JUSTICE IS SERVED. JUSTICE IS SERVED. JUSTICE IS SERVED. JUSTICE IS SERVED. JUSTICE IS SERVED.

Peters snorted. "Must be a weird lawyer joke."

Defying all odds is what #1 *New York Times* and international bestselling author **Sherrilyn Kenyon** does best. Rising from extreme poverty as a child that culminated in being a homeless mother with an infant, she has become one of the most popular and influential authors in the world (in both adult and young adult fiction), with dedicated legions of fans known as Paladins—thousands of whom proudly sport tattoos from her numerous genre-defying series.

Intense gamer, former Japanese teacher (and resident of Japan), and current mastermind of all around mayhem, **Madaug Hishinuma** first started writing in grade school ... on his mother's walls. Deciding that near death experiences weren't exactly his thing, he traded his crayons for a computer, and once he broke away from his severe gaming addiction, realized that his keyboard could also be used to create his own worlds. He's been doing that ever since.

EVERYDAY THINGS
SYLVIA STOPFORTH

They call me things. Gormless. Want-wit. Dolt.
Other things too. Things I can't say, or mama'll switch me.

But I did something right, once. Out-smarted smart, I did.

It started on account of a puddle. I get to looking in 'em, after a fresh rain. You can see right through then, t'other side. Looks like ours, but ain't. Clouds're different. That's how you can tell.

So anyways, I was looking, and over the head of the like-me, in the puddle, I see the witch flying. And she's got my little brother. And that was bad. 'Cause I was to watch him, see, while mama went to the market to sell the rainberries and charnuts we'd foraged. And, too, 'cause everybody knows that witches want nothing with babies but to eat 'em.

I felt it in my bones, that this was one of those things that'd work same-wise in both places, so I scrammed for home. Sure enough, his straw mat, there in the corner, was bare and empty. And on his little pillow was a hair, gray and bristly, from nowhere else but a witch's chin.

I knew I had to go. I was skairt so I could hardly think. But I knew I had to, even in spite of that.

So I pulled on my boots and stuffed a stale bread crust in my pocket.

And I went.

It was a long way, with lots of puddles on it. But I didn't stop to look in even one. At the fork in the road I turned right-wards, scrabble-hand, into the dark woods, 'cause that's where witches abide. When I got hungry, I et my crust, and when I got thirsty, I stopped to drink out of a chuckle. But still I wasn't there, where I was going. So I kept on. And finally, when the sun was all but winked-out, I came to it. I could tell it was the witch's house, 'cause there she was in front of it, using her broom to sweep the front stoop. Like it was just an ordinary broom. Like she was just an ordinary old woman.

There were rows of turnips and taties and carrots along the one side of the hillocky path, and sunshiney flowers on the other, half run to seed. Like it was just an ordinary garden.

But that's how they get you, ain't it.

She looked to me where I'd stopped, at the edge of the clearing. I was pondering on just how far a witch could throw a hex, see.

"Why're you here, girlie?" she said, like she didn't know.

"You got my brother," I said.

"The one don't necessarily lead t'other," she said.

That befuddled me.

She rolled her eyes. "The you being here don't necessarily follow from the me having your brother. Unless there's a string, holding 'em together. What's the string?"

I thought, and tried again. "'Cause I'll get switched, and worse, if mama comes home, and finds I've let a warty old witch have my brother for supper."

The witch frowned at that, all thundery. "Well," she said,

"if that's all you care about, saving your own hide, then hop it. I've got better things to do." She shook her broom out at me and made as if to go in.

Well. I sat down on the ground, right where I was, and bawled.

She turned around and looked at me. "What else is in there, then, girlie?"

"I got nothing else," I wailed. "Only he's my brother, and I love him, and I don't know what I'll do without him to hold and kiss, and without his toes to pinch, to make him laugh."

The witch snorted. "You love him? Prove it's so."

I forced myself to stand up, on legs didn't feel like mine. "I'm here, ain't I? And it was a long way. And I'm so skairt my bones're watery. But I'm here, even in spite of that."

She put her head to one side, the way a robin does, when it's listening for worms 'neath the grass. "All right then. I'll give you your brother back."

"You will?" I near-about hugged her.

But she held up a crookit finger. "Not so quick," she said. "Don't you know the rules? You got to do something for me, first. Three somethings, in fact."

"All right then. I—I can wash your dishes, or scrub your floors. I can gather mushrooms for you. Or charnuts. Mama says finding things in the woods is something I'm near-wise good at. I can shell your peas,"—but I saw her vines were all done and spent—"or I can clean the muck off your boots, or I can chase all the spiders from out your privy."

She shook her head. "Those're everyday things," she said. "Everyday things don't win back a brother. Everyday things don't prove love."

I didn't know how to do anything but everyday things. And plenty of 'em, not so well. "What, then?" I asked.

The witch tapped her nose with her finger. "First thing," she said, "I want a horse. A horse that can fly me over the moon."

My heart fell clunk, into my belly. I'd never even heard of such a thing. And if someone had such a wondrous beast, they'd sure not be giving it to me.

"Second," she grinned, toothless, "I want hair from a bald man. A whole passel of it."

My heart climbed down into my toes, for even I knew that bald men haven't any hair. Else they'd not be bald.

"And third," she nodded like she was agreeing with herself, "I'm getting on. Could use some help 'round here. Any girl will do."

I perked up a bit at that last one. "Any girl? I'm a girl. Take me."

She shook her head.

"But you said ..."

"I know full well what I said, girlie. Not just any girl. Any girl. Pay attention."

"I don't understand." I wiped my nose on my sleeve.

"That's not my problem." The witch turned to go. "Oh," she squinted up at the night sky, at the sliver of Bright Lady hung there. "See to it you bring me all these somethings before midnight of the next full moon."

"But that's just," I counted on my fingers, "that's just three weeks!"

"So you're not the complete dolt they've named you, then," she said, and stepped over the threshold.

"Wait! Promise!"

"Promise what?"

"Promise you won't eat him until then."

She soured her mouth at me. "I won't eat your brother before the next full moon," she said, and went in, slamming the door so the shutters rattled.

I plopped myself down on her stoop, too miserable even to cry. I heard her bustling about, and making cooing noises, and my little brother crowing and squealing. It seemed an odd way to treat your supper. But I knew people to be full of contraries.

A fine smell of cooking commenced to mix with the smoke from her fire, and my belly grumbled. I wondered if she'd turn me to stone for nicking a carrot from her garden.

The door opened and I jumped. But the witch only pushed a bowl of stew at me, and went in again. It came to me to wonder if she'd poisoned it. But I figured, hexing or starving, it'd come to the same end, and so I et it. When I was done I licked my fingers clean, it was so good, and the bowl too. Then I laid myself down, right where I was, and went to sleep.

I woke the next morning with the sun in my eyes. So that was all right then. I figured you don't wake with the sun in your eyes if you're dead.

I thought to thank the witch for the supper. But also, too, I was ireful on account of my brother, and the three impossible somethings. So I nicked some carrots from her garden, and I went.

At the fork I took the way that didn't lead to home. 'Cause I knew the way to home had no flying horses on it, nor hairy bald men neither. Though I wasn't sure about the any girls. That was a stumper, for sure and certain.

I got to thinking that something the witch'd said wasn't right. It was like an itch down deep in my ear. But I couldn't get at it, and thinking ain't my strong suit, mama says. So I gave it up and kept on.

About midday I came to a field full of nothing but buttercups. Well. Buttercups and the sorriest-looking horse I'd ever seen. His ribs stood out sharp. And his dull, dirty coat was rubbed raw in places. I took the carrots out of my pocket and sighed, 'cause I'd been saving 'em for my supper. But Horse looked worse-off than I felt.

He et 'em all, and I stroked his mole-soft nose. And then I had a thought.

"Say," I said, "I don't s'pose witch-carrots give horses wings?"

He just eyed me, 'til I had to look away.

"All right," I said, "it was only just a thought. Anyways. I need to get on. I have three impossible somethings to find before the moon fills."

I'd only gone a few steps when I heard such a ruckus.

Horse'd kicked the fence clear over. He stood there, puffing, and then was clippity cloppiting over to put his nose on my shoulder.

"I ain't got any more carrots," I said.

He lipped my hair.

"You can't come," I said. "Your owner'll come after us. You'll get beat and I'll get worse, for thievin'."

He shook his head and sidled me near off the lane.

"It's no good," I said. "I ain't never rode a horse."

He groaned and got down on his knees.

"I'm heavier than I look," I said. "Big bones."

He put his ears back, so I climbed on, and he staggered back up to his feet, and off we went. It was a lot higher up there than it looked from down below, so I closed my eyes and thought cocklebur thoughts.

After a while, my stomach commenced to grumble. Horse walked us right under a wild apple tree. From off his back I could reach to pick some, and so I did, and we both et our fill. They were some tasty. Mama always says hunger is the best seasoning. I wouldn't know, never having tried another.

Horse got more lively then, picking his feet up and flicking his ears.

'Round about the time mama would've been putting my brother to bed, we came across a sight. There was a man sitting on the front step of a run-down old house, crying like a baby. I couldn't bear it, to hear such misery, so I asked Horse, and he stopped.

"What's the matter?" I said. From off the top of the Horse. 'Cause you never know.

The man held his lantern up so he could see, then he set to howling again.

"Stop that!" I shouted. Sometimes, with my brother, it helps to surprise him.

The man's mouth snapped shut, and he looked at me, his eyes big.

"What's ailing you? I ain't good for much, but maybe I can help."

The corners of his mouth turned down. "I lost my comb," he said.

Well. That was a stumper. For he was as bald as an egg.

"Where'd you lose it?"

"I was mucking out the barn."

"But if you lost the comb in the barn, then why ain't you in there, looking?"

"Well it'll be in the mess-pile, won't it," he said, and then he set to wailing again.

He was crying too hard to murder me, so I clambered down off Horse, which set to munching the long, untidy grass around the house.

"So look in the mess-pile then."

"You slow, child?" he said.

"You have hit that nail directly on its top."

He took up his lantern and led me 'round the back of the barn. And there was the most ginormous pile of cow-muck I'd ever seen.

"And the comb," he said with a little hitch, "is tortoise-shell!" With this he sat down on the ground and sobbed like his heart had broke in two.

"Well," I said, "thinking ain't my strong suit. But I'm

pretty good at certain everyday things." I found a shovel, turned up the wick on the lantern, and commenced to dig. "What's this comb look like? Any turtles I've ever seen came in a sort of a lumpy green color."

"This one," he whispered, "was brown."

I stopped. "Muck-brown?"

"Muck-brown."

I began to see why he'd been carrying on so. "Say," I said, "don't most farm-folk spread this around every now and then? To make things grow?"

He sniffed. "I got more important things to do."

I thought about important things. Like my baby brother. And the moon rolling her way 'round the sky. And then my stomach grumbled. First things first, mama always says.

"Look," I said, "I could prob'ly shovel better with a bit of supper in my belly. Do you have a crust of bread, or a rind of cheese, spare?"

He cheered right up at that.

"It's been ages since I've had a dinner guest," he said.

The sink was heaped-full of dirty dishes, and the wood box was near-empty, but didn't we have the best supper? First, fresh greens with nuts and crumbly cheese and pickled beet-root. Then barley soup alongside thick slices of buttered bread, and the bread still warm. Just when I thought I couldn't eat another bite, out from the oven came a pan of spiced apples.

While I licked my bowl clean the man commenced to tell his story.

In his courtin' days, he'd been a fine figure of a man. Strong back and legs hardly-bowed. Had thick, black hair down to his waist, and was ever-so vain about it. Every night he tended it with a tortoise-shell comb his mother'd left him.

At a dance one night, some swagger-git knocked him down and sawed off his hair with a pocketknife. The girl he was sweet on took one look at his crook-shorn head and went off with the git.

Good riddance, I thought, if that's all she cared about.

Next thing, all the man's hair fell out, on account of his dreams being dashed to smithereens, and it never grew back.

He opened a dresser drawer to show me a thick hank of black hair, tied at one end with a blue ribbon.

"Every night I sit and recollect the wrongs done me, and tend my hair with the tortoise-shell comb."

"It's awful pretty," I said, "but why keep the shell when the nut's long gone?"

He shrugged. "It's all I've got."

"But that supper," I said, "you could cook for a queen!"

He smiled at that, and his cheeks pinked. "Well, that's about the nicest thing anybody's ever said to me."

I got to my feet. "I'm going to find that comb of yours, and then I've got to be on my way."

"Hold up a minute," he said. "I told you my story. Now you got to tell me yours. What're you doing all the way out here on that old nag, don't belong to you?"

"How d'you know he don't belong to me?" I asked, all skairt.

"'Cause he's not been well looked-after," he said, "and I reckon if you had a horse of your own, you'd take some care with it."

"Oh," I said. And I sat back down, and I told it all, from the puddle on up. And when I was done, he threw his head back, and laughed as hard as he'd been crying, before.

"What's funny?" I felt a bit riled, truth be told. I'd not laughed at him, for all his silliness over his hair.

"Well, ain't it obvious, child?"

"Mama says there ain't much in God's green world is obvious to me," I said.

"This here," he took up the beribboned hair, "is hair from a bald man."

It took a full tick-tock of a grandfather clock for that to sink in.

"That's one of my impossible somethings, ain't it!"

"You have hit that nail directly on its top," he said.

"Oh, but you wouldn't want to give it to me."

"Did you mean it, when you said I could cook for a queen?"

"'Course I did. I never say things I don't mean. Too hard to keep track, else."

"Well then. You take this hair, and that'll put a sad chapter to a good end. And maybe I'll hitch my cows to my wagon and find myself a peckish queen with a fat purse."

"Oh thank you!" I threw my arms around him and something clattered to the floor. It was a shining comb, all motley brown.

The man took it up and stared at the one gray, bristly hair caught in its teeth.

"Well, ain't that the oddest thing," he said.

"Hmmm," I said. For I recognized that hair. It could've come from nowhere else but a witch's chin.

I slept cozy that night, my belly stretched tight over all that good food.

The next morning the man gave me a rucksack he'd filled with dried plums, a wedge of cheese, and a fresh loaf of bread. The hank of hair was curled at the bottom of the sack, where it'd be safe.

I climbed aboard Horse and off we went, clippity clop-piting down the road, the man and me both waving like friends parting.

We travelled eight days and the same exact number of nights. The cheese was gone, and then the last piece of bread. Altogether, I had three plums, and no flying horse, and no any girl. And despite the impossible hair in the rucksack, my spirits were pretty low, I don't mind saying.

"Soon we'll have to turn around, Horse," I told him, "and I'll give the witch the one thing I've got, and beg her to send my brother back home, and eat me instead."

Horse flicked his ears to say he had his doubts.

We passed through a bramble-wood and rounded a bend to find a vasty farm, with fields and a barn and a house with two layers. Near the lane a girl was emptying slop buckets for a jostling passel of pigs. She had on a patched dress, and a straw hat with a bite out of it. The skin of her hands was cracked and raw, and she was so scrawny, one of the pigs clear knocked her over.

I asked Horse and he stopped, lickety-split. I scrambled down and offered my hand.

"Thanks," she said, and looked me over sharpish, with a pair of black eyes.

"I ain't good for much," I said, "but maybe I can help. Looks like you got a fair amount of work here."

"Nothing gets by you, I can see," she said.

I shrugged. "I got big bones. So there ain't much room."

Her eyes squinched down. "You funnin' me?"

"Wouldn't know how," I said, and she snorted.

"Feeding the pigs is a sight easier than taking care o' my brothers." She commenced to gather up the empty slop buckets. "There's nine, all told. Each one worse'n the last."

"Sounds like a trial."

"That's a truth."

I followed her on up the hill to the barn.

"Fine farm you got," I said, admiring tidy rows of pick-ready corn.

"Oh sure. Everything a body needs. Just no time for

anything a body might want. Like flowers, say. Or stories. Or time to look at the stars." She sighed.

Right then, two boys came barreling around the corner of the barn. One knocked the girl's hat off and the other pulled her hair and yelled, "Outta the way, Annie-girl!" And they were off and away, quick as blinking.

Horse whickered.

"See what I mean?" The girl bent to take up her hat.

Right then a hay wagon came rumbling over the ridge behind the house. Three boys tussled in the box, scuffling hay every which way, until there was more outside of the wagon than inside of it.

"Boys, mind the hay!" the girl called.

"Mind it yourself, Annie-girl," one of ' em hollered back.

Horse whickered again, and nosed me.

The girl took up two clean buckets from the barn and I followed her to where a bleat of nanny goats grazed in a fenced meadow.

"Can I help?" I said. "I'm fair at everyday somethings like milking, even if impossible somethings ain't my strong suit."

The wrong thing the witch'd said itched at me again. I stuck my finger in my ear, but it was gone.

"What's an impossible something?" the girl asked.

"It's a long yarn," I said. "Ain't coming to a good end, neither." My stomach grumbled.

"Oh, tell it me," she said. "Since ma died, no one tells me stories."

So while we worked I told it all. From the puddle on up.

"What're we waiting for?" she said, when I was done.

"I don't take your meaning," I said.

"When I was born, ma wanted to call me Amy, a-m-y, after her sister. But when pa went to register me, he spelt it wrong. He wrote down Any, a-n-y. So now everyone calls me 'Any Girl.' I'm the Any Girl your witch wants. I'm sure of it!"

Horse snorted.

"You knew all along, didn't you?"

He just looked at me.

I took up my pail and right there, atop the milk, floated a wiry gray hair.

"That's odd," Any Girl said, looking at my brown braids.

"Hmmm," I said.

"C'mon. We'll set out first thing in the morning," she said.

"But did you hear the part about her being a witch? About how she flies on a broom, and lives in the dark woods, and—"

"She got kids?"

"No. Well. Just the one, far as I know. But I'm trying to get 'im back."

"She got pigs need feeding, goats need milking, a bull needs to charge you any chance it gets?"

"Just a garden's all I saw."

"A garden! Fruit trees and berry bushes and vegetables, all sorts?"

"Well, I can't say I took it all in, proper. But there's vegetables. Flowers too."

"Flowers!" the girl's eyes grew big. "Ma used to plant flowers. But I ain't never had time. C'mon!"

Up at the house, Any Girl set a ginormous pot of stew to simmering. I helped her bring in the washing, make the beds, and sweep the floors. Then she went to the front step and jangled a clutch of cowbells.

A squall of boys roared in. They thundered and stomped and slopped and spilled. And when it was all done, they jumped up to go.

"Hold up!" Any Girl hollered.

They held.

"Sit you down!" she hollered.

They sat.

"This here's the last supper I'm going to cook for you lot. I've set you up real nice, so you'll have to work hard at going hungry, though I don't doubt you could manage it. I've wore myself thin for you, and now that you're all growed up, I'm off to 'prentice myself to a witch. This here girl," she pointed at me, "she's come from there to fetch me. And she knows all about brooms and hexings and impossible somethings."

They looked at me like grub-fed gobblers eyeing a sleeksty fox.

"Now you can go," she said.

They went.

All but one.

He sidled up to her and she hugged him, quick, then took his face in her hands.

"You'll be fine," she said. "Just remember to say 'please' and 'thank you' once in a while. And if you're ever in dire need, you come lookin' for me, with your best layin' hen as a gift, and I promise I won't hex you. All right?"

He nodded and skittered off.

"Nice horse," Any Girl said the next morning.

And sure 'nough, he was. His coat was coming in all thick, and his belly had rounded, and he held his head like someone was watching. He was strong enough to carry us both, and so it came about we fetched up at the witch's house the very night of the full moon.

The rain had just let up, and the chuckle was running high in its banks, and the humpty garden path was puddle-pocked.

My heart was awful low, on account of I didn't have all three impossible somethings.

"This'll do right fine," Any Girl said, looking about with her black eyes.

The door of the house opened and out came the witch, my baby brother on her hip. He was fat and happy, though he had no business to be.

"Well?" said the witch.

We clambered down off Horse.

"This here's the Any Girl you were wanting," I said.

"She'll do," the witch said. "What else?"

I dug around bottom of the rucksack. "And this here's the hair off a bald man."

The witch took off her kerchief, and she was hairless as a toad! She stuck the hair on her head, and tied her kerchief overtop of it, and I'll be jiggered if she didn't look right handsome.

"What else? That's a fine horse you stole, but he don't look like he could fly me over the moon."

"But I got two whole impossible somethings. And there's me. You can." I swallowed. "You can eat me. If it's needful to be eating folk. Or I can work for you. All the rest of my days."

"What would I need with you, when I got me my Any Girl?"

I couldn't help it. I commenced to cry.

"Come in for some vittles," the witch said. "Then I'll send you home to your mother, and the horse to his master."

Horse shook his head and stamped.

"Can't say I blame you," the witch said. "That old skinflint don't care for nothing and no one but his own ferrety self."

"Can't I hold my brother? Or pinch his toes, just once, to make him laugh?"

The witch shook her head. "He's mine now, and that's all there is to it."

"But you ain't going to eat him!"

"It's none of your business what I do with him. Now, come in. Or don't. It's all the same to me."

My last hope drained out of me and I sank to the ground. And right next to me was a puddle. With a wiry grey hair floating on it.

Hmmm. I thought. And then it came to me.

"Get up on Horse!" I said.

"You givin' me orders, girl?"

"But it's the third thing!"

The witch squinted at Horse. "I don't see no wings. Nor legs so strong he can bound on over Bright Lady, neither."

"Please."

The witch rolled her eyes, but she handed my brother to Any Girl, hitched her skirts, and scrambled up onto Horse.

"Well?"

I stroked his mole-soft nose, and asked, and he clippity cloppited down the path to a puddle brim-full of moonshine. He gathered himself, then sprang over the puddle, the witch clinging on tight as a tick.

"You didn't never say it had to be our moon," I crowed. "He just flew you over t'other-side moon."

And with that I took my brother, and I wished Any Girl luck, and off I went.

Behind me the witch muttered something, then the door of her house slammed so hard the shutters rattled.

"What'd she say?"

"She called you Clever Clogs," Any Girl said, laughing. Then she waved at me and went along inside too, like it was an everyday thing to go live in a witch's house, in the middle of a dark wood.

And then the itch came back, and this time I caught it.

I went back, and knocked.

"Two things more," I said to the witch.

"Ain't got all day."

"First, you got to watch out for wolves, on account of you soon won't have any hairs left on your chinny-chin-chin."

She soured her mouth at me. "And?"

"And second, you said everyday things don't win back a brother. You said everyday things don't prove love. But I ain't done nothin' but feed a hungry horse, and shovel muck, and help with choring, and listen to folk. And all those everyday

things, together, they add up to a kind of love. And they got me my brother back, what's more."
And I swear, that witch, she winked at me.
I pinched my brother's fat toes, and he squealed. And then I left, my heart as full as the moon.
We weren't far along, when from behind me came a clippity cloppit, and Horse about sidled me right off the lane.
"Shouldn't you go home too?" I said.
Horse nodded. So I climbed up.
And home was right where we went.

Sylvia Stopforth is a librarian by training, an archivist and editor by happy accident, and a writer by choice for sheer love of the thing.

She is the child and grandchild of Mennonite refugees and immigrants, grateful to be living and working in the southwest corner of Canada on the traditional lands of the Semiahmoo First Nation and the broader territory of the Coast Salish Peoples.

She has a degree in English Literature, which her mother suspected was merely an excuse to read (a wise woman, her mother). She also holds a Master's in Library and Information Studies. Her fiction and creative nonfiction have appeared in publications including *Room*, *The New Quarterly*, *Pulp Literature*, and *Shy: an Anthology*. For nearly twenty years, she edited a regular column for British Columbia History magazine.

Sylvia is currently working on a YA speculative fiction trilogy.

THE VESSEL OF THE NAMELESS GODDESS
SOON JONES

In the cool, early morning of spring's first new moon, Madam Yim brought her young wards onto the Lake of the Nameless Goddess on a boat, pushing off the lake's bottom with a long bamboo pole until it could no longer reach. As the first rays of sunlight rose over the tops of the trees, they drifted into the thick fog until their temple home on the shore disappeared.

The wards, all girls, wearing plain hanboks, huddled in the center of the boat for warmth. Except for Chohee, drawn to the edge of the boat, gripping the side with both hands as she slowly lowered her face closer to the water. Madam Yim smacked her fingers with the pole, and she snatched them back with a yelp.

"Not yet," Madam Yim said. "Wait your turn."

Chohee sat back down in the boat, rubbing the pain out of her knuckles. Her best friend gently nudged her shoulder.

"Sorry, Madam Yim," she murmured.

Chohee and the other six girls had all been born during the once-a-century arrival of the Great Heavenly Comet, marking them as a potential vessel for the Nameless Goddess whose spirit resided in the lake. After their tenth winter, they had all left their families' homes to live together in the village temple with Madam Yim to purify their bodies and strengthen their ties to the spirit world. Now, ten long years later, one of them would become the next vessel, and the rest would be commoners again.

The Nameless Goddess had resided in her lake for thousands of years. She blessed her people with favorable rains for their harvests and abundant, delicious fish for their tables and markets, sought out by even royal chefs for the king's table in the distant capital city.

Like their goddess, the seven wards had kept their names to themselves during the entirety of the decade they had served in the temple, if they had been named at all. Chohee didn't even know the name of her best friend, with whom she had eaten every meal, stolen wine from the kitchen, and sneaked out of the temple into the village late at night just to see if they could.

Madam Yim looked to the heavens, waiting for some sign, then tapped the fishmonger's daughter with the pole.

"You. Go," Madam Yim said.

With trembling hands, the fishmonger's daughter approached the edge of the boat and looked down at her reflection.

"What do you see?" Madam Yim asked.

"I only see fog," she confessed.

"Very well. Next," Madam Yim said.

The fishmonger's daughter returned to the center of the boat sniffling, big tears rolling down her cheeks. Her friends comforted her with gentle words. She was just another commoner now.

"Silence!" Madam Yim barked. "Do not distract the others."

The second girl went forward, and she, too, saw only fog. The third as well. The fourth girl, her dear friend, was the first to see.

"A fighter, with a face covered in blood, surrounded by flames," she said, her voice shaking. She looked up with wonder in her eyes. Madam Yim smiled.

"Our Nameless Goddess has chosen to show you a vision of your future son. Rejoice, for he will surely be a great general of whom many songs will be written. Next," she said.

But her friend did not look happy. She looked disturbed.

The fifth girl saw a beautiful young nobleman, and Madam Yim declared it would be her future suitor. Finally, Chohee was allowed to approach, and once again she peered down into the water, keeping her sore hands close to her stomach. A patch of fog stirred and cleared away, and she held her breath as she leaned farther over the edge.

The boat gently rocked, yet the water was as still as glass. A featureless face, a flat brown oval matching her own sun-darkened skin appeared. Slowly, her own face was etched into the lake's surface, wearing an expression she could not decipher. Her own eyes were wide, but her reflection's eyes were hooded, as if she held mysteries that she did not care to reveal.

"Well? What do you see?" Madam Yim demanded.

"I see myself," Chohee said, leaning so close to the water that her nose nearly touched.

A rough wave suddenly struck the boat, and she fell headfirst into the cold lake. The weight of her layered hanbok pulled her down into the depths, and she flailed her arms and legs, though she had never learned to swim. She tried to hold her breath, but her lungs screamed for air and her traitorous mouth opened anyway, sucking in water.

An intense loneliness seized her as she watched the bottom of the boat drift away while she sank. Somehow, she had always known that she would not survive past this day. Her own family had fallen ill and died of sickness only months after she had joined the other girls in the temple, and now she was dying, alone and unwanted. She stopped struggling. At least death would be better than this loneliness she felt.

Something struck her hard in the chest: the end of Madam Yim's bamboo pole, searching for her in the depths. It struck her side, and her hands grabbed it automatically. She flew through the water and broke the surface with a gasp. Some of the other girls were there at the edge of the boat, grabbing her hanbok and her arms, pulling her to safety. The feeling of loneliness subsided as she left the lake.

The fishmonger's daughter turned her on her side, and her friend struck her back hard. She threw up all the water she had swallowed, and the other girls squealed and jumped back, rocking the boat even more. Only her friend stayed.

"Steady, steady!" Madam Yim called, kneeling beside Chohee. "Do you live, girl?"

Chohee's nose and throat burned. She nodded, too weak to speak.

"Did you see anything in the lake?"

Chohee shook her head.

Madam Yim picked her up and leaned her against the front of the boat, where it pinched into a point.

"Stay there and don't fall in again," she commanded.

When the other girls had settled, Madam Yim tapped the last girl, the nobleman's daughter. No one was supposed to know she was a nobleman's daughter, but it was obvious by her pale, glowing skin, untouched by the sun even though they all had to do outdoor chores, and how her long black hair always shone in any light, healthy and lustrous. Her features, too, were beautiful: a small, petite face carved from ivory.

She approached the edge of the boat and peered down at her reflection.

"I see a beautiful woman crowned with seven stars, holding a scepter of twin dragons around a pearl."

Madam Yim clapped her hands together and covered her

face, then got down on her knees and bowed low to the nobleman's daughter. The other girls did the same, except for Chohee. She locked eyes with the nobleman's daughter over the others' heads. Envy burned in her heart.

The Nameless Goddess had chosen her next vessel.

There was a festival in the village that very night, celebrating the next cycle of the Nameless Goddess. Colorful silk and paper lanterns were hung from every home and along the streets and alleyways, some folded into the shapes of lotuses, frogs, and dragons. At the temple, villagers brought offerings before the stone statue of the Nameless Goddess, with her seven-starred crown and scepter of twin dragons entwined around a pearl. A fan covered her face, etched with the story of how she had angered the other gods through insolence and so was cast from the heavens into the lake, losing both her name and face in the process. Now she protected the villagers as part of her divine penance, forever separated from her celestial family.

The offerings were stacked plates of fruit and confections, cooked rice, the best catches of fish, and spring wine that had been fermented throughout the long winter. The spirits, ancestors, and local household gods would come and feast on the offerings, draining them of their energy, and later the villagers would share and feast on the same food.

Chohee played her part with the other five unchosen girls by arranging the offerings to their proper place while shamans in colorful robes danced with knives and bells, calling down their gods into their bodies. They walked unharmed on beds of nails, ran sharp swords along their tongues, and then with grins showed their uncut tongues to the villagers. They re-enacted stories of the gods and of humans who had walked the spiritual plain, some full of joy and laughter, some of tragedy and sorrow. Their apprentices, lovers, and village musicians beat complex rhythms on animal-hide drums and cymbals and loudly sang old folk songs.

The nobleman's daughter, dressed now in a vibrant silk hanbok, her hair done up with jewel-encrusted combs and tiny bells, sat cross-legged at a table to the side and heard the villagers' wishes and prayers as they brought their offerings. Royal emissaries and stone-faced monks from the capital, unamused by the shamans' raucous performances, sat on either side of her, whispering words from the king into her ears. She was not the vessel yet, but already she was elevated to godhood in everyone's eyes.

When the last of the offerings were at last placed, Chohee slipped away. She climbed the old, crooked pine tree growing beside the courtyard walls as she had a thousand times before, sitting in its branches and watching the shamans dance in peace. It didn't last long. She had just gotten comfortable when her dear friend walked up to the base of the tree.

"May I join you?" she asked, raising a ceramic jug and a clay bowl. "I brought wine."

"If you can climb on your own," Chohee replied.

Her friend grinned and quickly made her way up the tree with only one hand, sitting beside Chohee. Balancing against the trunk and bracing her foot against an opposing branch, she poured cloudy rice wine into the bowl, took a deep drink, then handed it to Chohee. The cool wine chilled her throat and stomach. She shivered, and her friend poured another drink for them both.

"I took this from the offering table," her friend said casually as Chohee took her second sip.

Chohee choked but did not spit it out. She smacked her friend's arm.

"You can't do that!" she said.

"The spirits have plenty. They won't miss one bottle," she said, shrugging, then removed a paper-wrapped package from the inside of her hanbok. "They won't miss a couple of honey cakes, either."

Chohee smacked her arm again, but she still took one of the cakes. She'd already drunk the wine, after all, and besides, she was just another unwanted girl now, with no family and no prospects. What more could the spirits do to her that hadn't already been done?

"So. Will you tell me your name?" the girl asked.

"My name?" Chohee blurted, startled. "Why would you want to know my name?"

"Because we've lived together for ten years. Isn't that enough? Don't you want to know my name, too? I'll go first," her friend said. "Lee Gangwol. My family lives to the south."

"I'm Chohee. Just Chohee," she said.

"Chohee," Gangwol said slowly and smiled.

She blushed. It was the first time she had heard her name spoken from someone else's lips in a decade, and maybe the first time she had ever heard it spoken with such care.

They climbed from the pine tree onto the courtyard wall and drank the rest of the wine together, hushing whenever someone walked by underneath their tree, laughing as they leaned into each other, and Chohee felt light as air. When the shamans had finished their rituals, the monks from the capitol at last were allowed to pray in long, monotonous chants none of the villagers could even understand. She leaned back on her hands, sleepy and content, and watched the stars instead.

"If I tell you something, will you promise not to share it with anyone else?" Gangwol asked.

"Of course," Chohee said.

Gangwol stared hard at the chanting monks, her arm resting on the knee of her widespread leg, looking anything but ladylike.

"The vision I saw. It wasn't a man's face. It was a woman's," she said at last. Then she breathed in deep, held it, and sighed. "It was mine."

Chohee sat up straight, wobbled a little from the wine, but Gangwol reached out and grabbed the back of her hanbok, keeping her from falling.

"What does that mean?" she asked.

"I'm not sure. But I don't think I'm ever going to be a mother. I think I'm going to die in battle one day," Gangwol said.

"A woman general," Chohee said in awe. "Madam Yim was right: they'll write songs about you."

"I wonder if they'll be good ones," Gangwol said, drinking the dregs straight from the jug. "Did you really not see anything when you fell in the lake?"

"Nothing."

Gangwol nodded, deep in thought.

"I thought for sure when you fell that the goddess was taking you then and there."

"I thought she was taking me, too, at first," Chohee said with a heavy sigh of her own. "If she had chosen me, I would never let you die in battle. I would follow you and keep you safe."

Gangwol laughed and nudged her shoulder.

"War would take me far away from here. How would you protect me from the lake?"

"There are rivers and springs. And rain. I would hop from puddle to puddle on one foot, like this," Chohee said.

She stood halfway up, balanced on one foot, when she toppled forward. Gangwol grabbed her by the waist and pulled her close, keeping her from falling again, laughing all the while.

"I'm glad you weren't chosen," Gangwol said. "It would be lonely without you. But now, we're both free. We can be whatever we want."

Chohee stopped laughing.

"I wanted to be the Nameless Goddess's vessel," she admitted. "I wanted it more than anything. Didn't you?"

Gangwol just smiled and shook her head.

The royal emissaries and the monks bowed to the nobleman's daughter as she was taken away by Madam Yim to prepare for her joining with the goddess. Then they made their way to the back of the courtyard, past the sleeping quarters, through the eastern gate, and toward the vessel's raft laden with flowers and ritual instruments, along with the other boats where lanterns and fish offerings would be carried out onto the lake.

Chohee jerked up: something was wrong. They should not be approaching the raft without Madam Yim or any of the shamans. It was a closed ceremony to anyone outside of the village.

"Look! Where do they think they're going?" Chohee asked, pointing to the emissaries and monks.

Gangwol watched the group and frowned. She stood up and held the jug like a weapon.

"Let's follow them," she said.

Quickly and quietly, they scampered across the courtyard wall on their hands and feet, dropped to ground, and followed the men from the shadows.

"Be sure to bless the wine," one of the emissaries said as they stepped onto the raft.

A monk pulled a silver vial from his robe, unstoppered the sacred wine, and upended the vial into the jug. He sat and chanted as the other monks spread some sort of dust in complex circular patterns on the raft.

"It is blessed now, my lord," the monk said. "When their goddess descends into her new body, she will be too weak to escape the dying vessel."

"Good. Soldiers should be here soon to stop any villagers who try to get in our way. Their heathen goddess will be cast to the underworld, and this sacred lake and all its power will belong to our Heavenly General and our king," the emissary said.

Chohee covered her mouth. The Heavenly General was a new military god from the capital who demanded sacrifice from the battlefield. How dare they come and supplant their goddess who had watched over their village since before the Heavenly General had even been born? Red-hot righteous fury boiled Chohee's blood, and she ran at them, ready to kill —but Gangwol yanked her back into the brush.

"What was that?" a younger emissary said, peering into the dark.

"The soldiers taking their positions, or a night bird catching its prey," a monk suggested.

"You heard them—soldiers are coming. We have to warn the others," Gangwol whispered.

"Aren't you supposed to be a general yourself in your future? We must kill them and protect our goddess," Chohee said, seething.

"We will only be killed ourselves, and then the new vessel will unknowingly go to her death and sever the Nameless Goddess's ties to our realm. Come, Madam Yim will know what to do," Gangwol said, pulling her back toward the temple.

A group of soldiers wearing tall black hats with purple imperial feathers stepped out of the trees and blocked their path, swords drawn.

"Little sisters, what are you doing out here without a chaperone?" a soldier asked. "It's dangerous to be out here alone."

"It wasn't dangerous until you came," Chohee said, and spat on him.

"We have holy business at the temple. Our gods will curse you if you hinder us," Gangwol said, raising her chin.

"How can I let you go when you have disrespected me like

this?" the head soldier demanded, wiping the spit from his cheek with a glare. "Don't you know that spitting on an imperial soldier is the same as spitting on the king?"

Gangwol stepped in front of Chohee, shielding her with her body. Lanterns lit up farther down the lakeshore, where most of the village would be watching the ceremony. Past the soldiers and through the open courtyard gate, villagers carried the nobleman's daughter on a plain palanquin, proceeded in front by the other four wards carrying silk lanterns on poles, led by Madam Yim. Behind the palanquin, more villagers beat on drums and sang in drunken celebration.

"It's a trap!" Chohee shouted. "They've poisoned the wine! It's a tr—"

The soldiers moved fast as serpents, grabbing both of the girls and covering their mouths. Chohee bit down hard and the soldier holding her grunted in pain but did not remove his hand, his blood filling her mouth as they were dragged into the trees. Gangwol smashed the jug on another soldier's head, and he collapsed, but two more grabbed her.

"Should we kill them?" one of the men asked.

"No—not until their goddess is dead. If their blood is spilled on the earth, she may sense the threat," the head soldier said.

The more the girls struggled, the tighter the soldiers held them, pulling them farther and farther into the woods. She kicked and bit even as the procession moved past them toward the raft, the music drowning out their desperate silent battle.

The royal emissaries and monks bowed to Madam Yim as they approached.

"Haven't you retired to your rooms?" she asked.

The eldest emissary smiled at her. "We humbly request you let us stay and observe the ceremony. We may never have a chance to witness a god fully possessing a mortal again. We will be sure to tell our king of this glorious occasion."

"Goddess," Madam Yim corrected. "Very well. For the sake of our king, you may stay and observe. From the shore."

"Could not one of our monks join the party on the raft, so we may give a more accurate account to our king? He would surely bless your village with many riches," the emissary said.

"With my deepest apologies, I must insist you remain on the shore."

The emissary gave a slight bow of his head and relented. Helplessly, Chohee could only watch as the nobleman's daughter, Madam Yim, and her fellow wards stepped onto the raft and pushed out into the water, the rest of the procession climbing into the other boats to follow.

Gangwol got an arm free, and she grabbed a sword from one of the soldiers holding her, running him through. She slayed another before the others could react. Chohee got a soldier's finger in her mouth and bit clean through the bone. The soldier let go of her, screaming, and she spit the finger onto the ground.

"Don't kill them yet!" the head soldier cried, even as he struggled to disarm Gangwol without spilling her blood.

Gangwol fought like she had been born with a sword in her hand, as elegant as she was deadly. She shoved Chohee behind her and waved the sword in the remaining soldiers' faces, backing away towards the water.

"I'll hold them off! Go!" she cried.

Trusting in the vision the Nameless Goddess had given Gangwol—that she would one day fight in a future battle—Chohee ran toward the water. She looked back once just as a soldier struck Gangwol in the temple with a rock, knocking her to the ground.

Tears stung her eyes, but she could not go back for her beloved. She had to save the Nameless Goddess. She screamed warnings as she ran to the boats, but her voice was lost in the drums and singing. A royal emissary grabbed her by her jeogori as she tried to run past him, holding her back.

"Little sister, where are you going? The raft has already left," he said.

Chohee quickly yanked her jeogori's knot loose and slipped out of the little jacket. She ran into the water, ignoring the shouts behind her. Perhaps it was her blind faith or sheer desperation, but for once her arms and legs carved a path through the water like the fins of a fish.

But the raft pulled farther away as Madam Yim uncorked the tainted wine and poured it into a bowl for the nobleman's daughter.

Chohee screamed again, but she sank and choked on water. She thrashed, using every last bit of strength she had to claw her way to the surface.

A hand reached down and pulled her up and into a boat, smacking her hard on the back. She coughed up the water and saw Gangwol, pushing hard along the lakebed with a bamboo pole in a boat left behind, her face covered in blood from the cut on her temple.

The emissaries and monks chased them on another boat. Three soldiers stood at the bow, swords drawn. Behind them, the trees lit up with flaming arrows. Panic seized her: they weren't going to kill the Nameless Goddess with poison. They were going to burn her and everyone else on the raft.

"Madam Yim!" she cried.

At last, Madam Yim turned around and saw them just as the nobleman's daughter lifted the bowl to her lips.

"It's poison!" Chohee screamed, jumping out of the boat and onto the raft. "Don't drink!"

Madam Yim spun around to yank the bowl back, but it was already empty. The nobleman's daughter looked up at her, startled. Chohee held her breath.

Silence hung in the air. The waters did not part. The Nameless Goddess did not appear.

"What is the meaning of this?" Madam Yim demanded.

The nobleman's daughter burst into tears.

"I'm sorry!" she cried. "I lied. I didn't see anything in my reflection. I only saw fog."

She threw herself at Madam Yim's feet and grabbed her leg, wailing.

"Please forgive me! My father told me if I didn't become the Nameless Goddess I could never return! I didn't know what to do!"

The other four girls gasped. The wrong girl had drunk the wine. The ritual had failed. The Nameless Goddess could not ascend for another hundred years, her protection and ties to the land severed. The emissaries and monks hadn't even needed to sabotage the ritual; they had already won the moment the nobleman's daughter had lied.

Flaming arrows fell from the sky like stars, striking the raft. Chohee and the others quickly stamped them out, but it only took one arrow to strike the circle of dust the monk had scattered, and a raging fire swirled up. The other boats in the water started moving towards the raft, but they were too far away.

Chohee and Gangwol grabbed Madam Yim and the other girls, guiding them to the small boat they had taken. Gangwol reached back for Chohee but when she stepped in, the boat began to sink, already at its limit. It couldn't support her weight and her friends' at the same time. She and Gangwol locked eyes, and then Chohee stepped back onto the raft and shoved the boat away with her foot, hard.

"What are you doing? Get in!" Gangwol cried as the water took her away.

Chohee turned away to face the flames. She had failed her goddess, but at least the others would be saved.

The raft suddenly dipped as Gangwol climbed on: she had jumped from the boat and swam back.

"What are you doing?" Chohee said, shaking. "You'll be killed."

"I'll carry you to shore!" Gangwol said.

Chohee held onto the back of Gangwol's jeogori, and they jumped into the water, but their soaked hanboks weighed them down. They struggled to keep their heads above the surface. Finally, they both took hold of the raft's edge, gasping for air.

"Go without me. Live for us both," Chohee said, but Gangwol shook her head.

"This is my fate. To die here with you, surrounded by flames," Gangwol said, her silhouette crowned with flames, tears streaking down her face. "I always thought we would have more time, that after tonight, when we were truly free, I could finally tell you I love you. I'm sorry, Chohee. I wasted the ten years we had."

Chohee held on tight to Gangwol, opened her mouth to say that she loved her, too, that every morning she had woken up looking forward to seeing her face, that none of it had been a waste—but something grabbed her ankle and dragged her into the lake. The water pulled her down faster than Gangwol could swim after her, bubbles covering her face as she screamed in frustration.

And then, all was still. From the bottom of the lake came a light, and a woman swam up like a fish, clothed in a plain, undyed hanbok, skin browned by the sun, her face a blank and featureless oval. She took Chohee's hands, and she was no longer choking on the water, but breathing it as freely as she did air. Features were etched onto the woman's face until it was Chohee's own reflection staring back at her.

And then she understood. The Nameless Goddess, who had lost her identity when she was cast from the heavens, took on the name and face of her vessels. The Nameless Goddess embraced Chohee as they became one flesh and one spirit, and she felt again her goddess's unbearable loneliness, eased by their joining. Through the Nameless Goddess, Chohee would at last have the power to protect her village and the ones she cared for. And through Chohee, the Nameless Goddess would no longer be alone, at least for a time.

Together as one body, she ascended through the water, taking Gangwol and placing her gently on the raft. She floated high above the surface of the lake and held out her hand, water swirling up to take the shape of her scepter. With a single sweep, storm clouds suddenly filled the clear sky, and a torrent of rain quenched the flames on the raft and the archers' arrows.

The emissaries and monks fell prostrate in their stolen boat, crying out for her forgiveness. Her twin dragons rose from the depths, made of lake water, and devoured the men whole. The dragons swept into the trees, swimming through the air, and tore the imperial soldiers limb from limb.

She felt the presence of the Heavenly General, her young nephew, angry that his followers had failed. This would never be his land. This would never be his lake. Her fellow celestial gods had believed tying her to the mortal world would make her weak and teach her her place, but it had only made her stronger and more defiant. She would never again bow to any god or king.

Across the lake and the shore, her villagers sang her praises and celebrated her return. All but Gangwol, standing on the raft and watching her with sorrow. When the dragons had finished their meals and returned once again to the lake's depths, she set foot on the raft as Chohee the human girl, not Chohee the Named Goddess. She stroked Gangwol's cheek with a tender hand.

"We were going to be free," Gangwol said, choking on tears. "Both of us. But now, you're going away from me, to somewhere I can't reach."

"But I am free. Truly free to walk the worlds of spirits and humans as I wish, with whom I wish," Chohee said, brushing a tear away with her thumb. "Will you walk with me?"

"Always," Gangwol said.

Gangwol kissed her deeply, and both of Chohee's hearts flooded with joy to love and be loved in return. The storm clouds cleared, and the lake shone with stars.

Soon Jones is a Korean lesbian poet and fiction writer from the rural countryside of the American South. Growing up, Soon spent much of their time in the library reading as many books on myths and fairy tales as possible. They dreamed of one day creating their own mythology. Not much has changed since then.

"The Vessel of the Nameless Goddess," while influenced and inspired by tales and accounts from their motherland, is based on that created mythology and should not be taken as historically accurate. Soon's work has been published (or is forthcoming) in Moon City Review, beestung, Typehouse Literary Magazine, and Emerge: Lambda Literary Fellows Anthology, and others. They can be found at soonjones.com.

WRITING UNTIL THE END
ROBERT J. MCCARTER

I was having a good day.

It was the Saturday Market in Portland, Oregon, a swirl of people and commerce and sounds and scents, and I was standing in front of a white pop-up tent with bright and fragrant fruit arrayed in wooden crates.

As the years have rolled on, I've found "good" to be a highly relative term. For me, today, that meant I was only mildly nauseous, just kind of tired, and only fairly melancholy.

But I had ventured out, and I liked it here because of the swirling of all those things, because I could feel like I wasn't alone and still have my anonymity. If anyone here asked me how I was doing, it was a perfunctory question and no one would challenge me for saying "just fine."

I wasn't fine. I was sick, and I was well and truly alone, and even introverts like me had their limits.

But it was a good day, and I was on a quest to find the perfect mango, enjoying a healthy helping of people watching, when a face jumped out of the crowd.

That is an odd turn of phrase, "jumped out of the crowd,"

when what happened was my roaming eye stopped roaming when I saw him.

He had a lean face with pronounced frown lines around his thin lips, his cheeks starting to hollow out, his broad forehead and bushy eyebrows leaving his blue-gray eyes to sink into his face. There were dark circles under those eyes, and a splash of brown and gray stubble on his face.

For a moment the jangle of sounds and smells and colors all receded, and it was just him and me as our eyes met and, I presume, my face jumped out of the crowd at him.

There was a good reason our faces were doing all this "jumping out." His face was my face, but not exactly. His was the face of a man who thought he was getting old, while my face was that of a man who knew he was old.

It was just a moment, and I couldn't be sure he had been really looking at me. And then he turned and melted into the swirling crowd of humanity.

I didn't have the knees or the energy to give much of a chase, but I put down the mango I had been examining, pulled up the hood of my rain jacket, and followed the man with my younger face.

I don't like pictures of the past. That annoying feature of smartphones where they want to share your old photos just irritates me. I don't take very many pictures because of it. I don't want to see my younger self. I am not him anymore, and yet I am living with his mistakes and the consequences of his naïveté, his laziness, and his foolishness—as well as all the good things my younger self did, but I don't find it easy to focus on those.

I, of course, understand that as I write this account that my older self will likely view it with similar disdain, having the twenty-twenty hindsight that I, unfortunately, lack.

As I followed the man who appeared to be my younger self through the colorful and crowded expanse of the Portland Saturday Market, my mind was a jumbled mess of thoughts. Things such as cloning, time travel, and other such nonsense that fiction writers such as myself often ponder flitted through my very active imagination.

He should have easily lost me, the man with my younger face, but I found him stopped at a stall examining colorful jars of homemade jams and jellies, but something about the stiff set of his shoulders led me to believe he wasn't paying any attention to the vendor's wares.

He was dressed all in tan with long pants and a many-pocketed long-sleeved shirt, the kind I was quite fond of because you could stash so many different things in it. On his head, covering his short brown, sliding-to-gray hair was an Australian slouch hat, one side of the brim pinned up to allow one to carry a rifle.

It was a sunny day, and in a crowd of shorts and flipflops, he stood out.

When he walked away from the stall, I realized what had first drawn my attention to him, besides the unusual clothing: his walk. It was quick and confident, the walk of someone who looked like they always knew where they were going even when they were lost.

An idea tickled the back of my brain, one much more interesting than time travel or cloning, an idea that terrified me but kept me walking long after I was tired. Past food trucks with delightful scents wafting out. Past flower vendors with colors so vibrant and scents so intoxicating. Past a man juggling machetes for a crowd. Past the sea of the white pop-up tents of the market into a small, treed park sitting next to the calm blue of the Willamette River.

The man was leaning against a tree staring across the river at the twin glass towers of the Oregon Convention Center.

"About time," he said as I approached, his eyes still on the towers. His voice too was familiar. It didn't sound the way I thought my voice sounded, but like it really was, like the recordings of my voice I have heard.

"Excuse me?" I asked. A wholly inadequate reply but all I had in me.

He turned and looked at me, his blue-gray eyes intense—it was like looking into a mirror, one that reflected the past. He looked me up and down, and his thin lips quirked into a brief smile.

I was tall and too thin, wearing cargo shorts and a blue T-shirt with a blue rain jacket on top.

"Somehow I thought you would be taller than me," he said.

I opened my mouth to speak, but I couldn't find any words at all this time.

He took a breath and sighed, pointing at the glass towers across the river. "We've got a room over there," he said. "Under the name Rogers International. Come see us all if you dare."

My knees went weak as he strolled confidently off.

Rogers International was the name of a fictional company from my most popular series of books. One featuring a tall, globe-trotting historian who always wore an Australian slouch hat.

The Oregon Convention Center was vast. The two glass towers let sunlight into the space, which was part of their sustainability initiative, the vast roof covered with solar panels. My feet echoed in the empty hall, the air smelling faintly of disinfectant, the hollowness of the space feeling somehow wrong or dangerous.

Of course people had approached me about Alan Rogers,

about the sixth book in the series where I gave him a happily ever after, the adventuresome professor meeting the love of his life and finally settling down in Greece. Readers could be strangely fascinated with my fictional worlds, and demands for more Alan Rogers books got to me occasionally.

I had received the strangest come-ons over the years. A rich Japanese businessman once offered me a million dollars to continue Alan's story. I always spurned such offers—this was not how I wrote—but I had never had anyone approach me with my own face and my own voice.

Despite what you might see in the movies, no disguises were good enough for what I'd seen, like I was looking into a mirror that showed the past. Such things were inventions of writers and the work of special-effects artists.

In the middle of the vast hall were three round tables with people sitting and milling about. I couldn't hear the words, but the tone of the voices and the frequent laughter made it sound like a gathering of old friends or family.

As I drew close, the talking stopped, and all eyes were on me. It was a strange assortment of people, young and old, men and women, none of them dressed like tourists.

An elegant older woman in a long gray skirt stood near one of the tables, a cane in her hand she clearly didn't need, blue-gray eyes shining forth from her deeply wrinkled skin.

A young boy with bright blond hair wearing dark blue shorts was swinging his legs hard enough they smacked the bottom of his chair. He looked up shyly at me, but only for a moment.

A shorter man with broad shoulders, his eyes shifty and his arms folded over a dark suit that belonged in the fifties, stared at me.

I stood there and stared, my knees going weak again. Each one of them stared at me with the same blue-gray eyes, and I knew each and every one of them.

The older woman was named Claire Page, a former

librarian who solved mysteries in the quaint seaside town where she lived.

The boy was Bobby Simmons, dressed in his boarding-school uniform, a troubled child who had seen his parents murdered and was wrestling with burgeoning psychic powers.

The shifty-eyed man was a gangster who, through his brutal tactics, thought he was what his inner-city neighborhood needed.

There were at least twenty of them, each one someone I knew well, because each one had sprung forth from my imagination and were a part of one of my stories.

I stood there, my jaw moving, no words coming out. This wasn't possible. This couldn't be. This could only mean one thing, that I was a lot sicker than I had thought. That the cancer had clearly gotten into my brain.

Alan Rogers unfolded himself from a chair and spoke quietly to the rest of them and headed toward me.

I didn't wait. I turned around and walked away as fast as my tired body would take me.

"How else would you believe me?" the fictional character Alan Rogers asked as he caught up to me, answering my unasked question.

I could hear the soft murmur of my character's voices behind me, but I didn't turn, I didn't look at the man with my younger face. I kept walking.

He, unfortunately, kept talking. "It's not like I could just walk up to you and say, 'Hi, I'm the guy from all your books and I need your help.'"

My hand shook as I opened the door to the conference hall and exited into the long curving hallway, glad to get carpet under my feet and for the echoing to stop. I pulled my phone from my rain jacket and brought up the ride-sharing app and called for a car.

"I needed to prove this to you," he said.

I finally looked at him, his face earnest and pain in his eyes, in my own eyes. Not all of them looked like me, like Alan, although many had some of my facial characteristics, but each and every one of them had my eyes. I hadn't written them all with blue-gray eyes—Alan certainly, and Claire—but not all of them.

Amongst the swirl of chaotic thoughts, that is the one that took over. "You all have the same eyes," I said, my voice sounding distant.

Alan smiled. It was a good smile, one that had served him well over the years. He nodded. "And I bet you're thinking about Robert Heinlein's book, *The Number of the Beast.*"

I nodded. "They had that ship with the 'continua' device, and they could travel into parallel universes. In it Heinlein posited that fictional characters all existed out there somewhere."

Alan nodded again, and I had a brief moment of hope. Maybe there was an explanation—not that it was a simple one, but one I could at least grok (to borrow a word from Heinlein). But then Alan's smile disappeared, and he bit his lip. "But that's not what's going on," he said, looking around. "We should talk, but not here."

The act of writing has often felt more like an act of discovery than one of invention, the stories slowly unfolding as I write, my job being to listen to my characters rather than telling them what to do.

One of the sublime joys of writing, for me, has been to write my characters into corners where no escape seems possible and watch them escape, nonetheless.

But it seemed my characters had escaped the bounds of their fictional world ... or my mind was well and truly gone. One or the other.

As Alan and I sat in the back seat of a Prius that smelled faintly of old Chinese food and the unusually sunny Portland slipped by, I decided to let go of the worry, to listen to my character, and to see where this particular story would go.

I was having a good day, which was why I'd come out to the market in the first place, and I might as well lean into it. I didn't have a lot of time left, so why not indulge my characters one last time? Even if they were just figments of my imagination.

If truth be told, I hadn't written a thing in three years. Not since my wife died. For decades it was a daily practice. Early in the morning, often when the sun was rising, I would get up, brew some tea, and go indulge my characters.

I sneaked a glance at Alan, and he was staring out the window. We were on I-5 heading north, and while the view wasn't inspiring, between the bland industrial buildings the grass was sparkling green in the sunlight, and the trees were tall and verdant.

I was never precious about writing, worked it like a job, and found that inspiration came to those who were actually doing the work. But grief was the one thing I found that can steal it away. Grace's death took all my words from me. She was my biggest fan, and she's the reason I wrote many of those books.

But I have missed them—my characters, that is. I, of course, miss Grace, and if my mind was truly gone, I'd much rather it be her I summon to life. But when I could write, my characters always provided me a much-needed escape into other worlds and created structure around my day.

"How have you been?" I asked Alan. He'd gotten all secretive with me at the convention center, but this was a totally normal question. "You got married, right?"

He gave me a quizzical smile, and his right eyebrow raised in question. I had finished Alan's series right when Grace got sick. He had one last rousing world-saving adventure, met the love of his life, and went off to his happily ever after.

"I did," he said, his face darkening. "As it turns out, I just wasn't built for a quiet life in Greece."

"No ..." I began. "But you and Grace. You were perfect for each other." And, yes, I named the love of Alan's life after the love of my life. Grace really adored those books.

As we talked, I watched the rearview mirror and the face of our driver reflected there. I could be fooling myself, but he appeared to be glancing back at both of us. I was too afraid to ask him if there were two of us.

Alan turned away and stared at the trees whipping by, a row of giant firs, tall and bristly, planted right next to the road. "We tried, god knows we tried. But ... I got bored ... and when I get bored ..." He trailed off.

"You started drinking again?" I asked. I had made Alan Rogers a recovering alcoholic to add some depth to the usual action/adventure tropes.

He didn't look at me and nodded.

A wave of sadness crashed over me, and the bright day was no longer a comfort. I sank down into the seat, pulling my raincoat close. I was grieving for Alan and his Grace. But it made sense. Alan Rogers wasn't a man to settle down. And then I felt guilty I had written an ending that wasn't true to the character.

The rest of the ride to my house was silent, too silent.

"I don't think I can write anymore," I said.

Alan and I were sitting at the breakfast nook in my house, the bay windows looking out over several acres of freshly mowed grass with dense trees beyond, the fluffy white clouds flitting by, casting shadows on the brightly lit scene.

Two steaming cups of tea sat on the table untouched. I breathed in the earthy scent, waiting for Alan to reply, but he was just staring out the window.

I liked the view myself. I had walked hundreds of miles on that lawn. With Grace. With our dogs when we had them. By myself, my brain sifting through story ideas as my body rambled over the gentle slopes of the land.

"Since Grace, I ..." I began. Surely he knew this. Surely I didn't need to spell it out. "And I'm sick," I added. "Today's a good day, but most are not anymore."

I was managing still. I had food brought in and house-keepers to clean, but I was still able to take care of myself. For how much longer, I had no idea.

Alan looked at me, the smallest of smiles briefly deco-rating his thin face. It was one of those bitter little smiles that lean toward a grimace. "I need you to write," he said, his words simple, his tone flat, but the energy behind it still apparent. "I need a different ending."

Guilt mixed with the strong brew of self-pity that was already swirling through me, and I looked away. "I can't," I said.

The wooden chair he was sitting in scraped against the tile of the kitchen. He walked away, and then the front door opened and closed.

A few moments later there were more steps, softer steps, and the wrinkled form of Claire Page entered, her gray hair piled into a tight bun on her head, her long gray skirt swirling around her as she walked in, carrying her cane but not using it.

"I need some kind of an ending," she said.

The cozy seaside mysteries Claire solved were all stand-alones, and I had stopped writing her about ten years ago when my brain got interested in writing other things.

She walked away and was replaced by Bobby Simmons in his dark-blue boarding-school uniform, his blond hair a tousled mess and falling into his eyes. "I need to find my parents' killer."

It went on from there, character after character asking for their own ending. Fortunately, not every major character I had created—apparently some were satisfied with where I left them—but many of my most vivid characters visited me. Asked me to start writing again, to start listening to them again.

In the end, Alan was back in that chair and took a noisy sip of tea. "We need you to write."

Earlier I said I have found "good" to be a relative term. As in a "good" day or a "good" thing. The same can be said for "bad." It too is relative.

Having your characters parade in front of you and ask you to write their endings could really go either way. And if we are talking in terms of story genre, this could easily be a horror story I found myself in the middle of. A dying man haunted by his characters who insist he write the endings they wanted, the endings they needed.

Horror indeed.

I have found that life doesn't easily fit into one genre, the themes and emotions as jumbled as the sounds and smells at the Saturday Market. There was horror in everyday life, to be sure, but also wonder, plenty of science fiction as reality caught up with imagination, romance, and even a mystery here or there.

After Alan came back, I Facetimed my friend Blake, another writer who lived in the drab desert of Phoenix, Arizona.

"Hey, how you doin'?" Blake asked. His round face was

bouncing on my smartphone as saguaro cactus and blurry desert views slid by. He was on a hike.

"It's a good day," I said. "An interesting day."

Across from me, Alan raised his bushy right eyebrow.

"Glad to hear it, brother," Blake said. He was a few years younger than me with a long graying ponytail and bulbous nose. "What can I do you for?"

"I just need a confirmation of reality," I said.

Blake stopped, the stark beauty of his surroundings coming into focus. We had known each other a long time and had many discussions about the pitfalls of following your imagination for a living. "I'm here," he said.

I got up and walked around the wooden table to where Alan was. He kindly stood, and I held the phone so we were both visible.

"Shit!" Blake said. "You gotta younger brother you didn't tell me about?"

My stomach did a few Olympics-quality gymnastics tumbling runs, and I couldn't tell if I was terrified or excited or both.

"Blake," I said. "I would like you to meet Alan Rogers. Alan, this is Blake Young."

Blake's brown eyes got wide, and he suddenly looked much younger, like a little kid who had just seen Santa Claus. He blinked, turned around, the desert swirling behind him, and started walking the other direction.

"Reality confirmed," he said. "I'll be there in five hours. Don't let him go anywhere."

"I still can't write," I said as Alan and I strolled the lawn in the back of my house. "Certainly not enough to finish all your stories. The cancer is back, and I'm not doing another round of chemo. Not without Grace."

Alan's stride was graceful and easy, while mine was slow and halting. Although this was a good day, my energy was waning, and there had been enough shocks for one day.

The air was perfumed with the smell of freshly cut grass, and birdsong emanated from the nearby forest, the sun still playing hide-and-seek with the puffy white clouds.

Claire was supervising in the house with several other characters. Apparently the housekeepers hadn't been keeping it sufficiently clean and "something simply has to be done about it."

"I have Dr. Ellen Carter on speed dial," he said with a silly grin.

Ellen Carter was a genius epidemiologist who had saved the world in multiple books. I did a crossover book she and Alan were both in once, the two of them having a brief fling, of course.

"Even she can't keep me from dying," I said.

"No," he said. "We all die, but I'm quite sure she can buy you some time."

I shook my head. "I'm tired, Alan."

We walked in silence, and I was painfully aware of how slow my pace was and how big some of these little hills had become. Despite the wonders of the day, despair had leached into my being, slowing me down even further.

Nestled behind a clump of trees was a bench, and when we came near, I walked over and sat on it with a sigh as Alan kept pacing, his hands behind his back as he stared at the ground.

Feeling like I needed reality confirmed again, I videoed him for a little bit and played it back. I texted it to Blake, asking him what the video was, and he texted me back, "Alan Rogers doing that pacing thing you always write him doing," followed by a Bible emoji and the brown crap emoji (i.e. holy shit!).

If this was a psychotic break, it was a massive one.

"What is going on?" I asked, more to myself than to the man with my younger face who shouldn't be here.

"I have a theory," Alan said without stopping his pacing.

I blinked and felt more tumbling routines going on in my stomach. If Alan didn't know what was going on, that didn't seem like a good sign.

"What?" I asked.

He stopped and stared at me, his hands shoved into his pockets, and his blue-gray eyes not quite meeting mine. He looked like a kid about to tell his parents something they wouldn't like.

He bit his lip, and it was a strange thing for me to watch. Sure, I had given Alan Rogers a version of my face. I had grafted on some of my own ticks and some of my own history. He was a character I had created early on when I needed to borrow a lot from myself. But to have that standing in front of me in the flesh was more than bizarre.

"How bad can your theory be?" I asked.

His smile was entirely a grimace this time.

"I remember everything," he began. "Growing up in Marietta, Ohio, and getting into trouble along the river. I remember college at Columbia and escaping class to roam 'round Central Park. I remember that first foray into the jungles of the Congo and that mission that went horribly wrong."

He started pacing again. "But I only remember bits and pieces, just crucial scenes and amusing anecdotes, with what happened in between only a few words in my memory. I only remember what you wrote. I did not come from Heinlein's parallel worlds. I am purely a construct of your imagination."

This wasn't helping. "Then what is going on?"

He stopped again and shoved his hands into his pockets, his face forming a half-grin this time. "I don't know, but you do."

"I do?" I asked. I didn't like the sound of my voice. I sounded like a lost child.

He nodded. "I only remember what you wrote and—"

"Well how do you explain this, then?" I asked, cutting him off. "I certainly didn't write *this*."

He smiled, and this time it was a real smile. Grace always loved my smile, and seeing it mirrored on my younger face, I could see why. It was the kind of smile that was hard to be sad around. "What I was going to say is, I only remember what you wrote and—this part is the theory—some of what you *will* write."

I sat there blinking, trying to take it in.

"You can feel it, can't you?" he asked. "The stories you still need to tell. They are trying to get out. Even the one we are living right now."

I felt a wave of dizziness and was very glad I was sitting down. I looked up at Alan, the character I had given my face and many pieces of myself to. "You ... you don't want a happily ever after," I said. It felt like the words were pushing their way out, like it often did when I was writing. "That's where I went wrong. You want to give yourself to something ... you want to die in the end and die for a good reason."

His smile widened, and I basked in the glow of it.

"You felt that way when you wrote my last book," he said.

I nodded. "But it would be a different kind of book, not the typical Alan Rogers adventure."

"But you've always listened to your characters," he said. "Listen to us now."

I swallowed hard and nodded. "And what about you and the rest of my characters and what's happening here?" I asked.

He smiled again. "You have to write this story, too. You'll figure it out as you write, just like you have so many times before."

And I could feel it. The mechanics of it were squishier

than what Heinlein had come up with, more about the collective unconscious and the power of story to change reality. It made sense that each character had my eyes because they were all a part of me, a reflection of me. The idea wasn't fully formed, but it was there, just waiting to be written about. The story ideas were swirling around my mind again, and I felt more like myself than I had in years.

I looked past Alan at the thick forest, the light alternating from dark to light as clouds passed over. There had always been something alchemical about writing to me, how stringing words into sentences and then sentences into paragraphs could create something that speaks to us as humans on a very fundamental level. Besides Grace's love, it's been the most consistent source of magic in my life.

But I knew this wouldn't be easy. This would mean another round of chemo and another fight with my failing biology, and at the end of all of this, I would still die. I looked up into Alan's blue-gray eyes, and he gave me a small nod like he knew how much he was asking and how very much I needed a little more magic before the end.

"I guess we'd best get Dr. Carter here," I said.

He nodded but didn't move and was still staring at me.

"But I don't know how to start, Alan," I said.

He shrugged. "Just sit down and do the work," he said. "One sentence at a time, like usual. Write us all the endings we deserve."

Robert J. McCarter is the author of more than ten novels and over one hundred short stories. He is a regular contributor to *Pulphouse Fiction Magazine*, and his short fiction has also appeared in *The Saturday Evening Post, Andromeda Spaceways Inflight Magazine, Everyday Fiction*, and numerous anthologies.

Robert writes in a variety of genres from contemporary

fantasy to science fiction and just about everything in between. His diverse background—including a career in software engineering, growing up on a ranch riding horses, and acting—colors the stories he tells.

He lives in the mountains of Arizona with his amazing wife and his ridiculously adorable dogs.

If you would like to find out more about which of his characters are demanding his attention now, head over to RobertJMcCarter.com.

COPYRIGHT INFORMATION

ACKNOWLEDGMENTS

This anthology was made possible with the support of Draft2Digital and Western Colorado University's Graduate Program in Creative Writing.

Special thanks to Victoria Lane, Keayah Pittman, and Alannah Tuell for their help with the slushpile.

IF YOU LIKED GILDED GLASS
YOU MAY ALSO ENJOY...

Monsters, Movies & Mayhem
Edited by Kevin J Anderson

Unmasked: Tales of Risk and Revelation
Edited by Kevin J Anderson

Eat, Drink, and Be Wary
Edited by Lisa Mangum

Our list of other WordFire Press authors and titles is always growing. To find out more and to shop our selection of titles, visit us at:
wordfirepress.com

facebook.com/WordfireIncWordfirePress

twitter.com/WordFirePress

instagram.com/WordFirePress

bookbub.com/profile/4109784512

9 781680 573459